"YOU OWE ME AN APOLOGY."

Despite Rebecca's outburst, Jacob didn't believe her for a minute. Not when the taste of her lingered in his mouth. Not when the warmth of her caresses still tingled where she'd touched him.

"In the past year, I've been nurse to dozens—*hundreds*—of young men," she continued, "and not one of them has presumed to do anything as—"

"You ever think that maybe that's because you never stopped giving orders long enough?" He knew the words were all wrong, nothing but a sad attempt at humor to keep from explaining the way she'd reawakened him.

She lowered her chin and glared up at him. "Well, here's another one. *Get out.*"

He picked up the bowl and stood, then opened his mouth, wanting to say something—anything—to make her understand. "I'm sorry if you think I took advantage. But I'm not sorry that we kissed . . . Rebecca."

She shook her head. "Under the circumstances, I'd prefer we go back to 'Miss Marston.' Perhaps that will help you remember I'm a nurse."

He went to the door and opened it. "I'll call you anything you like, but I don't expect I'll ever forget the most important thing—that you're a woman, too."

TRUST TO CHANCE

Gwyneth Atlee

ZEBRA BOOKS
KENSINGTON PUBLISHING CORP.

http://www.kensingtonbooks.com

ZEBRA BOOKS are published by

Kensington Publishing Corp.
850 Third Avenue
New York, NY 10022

All Kensington titles, imprints and distributed lines are available at special quantity discounts for bulk purchases for sales promotion, premiums, fund-raising, educational or institutional use.

Special book excerpts or customized printings can also be created to fit specific needs. For details, write or phone the office of the Kensington Special Sales Manager: Kensington Publishing Corp., 850 Third Avenue, New York, NY 10022. Attn. Special Sales Department. Phone: 1-800-221-2647.

Zebra and the Z logo Reg. U.S. Pat. & TM Off.

First Printing: December 2001
10 9 8 7 6 5 4 3 2 1

Printed in the United States of America

*To the women who pushed beyond their
boundaries . . .
and the women who are doing it today.*

ACKNOWLEDGMENTS

I'd like to acknowledge several people for their contributions to the writing and production of *Trust to Chance*. First and foremost, thanks to my husband, Mike, and son, Andrew, for their support and enthusiasm. I greatly appreciate the advice and assistance of my agent, Meredith Bernstein, and editors Tomasita Ortiz and Amy Garvey.

Special thanks to Joe W. Smith for generously sharing information regarding the bands of raiders that plagued Arkansas and Missouri throughout the 1860s. Thanks also to the members of the Association of Sultana Descendants and Friends for their assistance with the facts of both this novel and *Against the Odds*.

I am continually inspired by the generosity of fellow writers. I'd like to thank members of the Woodlands Writers' Guild, the Northwest and West Houston Chapters of the Romance Writers of America, the To Beez, and Guida Jackson and Bill Laufer's Friday Nighters. In particular, I appreciate the tireless reading and helpful criticism of Kathleen Y'Barbo and the Midwives: Barbara Taylor Sissel, Wanda Dionne, Betty Joffrion, and Linda Helman.

Chapter One

*The sword of murder is not the balance of justice.
Blood does not wipe out dishonor nor violence
indicate possession.*

—Julia Ward Howe

April 26, 1865

Stupid Yanks were having a damned picnic. A
picnic, while loyal men starved not fifty yards away.

With the use of his remaining eye, Asa Graves
peered through the screen of underbrush and
focused on the lone man, clad in a uniform of
Union blue. His attention narrowed like a ray of
sunlight through a magnifying lens, excluding the
three women with the fellow, blotting out their
easy laughter and the Yank's infectious grin.

Didn't help to think on who they were, just what
they had. A team of sleek brown horses, a solid-
looking wagon, and of course, that picnic lunch.
They had what he needed, and they were the
enemy.

His focus shifted to two of the women, both
young-looking and slender, and he smiled to himself. From time to time, the spoils of war were sweet.

Turning carefully, Asa nodded to his compatriots. And his heartbeat quickened in anticipation of the bloody rebel yell.

Not a single drop of blood here. Rebecca smiled, allowing the budding glade with all its myriad greens to soothe her eyes and ease a strain she'd felt so long, she hadn't recognized its full extent.

As Drew halted the team of dark-brown horses, Rebecca leaped down from the wagon without awaiting help. It felt so good to escape the makeshift army hospital, to feast her eyes on the verdant shoots, to listen to the tree frogs peep and the birds sing songs of birth, of growth and life. Not far from the clearing, the Mississippi River meandered southward, its moisture softening the eastern sky to a hazier shade of blue.

Thank God for her cousin's idea of a country picnic to celebrate her birthday. Rebecca hadn't known how much she'd needed to escape the ward, with its rows of faces pinched with pain, of empty sockets, and limbs that ended too abruptly. She hadn't guessed how badly she'd needed this distance from her failure.

"No one eats until she opens her present!" her blond friend, Sarah, called cheerfully.

Drew helped Sarah from the wagon, his touch lingering a bit too long at her slim waist.

Rebecca had long suspected a growing bond between the two, in spite of Sarah's laughing assertions that she'd rather wed a spotted hog than an almighty army surgeon. As Drew set her down, a peculiar look passed between them. When the two caught Rebecca watching, their glances skittered apart, and Sarah's fair face colored. During the ride here, the normally effervescent blonde had been far quieter than usual, as if she were attempting for some reason to contain all her emotions.

Aboard the wagon, Eleanor loudly cleared her throat, and Drew quickly turned to help her down, too. Rebecca thought she heard him grunt under the strain. The ward matron's physique, like her manner, was about as delicate as the average army mule. Yet, like Sarah, she'd been uncharacteristically quiet during the drive.

They're worried I'll turn my nose up at their gift. Rebecca sighed. She wore the same dark, austere clothing as the other nurses, but even here, in eastern Arkansas, she could not escape her family's fortune. Drew hadn't helped, eager as he'd been to tell everyone his cousin was Rebecca Marston of *the* famous Philadelphia Marstons. Rebecca supposed he'd only done it to impress the other surgeons (and possibly Sarah, despite his protests to the contrary) about his family connections, but in her opinion, someone ought to suture his mouth shut.

Rebecca had wanted only to offer up her hands to this conflict, to ease the suffering of those boys injured while they wore the Union blue. Early in the war, she'd been content attending patriotic speeches, rolling bandages, and gathering relief supplies to help both the soldiers and the newly freed slaves who fled northward in droves. But ever since her only brother, Thomas, had been killed at Cold Harbor, she'd grown increasingly eager to find a more active method to support this war.

Her parents had been mortified by her idea of enlisting as a Union nurse.

"Merciful heavens!" her mother, Harriet Wells Marston, exclaimed. "You mean to scrub sheets and wash filth from the wounded? How would you ever hold your head up to the servants after that? And how can you even think of consorting with common soldiers and the men that run those hospitals? It's challenge enough finding a girl of your age and temperament a proper husband without your ruining your reputation."

As always, Mother ignored Rebecca's insistence that she fully intended to remain unwed, like Aunt Millicent.

Her father, Winfield, had been even more direct. "I forbid it, absolutely. No daughter of mine will work for wages. I've been entirely too lenient, allowing you to dabble about with all these social reformers my sister's so taken with. But I draw the line at this ridiculous notion. If you persist, I wash my hands of you."

Remembering his comments, Rebecca winced. She didn't know which hurt worse, being called a ridiculous dabbler or admitting that her parents had been right. She tried to imagine how it would feel returning home to spearhead some committee, knowing that she'd failed at the important tasks that humbler women mastered with such ease. Thinking of her father's threat, she wondered whether it was possible that she might not be welcomed home at all.

She swallowed past a lump. Surely not. Despite her disobedience, she was still a Marston . . . wasn't she?

Drew chucked her beneath the chin. "Cheer up, Rebecca. It's not every day one celebrates a twenty-sixth birthday."

His other hand held the bottom of a fairly large box, festooned in yellow ribbons.

A few steps away, Sarah and Eleanor were spreading out a blanket for their picnic.

"Why not celebrate?" Rebecca forced a smile. "Now, at least, I've moved beyond the 'verge of spinsterhood,' as Mother puts it. Perhaps she'll at last give up on the idea of a 'suitable match.' "

Drew laughed. "If I know Aunt Hattie, she's this

very moment negotiating a dowry large enough to offset your odd political sentiments."

Rebecca smacked his arm while the two nurses looked on. She saw nothing in the least odd about the idea of obtaining the right to vote for women, nor of abolition, for that matter. She was about to remind him that poor Mr. Lincoln had recently been sacrificed on the altar of the latter "sentiment," but Drew spoke again before she could reply.

"Careful." Her cousin dropped his voice. "They're worried that you'll break their gift. They've put a lot of thought into it."

Rebecca lowered her hand, more concerned with the women's feelings than with having her say—at least for now.

"Mother hates it when you call her Hattie," she said, unwilling to be completely silenced. "Even my father calls her Mrs. Marston."

"I *know.*" Drew grinned disarmingly, the spring sunshine illuminating the reddish tones in his dark-auburn hair.

Rebecca wished her own more vibrant locks were as subtle. "Red as a Viking's," her mother often said. Inevitably, on doing so, she'd pulled the brush harder through the thick waves and shaken her head with disapproval. "No wonder you're so stubborn. . . ."

Self-consciously, Rebecca adjusted her bonnet. Her red hair, like the Marston name, was only one more impediment in her war to be taken seriously.

She remembered the first time she'd try to sign up for Dorothea Dix's nursing corps, how the woman's gaze had locked onto those bright tresses.

"Don't bother writing me again, and don't come back," Miss Dix had told her bluntly. "I have seldom seen such a supremely unqualified applicant to nursing. You are altogether too young, too attractive, and too used to being waited upon to be considered for such a responsibility."

That last comment made Rebecca wonder whether her father had communicated with Miss Dix. Only later in the war, when need had helped relax the standards, did she learn that the outspoken Dorothea Dix had been as strict with everyone.

Both Dorothea Dix and Winfield Marston, however, had underestimated Rebecca's willfulness. She had immediately—and secretly—written her cousin, Drew, who was chief surgeon in an Arkansas military hospital along the Union-occupied shoreline of the Mississippi River. In short order, he hired her, more because he enjoyed goading his "aunt Hattie" than because he thought Rebecca qualified.

Her age and so-called personal attractions notwithstanding, Rebecca had quickly proven Miss Dix's direst warnings correct. Although she was keenly interested in nursing wounded soldiers, she had almost no idea of the practical aspects. Quick learner that she was, that in itself would have proved only a temporary inconvenience. It was her compassion, the very quality that led her to speak out for slaves and the impoverished wives of drunkards, that caused her so much trouble as a nurse.

She simply could not look at a wounded man without, in some deeply affecting sense, *becoming* him. In her mind, his blood flowed from her wounded body; his amputation shocked her as if the loss had been her own. She soaked up the suffering around her like a sponge until every groan and scream resonated painfully inside her.

Time after time in those first weeks, she'd been ill or fainted in the ward. For months afterward, she was repeatedly led outside for fresh air, usually by Sarah, who took a devilish delight in teasing her about her weakness. Rebecca might never have learned to endure the terrible sights and smells of the hospital had she not overheard the ward matron, Eleanor. Despite her penchant for mothering the nurses, the middle-aged woman suggested Rebecca be put on the first train back to Philadelphia. Sarah, whom she'd imagined a great friend, had agreed.

The idea of returning home and—worse yet— admitting that her parents had been right, terrified Rebecca. As a result, she had walled off her internal horror from the world beyond. Brick by brick, the barricade gradually allowed her to perform her duties with unimpeachable exactness.

Even as it was slowly killing her inside. Her tears, so long unshed, dried until her soul felt parched and dusty as a desert, and twice as barren.

Rebecca knew now she'd been wrong to come west. Despite all outward appearances, she felt the cracks in her composure deepening each day, heard her brick wall rumbling, threatening a breakdown so complete there would be little left of her but rubble. She was finished as a nurse. Now all she had to do was tell these people she was leaving. She'd have to admit to Drew and Sarah, who faced their grim duties with ghastly good humor, and Eleanor, who relied on prayer, that she had not found a way to cope. After more than a year of suffering in silence, she was going home.

Sarah set down the picnic basket and straightened with a bounce. Her green eyes sparkled with excitement. "The gift, Rebecca, please! I'm starving, and we can't eat until you open it."

Rebecca nodded, and the four of them knelt upon the blanket. Drew, who still had possession of the ribboned box, held it out toward her.

Smiling, determined to like whatever the three of them had brought her, Rebecca lifted off the lid . . .

And stared in horror at a severed male hand, clenched in a fist and lying in a bed of yellow straw.

Blood pooled at its wrist, just as gray dots pooled in Rebecca's vision. Until she saw the fingers open, revealing both a tiny wrapped box and the unmistakable sounds of Drew and Sarah's laughter.

Her eyes snapped open, and she glared at Drew, whose "severed" hand poked through the bottom of the box.

"Doctor Wells—Sarah, of all the appalling bad taste!" Eleanor began indignantly.

"*You!*" Rebecca accused both Drew and Sarah. "You two, you—"

But Rebecca never had the chance to choose what names she would call the pair, for at that very moment, the clearing erupted with the most bloodcurdling sounds she had ever heard.

Chapter Two

In the new code of laws which I suppose it will be necessary for you to make I desire you would remember the ladies, and be more generous and favorable to them than your ancestors. Do not put such unlimited power into the hands of the husbands. Remember all men would be tyrants if they could.

—Abigail Adams
From a letter to John Adams,
March 31, 1776

April 27, 1865

Each time Jacob Fuller managed to rouse himself enough to call out, fewer answered. One after another, the survivors fell victim to the long, dark hours spent clinging to the floating stage plank. Men who had endured the starvation and disease of Cahaba and Andersonville, two of the South's most notorious prisoner-of-war camps, gradually succumbed to burns, exhaustion, and the chill waters of the flooded Mississippi River.

They had been finally going home, finally putting the cursed South behind them, when the riverboat exploded in the dead of night. Jacob thought back to the repairs he'd seen in progress the afternoon he'd boarded the *Sultana*. The engineer had been slapping thin metal over a bulge in a worn boiler.

"Don't worry," the mechanic had reassured him. *"We'll have this patched and get you home in good time."*

Jacob wondered if the fool who had made that promise lived, or if he'd been blown to bits by his own shoddy workmanship. If that had even been the cause of the disaster. For all Jacob knew, it could have been a parting shot from the rebs. Lee might have surrendered at Appomattox weeks before, but Jacob had heard talk that not all the damned secessionists had given up their cause.

He made an effort to rekindle his anger, hoping that its fire would send warmth flowing through his tired limbs. Too numb to feel anything on his own behalf, he conjured images of his brother Zeke and their two friends, Gabe Davis and Seth Harris, all of whom had been aboard the steamboat, too. Jacob had seen only Seth leave the *Sultana* alive, and not even that guaranteed the man remained so. Yet even those grave losses failed to resurrect his strength.

Beside him, Jacob heard a splash. With one hand, he groped at the dark water, trying to snag a sleeve or pant leg or even the hair of the man who'd slipped off the floating plank. He fought the stiffness in his unfeeling fingers in a desperate attempt to make them grasp. But it was too late; the man who'd clung beside him had utterly vanished.

Jacob hadn't even asked his name. The fellow had been speaking just an hour before, offering up prayers, camp songs, and finally grim words. He'd told Jacob that escaping steam from the *Sultana's* ruptured boiler had badly scalded his left side, but eventually his words slurred into whimpers . . . then finally silence as one by one, the rescue boats had missed them and they'd floated south of Memphis, south of hope.

It had been the loss of will that killed him, Jacob realized. And that realization sent a jolt of pure fear up his spine to infuse him with the warmth that anger had denied him. If he gave up, he would die, too.

He thought of joining Hope, thought of how it might be fitting. But he'd already failed her—or they had failed each other—and others still remained who needed him. Zeke came to mind once more, his leg badly wounded. If his brother had survived, he'd need help to make it home.

Jacob knew if he stopped fighting for an instant, he would fall asleep and sink, beyond the chance of helping Zeke or anybody else. So instead, he marshaled his resources to call again for help.

Finally, at long, long last, exhaustion robbed Rebecca of the strength to shake. The utter stillness of her body surprised her, after so many hours spent trembling.

Still, she was not completely motionless. Lying in the hard bed of the army wagon, she was bounced and bruised painfully by the deeply rutted road. One of these jolts had long since caused her blindfold to slip down, uncovering her eyes.

But that made little difference, for the night enveloped her as fully as any hangman's hood. Above, a curtain of clouds shrouded all but the most stubborn stars. At one point, she flinched at what she thought to be a murmur of thunder, but no flash of lightning ever came, so she was spared the sight of the bloodstains she knew must spatter her dark-gray skirt and shirtwaist.

Dizziness washed over her at the specters raised by that last thought, and she knew that if she focused on each separate image, she would surely be sick. With her wrists so cruelly bound behind her, she might spend hours lying in the stinking pool of her disgust.

Only that repulsive thought allowed her to shut her mind to danger. Turning from the horror that followed the attack, she thought instead of her future.

And found it no less terrifying.

Would these rebel scavengers live up to their promise to release her once her father paid? Or did they only mean to take her to some filthy camp to commit outrages on her body?

She heard another horse's hoofbeats coming near the wagon.

"Bear right, toward the river. Remember that abandoned place we seen?"

A murmured reply came from the front of the wagon. Then the hoofbeats receded, and the sounds of the creaking wagon and the trotting team were all that she could hear.

Despite her attempt to keep from recalling what had occurred this afternoon, Rebecca pictured Sarah's face, her normally fair skin as pale as undyed cotton, her eyes white-ringed with terror. Rebecca whimpered as she pictured the ugly rebel with the ruined eye dragging the blond nurse off into the woods, his foul hands tearing at her shirtwaist. The more desperately Sarah had cried out and struggled, the broader the beast's grin.

A long-limbed, tan hound pup had leaped, snapping playfully at Sarah's skirt. The raider had kicked at it and laughed.

"Get off, dog. I ain't sharin' with the likes of you."

He'd meant to ravage Sarah, and the others would have let him, maybe even taken turns, if not for her desperate cry.

"She's Rebecca Marston from Philadelphia!" Sarah had screamed, pointing toward Rebecca. "Her father has a fortune; I swear it! He'll pay you well if we're not harmed!"

Another soldier stepped forward then, a tall man who held himself with an almost aristocratic bearing, despite a heavy limp. Unlike the other raiders, his black beard was neatly barbered, and he wore a gray uniform jacket only slightly torn at one shoulder. Rebecca knew little of Confederate insignia, but the stars on his collar appeared to mark him as an officer.

He glanced down at Drew, who lay prostrate in a spreading pool of scarlet, and at Eleanor, who knelt beside him, rocking on her knees and weeping. Moving past both without reaction, he continued beyond Rebecca. She remained absolutely silent and on her feet, despite the fact that the world was swaying as if she were aboard a ship at sea.

"Bring the girl back, Asa," the officer ordered the rebel who was holding Sarah.

"Goddamn it, she's *mine*, colonel," he spat. "Ain't nothin' them Yankees haven't done to our women time and time again. Spoils of war."

The officer drew a pistol in the space it took a man to blink an eye. "I don't care if they abused your *mother*, sergeant. We are Southern *men*, not Yankee animals, and we do no harm to ladies."

The sergeant, who was apparently called Asa, swore and glared, but he took Sarah no farther from the clearing. Neither did he bring her back a single step.

The colonel turned his attention to Rebecca. "Your father—he's the textile millionaire, *Winfield* Marston?"

She didn't answer, more out of shock than stub-

bornness. Her gaze drifted back and forth from
Drew's still form to Sarah's impossibly white face.

Ignoring Rebecca, the man with the neat black
beard stalked past her, his limp slowing him but
little.

"Is she Winfield Marston's daughter?" he asked
Sarah.

Sarah glanced at Rebecca and appeared to hesitate. Then she shook her head, her lips pressed
close together, as if a refusal to answer might undo
the words she'd blurted earlier.

Rebecca could not see the officer's expression,
but she could hear sternness descend over his voice
like a heavy frost.

"Answer me," he ordered.

When she did not, the colonel spoke again.
"Then God forgive me, I shall let him take you.
He's a rough man, as they all are."

He gestured at the other six raiders, who were
watching the proceedings with palpable interest.
One man leered through brown teeth while
another moved to loosen his begrimed gray trousers.

"They've been without a woman for a good, long
time. I only hope that they don't hurt you too
badly."

The threat evidently shattered Sarah's nerve, for
she screamed, "Yes! *Yes!* She's Winfield Marston's
daughter! And I swear to you, he'll pay! Only
don't—please, dear God, don't—"

Deep sobs fractured her words, and her knees
buckled. Asa let her fall, his own gaze riveted on
the officer, as if seeking permission. The glade,
which once rang with birdsong and with laughter,
echoed with the sounds of Sarah's and Eleanor's
weeping. The spring air, which had been scented
with the fragrance of new growth and the nearby

river, now hung heavy with the thickening stench of spilled blood.

Drew's blood. Her cousin's, who had served his nation healing wounded men, who had died the instant the bullet pierced his chest.

Anger pulsed in Rebecca's temples, and, oddly, she blamed Drew. Not the man who'd shot him, but the thirty-year-old who had been her friend and cousin, who'd brought her out here for a foolish birthday prank.

Now, as she bounced against the wagon's side, she wished he were alive so she could scream at him.

Why did you have to reach for the revolver, Drew? Otherwise, they might have let a surgeon live.

But it was no use blaming poor Drew, no more use than it was condemning Sarah for her betrayal. For all Rebecca knew, all three of the women would have been degraded and murdered, had it not been for Sarah's desperate exclamation.

The colonel had ordered his men to allow Sarah and Eleanor to go free. As long as they were unharmed, he'd explained, Winfield Marston could reasonably believe his daughter would be returned in safety. . . .

Once he'd paid twenty-five thousand dollars ransom to the men now holding her.

Despite her grief and terror, Rebecca must have slept, for the sounds woke her. Splashing and then shouting, somewhere to the right.

"They're in the river, colonel!"

"Holy hell, they's clingin' to some sort of wood."

"Who goes there?"

Her captors' voices blended into a confused cacophony. Rebecca strained, trying to lift her head high enough to see over the buckboard's side. The sky had lightened to a dismal predawn pewter, but she could make out nothing else.

Footsteps thudded toward the right. Were the raiders now abandoning her? Could Sarah and Eleanor have sent soldiers to save her? Her heart thudded in joyful anticipation of the end of this ordeal.

A hand pressed down on her neck, prompting her to shriek in terror.

"Shush, little princess. You just lay real still."

He leaned above her, and she smelled his fetid breath. His silhouette loomed over her, a figure cut from shadow. Yet despite his apparent lack of features, she was certain that she recognized the rebel.

He was Asa, the one-eyed sergeant who had meant to rape her friend. And now his hand was taking off her bonnet, tossing it away, and then removing the pins that held in place her hair.

Bile rose to choke her as she felt her tresses tumble free.

"Damned if that ain't a sight to set a man afire," he whispered.

Revulsion transformed her into stone, making it impossible to move or speak or even breathe . . . until the moment that his fingers grazed the top buttons of her shirtwaist.

"Who goes there?" came the shouted question.

Jacob peered in the direction of the new voice. Unlike the river's surface, which reflected the dim sky, the area to his right was completely dark and solid. *Land!* The voice had come from land!

One of the men clinging to the stage plank cried out, "Help us!"

Jacob, too, called, "Over here—and hurry! Our riverboat burned up!"

Another of the survivors, his voice gone, feebly splashed in an attempt to attract the attention of the man whose voice they had heard.

The stage plank had lodged amid a tangle of dead branches, holding them in place. Thank God they wouldn't drift beyond the reach of help this time.

Jacob strained his ears, listening for the echo of an answer or the sound of a man's boots tramping through the shoreline underbrush. Instead, a bird trilled to greet the coming dawn. One by one, its fellows answered brightly, utterly oblivious to the slowly dying men.

Jacob repeatedly shouted, "Hello!" until his throat felt shredded.

Had the man on shore abandoned them? Or, even more alarming, had he merely imagined he had heard the voice? Was it a part of some delirium, a harbinger of death?

But the survivors nearest Jacob seemed as agitated as he felt. One tried to call out, though his voice lacked the power to carry much beyond the stage plank. The fellow who'd been splashing allowed his free arm to sink beneath the water's surface. Now, instead, he cried out, "Please . . . please . . . please . . ." as a lost child might call for his mother.

As the sky gradually silvered, Jacob could for the first time count his fellows. Besides him, only four remained. Four, out of the dozens who had swarmed over the plank as it was thrown off the burning steamboat. Four, out of the masses aboard the doomed *Sultana.*

Where were the rest now? Had they all burned or drowned, or had most of them been rescued? Had his brother or his friends managed to escape with their lives?

Anger gathered into a molten ball inside his

chest. Three years of mud and blood and battle, followed by five months penned like animals to starve—and all of that to die here. Was God no better than a cruel boy who tore the wings from flies?

The sounds of splashing toward the shoreline attracted his attention. At first, he wondered if it might be a fish jumping or a diving bird, but the sounds were regular and rhythmic—an oar stroking the water?

"Hallo! Can y'all hear me?"

"Shout out, boys, so we can find you!"

The man had come—and from the sounds of it, he'd brought help.

"Over here!" Jacob called back. He waved his free arm wildly.

The two other survivors who were sufficiently conscious did the same, though both were so weak their cries were barely audible. A fourth man clung to the stage plank, his eyes closed and his face pale as a moon above the water.

Somehow, in the last few seconds, the fifth man had disappeared.

"Grab onto him," Jacob shouted, gesturing toward the unconscious man, who was out of his reach. "We can't lose another one—not now!"

The other two ignored him, so Jacob moved hand over hand down the length of the stage plank until he could grasp the fellow's collar to keep his head above the river's surface. He'd be damned if he'd let the Mississippi swallow one more man.

The sounds of a blade splashing and men's voices rose and fell with the movement of the waters. So much so that it was impossible to tell how much farther the boat was, or if it had moved past them. Jacob's arm, extended to hold up the insensate soldier, throbbed with the strain of the awkward position. He fought a cramp in the same hand, an agonizing tightness that begged him to let go, if only for a moment, so that he might flex his tired muscles.

A silhouetted figure rose above him, gradually materializing from the dimness.

"Here!" Jacob called to it.

"Grab hold of this here oar," the man responded.

Jacob glanced at the man beside him. "Better get him first. He can't hold on by himself."

A second man came into focus, his hands filled with a pole he'd apparently been using to help guide their movement. They stood aboard some sort of flatboat.

The man with the paddle knelt to grasp the unconscious soldier. Jacob helped push him onto what he now recognized as a crude raft.

The man's body was halfway aboard when his rescuer abruptly stopped pulling and glanced back at the second man.

"These is Federals, colonel. Yanks."

An image flashed through Jacob's mind. A stack of delicate flies' wings, just grown larger. Their "saviors" were rebel soldiers. The first man wore a torn jacket made of butternut.

The second man, the one called "colonel," moved forward and stooped to finish the task of pulling the limp form onto the raft.

"Just let's bring them in to shore," he told his fellow. "None of them look too dangerous right now."

The first rebel hesitated while the officer, assisted by Jacob in the water, helped the next two survivors crowd aboard.

"Damn it, Simms, lend a hand here!" the colonel barked.

Simms squatted and reached down for Jacob.

As Jacob clambered aboard the sloped and splintery deck, he looked into small, mean eyes set above a nose that might have once been flattened by a fist.

"I reckon we can figure out later how we want to kill 'em." Simms was speaking to the colonel, but his gaze never veered from Jacob's face.

"Remove your hand," Rebecca ordered the raider. She struggled to sound as stern as Eleanor at the hospital. Her effort fell short, though, so that her voice quavered like a child's.

Her heart was hammering so hard, she was certain Asa could feel it beneath his fingertips. His touch burned into the thin skin covering the V between her collarbones. The heat from that light contact spread through her like the puddle of Drew's blood. Then she recalled this man's repulsive grin at Sarah's panic, and she shivered, as if a sudden fever had beset her with a chill.

"Your father always asks why I never chose to marry," Aunt Millicent once commented. *"And I tell him it is because of man's wish to rule over and diminish woman for the sense of power it gives him."*

Unlike Aunt Millicent, Rebecca doubted that assessment suited all men, but if it described any man at all, it was this lowbred criminal. She *must* master her fear, if only to rob him of the pleasure that her screams would elicit.

Be Aunt Millicent, she told herself. Aunt Millicent bowed to no man, not even Father, who was known to intimidate nearly everyone, male or female, who crossed his path.

"Your colonel has a fine plan," Rebecca said, her voice so firm and calm that it surprised her. "My father will make each of you rich—but only if I remain untouched. Winfield Marston is a harsh man as well as wealthy, and I tell you he'll pay not a penny for a ruined daughter.''

Asa lifted his hand from her throat. With a great deal of effort, she could just make out his face. He appeared to be staring at her in utter disbelief.

"How's your Big Man daddy gonna know a thing till you get back? *If* we don't kill you?"

Rebecca winced at the hole in her logic. She felt insulted to have it pointed out by this untutored brute.

Be Aunt Millicent, she admonished herself more fiercely. She could scarcely be expected to develop a rational argument with her heart pounding its way through her chest wall. This might be a deadly game she played, but she must play it to the very best of her ability.

"When he finds out, he'll hunt you down like the dogs you are. He'll stop at nothing to destroy you." Rebecca's voice remained steady, despite her doubts about the verity of what she'd said. The idea of her father abandoning his business to avenge her honor was too incredible to fathom. But perhaps he'd hire men to see that it was done.

"Sounds like we oughta use you like we want, get the money, and then kill you. Him bein' a Big Man like he is, he'll prob'ly wanta run us down anyhow on account of this whole scheme."

Rebecca cursed herself. He was thinking more rationally than she was. She could feel panic eating away at her reason, trying to reduce her to a shrieking, quivering animal.

No! She refused to give in to her terror.

She tried another tack. "Your colonel will punish you for disobeying orders."

"God *damn!*" Asa erupted. "I pity the poor bastard what has to marry you. Don't you *ever* give up arguin'?"

At his outburst, a dog began to whine.

Ignoring it, she answered, "No." Her parents could both attest to that.

"I got a good mind to give you somethin' to shut you up for good."

He yanked her shirtwaist with enough force to send buttons flying, and Rebecca's thin veneer of courage cracked wide to emit her scream.

But Asa went no further. She heard him chuckling as he paused, and her face burned with her defeat. She'd been fooling herself to think she could fight brute force with a show of intellect, as if this were a civilized debate in some lyceum.

His head jerked toward a voice off to her right.

"Asa! Quit pawin' her and bring on up that wagon! We got company!"

Rebecca struggled to sit up, convinced beyond all reason that her rescue was at hand.

Asa roughly shoved her down and then spoke in a voice that chilled her to the marrow. "You better hope that it ain't soldiers, princess. Cause if any one of us is dyin', I swear to God you'll lead the way."

Jacob had never been so cold in all his life, not even in the Indiana of his boyhood, where snowstorms blanketed the farm in white. Not even in Andersonville Prison, where he'd fought the elements in addition to the twin specters of starvation and disease. He realized his wet clothes were the culprits, but he had no means of drying himself as the raft moved steadily toward shore.

Beside him, the other survivors shuddered miserably, with the exception of the unconscious man, who had not yet awakened. *Too far gone to shiver*, Jacob thought as he stared at the bedraggled beard and sodden hair, whose darkness only served to accentuate the sickly pallor of the man's face.

"Wake up," Jacob told him. "They'll have us on land soon. Don't die on me now."

Reaching out, he shook the fellow's upper arm—and jerked back in horror as the man's flesh peeled away in thick, dark layers, like roasted meat. The better part of the blue jacket had burned, and now the skin beneath would slough off at the gentlest touch. Jacob had seen a lot in the past few years, but he had to turn away. Better that the man should never wake than face such pain.

As dawn washed the eastern sky in scarlet, the raft bumped against the river's muddy bank.

The colonel shouted to a group of men on shore, "Get the woman. These boys'll need a bit of help."

No one moved. Instead, unyielding gazes locked onto the four newcomers. Every rebel held some sort of weapon. Jacob noted several rifles, a shotgun, and a pistol. One razor-thin man brandished an officer's saber as if it were a club.

"Enemies." Simms answered the question that none had asked aloud. "Half-drownt Yankees . . . said their steamboat burnt."

"You want that woman to play nursemaid?" The rebel with the saber lifted its point higher. "What the devil for? If you don't want to waste the bullets, let me run 'em through."

"These aren't worthy enemies, and we aren't soldiers in this case," the colonel told them. "We're men. Decent, honorable men. Or have you forgotten the reasons you joined up with this unit?"

"Yeah!" another man called. "To kill some goddamned Yanks!"

But his retort provoked first a burst of laughter and then murmurs of consent. In the wake of both, the men helped move the injured soldiers onto shore.

"We'll need some blankets," the colonel ordered, "and one of you should ride ahead and start a good fire if you can find dry kindling. Go on, Simms, and take Billy. Chop up some furniture if you have to. These boys need to get warm right away."

Two men left, and another rebel dragged forward a woman whose hair tumbled in thick waves to her waist. The first rays of the morning sun lit her tresses fiery red, and she shrieked and struggled as if her temper, too, had been ignited.

Jacob noted her shirtwaist, which hung partly open, the wild mane, which obscured her features, and decided she was some sort of camp follower, awakened from slumber after a night spent servicing the men. But most of all he noticed the color of her hair, the same shade as Hope's had been. The resemblance lanced through him like pain.

"I absolutely refuse to be manhandled in this fashion!" the woman complained, wrenching her arm free of the one-eyed man who held her.

Pretty highfalutin' talk for a camp whore, Jacob thought. But whoever she was and whatever her problems, he didn't give a tinker's damn right now.

The colonel limped toward her and said, "Compose yourself, Miss Marston. These are your countrymen, and they need you. Apparently, their riverboat exploded."

She shoved her thick hair from her face to look at the injured men for the first time. And her blue eyes filled with such a look of sympathy and horror that every shred of anger vanished from her face.

The colonel's gaze swept over them as well. "We'll take them to a place of shelter, but we're not about to spend time coddling the enemy. If they're to have any chance at all, it's you. Their lives are in your hands."

* * *

Rebecca stared at the sodden men in disbelief. In her hands—oh, dear God. She couldn't! Not now, only hours after she had watched her cousin die, only hours after she had been abducted!

She couldn't do this anymore. She'd seen too much, given too much of herself already, to face more suffering.

Yet three of them stared up at her weakly, shivering so hard they looked as if they might shake themselves to bits. The fourth appeared completely unconscious. All of them were thin and pale . . . and all of them wore at least the remnants of dark-blue uniforms.

"They're your countrymen, and they need you." The words resonated in her memory, reminding her of why she'd defied her parents to come west in the first place. It was disgraceful even to think that she might turn her back on them.

Swallowing her misgivings, Rebecca struggled to find her voice. "Quickly, they need blankets, jackets, anything you have to get them warm."

The rebel soldiers hesitated, clearly unconvinced.

She had to do better. Instead of her Aunt Millicent, Rebecca now called upon her memories of Eleanor, who ran the ward with brusque efficiency. *Be Eleanor,* she told herself firmly. Be anyone except Rebecca, whose soul wept even though her eyes were dry as dust.

"You heard me," she told her kidnappers. "We need blankets—*now.*"

Several of the rebel soldiers shuffled off, grumbling and swearing loud enough that she could hear. Rebecca glared a challenge at their leader.

"I'll take that frock coat, colonel."

To her surprise, he nodded and removed it, exposing his waistcoat. Even more shocking, Asa took off a threadbare jacket and tossed it at her feet.

When the colonel handed her the garment, Rebecca knelt to pick up the one-eyed rebel's jacket. Ignoring the two Confederates, she turned her full attention to the wounded men to assess their condition.

She struggled to mask the extent of her surprise. Exposure had clearly weakened all four, and two suffered visible burns. Both conditions were indicative of an explosion and time spent in the water, but it was the full extent of their gauntness that came as such a shock.

Hunger had carved hollows beneath cheekbones and painted deep shadows between the exposed ribs of one bare-chested man. Not just hunger, either. This hadn't been the work of a few days' want, but of weeks upon weeks of deprivation.

Carefully, she draped the frock coat over the unconscious soldier. Then her gaze settled on the tallest and strongest-looking of the others, a man who was struggling to control his shivering. He rubbed his arms briskly, his movement shaking the damp brown curls atop his head. She could not help noticing that, though thin, there was something quite compelling in the man's face, something that drew her gaze and held it.

"You were prisoners?" she asked him. Dreadful rumors had come north from Vicksburg, where paroled prisoners of war had massed, awaiting transport home.

"Guests of the Confederacy," the soldier answered grimly.

Rebecca noticed the broad, masculine planes of the man's face, the strong chin, and the square, set jaw. To disguise her reluctance to look away, she passed him Asa's jacket. He gave it to the shirtless man instead.

"I didn't come this far to wear a rebel uniform," he told her, his tone steeped in both stubbornness and pride.

"You'll take what help you're offered—without argument," she told him sharply, mostly to disguise her annoyance with herself. Was she some insipid coquette, to be so affected by a handsome face? Or had yesterday's events combined with the daily horrors of the ward to push her irrevocably beyond her limits, so far outside herself that she might never find her way back?

"I know the rebs have fallen on rough times," he answered, clearly irritated with her tone, "but it's hard to imagine they're giving sergeant's stripes to *ladies* these days."

His expression left no doubt what sort of "lady" the soldier took her for. With her hair undone and her shirtwaist hanging partially open, she must look thoroughly disreputable. Asa gave a sharp bark of laughter, and Rebecca felt her cheeks flame with humiliation.

Rather than explain the curly-haired man's error, Rebecca glared at him instead. "Very well. I'd prefer to expend my energies on men worth saving, anyway."

Footsteps thudded in the sand and diverted her attention. It was another of the rebels, who handed Rebecca several jackets and blankets.

The big, tan pup leaped forward and snatched an old quilt in its teeth.

"Git on outta here!" When Asa raised his hand, the animal dropped its prize and bounded a few steps away, tail wagging.

Rebecca could hardly blame it. The assembled items looked more fitting for a dog than for men. The pile reeked of old sweat, and the cloth felt gritty with dirt, but at least the items would provide

warmth to keep the soldiers alive until they could
be moved to shelter.

Rebecca offered the filthiest, most tattered blanket to the curly-haired soldier who'd mistaken her
for a harlot. She thought for a moment of withholding even that to repay his rudeness, but in the end
his shivering made her relent.

His shivering . . . and her need to look at him
once more.

Jacob thought it strange the way she watched
him, as if she were as hungry as he was. But not
for food, for something other. Something he could
not begin to fathom.

She was not a whore, despite the wild locks and
the torn bodice. If he'd been in his right mind,
he would have known it in an instant from the way
she spoke, the way the officer had called her Miss
Marston, and the interplay between her and the
rebel soldiers, which smoldered like the kindling
tucked beneath a log. Like something that might
ignite at any moment. Even her hair color reminded him of flame.

Flame, but different from his wife's. He'd been
wrong in thinking that before. This woman's hair
was a shade brighter, her eyes blue and not Hope's
green. She was taller, too, yet finer-boned. Not the
same at all, for her words were fire to Hope's cold
flint.

Thinking of fire, Jacob wished to God he had
some now. In the back of the wagon, he huddled
in the blanket, his jaws aching with their frigid
chattering. One of his fellows, a man with dark,
matted hair and a coarse beard, leaned against
him, quietly imploring, "Please . . . please . . .
please," just as he had called out in the water. Jacob
doubted that he even knew what he was saying or

that he would ever again stop. He tried to concentrate upon the early birdsong, to pretend that the unsettling cries were nothing but the calls of mourning doves.

The wagon's driver ducked to avoid branches that overhung the path. Some scraped the back of the buckboard's driver's seat, then whipped backward, flinging flurries of pale green, tender leaves and caterpillarlike gold strands of pollen. The rising sun made shadowed bars of myriad trunks and tree limbs, but rays splintered through their ranks to paint the underbrush with verdant light. The wood smelled of new growth and the morning, all overlaid with the rich dampness of the nearby Mississippi.

Too beautiful to be real, Jacob thought. He'd never been a man to appreciate such ordinary things before, but after five months in the fetid quagmire of a prison pen, he'd forgotten the flamboyant extravagance of spring. Now he had to face the hard facts that his brother and his friends might be dead to all this . . . and that he had again fallen into rebel hands.

The man leaning on his shoulder was weeping now, with tears that felt hot as they dripped on Jacob's hand where it held the blanket. Jacob wished the bearded man would move away. He wanted—no, *needed*—to retreat into isolation, to keep the grief and exhaustion from bubbling up inside his own throat, too.

The woman, who'd been tucking a bedroll around the unconscious man, turned her head to look in the direction of the crying soldier. But as it had before, her gaze found Jacob's and held it. This time he looked just as hard at her.

Anguish shadowed her blue eyes—pain so deep that he had to look away to keep his thoughts from the last time he'd seen so deeply into a woman's soul.

On hands and knees, she crawled to the man beside him. Avoiding her gaze, he watched her enfold the weeping soldier's hand in hers. He listened to her whispering a prayer. And all the while, the horses' hooves crunched gravel, and the branches scraped the wagon's sides with leafy, sweeping noises.

And all the while, he wished that she were holding him instead.

Chapter Three

time he'd seen so deeply into a woman's

No young ladies should be sent at all but . . . those who are sober, earnest, self-sacrificing, and self-sustained; who can be calm, gentle, quiet, active, and steadfast in duty, also those who are willing to take and execute the directions of the surgeons. . . .
—Dorothea Dix, superintendent of women nurses, Union Army

"Them wagon wheels is gonna mire in all that mud," Asa told the colonel, who rode beside them aboard a coal black mare. "We gotta move them in on horseback."

Move them into where? Rebecca peered around the seat, where Asa perched alone, to look ahead. Before them, the rutted road vanished beneath mud brown waters that spread into the underbrush on either side. In the distance, a two-story wooden farmhouse rose above a tiny island like a castle surrounded by a swollen moat.

A castle for a rat king, maybe, or perhaps his rodent courtiers. Shutters hung askew on all the upper windows, and not a speck of paint adorned the weathered outer walls. The porch posts all tilted toward the left at such an angle that collapse looked imminent.

A cluster of about a dozen trees and a narrow fringe of mud-stained grasses shared the islet with the house. Bright-green willow leaves fluttered in the morning breeze. Somehow their lively dance made the abandoned house appear even more forlorn, despite the curl of smoke rising from the chimney.

"You cannot possibly mean to take sick men there," Rebecca told the colonel. "Why, that place looks as if no one has lived in it for ages. It will come down around our ears."

"We've stayed there a time or two," he told her. "The house is sound—and isolated enough that no one will bother us."

"No one except vermin," she said. "And these men absolutely must not be moved on horseback. They're far too ill to—"

"On that point, I'll agree. We'll try the wagon. We've men enough to push if it gets mired."

"Damned if I'll stand hip-deep in the muck to shove loose a bunch of Yankees," a nearby rider complained. His brown teeth glistened darkly, and heavy brows brought to mind a scowling bear.

The colonel touched his gun butt and stared at him intently. "You'll follow orders."

"We could take 'em to the barn instead," another man suggested. He gestured toward a structure Rebecca hadn't noticed earlier. Although reaching it would not necessitate crossing the water, it looked in as much need of repair as did the house.

"I've made my decision," the officer responded.

The soldier looked away, a frown twisting in the harsh nest of his beard.

Asa hesitated, then called out, "C'mon, dog."

When the big pup leaped onto the wagon seat beside him, the raider chucked the reins across the backs of the two horses. The animals refused, even after Asa slapped them twice more with the lines. The colonel ordered another man to lead them, and in this way, the team moved forward into water that soon rose to their chests.

The wagon lurched, then floated, though water seeped through its bottom slats. The handsome Union soldier with the curly hair was the only one strong enough to sit up. Rebecca could do nothing to keep the other injured men dry, and her skirt soaked up moisture like a lantern wick.

One of the harnessed horses squealed and began rearing, spooking its teammate. The raider leading the two animals fell off his mount, which struggled back in the direction they had come.

The wagon pitched, and Rebecca reached for the seatback to keep from falling. She missed, but someone grabbed her firmly from behind and held her upright. As the colonel and another rebel helped subdue the frightened horses, the man who'd been thrown rose. He began shouting and pointing at a spot beyond him in the water.

Rebecca's gaze followed the direction of his outstretched hand until she saw it. A dark, sinuous form undulated across the water's surface, forming and reforming a long S. If straight, Rebecca guessed it would be nearly five feet long.

"It's a goddamn cottonmouth!" shouted Asa. "Don't get near it!"

He drew a revolver and aimed it toward the snake, but the colonel held up his hand and shouted. "No! The horses!"

Asa fired anyway, further upsetting the already frightened team. The horses tried to bolt, and would have, except that the colonel and the second man kept a tight hold on their headstalls.

"Put that gun away—now!" the colonel shouted back at Asa.

"At least that damned snake skedaddled," Asa told him, but he stuck the revolver back inside his waistband.

The colonel's face reddened, emphasizing the pale gray of his eyes. "You idiot! That was a common water snake. Nothing poisonous about it!"

"Tell that to them horses," said the soldier who'd been thrown. His long hair and beard dripped from his drenching, and his gaze searched the water, as if he expected another snake to glide toward him at any second. He looked distinctly unhappy about the prospect.

An awkward silence lengthened, and tension stretched between the colonel and his subordinates. Asa snapped the reins across the horses' backs to start them moving. Further argument was postponed, at least for the time being.

"The horses sensed his panic," a voice said, too softly for any of the rebels to hear.

Rebecca felt the breath of the man's words warming her ear, just as she still felt his arms around her, holding her securely from behind. She sensed, rather than saw, that it was the soldier with the curly hair who had grabbed and steadied her. Blood rushed to heat her face at their closeness.

But at the same time, his nearness felt good, reassuring and quite solid, especially in consideration of his physical condition. Mindful of propriety, she knew she should free herself from his embrace, but something made her linger, content in the security he offered her aboard the moving wagon.

"Men never give without expecting something in return," Aunt Millicent once told her. *"If you wish to avoid becoming either a doll or drudge, keep that ever in your mind."*

With as much dignity as she could muster, Rebecca pulled away. Almost at once, she missed the contact. She thought again of the possibility that her recent shock had left her altered. More likely it was a temporary weakness, like a chill draft that might leave one susceptible to catching cold.

"Thank you for keeping me from falling," she told him, turning just enough to see his face.

"It was my pleasure, miss." He offered her his hand. "I'm Jacob Fuller. Sorry we got off on the wrong foot earlier."

She accepted his hand, meaning only to shake and then release it. Instead, she held onto it.

"You're still very cold," she said, squeezing his fingers. She felt it, too, stronger than ever, that sense that *she* had been the one pulled from the river, that *her* bones now ached with the long chill.

"I'll be all right," he assured her. "I'm more worried about these other fellows."

"Are they friends of yours?" she asked.

"They are now." He might have smiled, but his expression changed too quickly to be sure. "But I didn't know them before the accident. I wish I knew my brother had made it through—and our friends from Andersonville."

When he spoke of his brother and his friends, some shift in his voice made images flash over Rebecca's consciousness. Drew, his body facedown, blood leaking from a hole that passed straight through his chest. Eleanor's escalating cries. Sarah's white-faced terror.

The cracks in Rebecca's composure widened into deep fissures, and she felt herself begin to tremble. Her throat constricted painfully, and she released the soldier's hand so he wouldn't feel what was happening inside her.

Quickly, she turned to adjust the blankets on the other injured men. Her efforts were in vain, though, for all of them were soaked.

Jacob touched her arm.

"What are you doing here?" he asked her. "Why are you with them?"

She didn't answer because she knew the words would lodge like spiny burrs inside her throat.

Go on as if there's nothing wrong, she told herself. _Just go on like always._

Yet this time the oft-repeated mantra failed her, and she raised her hands to cover her face. She felt lost within a foreign landscape deep inside her, lost without a compass or a navigator's chart.

"I can't talk about what happened, and I—I can't help any of you," she said, whether to herself or Jacob she had no idea.

The wagon's wheels bumped land, and Rebecca felt them roll up onto the flood-spawned island of the decaying house. Felt, but did not see, for she could not lower her hands to bare her dust-dry eyes.

His voice gave her direction. "You can," he told her softly. "You can because you have to."

Jacob recognized the woman's struggle to master some internal tempest. He knew it because he so often fought the same battle, hiding grief and rage enough to fuel a dozen storms.

Miss Marston would not be so strong. Perhaps because she was a woman, or maybe because of some fundamental weakness, she would clearly crumble soon, the same way Hope had after he had failed her. And it was a damned shame, too, for this woman was all they had. This undisciplined band of rebels couldn't be counted on to expend the energy to dig their enemies decent graves, much less try to save their lives.

She dropped her hands and appeared to stare at the mud and grass clinging to a waterline that ringed the outside of the house. Then she blinked twice, rapidly, and regained control—at least for now.

One of the rebels who had ridden ahead stepped out onto the leaning porch.

"Hell of a time we had layin' a fire," he said. "Nothin' but wet wood all around. We done it, though. We done it, and it's warmin' up real fine."

"This building was flooded," Miss Marston said, gesturing toward the waterline, which reached waist level on the soldier standing on the porch. "I shudder to imagine the conditions inside. It's totally unsuitable for sick men."

Paying her no heed, the rebels carried the injured men into the house. Jacob climbed out of the wagon on his own, but the moment his feet hit the soggy ground, his knees buckled.

The woman hopped down beside him and firmly grasped his upper arm.

"Here, now. Lean on me," she said.

It warmed Jacob to hear a soothing female voice, so reminiscent of his family's farm, where his mother or his sister would have helped if he fell ill. The accompanying pang of homesickness made him hesitate.

As always, when he remembered home, the farm, his family, his thoughts veered dangerously toward Papa and to the letter his sister sent before he left Vicksburg. *Please hurry,* she had warned him. It galled him that at the moment there wasn't a damned thing he could do to get home faster, so he shoved aside the worry to let it fester with the others.

Miss Marston slid her arm around his waist as if it were something she'd done many times before. "Let me help you."

Jacob realized that although her words reminded him of his mother and Eliza, her touch in no way did. Something long dormant in him awakened to the softness of her loose red hair as it brushed his arm, and the pressure of her hand where it touched his side. He remembered, too, the pain that he'd seen welling in her tearless eyes, eyes that seemed too old for her unblemished face. He suspected it was sinful to find even a moment's pleasure in the nearness of someone so distressed, that he found any kind of pleasure when the men around him might be dying, when he had lost track of his own brother and his friends.

It was especially wrong because of where he'd found her: with this raider band. Although tension rumbled like thunder between her and the men, it might well be no different than the threat of insubordination that lay coiled between the rebels and their leader. It was altogether possible she was the lover of one of his captors, and, as such, his enemy.

As they mounted the rotting wooden steps, Jacob tried to divert his thoughts from the woman to their shelter. After dividing most of the past three years between tents and the open, he was grateful to have a roof over his head, and any building with a working fireplace sounded downright luxurious. He stepped inside the door ahead of Miss Marston.

To his way of thinking, the noticeable rise in temperature offset the layer of dried mud that covered everything below waist level, the corded cobwebs that hung from each ceiling and corner, and the unpleasant, sour odor of old dampness.

"Oh, dear," Miss Marston muttered, her tone indicating that she did not share his opinion. Her gaze swept the room, and he imagined her mentally assessing each inadequacy and forming a battle plan against it, just as the women of his own family would have done. Her attention appeared to focus on a sofa with matted stuffing leaking from several large tears. An overturned, warped table and a pair of ladderback chairs were the only other furnishings in sight.

Jacob sank wearily onto the mud-crusted floor in front of the huge stone fireplace, beside the other three men from the river, all of whom were lying motionless and quiet. He noticed pieces of a smashed chair and old newspapers had been used to lure the flame. With an effort, he forced himself to face the fire, as if that shift in direction could banish the woman from his thoughts. Closing his eyes, he watched warm colors flicker across the insides of his eyelids. The blood flowing through the thin veins deepened the yellow firelight into shades of orange, even red. He felt exhaustion tugging him toward a deep, unbroken sleep, but her voice cut through the cocoon of fatigue and demanded his attention.

"Our first order of business will be to warm these men," the woman said. Jacob supposed that she was speaking to the rebel officer. "We'll need to make hot warm broth if we're to save them. I'll also expect your men to help gather clean water, bandages, and locate some morphine for their pain, quinine for potential fever—"

"Miss Marston . . ." The colonel began.

She paid him no heed, but simply went on talking rapidly, as though she outranked the man. "We'll need some good salve for those burns, too. Then we can begin to set this place to rights, starting with the—"

"Miss Marston!" The officer sounded angry this time. "You forget you are our prisoner! That all of you are prisoners. You will *not* order us about."

Jacob opened his eyes. She was a *prisoner*? Damned bossiest one he'd ever seen, if that were true. He was surprised to feel relief creeping up on him at the discovery that she did not ride with these rough men willingly. It made sense as well, for her speech was educated, her accent Northern.

She glared stubbornly at the colonel. Again, Jacob's attention drifted to her torn bodice and loose hair. He thought about what he'd glimpsed earlier in her blue eyes. He remembered how he'd failed Hope when she had looked at him that way four years before.

"Son of a bitch," he swore under his breath at both the memory and another thought.

Had the raiders captured Miss Marston for their pleasure? The image of their filthy hands upon this beautiful woman, using her against her will, sickened him in a way that somehow shocked him. He'd seen nearly every type of ugliness a person could imagine in these past few years, so why should her pain affect him so deeply? Didn't he have troubles enough of his own?

The colonel raked his fingers through his black hair. Pulling a pipe out of his waistcoat pocket, he felt around for a tobacco pouch. He looked distinctly uncomfortable, as if he weren't accustomed to speaking so insultingly to women. "You're the nurse. If you want them saved, you save them. Otherwise . . ."

He shrugged. His manner, along with the way he'd insisted that the Union soldiers were not now "worthy adversaries," convinced Jacob that he was no rapist, but rather the sort of gentleman officer who turned a blind eye to his men's sins. Perhaps he felt that letting them use a captive woman would be good for camp morale.

He'd called her a nurse, Jacob realized, and he thought about the kindness of the Sisters of Mercy who had helped him and his friends and brother back in Vicksburg as they'd awaited transport home. They, too, had been nurses, women who had gone to war for no other reason than to bring men kindness. If these bastards were using this one for a whore . . .

Jacob's right hand knotted into a tight fist. Despite months of starvation and the disaster on the river, his arms were still powerful from years spent as a farrier, shoeing horses and hammering metal into useful forms. He wanted to test their strength, to find out if it was enough to knock the colonel's teeth down his throat.

A wave of exhaustion convinced him of the foolhardiness of that idea. That, and the armed men who were rummaging throughout the house. The fact was, though the war seemed all but over, the rebels held the upper hand here. He couldn't even keep himself safe, much less this strange female.

Jacob should think by now he would be used to the grief and rage glowing hot inside him, hidden only by his will to survive. He should think by now it wouldn't be so difficult to bear. But somehow the presence of one woman in this hell fanned the long months of frustration into a blaze so fierce that he knew he would no longer be able to conceal it. Not even if it cost him his last chance to go home.

Chapter Four

*We hold these truths to be self-evident: that all men
and women are created equal . . .*
—From "Declaration of Sentiments"
Adopted at Seneca Falls,
New York, 1848

Rebecca had done what she could, peeling off
each article of the wounded soldiers' soaked clothing and carefully washing the burns that had
injured three of them. All four men slept now, lying
on the dusty floor before the fire, each covered
only by a coarse blanket. After what they'd been
through, sleep was their most crucial need. But
she knew it wouldn't be enough. They required
nourishing food, clean water, and a wholesome
environment, along with medicines to treat the
burns and the fevers that would likely ensue. Her
stomach felt hollow, not only with hunger, but with
the certain knowledge that on her own, she had
no means of keeping any of these four men alive.

The colonel, with his trim black beard and hair,
limped in from the doorway that led to a simple
kitchen.

"The pantry's been stripped of anything edible,"

he announced, nodding toward the room he had just left. "But the stove, at least, is usable, and a few pans and such were left behind. I'll have wood cut for you, for cooking and for heat. There's water in the cistern just outside, too."

Her hands fisted with frustration. "These men need a doctor and a modern hospital. It's inhuman to insist they remain here under these conditions."

The colonel picked up first one ladderback chair and then the other and placed them beside a scarred worktable. He dusted off the second chair and motioned toward it. "Please, sit down, Miss Marston. There's no reason the two of us cannot carry on a civilized discussion."

Rebecca ignored the chair. "Oh, really?" she asked. "I can think of several. Beginning with the fact that one of your men murdered my cousin."

"War is little more than a chain of regrettable events." His face was shadowed with fatigue and what looked like sadness. He paused, as if he were recalling some especially troubling episode. "Regrettable, but necessary. Your cousin reached for a weapon. I saw him myself."

"Drew Wells was a surgeon and one of the gentlest men I ever knew!"

"Perhaps he should have conducted himself as such, then." The officer rested his arms atop the chair's back.

Rebecca suspected he would have preferred to sit but didn't since she had refused. That habitual courtesy, along with his manner of speaking, convinced her he'd been raised in a genteel environment more in keeping with her own than that of the rough men in his company. A more docile woman might have dropped daintily into the chair to avoid discomfiting him further, but at that moment Rebecca would not have spat upon him if he were afire.

"What choice did you leave Drew," she railed, "charging into the clearing with all that awful cater-wauling? He was only trying to defend the other women and myself! He was only—"

"A great fool," the colonel interrupted. "Other-wise, he never would have taken three ladies so far from protection. Ours is not the only group of raiders in the area, only the most civilized."

"Civilized? How can you possibly call yourself—"

"Others would have hanged the lot of you for your Union ties, after abusing all the women."

"Something your own men would be only too glad to do."

"The rules are different here, Miss Marston. Each of us has seen Union sympathizers commit so many atrocities against civilians and their property that a different sort of system has come into play. Whenever possible, I remind my men that inno-cents should not be harmed, that people must have something left to eat, that medical personnel on both sides are normally off limits. But my men have suffered such loss, such pain, that after a time, they understand only one law: an eye for an eye."

"If that's the only rule you know, then follow it," she challenged. "I'm no soldier. I'm a nurse, and I've done nothing to you, so why hold me against my will?"

"You're correct," the colonel told her, "but your father is another case entirely. He's the one this is about, not you."

"My father? How would you even be acquainted with him? Why on earth would—"

He lifted a palm, signaling for silence. "There are things you must not know. Our names, for one, and any information that might be used to find us later. If you learn too much, you will become another regrettable event."

As his meaning became clear, a wave of dizziness

washed over Rebecca. She sank into the empty chair farthest from the colonel and reminded herself to say nothing of those few names she'd heard already.

He reached into his waistcoat pocket and pulled out a flask.

"Whatever you might think of me, I consider myself a gentleman," he told her, offering the flask first.

She shook her head, and he withdrew it.

"I have no wish to harm a lady, only to see justice served. For that to happen, you must cooperate."

She wanted to protest that nothing about this situation had a thing to do with justice, but she remained silent instead, too unnerved by the fact that no matter how politely he had couched his statement, he had just threatened her life.

He unscrewed the flask's lid and sipped. When he had finished, he carefully replaced the top.

"First and most importantly," the colonel began as he slipped the flask into his pocket, "you will not attempt escape. Several of my men will be outside at all times, hoping you'll set foot outside the boundaries."

He did not say what those men might do; he didn't have to. Yesterday was still too fresh in Rebecca's mind; she could still feel the searing pressure of Asa's fingertips. Nausea fluttered in her belly.

"Secondly," he continued, "you will speak to me but not to my men. After they finish their search, they will not be permitted inside this house. That way, you'll never learn their names. And you'll be safer."

He's trying to protect all of us, his men from me and me from his men. For a moment, her anger ebbed, and in its place gratitude flowed forward—until he gazed meaningfully at the men lined up before the fire.

"If you choose to disobey me," he continued, the coldness of his voice freezing her goodwill almost before it started, "if you do anything to thwart my purpose, I'll have all these men killed, one by one."

Though on some level Jacob knew he lay before a fire, wrapped inside a blanket gritty with both sweat and Southern soil, at the same time he walked the farm in Indiana. The ripe odors of the cows, manure, and soured, spilled milk warred with the sweeter scents of hay and corn and cream. His eyes feasted on the green and gold of feed crops and the soft brown eyes of Jersey cows. As he touched warm udders with his callused hands, the cows lowed softly, as if in bovine bliss at the relief of giving milk. Jacob's feet measured acre after acre of dark and fertile soil, acres that ached like throbbing jaws until he pulled out stumps and stones to soothe them, acres that sighed in earthy exhalations scented with the richness of potential.

Sometimes Hope walked beside him, her hand cool inside his. But mostly Hope was no more than the breath of wind that moved the tassels of the growing corn—the chill that rippled through the creek.

Jacob did not see his father pouring warm, white rivers into heavy canisters. He didn't hear him, either, wheezing with the grain dust or humming old church hymns. Yet he understood that Papa permeated every level of his long walk—that the barn, the pastures, and the fields *were* Papa in some sense.

With that understanding, the cornstalks browned and withered; the cows' plump udders shrank and dried. Eliza stepped off the porch and jabbed her broom in his direction as she asked, "Why didn't you come sooner?"

Jacob lurched awake, his heart thumping with a woodpecker's staccato rhythm, his mouth as parched as pastureland in drought. As he lay on his side, Jacob's vision focused on an unfamiliar landscape. Yellow flames augmented the daylight slanting through filmed windows. The table and chairs, lying in disarray before, had been righted; the shredded sofa was no longer visible. A haze of dust sparkled golden in the air, and the scent of cooking meat flooded his dry mouth with hopeful moisture.

The illusion of perfection frayed as his vision cleared enough to focus on the cobwebs that still formed swags in every corner and on the smeary dirt trails where someone had tried to sweep. He rolled onto his back and took in the sight of the woman tending an unconscious soldier. She was using a rag and a shallow basin of water to bathe the horribly scalded flesh of his upper arm and shoulder. Jacob winced, remembering how the man's skin had fallen away at his touch. It seemed unlikely that the soldier would survive, but at least he had someone here to offer comfort. At least he wouldn't have to die alone.

As he watched the nurse, he noticed how her hands shook as she went about her work. Her red hair had been twisted into an untidy knot behind her neck, just as Hope did when she was too busy to spare hers much attention. But this woman was busy working to save him and the other injured soldiers, apparently alone. Despite his condition, he wanted to get up, to offer her some share of comfort, for in her own way, she appeared to need it as much as any of the men.

He reminded himself this had nothing to do with the disastrous time he had failed to offer enough compassion—that this woman was a stranger, not his wife.

Pushing aside the impulse to do more, Jacob instead heeded his grumbling stomach.

"Something sure smells good. Is that beef tea?" he croaked hopefully, his voice hoarser than he'd expected. His mother had always made beef tea when he'd been ill, and the thought of its rich, salty goodness made his mouth water anew.

She jumped as if she hadn't expected anyone to speak. Her face turned toward him, and for a moment he once more saw such naked pain that he could hardly bear it. Almost instantly, she masked the expression with one of professional concern.

"I'm afraid not. There's no fresh meat to be had, but I've boiled some jerked beef. The liquid should be cool enough to drink. Would you like to try some?"

He nodded, and she left the room. In less than a minute, she returned with a metal cup. His stomach rumbled at the steaming fragrance. It might not be real beef tea, but if this war had accomplished nothing else, it had accustomed him to making do.

As she knelt beside him, he noticed the dirt ground into the knee level of her skirt, indicating that she'd been kneeling for long hours.

"How are you feeling?" she asked.

"Tired and sore and almighty glad to be out of the river. Where are they?" Jacob asked, referring to their captors. He couldn't afford to forget about them, couldn't breathe easy until he knew what they meant to do.

Slowly he sat up, and as he did, his gaze swept over his fellows, and he counted quickly. Reassured that all still lived, he took the cup from her and sipped. He could hear them breathing and the burned man moaning in his sleep. The brew was weak and probably not much in terms of nourishment, but both the warmth and wetness in his parched mouth felt heavenly.

"The raiders?" the woman asked him. "A few of them are outside cutting wood. I heard at least one ride off a while ago. The colonel was careful to let me know they'd be keeping watch. He said . . ."

"What did he tell you?" Jacob prompted.

"He said he'd have you all killed if I tried to escape."

She shuddered, and Jacob wondered if that was all the son of a bitch had said—or done—to her.

"What time—?" he began. "How long did I sleep?"

"It's late afternoon now. You've slept since this morning. The others haven't yet awakened." She turned, and her gaze lingered on each one.

Jacob guessed that she was checking to see if they still breathed. She looked so exhausted, so very nearly ill herself, that he wanted to brush the loose hair from her face, to smooth the darkness from beneath those beautiful blue eyes. Instead of acting, he reminded himself that he knew nothing of her, and that he had pain enough to bear without shouldering hers, too.

The blanket slid down his chest to gather near his waist. That was when he realized that underneath it, he hadn't a single stitch of clothing.

"Good Lord, woman," he said, hastily adjusting the blanket. "You've plucked me like a rooster."

Her hand flew to cover her mouth, but not before he saw the quick flash of her smile.

"All of you were soaked to the bone," she explained, serious once more. "It was important to get you out of those wet clothes so you could warm up."

"You stripped us on your own?"

A blush darkened her cheeks, and her red brows pulled together. "I'll thank you to remember I'm a trained nurse, Mister Fuller. I can assure you that doing so without assistance was quite a struggle, and I had neither the inclination nor the energy to enjoy the task.''

Her glare defied him to argue.

''Sorry, miss. It just took me by surprise, that's all.''

''You're forgiven, then. Your clothes are drying on the porch. I rinsed them as best I could with water from the cistern.''

''Thank you for that—and for everything you're doing.''

She said nothing, and he drained the remainder of the cup's contents. When he risked looking at her again, she was staring toward the window, her gaze unfocused. Her hands, resting on her knees, were close enough to touch if he reached for her.

He reminded himself that he'd already offended her on more than one occasion. Still, his words slipped out too suddenly to bridle.

''Why do they have you?''

His repetition of the question took him by surprise. He'd never been a man with much to say, especially to women. Hope had often complained about his unease with words, and by the time he'd finally found some, they sure as hell hadn't been what she'd needed to hear. The way he saw it since then, the less said, the less risked.

So why was he so interested in talking to this woman? Jacob reminded himself that he needed to concentrate on surviving. He couldn't afford to stir up the anger that had so nearly overwhelmed him earlier.

She hesitated so long, he began to think she would not answer. As she reached to tuck a wavy strand into her loose chignon, her trembling increased visibly.

Just as Jacob decided, almost gratefully, to let

the question drop, she spoke, her voice little louder than a whisper.

"They're holding me for ransom."

"For ransom?" Jacob could not have been more astonished. But relief, too, crept into the mix of his emotions. He'd been afraid she would tell him her situation was exactly what he'd feared earlier: that she'd been taken for their captors' pleasure. Yet her true status was nearly as alarming.

"The government will never pay, not even for a woman hostage," he said too bluntly. "Especially not when everyone knows the war is all but over."

She shook her head and interrupted. "The government won't, but my father is a wealthy man. It's his money they're after. I can only trust to chance they'll let me go once he has paid."

Despite her statement, the cynicism in her voice matched his opinion. Trust and rebel irregulars did not go hand in hand. Whether or not the raiders achieved their goal, they'd likely murder her to protect themselves from hanging.

"How long since they took you?" he asked.

"It was only yesterday afternoon." The mask slipped further to expose her sadness.

He warned himself to stop, but the questions refused to wait in silence. "How did it happen? Where?"

She shook her head and turned her face from him. "I need to check the others."

He understood, then, that she wouldn't answer, or she couldn't. He had bumped against a boundary with his questions, and as much as he wanted to, he knew he could not push past it. Not while his life and the lives of the other injured soldiers remained in her unsteady hands. And not when he had so many painful borders of his own.

In Andersonville, he'd tried to keep himself contained by limiting his focus to his brother and their two close friends. It was the only way he could survive in the face of all the suffering, all the death around him. He'd seen far worse pain than hers before, so what was it about this woman that so compelled him?

She bent to adjust a soldier's blanket, and the heavy fabric of her skirt draped over a nicely rounded bottom—and his answer. Jacob nearly laughed aloud at his own foolishness. Neither her tailored pale-gray shirtwaist nor her charcoal-colored skirt could be construed as provocative dress, but how long had it been since he'd shared close quarters with a woman? The only wonder of it was that he hadn't propositioned the elderly nun who'd cut his hair and shaved him back in Vicksburg.

This woman was nearly as unsuitable. She might have taken the notion to become a Union nurse, but she came from the kind of money that prompted these Confederate bastards to demand a ransom. The same kind of money built a barricade between her and a man who'd made his living hard, by shoeing horses and shaping metal back in Indiana.

Still, as if he were a moonstruck adolescent, he could barely take his eyes off her graceful movements, the swish of her full skirt, the slender curves of her bodice, the way her hands settled on her hips—just as Ma's did when she was angry. His gaze rose quickly to her face, which had arranged itself into a no-nonsense frown.

"Is there something that you need, Mr. Fuller?"

Jacob cursed himself, feeling even more embarrassed than when he'd realized she'd undressed him. If he were half the talker his younger brother, Zeke, had always been, he'd spin out some smooth words about how beautiful she was. Instead, he grappled for the first excuse that he could think of.

Lifting his cup, he told her, "I'd be much obliged if I might have a little more . . . if there's enough left."

Food—and its absence—were never far from his mind, and as poor a soup as the weak broth made, he couldn't drink it without knowing how far it had to stretch.

"They brought some hardtack, too. Do you think you could eat some if I softened it with broth?"

His stomach growled at the suggestion. The hard biscuits may have inspired such uncomplimentary names as "teeth-dullers" and "worm castle," but they'd soothed the ache in his belly more times than he could count. "I'd like that, Miss Marston."

She smiled. "We may be together for some time. I think we can dispense with the formalities. My name is Rebecca, Jacob."

He felt as if she'd entrusted him with something precious, just by telling him her name. He spoke quickly, eager to repeat it. "Thank you . . . Rebecca."

Caution trod on the heels of his enthusiasm. It was only natural for her to seek a temporary ally to help her through this situation. If ever they regained their freedom, she would cease to be Rebecca. Instead, she would resume her rightful name—Miss Marston. She would flee to her rich father. In later years, the story of her daring adventure would make her a popular fixture at the big bugs' dinner parties. She might whisper and laugh with the other ladies about the curly-haired Indiana farrier who'd fancied her, but one thing was for damned sure. She would never consider, even for a moment, continuing any sort of relationship with him—not even if he were the sort of man who could afford to risk what Hope had left of his heart.

Chapter Five

*A woman is nobody. A wife is everything. A pretty
girl is equal to ten thousand men, and a mother
is, next to God, all powerful. . . . The ladies of
Philadelphia, therefore, under the influence of the
most serious, sober second thoughts, are resolved
to maintain their rights as Wives, Belles, Virgins
and Mothers, and not as Women.*

*Philadelphia Public Ledger and
Daily Transcript*, 1848

April 28, 1865

Rebecca hung the blankets she had washed over
the porch railing to dry. She should have attended
to this chore hours earlier, but her day had been
a desperate blur of chores to help the wounded
men. Around the tiny island, darkness had settled
heavily, cloaking the world in deep shadow punctuated by the secret speech of insects, the lonely
hoots of a hunting owl.

This evening she knew how the mouse must feel,
hearing that reminder of the dangers of the night.
Gazing blindly outward, she wondered which of
the raiders was now watching her, silhouetted as

she was by the firelight leaking beyond the open door. At any moment, she expected to hear the eerie Rebel yell and see men swooping in to hurt her.

Swallowing hard, she hurried back inside and closed the front door. But the house offered little comfort. Instead, she felt the same apprehension she'd experienced when she'd first seen the deserted place.

Her imagination tried to reconstruct the family who'd once lived here, leaving behind both their home and a number of possessions. Had the flooding Mississippi driven them away? Or had raiders— maybe even *these* raiders—come and murdered them for what they had? As the firelight flickered across the mud-stained walls, she heard muted voices or their echoes, and she felt the hair rising on her arms and neck.

With a shudder, Rebecca crossed the room to check her patients and found them all still sleeping as they should be, for the hour was very late. Though she knew better, she could not resist the feeling that as long as she watched over them, they would continue drawing breath after breath in the endless healing cycle of deep sleep. Once again, she wondered how long she could hold out against her own need for rest, and what nightmares lay in wait when finally, inevitably, she succumbed.

Weary to her bones, Rebecca sat behind the row of men arranged before the fire and watched the dying flames settle into a warm glow. She ought to put on one more log against the night's chill, she realized, but her mind was powerless to force her arms to move. She'd just rest for a moment, and close her eyes before she . . .

Despite the swirl of violent memories from the raiders' attack, despite her fears for the injured men entrusted to her care, Rebecca slept too

deeply to be reached by the sharp claws of evil
dreams. As she woke, her nose itching with the
thick dust from the floor, she thanked God for
that small mercy.

And for one other as well. Someone had thrown
a blanket over her. She clutched it tighter, for the
morning air was chilly, and tried not to notice the
odor of old sweat, damp wool, and ground-in dirt.

Her eyes slowly opened, and she thought of how
very far she'd come to be content with such thin
comfort. She could barely believe she was the same
person who had taken for granted her soft feather
bed with its fine linens, the elegant Spruce Street
mansion back in Philadelphia, and the summer
estate along the banks of the Delaware River. She
doubted whether her old friends, nearly all of
whom had married, would recognize her now, and
she wondered if, after all she'd seen and done, she
would ever again have anything to say to them.
The problems of selecting the right gloves to match
a dinner dress, or choosing which set of china to
use for an afternoon tea, paled to inconsequence
when compared to working to save the lives of
men. But they wouldn't understand that, and she
wouldn't know how to explain to them the price
she'd paid for the failure of her courage.

Small, bright flames danced in the fireplace, and
a dark-haired man stooped to feed them several
split logs. Her heart skipped a beat as she wondered
which one of the raiders had slipped inside while
she slept—and what harm the man intended.

When Jacob turned, Rebecca Marston was staring
at him, his blanket clutched in both her hands and
her blue eyes wide with apprehension.

Silence stretched between them, lengthening in

brittle strands. Then he heard the hiss of her pent-up breath escaping.

"I thought at first you were one of the rebels," she told him. "You frightened me half out of my wits."

"I could tell you were surprised."

"How?"

"No orders. If you'd been yourself, you would have probably had me out chopping more firewood by now." He grinned, remembering yesterday. "I have to say, I kind of enjoyed hearing you put those Johnnies in their place."

"For all the good it did us," she answered. Sitting up, she yawned and stretched her arms. "Thank you for the blanket. I assume you were the one who covered me."

"It's a pleasure sharing a blanket with you, Rebecca."

He felt a rush of shame as he realized exactly what he'd said. Quickly, he added, "I—I meant—that is—I didn't mean—"

Rebecca laughed. "*I* have to say, I rather enjoy hearing *you* stammer. Why it's almost as gratifying as issuing orders."

Jacob sighed. "I reckon I deserved that."

"I dare say you did—and more."

One of the men groaned, and Rebecca's expression grew instantly serious. As her gaze swung past the injured man and toward the body, Jacob wished uselessly that he could shield her from what had happened while she'd slept.

A stained quilt now completely covered the man farthest from her, the one who'd been so badly burned about the upper arm and shoulder. Her hand rose to her mouth, but not fast enough to block her cry of dismay.

The sound brought the other two men awake, and all three stared at her, the two who'd been asleep blinking their confusion. Noticing their scrutiny, Rebecca blushed fiercely, and Jacob could see from her expression how she struggled to dam the leak in her emotions.

"I shouldn't have slept." Grief cracked her voice.

Before he could warn himself against it, Jacob closed the distance between them. He knelt beside her, and his hand reached out to touch her arm. Yet he hesitated, unsure whether she would welcome that degree of intimacy, especially with the other two men watching. Even so, he wanted— needed—to wrap his arms around her. The wave of longing took him by surprise.

"No one could have saved him," he told her quietly. "You did all you could."

Despite his body's weakness, strength suffused his voice with all the surety that so often made men follow his lead. He might not be able to hold her, but he could at least offer her that much.

She continued staring at the hump formed by the dead man beneath the dirty shroud.

"He should have had a hospital and doctors," she said. "With the right medication—"

"With decent food, solid shelter, and good medicine, God knows how many men would be alive today," Jacob interrupted. Anger colored his words, frustration with the terrible destruction, the blasphemous waste of life he'd seen. "And without this damned fool war to send us traipsing all over creation to force traitors back into the Union, we'd all be better off."

Her gaze sharpened as she looked into his eyes. "You can't possibly mean that you don't think this war was worthy."

He saw her disapproval and found that he preferred it to the desolation he'd seen moments before. Enough so that he did not soften his opinions to appease her. Instead, he thought of all the bodies he'd helped cover, and he allowed those men a voice. "I mean exactly what I said. This whole thing was started by a bunch of useless intellectuals spouting off about rights and freedoms, never giving half a thought to the poor men who'd be pulled from farms and businesses to fight out their squabbles. Who'd be shot and starved and afflicted with diseases they'd never heard of."

Her jaw looked set for battle, but instead Rebecca turned away from him. She dusted herself off and rose to tend those men still living. The first, a fellow Jacob judged to be in his late thirties, had scattered burns across his neck and chest, as if flying coals had struck him. His coarse black hair and beard, too, had singed patches. Today, at least, he'd ceased crying the endless, beseeching chorus of "Please," but he groaned loudly and was so disoriented that he fought Rebecca's efforts to give him water.

Jacob held his arms and said, "You'll need to drink now."

The burned soldier's hazel eyes turned toward Jacob, and he took a deep breath. Jacob braced himself for an earsplitting wail. Instead, however, the man seemed to recover his senses, at least enough to nod and allow the nurse to give him water.

"If you can stay awake until I get the stove lit, I'll bring you some warm broth and hardtack," she offered. "Can you do that for me?"

But the soldier's eyelids were already drooping, and in a few moments he had fallen back to sleep.

"We'll wake him later," Jacob said as Rebecca helped the second man sip water.

"Thank you, miss," the other soldier said, once he had finished drinking. He scratched at his cheek, which was faintly stubbled with blond whiskers.

Not even old enough to grow a decent beard, Jacob thought. And already, he had survived so much. Jacob tried to judge the fellow's age. Seventeen or eighteen, he imagined. The blond boy had spent his youth on pointless suffering.

The young man's blue eyes scanned their surroundings. "Where *is* this?" he asked.

"Don't you remember yesterday, when you and these men were pulled out of the river?" Rebecca asked him.

His gaze settled on the shrouded soldier for a moment before he looked away. "The explosion . . ."

"Yes," she continued. "How are those burns today?"

While Rebecca slept, Jacob had checked a blistered swath across the boy's stomach. The reddened skin appeared to be the result of steam exposure. The burns covered an area about the size of an open bible, but they weren't nearly as deep as those of the sleeping soldier or the man who'd died.

Jacob Fuller was the only soldier of the group not burned, and for that he was profoundly grateful. He may not have regained all of his strength yet, but Rebecca would need his help to save these men.

The blond soldier lowered the blanket to expose his stomach and peered down at the oozing wound. He hissed through his teeth at the sight of it.

"It's plenty sore," he explained, not appearing in the least bothered by his lack of clothing, though only the blanket covered his thin lower body. "I reckon it'll hurt like the dickens when I walk back to find my unit."

"I'm afraid you can't leave for a while," Rebecca told him.

"Course I got to. Me and my messmates, why,

we always stick together. Wonder where them fellas will meet up.''

"We're stuck here for the time being," Jacob told him. "We've all been captured by reb irregulars, and they're holding her for ransom.''

The younger man's mouth formed an O, and his expression hinted at a cascade of returning memories.

"Well, hell," he finally said.

"Pretty much," Jacob answered. Sticking out his hand, he introduced himself and then Rebecca, although he called her Miss Marston.

"I'm Private Nate Gordon, Fourth Kentucky Infantry. What's your unit?"

Jacob shook his head. "I'm through with units, through with rank. All I want to be now is Jacob Fuller, the best farrier in West Deerfield, Indiana.''

For some reason, Rebecca glowered at him, then spun on her heel. "I'll be in the kitchen—cooking.''

With that, she vanished with a dark swirl of her skirt.

Jacob stared after her, confused at her anger, but altogether sure it had something to do with what he'd said. And he wondered, when it came to women, how a man of so few words could so often find the wrong ones.

He couldn't care less if the rest of the country went straight to Hades, thought Rebecca, as long as he was left in peace. Jacob Fuller's statements shouldn't bother her, she knew, yet for some reason they did. Perversely, her mind dredged up the gentle pressure of his arms around her in the wagon, the remarkable sense of peace she'd experienced those few moments when he'd held her. She felt bereft as a desert traveler who has just discovered that a glimpsed oasis is nothing more than a mirage.

Using some matches the colonel had left yesterday, she lit the stove and reheated the poor broth. She'd swept last night, but in the wake of the floodwaters, her efforts had been nearly useless. Gazing across the mud-stained floor and the warped cabinets, she thought of scrubbing, and her mind rebelled.

She couldn't possibly do all this by herself. Not without shattering into a thousand jagged shards, each one with razor edges that would slice into her heart. Gazing into the battered pot she'd found atop a cabinet, she looked in disgust at yesterday's nearly worthless brew. The idea of surviving on the broth and old hardtack left her nauseated. The idea of serving it to sick men was even worse.

I can't do this, she told herself. *I have no business even trying.* Certainly, she'd worked hard at the hospital, but at her heart, she was still a woman unfamiliar with the rudiments of cooking and housekeeping. She might speak French and read poetry and discourse intelligently on a wide variety of topics, but right now she'd trade all those skills for a thimble-full of the practical knowledge needed to keep herself and these men alive.

That is, the three who were not dead already.

She jumped when a tap came at the back door behind her. The colonel walked in, carrying something wrapped in dark burlap.

Anger flared at the sight of him, for she had so many questions she wanted to ask. But yesterday's warning still echoed in her mind.

If you learn too much, you will become another regrettable event.

So instead she told him, "One of them died last night."

He dropped his burden on the tabletop and

looked at her for a long while. His scrutiny
unnerved her, and she wondered if the accusation
in her voice had angered him.

But when he spoke, his words were almost gentle.
"I'll have my men remove the body and see that
it's buried properly. I'm sorry you had to witness
such a thing. A lady shouldn't have to tend to
wounded men. I've never understood why the Yankees don't treat their women with the respect they're
due. If you were mine, I'd never let you—"

"Fortunately, that will never be the case," she
snapped. Her gaze flicked to the table to the blood
that seeped out from the burlap. She couldn't take
her eyes off the spreading puddle.

Disjointed memories assailed her: Drew's "severed" hand inside the box, the dull thump of an
amputated leg as it fell onto the floor of the hospital
surgery, the hot spatter of her cousin's blood when
he'd been shot beside her. Image after image burst
upon her, leaving her with nowhere to retreat.
Nowhere but the blackness that roared up from
the floor to swallow her alive.

When Jacob heard a metallic clatter and a thud,
he rushed into the kitchen without a moment's
hesitation, only to find the officer kneeling beside
Rebecca, who was lying, apparently unconscious,
on the floor.

"What in God's name did you do to her?" Jacob
demanded, anger pounding so hard at his temples,
he didn't even stop to consider the revolver
strapped beside the colonel's waist.

The pan lay close beside her, its brownish contents soaking into the already filthy plank flooring.
His mind skated dangerously close to a scarlet puddle spreading on another wooden floor, and a dif-

ferent crumpled woman. Another time, another
nightmare . . .

The colonel held Rebecca's limp hand in a manner that made Jacob's gut clench.

"One of the men shot a fine buck this morning.
I brought a haunch of venison," the colonel
explained. "When she saw the blood, she fainted."

It seemed unlikely that a little deer blood would
cause a nurse to swoon. Jacob glared suspiciously at
the colonel, but even as he did so, he remembered
Rebecca's fragility, her borders. She was everything
and nothing like Hope all at once.

"I'll take care of her," Jacob told the other man.
Anything to get his filthy rebel hands off her.

The colonel ignored him, instead touching her
cheek. "Rebecca?"

When she didn't stir, he scooped her into his
arms, then rose. "There's a bed upstairs where she
would be more comfortable," he said as he passed
the unconscious redhead to Jacob. As he looked
after her, regret darkened his gray eyes. "I'll expect
her to be treated honorably."

Jacob snorted. "That's a hell of an odd thing for
you to say, seeing as how you're holding her for
ransom."

Though Rebecca was fairly slender, she was a
heavy burden for a man weakened by both hunger
and exposure. Jacob leaned against the pantry door
and shifted her weight carefully. His muscles might
ache, but he liked the way his arms fit around her,
and the sound of her breath, warm and even, as
she slept. Holding her this way made him feel as
if he had the power to protect her, and he had to
admit it was a sensation he liked.

"I have no wish to cause her more distress than
necessary." The colonel's expression was somber,
ill at ease. "Unfortunately, war sometimes necessi-
tates distasteful actions."

"Distasteful—or disgraceful?" Jacob asked.

"Make no mistake. Winfield Marston is the enemy and not his daughter. But we'll do what we must to be repaid, even if it comes to killing."

"You've already killed by trapping us inside here without medicine or any means to get it. And all for a war you know damned well you've lost already."

The colonel shook his head. "The greater war is not the point here. I'm only interested in settling an account that's come past due. And I don't know the last time I saw morphine or quinine or any sort of modern drug. You'll have to make do the same as we do."

"I've done a lot of making do these past few years," Jacob told him, though he was distracted by the outline of Rebecca's thigh against the fabric of her skirt. He warned himself to concentrate. He might not get another chance to convince the colonel that they would need more to survive. "Andersonville was no picnic."

The colonel raised one sleek, jet eyebrow. "And Union prisons *are?*"

Jacob shook his head. There was no need to make a contest of their suffering, especially not when he imagined there had been so much of it to go around. Instead, he tried a different approach. "I don't reckon you pulled us out of that river because you meant for us to die. I'm not asking you to ride to an apothecary and place an order for us. I'm asking permission to go out and forage for our needs."

"You think I'm going to let you?"

"I won't go far. I saw some willows in that little stand of trees outside the house. I want to get some bark for a painkiller."

The colonel nodded. "I'll tell you what, Yank. You—and only you—can leave this house. But stay on the island. You try to cross the floodwater, and

I'll have you shot. And if you somehow manage to slip away, we'll kill all of them. . . .''

His gray-eyed gaze lingered on Rebecca, whose hair had fallen loose. There was a momentary softness in his expression, but it hardened so quickly that Jacob couldn't be sure he'd seen it in the first place.

"Including her. You have my word," the colonel finished.

Jacob had seen enough during this war that he didn't doubt it for a minute. With a stiff nod, he turned and carried Rebecca from the room. And he wished for all that he was worth that he could somehow carry her from danger.

Asa Graves felt a sneer curling his lip as he watched Colonel Hall leave the farmhouse. The smug bastard kept them from the woman, but he'd bet his last dollar the man was romancing his way to what every mother's son of them ought to have a share of.

The colonel swung aboard his fancy black mare and rode through the water that isolated the two-story building. And all the while Asa glared at him until his one remaining eyeball felt like a smoldering coal inside its socket.

Down Louisiana way, Colonel Lewis Hall was a Big Man. Asa had heard talk that he owned a huge cotton plantation, every acre of it dotted with slaves to do his bidding. But despite his high-dollar East Coast lawyer talk and fancy manners, the son of a bitch rode like an Indian and drew a gun as fast as any outlaw. After a series of catastrophic decisions by his superiors in Tennessee, Hall had grown disgusted enough with the Confederate leadership to turn his horse's nose toward home. He'd made it only as far as Arkansas when conscience prompted him to find a different way to aid his cause.

Within a short time, Asa joined him, along with the remnants of his home guard and a handful of Confederate deserters. Most of them, Asa included, would have been content to continue taking what they wanted and killing whoever got in their way, but the colonel convinced the group to organize into an effective guerrilla force. Together, they'd disrupted Union supply lines, attacked occupied towns, and hanged as many Northern sympathizers as they could lay their hands on.

This kidnapping was something new for them, though, and the idea of it frustrated Asa deeply. This Marston fellow might be richer than pig shit on a wheat field, but it would take time to collect a ransom, time that they would all be forced to wait here, to give the Federals plenty of chances to hunt them down. For all he was worth, Asa couldn't figure out why Hall was so set on the plan.

One thing he knew for sure, though: the whole caper must have something to do with Hall's over-active sense of honor and the amount of ransom that he'd asked. He'd been stubbornly exact about it. Twenty-five thousand Yankee greenbacks. Asa could think of roughly the same number of reasons this was all a bad idea.

Starting with those Yanks they'd pulled out of the river. It would have been hard enough keeping one hostage quiet and subdued, much less four or five. Soldiers, too, would be less liable to go all scared and quiet and not make any trouble. If Hall had really wanted the kidnapping to come off, he would have let them fill the bastards' pockets with rocks and tossed the whole damned lot back in the river. Or maybe they could have had a little sunrise target practice.

The woman was another matter. She might be

mule-headed as they came, but she was no fool. Soon as she got loose, she'd figure some way to send troops after them, sure as he was Asa Graves. And that might turn out all right for Colonel Hall, who'd hide out on his high-dollar plantation down in Louisiana, but they'd have a damned good chance of finding him and the other Arkansas boys if they looked hard enough.

He remembered the snotty look on the woman's pretty face when she had threatened him with her old man.

"When he finds out, he'll hunt you down like the dogs you are. He'll stop at nothing to destroy you."

"You hear that? Gonna hunt us down like dogs," he told the pup, which shadowed him the way it had since the day he'd helped string up its Yankee owner.

The hound whined and sidled closer, fanning its tail until Asa scratched the floppy ears. The pup might not be concerned about the possibility of a rich man's revenge, but Asa didn't like the thought of it at all. The woman might promise later, sweet as you please, that she'd keep her mouth shut, but he damned sure knew better, didn't he? And Big Men didn't like you fooling with their daughters.

Asa Graves knew that for a fact. He'd done hard time learning it was gospel.

If they caught up with him now, there'd be no jail to bust out of. There'd only be a noose, and that was final as they came. Big Man Colonel Hall and his honor be damned; Asa wasn't about to swing on account of any woman.

Not when he could have his fun and then shut her mouth but good.

As Jacob peeled the bark from a willow tree, he had to force himself to keep his full attention on the job at hand. He knew he was being watched, not only from the colonel's warning, but from the chill creeping along his spine and gripping his empty stomach. Glancing back over his shoulder to see whether or not some Reb had a gun aimed in his direction wouldn't help. It would only give the raiders the satisfaction of knowing the idea made him uneasy. Imagining their laughter, he steeled himself against temptation.

Until he heard the splashing of a rider crossing the expanse of water. He turned, staring in disbelief at one of the rebels, a man grinning ear to ear with dully glistening brown teeth. Stranger still, he held a dead skunk by the tail. Its rank odor preceded horse and rider.

The chestnut gelding emerged dripping from the water, then trotted a few steps to bring it within a few feet of where Jacob stood.

"Colonel says we oughta feed y'all," the rebel told him, and the smile turned mean. "Brought ya s'more fresh meat."

With that, he tossed the dead skunk into the dirt at Jacob's feet. The smell from its black-and-white carcass rose in a thick cloud.

Satisfied with his gesture, the rebel wheeled around the horse and urged it back into the water. Beyond the harsh sound of his cackling, Jacob could hear the distant laughter of his fellows, who stood near the old barn, where they apparently were staying.

Looking down at the skunk, which had a bullet hole through one shoulder, he sighed.

"Well, Stinky," Jacob told the carcass. "You might not make dinner, but I suppose we have a use for you."

Chapter Six

I started with this idea in my head, "There's two things I've got a right to . . . death or liberty."
——Harriet Tubman

Rebecca dreamed the house a home, as it had been once. A young couple laughed, their backs turned to her, as the sheet of wallpaper they were hanging slid down, then collapsed to drape over their upper bodies. As they struggled with the flowered paper, sunshine filtered through translucent curtains to suffuse the scene with an ethereal glow.

Across the room a door swung open, and a red-haired boy grinned in obvious delight, exposing two missing front teeth.

"Mama and Papa made a tent!" he squealed.

Something shook Rebecca, and the scene dissolved.

"Miss Marston—Rebecca?"

Was she late for her shift? She fought toward alertness, but sleep pulled at her like an anchor, dragging her toward the bottom, beyond the reach of light.

Until she smelled a rich aroma and her mouth

began to water. Her stomach woke next, rumbling demands, reminding her she'd had only a little broth and hardtack yesterday and none at all this morning.

And then she remembered the men counting on her efforts to provide them food and succor. The one she had already failed when she'd succumbed late last night. And now she was asleep again, her mind weaving pleasant fancies about the family that had once lived in this house.

Guiltily, she forced her eyes to open and then struggled to sit up. She mustn't lose another of the soldiers. There was so much, so very much, she had to do.

A strong hand pressed against her shoulder and prevented her from rising. Remembering the raider called Asa, Rebecca opened her mouth to scream. But before the sound escaped, her vision focused on Jacob Fuller's face.

Her mouth snapped shut, but her heart attempted to beat its way free of her chest. As in her dream, a ray of sunshine shone through the worn muslin curtains covering the room's sole window, and she realized she was lying on a bed, beneath a cream-colored woolen blanket. Rebecca recognized the scarred dresser, along with the cracked mirror and chipped chamber set, from yesterday's search for linens on the upper floor. Her gaze lingered for a moment on the peeling floral wallpaper, now yellowed with age.

She shivered lightly, remembering how that detail had worked its way into her dream. Dismissing her discomfort, she realized she had far more important concerns than the strangeness of this house—such as the startling fact that she was alone, inside a bedroom with this man.

"It's all right," he told her, and once again his

voice worked its strange magic. "You're safe enough for now."

Thin curls of rising steam undulated in the afternoon sunlight. Rebecca's attention focused on an earthen bowl atop the dresser, on the glint of light from the dull silver handle of the spoon that slanted into the warm liquid. Her stomach growled in response to the aroma, which smelled far better than her poor attempts at cooking.

Still, there were questions she must ask. "How did I get here? The last thing I remember, I was in the kitchen, speaking to the colonel."

"You fainted. Apparently, you didn't appreciate the venison he brought." Jacob rose and retrieved the bowl from the dresser. "Maybe you'll like the cooked version better. I made some soup for us."

Her mouth watered, but a pang of guilt reminded her of the injured men downstairs.

"We'll feed the soldiers first," she told him.

He shook his head. "You eat now. I fed Nate a while back, and the other one's still sleeping. You probably passed out in the first place because you've been so busy taking care of us, you've barely slept or eaten."

"I rested long enough to lose one man." She sat up more slowly this time, so she could take the bowl. Her hands, as she reached toward it, trembled visibly.

"That's the worst of your type," Jacob told her. "You're so intent on running things that you can't see the obvious. Now put down those shaking hands and let me help you. It's hot enough that I don't expect you'd enjoy spilling it down your dress."

Rebecca glared at him. He'd already made it clear he thought her no more than a useless socialite. She wanted to rail at him that she was perfectly capable, but the warm scent of the soup was entirely too tempting. So instead, she fumed in silence and allowed him to feed her spoonful by spoonful, as if she were a small child.

In spite of all the arguments still boiling inside her, she couldn't help appreciating the almost tangy flavor of the broth, the rich succulence of the tender bites of meat. "What's in this?" she asked.

"I talked the colonel into letting me walk around a bit outside. While I was there, I saw some onion sprouts along the water's edge."

"Onions grow wild?"

He nodded slowly, and his gaze drifted. "When I think of how many springtime Saturdays my brother and I spent pulling them out of the pastures . . . Our hands stank for a week afterward, no matter how we scrubbed them."

"Did your mother cook with them as well?" Maybe he would teach her, too.

Jacob shook his head. "Not my mama. My grandmother taught me that trick. That woman knew more about living off the land than an old Indian, but Mama wouldn't allow wild cooking in her kitchen."

"So why did you pull the onions, then?"

He made a face, then grinned. "Our cows dearly loved to chew the tops off, but it made their milk taste awful. If Zeke and I sneaked off and didn't get to pulling before it was too late, we'd have to dump the whole day's milking in the creek—and afterwards, face Papa and his switch."

His expression hinted at such longing that it reminded Rebecca of what he'd said before about his brother.

"Zeke," she ventured. "Was he the same brother aboard the steamboat with you?"

His dark-brown eyes glanced at her, and their gazes locked. In that moment, the walls seemed to close in around them. There was only his pain,

not physical, but stronger, and it brought back to
Rebecca all the suffering she'd seen.

She wanted to detach herself, to look away and
break the spell. To stop imagining the two boys
pulling smelly weeds out of a pasture while scheming ways to slip out of the tiresome chore. To stop
imagining how Jacob felt, not knowing if he would
ever again see his brother, the same brother with
whom he'd shared so much family history.

But she couldn't stop the flow between them,
no matter what it cost her. So instead she told him,
"I lost a brother to this war . . . and, two days ago,
my cousin."

She said it in the hope that he would understand
that she, too, had known losses, that she, too, had
sacrificed. She'd done more than loose a gale of
words against a war that cost her nothing. She had
not come west to run things, as he thought, but
to serve with both her hands, with all her heart.

Even though the war had left it broken.

He put down the bowl, and then slowly, as if he
were having—and discarding—second thoughts,
he reached for her and took her in his arms. They
said absolutely nothing as he held her tight against
him, as she felt the warmth thrumming through
his body, the strength infusing her.

And Rebecca, so at home in her world of words,
felt as if she'd just entered a new realm, one in
which the only language was that which passed
between their bodies. She suspected, too, that this
place used a currency that her father, with all his
riches, would never understand.

A wave of pleasure rocked Jacob, spinning him
within its current. Here was life, within his grasp,
as if to make up for all he'd seen of dying. One
callused hand sleeked back the coppery silk of her

hair while the other stroked the warmth of her back, feeling—marveling at—the movements that marked the subtle ebb and flow of each one of her breaths.

Remember Hope, he warned himself, but this close, Rebecca filled his mind the way she filled his arms, crowding out all thoughts of anything but her unruly words and wounded eyes, her compassion and her courage.

How long had it been since he had held a woman like this? Jacob had missed so many things during the long months of his imprisonment. But always his mind had focused on his need for food, shelter, or some escape from filth. He'd never thought of what the lack of human contact cost him—never even known how much he'd missed it until this moment.

He stilled his hand upon her back and concentrated, then felt a smile pulling at the corners of his mouth. Beneath his fingertips her heart beat, a little fast but strong and steady. Some long-forgotten part of him followed up that rhythm to rejoin the larger world.

Jacob was afraid to speak, to move too quickly, to do anything that might prematurely break this spell. So he soaked up each sensation as if the pain in Rebecca's expression had given him some right. He held his words as though his silence might prevent her from tearing free of his grasp and decrying his lack of restraint.

Despite his fears, she said nothing, only hugged him to her, and Jacob wondered if she'd forgotten he earned his living with his hands. Or was her apparent affection only pity, the same as she might feel for any soldier? But then he thought of what she'd told him about her brother and her cousin, and of how she'd refused to share what happened during her abduction. Family money couldn't

shield her from her pain, so was it so strange to
think that she might welcome comfort, too?

Even so, the right thing to do was pull away, but
not too abruptly. Pull away and forget this ever
happened, so neither of them would have to
acknowledge the moment or feel the sharp sting
of regret. Hers, for being too familiar with a man
so far beneath her; his, for realizing that he'd never
get to hold such a woman in his arms again.

He began to draw back from her, but his body
wasn't quite in tune with his mind. For he pulled
away just enough to press his lips against hers gently, cautiously. He wondered if he had lost his mind,
because by kissing her, he'd completely destroyed
the excuse that he meant to offer only consolation.
But Rebecca erased his fear when she kissed him
back with such warmth and sweetness that he
couldn't help but think she meant it, too.

Like his emotions, Jacob's body thrummed to
life, so that he could not help opening his mouth,
then deepening the warmth that flowed between
them, pressing his tongue to her full lips until he
felt them open, too.

Her hands slid down his arms and pulled him
even closer. Just as his hands found, and partially
encircled, Rebecca's narrow waist.

Instead of slaking his desire, those caresses
inflamed the hunger roaring to life inside him,
blazing like a great inferno, barely under his control. Dear God, how he wanted her, to run his
hands beneath the layers of her clothing, to see,
to touch, to taste every inch of her pale flesh. Not
to stop until this appetite was sated, until he could
extinguish the aching lust that she ignited.

Yet when she pushed against his shoulders, he
pulled away, appalled by the speed and the direction of his thoughts. She was not the type of woman
for a quick tumble, even though their closeness

had convinced him her body was a soldier's fantasy. He gazed at her, fearing she would slap him and make a mockery of everything he felt.

She didn't. Instead, she stared up at him, her blue eyes slightly widened, her nostrils flared, as if she were a filly who scented danger. Her chest heaved, for her breaths came quickly, as did his own. This close, he noticed the faint trace of freckling across her forehead and the bridge of her nose. A light sheen of perspiration highlighted her rising color. She looked shocked by what had happened, and he began to wonder if their kiss had struck her speechless.

"I—uh—didn't intend for that to happen," he offered, and even to his own ears, the explanation sounded lame. He struggled to find more words, polite words he could offer. But before he could think of anything to say, he noticed the focus returning to her expression, which changed all too quickly from confusion to fury.

"Th-that is—is as far from an acceptable excuse as anything I've ever heard." Her words were angry clipped-winged birds flapping against the bars of indignation. "First of all, you owe me a profuse apology."

Despite her outburst, Jacob didn't believe her for an instant. Not when the taste of her kiss lingered in his mouth. Not when the warmth of her caresses still tingled where she'd touched him. Or perhaps he was only refusing to believe, not wanting to imagine that what had meant so very much to him had only made her angry. Apparently, he didn't tell her he was sorry fast enough, because she began speaking once again.

"In the past year, I've been nurse to dozens—hundreds—of young men, and not one of them has presumed to do anything as—"

"You ever think that maybe that's because you

never stopped giving orders long enough?'' He knew the words were all wrong, nothing but a sad attempt at humor to keep him from explaining the way she'd reawakened him.

She lowered her chin and glared up at him. If she'd been a heifer and not a woman, he'd get out of the way before she charged.

"Well, here's another one,'' she said. *"Get out."*

He picked up the bowl and stood, then opened his mouth, wanting to say something—anything— to make her understand. But the expression on her face snatched the words away, leaving him to stammer only, "I—I guess it's true, then, what they say about redheads and their tempers.''

She stood quickly, perhaps too quickly, for she swayed and then sat down again. Jacob cursed himself for his stupidity. He had no idea what to tell her that wouldn't make things worse.

"I'm sorry if you think I took advantage,'' he finally said. "But I'm not sorry that we kissed . . . Rebecca.''

She shook her head. "Under the circumstances, I'd prefer we go back to 'Miss Marston.' Perhaps that will help you remember I'm a nurse.''

He went to the door and opened it. "I'll call you anything you like, but I don't expect I'll ever forget the most important thing—that you're a woman, too.''

The hinges creaked as he left her, and Rebecca listened to the fading thuds of his footsteps on the warped stairs—listened, almost hoping he would think of some excuse to turn around. Turn around, come back, and kiss her once again. Her imagination replayed in vivid detail every touch and each sensation until her body tingled as though it had been plunged into a bath of chilled champagne.

So *this* was the great mystery to which her married friends alluded. This was what it had been so often hinted that she'd be missing because of her choice never to wed. Unexpected as it had been, Jacob Fuller had initiated her into the secret world with this one kiss.

She'd been kissed before a time or two. Once, when she and a boy were both sixteen and walking in the garden, he'd interrupted their debate and shocked her with eager lips. She'd slapped him and gone back to her argument without further comment. He had not repeated the attempt. The second time had come two years ago, when one of her father's friends had cornered her in the library. But the kiss he'd forced on her had felt anything but paternal. Instead, the sixty-year-old banker's touch made her feel soiled—and howlingly furious. She'd hissed a threat that drained the color from his face before she'd stormed out of the library. He, too, had never bothered her again.

Certainly, neither experience had prepared her for what had passed between Jacob and her, either its gentle sweetness or the ravenous hunger it awakened. This time, neither an awkward boy nor a lecherous old fossil had kissed her, but a man. She closed her eyes, allowing the sensations to repeat themselves.

It had been a fine thing, she decided, a kiss to tuck into the basket of her pleasant memories, to take out now and again to reexamine with a smile. Running her fingers through her hair in an attempt to unravel the worst tangles, Rebecca decided she wasn't at all sorry she was now a woman who'd been kissed in earnest.

She shook her head, hoping to reawaken her lost senses. She was twenty-six, not sixteen, yet here she was, daydreaming like a child. Downstairs, two wounded men needed her intelligence and professionalism to help keep them alive, and she was dawdling up here, giddy with romantic daydreams.

And over whom? A man who saw no merit in this costly war, a man who wanted nothing more than to bury his head in the dirt of some farmyard. A man who'd made it quite clear he considered her an overbearing, interfering irritant. It was hard to imagine why he'd ever kissed her in the first place.

Yet he had, and she sensed he might again unless she remained firm in her limits. Even though she burned to feel his lips on hers once more.

Clouds were rolling in, one atop the other, obscuring the bright sunshine that had made the afternoon so pleasant. Colonel Lewis Hall smelled rain closing in on them, and as a third-generation plantation owner, his instincts about weather rarely strayed far of the mark.

He tucked the drafts of two telegrams into his pocket—two telegrams that he must see to personally. He had no intention of allowing his men to read either, even though only one or two were sufficiently literate to do so.

"Saddle up, Simms. I'll want a good man with me."

Simms glanced up, his small eyes dark with suspicion. He shifted the knife he'd borrowed, which he'd been using to carve thin slivers of leftover venison, and wiped the blade against his grease-stained pants. Then he offered it, haft first, back to Hall.

"Gonna rain," he pointed out, reminding Hall that he used to be a farmer, too.

"Why the hell else d'you think he picked you?" Billy grinned the question from around the hind-quarters of the army horse that he'd been brushing.

Though his voice still sometimes squeaked reminders of his boyhood, a singular patch of white hairs at his left temple looked like a spider's web against his dark-brown hair. "Colonel's probably hopin' the rain'll drown some of them critters you been so busy scratchin'."

"You come along, I might drown *you* while I'm at it," Simms replied, but the threat held no real malice. Simms saved his hatred for Yanks and those he thought might be in league with them.

Which was exactly the reason Hall had chosen him to come along. If he were left behind, Simms would kill the prisoners. Nothing would change that simple fact—not explanations, bribes, or threats. In Simms's mind, all those sympathetic to the Yankees were the enemy: women, children, old men, anyone at all. He wouldn't differentiate the innocents from the pro-Union mob who had beaten him halfway to hell and burned his house two years before. Or perhaps he couldn't, because his six-year-old son had been inside. Later, Simms's wife had found the small charred body curled beneath what little had been left of his parents' bed. She had blamed Simms's loyalty to the South for their son's death, and shortly afterwards she left him, taking their three surviving children with her.

Like most of the others, Simms never talked about his losses. Lewis Hall had heard what happened secondhand from young Billy. It sure as hell explained the grim determination with which Simms went about his business.

As Hall tucked away the drafts of his telegrams and saddled his black mare, he wondered if his prisoners would be in any better hands once he left them in the care of the remainder of his band. An image flashed through his mind: Asa Graves dragging away the terrified blond nurse.

He glanced at the sergeant, who was sitting cross-legged with his chest bare and his crumpled shirt in his lap. His single green eye peered intently at the needle he was struggling to thread. That flop-eared pup he'd adopted was making matters more difficult by bumping at his elbow in a bid for attention. Asa swatted at it with a laugh.

The man didn't look too dangerous at the moment, but Hall certainly knew better. Yet he couldn't take them all with him.

"Sergeant," he said, and waited until Graves looked up in response. "You'll be in charge here when I'm gone. I'll expect the wounded men to remain unharmed."

Asa stabbed his needle into a split seam. "Reckon it's a good idea leavin' witnesses to a kidnapping?"

"We'll talk about it when I get back. Until then, I expect—"

"They won't get hurt," Graves allowed, "unless they make trouble or try to run off."

Hall nodded. The others, having heard this, would follow Asa's lead. "That's as much as any of us could expect in similar circumstances."

Asa said, "I wouldn't expect that much from any of those sorry sons o—"

"There's one more thing," Hall interrupted, thinking of the matter that most concerned him. "Whatever she says, whatever she does, Miss Marston is to remain untouched."

"Damn, colonel. She'll likely order us to build them hurt Yanks some fancy gazebo, so's they can take in some fine spring air."

A couple of the others laughed, and even Hall had to smile. Rebecca Marston might be beautiful as a bayou sunset, but that lovely mouth of hers had more bite than an alligator's.

He drew out his knife, with its long and gleaming blade, and used it to slice off several strands dangling from his saddle blanket. "Nevertheless, she must be treated with the deference due a lady."

Asa's single eye narrowed wickedly, and he grinned. "How 'bout if some fella was to make her glad she's a woman instead?"

The colonel still held the knife, but he resisted the temptation to use its point to gesture. He didn't need to, for every one of his men had seen the easy competence with which he handled the weapon, just as they'd noted his proficiency with his gun. His skills, far more than his rank, were responsible for keeping order in this group.

"We raise a lot of fine horseflesh back on my plantation. I've gelded many a colt before to keep him from getting too rambunctious. I could do it to a man as well." Hall gave his words some breathing space to let them sink in. "And I will do it, on my honor, to any man among you who soils that young woman."

He was gratified to see by their expressions that they believed him. He only hoped to God his threat would be enough.

Jacob hadn't precisely expected Rebecca to show gratitude for his help, but he sure as hell had not anticipated *this* reaction.

"What in heaven's name is that horrible odor?" she demanded only moments after coming down the stairs.

"Skunk," Jacob told her. "One of the Johnnies brought us a dead skunk."

Her color, which had looked much better after her rest and meal, faded in an instant. "Tell me that's not what was in that soup you brought me."

He laughed. "Of course not. You don't *eat* skunk. You render the fat."

She folded her arms across her chest. "To what purpose, pray tell?"

"Why, for medicine, of course. Didn't you have a grandma, Miss Marston?"

"I had two, thank you, neither of whom would be caught dead cooking skunk fat." Suddenly, her head whipped toward the two men lying before the fire. "Surely, you haven't dosed these poor men with your barbaric country cure, have you?"

The young private, Nate Gordon, opened his eyes before he piped in. "He sure did. Rubbed it on our burns, and I can tell you mine feel better. My Aunt Gert used to swear by skunk oil. Now I can see why."

Rebecca wrinkled her nose, displaying her disgust. Striding purposefully toward the window, she opened it wider. A cool breeze fanned out her red hair, which she had left loose.

"Some say the oil works better if you cover it with flannel," Jacob told her, although he had the distinct impression that it wouldn't help his case.

"Red flannel's the best," Nate added. "Works wonders for sore throats, too."

She stared at both of them as though they were insane. "This is ludicrous! Here we are, in the age of modern medicine, and you're poisoning men with melted skunk fat and talking about cheap cotton fabric as if it had some magical healing properties!"

"Rebecca—" Jacob began, until he noticed her brows beetling in annoyance. "I mean Miss Marston, we don't *have* any modern medicine available, so what's the harm in making do?"

She put one hand on her hip and thrust her chin forward in defiance. "The harm is in the risk of introducing filth into the systems of already weakened men. You'll kill them with your barbaric 'treatments.' We must immediately wash off that disgusting substance. I heard you say before that you're a farrier. Might I suggest you confine your doctoring to horses?''

"Miss Marston," Nate complained, "you ain't going to make us stop taking the willow-bark tea, too, are you?''

"It's of absolutely no use, Mr. Gordon. You need laudanum, not some foolish recipe from an old wives' tale.''

Her haughtiness annoyed the hell out of Jacob, enough so that he wondered what had ever possessed him to kiss her. "What's foolish is being too stubborn to use whatever nature offers.''

Her blue eyes narrowed dangerously. "I'll make you a deal, Mr. Fuller. You're clearly the better cook, so you're assigned to that detail. But make no mistake. *I* am the nurse here, and I will have the final say on all medical decisions, or at least those affecting human beings.''

Jacob retreated to his assigned domain—the kitchen—before he exploded into language that would scorch the ears of the red-haired tyrant. Not that she didn't deserve to hear it. She had to be the most overbearing, irritating female ever born! One thing was for certain: She'd cured him of the urge to hold her in his arms. He wasn't about to ever again repeat the mistake of kissing Miss Rebecca Holier-Than-Thou Marston. He'd sooner kiss the damned dead skunk.

Chapter Seven

Heedless of the rain that blew against him, Asa Graves stared out the open barn doors.

"Close that, sarge," called Billy. "It's gettin' damn chilly in here."

But Asa didn't move. Instead, he watched the column of smoke rising from the house's chimney. Smoke from the firewood he'd been ordered to help cut.

Lightning flashed, and thunder followed, big and booming. As the pup whined and leaned against his leg, Asa grinned at the thought of the colonel soaked and shivering, fighting to control that high-strung mare of his. Weather didn't pay no heed to Big Men. Colonel Hall and Simms would both get a hell of a lot colder than the men inside the barn.

And the whole damned lot of them could think on those bastard Yankees lying up all snug in the house.

Asa wished they could risk a fire, but the old barn, with its leftover hay and bone-dry wood, would go up like kindling if they tried it. He peered back at a couple of the boys, who were burrowing in some straw they'd scraped together to try to warm themselves.

Shivering, he pushed the doors shut. As he rubbed at the sleeves of his newly mended jacket, Asa kept thinking on how warm it would feel inside that house . . . and how slick and hot inside Rebecca Marston.

He'd be damned if he'd stay freezing inside this barn much longer.

A gust of wind puffed through the front windows, though the open porch sheltered them. With it came the rhythmic hiss of falling rain. Rebecca spared a glance through the opening, wishing she could fly out beneath that warped sash to soar up through the thick clouds and far away.

A rumble of thunder and a flash made short work of the fantasy. She'd hated storms since childhood, when a bolt of lightning had struck her family's ornate stone fireplace, sending a shower of debris across the sitting room, where she'd been playing jackstraws with her brother. With a shudder, Rebecca sighed, determined to take matters well in hand before that horse doctor, Jacob Fuller, could do any more to harm these men.

She'd already washed off the abomination Jacob had slathered onto the young soldier's wounds. Nate Gordon had gritted his teeth against the pain until he'd finally lost patience and erupted with a string of curses. Afterward, he apologized for his language, but he'd rolled onto his side, away from her. She hoped that he was sleeping, but she couldn't tell for certain.

Now she turned her attention to the wounds of the unconscious soldier. As the cool rag touched the burns on his neck, the black-haired man's head swung from side to side. He began to groan and whimper, "Please, God. No, don't . . ."

The hazel eyes slid open, gazing at her with an expression that begged relief, for anything at all to ease his pain.

"Help me," he said weakly. "Please, Miss . . . help me die."

Unlike his earlier requests, this one sounded coherent, and the sadness in his gaze convinced her he understood exactly what he asked. At that moment, Rebecca felt overpowered by all the suffering she had witnessed. Some part of her almost wished she could faint again so Jacob Fuller would carry her upstairs to feed her soup and hold her.

She pushed aside the ridiculous notion. She might be a poor nurse, but she was all these men had—unless she wanted to leave them to rely on Indian roots and skunk oil. Besides, judging from Jacob's expression when he'd strode out of the room, the only way he'd ever hold her again was to wring her neck like a red hen.

After a brief battle to shove back her emotions, she spoke gently. "I promise, you'll feel better after I wash your wounds in this cool water. And I want you to try some broth as well."

The soldier tried to push away her hand. "No . . . it's finished now. I'm ready. I tried so hard to get home, but I can't stand any mo—"

"Shhh . . ." Rebecca wiped his brow with a damp cloth and took his hand in hers. "Tell me your name. I'd like to know what I can call you."

"I—I'm Jonah—Jonah Pierce."

"Where's home, Mr. Pierce? Where's your family?" If she could focus him on those waiting, perhaps she could revive his will to live.

"Indiana—Monroe County. My—my wife's back there. . . , Elizabeth, with my daughters."

"How many girls do you and Elizabeth have?" The moment that she asked the question, she saw something shift in his expression. A soft light came into his eyes.

"Four—four of the prettiest little things you ever did see. But all of them'll be so grown up now, I won't hardly recognize them." The voice was wistful, but slightly stronger. "Mayhap they wouldn't know me either. It's been near to three years since I left home, and I'm considerably worse for wear."

Jacob must have heard them talking, for he drifted back into the room, a cup held in his big hands. Kneeling beside Rebecca, he passed it to her. As she took it, their gazes locked for an instant before skittering apart like startled mice.

Rebecca narrowed her eyes when she noticed the color of the liquid in the cup. As if he'd never heard her orders, stubborn Jacob Fuller had brought willow-bark tea. She decided she could wait till later to give him the rough side of her tongue. For now, she had to concentrate on getting liquid into this man while he remained conscious.

"I'm certain that your daughters miss you very much," she told the burned soldier. "They want you to get better, and they need you to come home and see how beautifully they're growing, and to help them sort out suitors and get ready to start families of their own. Please don't disappoint your girls, Mr. Pierce. You'll need to drink now. Mr. Fuller here will help you sit up a bit so you can take some liquid, and then I'll write a letter for you to Elizabeth."

Though she had neither pen nor paper, she promised herself she would memorize every one of Mr. Pierce's words. Moments later, as Jacob carefully moved him, his painful cries made Rebecca's vision swim with unshed tears. She swallowed past a thick lump and held the cup to his lips. Jonah Pierce swallowed, too, until he'd nearly emptied the battered tin cup that she held.

As Jacob lowered him, the wounded soldier moaned. His eyes rolled back, and Rebecca couldn't wake him to take soup. But at least he was breathing steadily, and he couldn't feel the pain of his deep burns.

Rebecca wished her own pain could be so easily avoided. The tears she'd held back for the past year threatened to spill. Bowing her head, she breathed a silent prayer for strength and courage. Please, God, let her father pay the ransom before she broke down completely.

"You all right, Rebecca?" Jacob laid his hand upon her back. When she didn't answer quickly, he continued. "That was a fine thing, the way you talked to him. Every time I'm about convinced you're a harpy out of hell, you say or do something to make me think you're almost human."

A fresh breeze from the open windows filled the room with the damp scents of springtime growth and the nearby river water. Outside, rain beat harder against the old house, and blue-white flashed in every window. Thunder detonated on its heels, rattling the windows, shaking Rebecca's tattered nerves.

Terror and grief swelled inside her chest till there was scarcely room for breathing. Squeezing shut her eyes, she waited out the onslaught, as wild as any thunderstorm she'd ever known. She felt shame knowing he could feel her trembling where he touched her, but she was helpless either to stop herself or move away.

"Hey, you're pale as snow," he observed. "It's just a spring shower. We're in a nice, dry house with a warm pot of soup while those rebs are stuck out in the barn dodging leaks. Who knows? Maybe the snakes'll move in with them, too."

She opened her eyes to see if he was laughing at her, but in his face she saw only kindness and gratitude for a scant handful of blessings amid the curses of their situation.

"Why are you doing this?" she asked.

"Doing what?"

"Confusing me like this. One minute, you look as if you'd like to shake me. The next, you treat me as if you . . ." She felt color rising, burning in her face. *"As if you'd like to kiss me again,"* she'd been about to say.

He turned her toward him, then pulled her tight against his chest.

"Seems to me that's the kind of woman you are, Rebecca," he murmured into her hair. "You're like one of those lemon drops I used to favor as a boy. Sour enough to make you pucker, but plenty sweet inside."

This time, despite his clumsy compliment, she didn't wait for him to take her by surprise. This time, Rebecca shocked herself. By seeking out his mouth with hers, by ignoring all the reasons this was wrong, and struggling toward some sustenance that only Jacob Fuller could provide.

Lightning again illuminated every corner of the old house, and the air trembled with the boom of nearby thunder. But Rebecca barely noticed, for the only storm that mattered to her was the one their kiss had spawned.

Jacob held her close against his body, allowing her to feel the way she'd stirred him. He half imagined she would scream and pull away the moment she felt his growing hardness. That would be best, wouldn't it? To make her understand he wanted her so badly, it was all he could do to keep himself from sweeping her off her feet and carrying her upstairs to that waiting bedroom. To make her understand she couldn't safely lose herself within their kiss.

He thought again about her father with his money and Rebecca with her high-minded arrogance—thought again of what a foolish thing it was to kiss a woman he didn't even like. A woman who'd be sure to turn her nose up at a man who returned after a long workday smelling of animals and sweat and the satisfaction of a job well done. A woman who was only passing time with him to keep herself from dwelling on her fear.

But damned if he didn't want her anyway, in a way he'd never wanted any woman in his life. His body ached with the urgency of his need, and his greedy mouth fed eagerly on hers, prizing her lips open, ravaging with his tongue. His hands, heedless of his better judgment, slid along her sides until he skimmed the feminine flare of her hips and groaned with pleasure and deep longing.

Pull away, Rebecca. He should stop, should tell her that. *End this before one of us gets hurt.*

As it had so many times before, a terrible image darted through his mind. Hope, the pistol still clutched in her pale hand.

But Rebecca's kiss, so sweet, so tentative before, had grown desperate, and her palms and fingertips blazed fiery trails along his upper arms. Again, she left no room for thoughts of any other woman.

It felt as if the storm and circumstance had spawned a vortex that pulled both of them inside a place where normal rules did not apply. Behind the heavy clouds, the sun must have set, for this land lay in darkness lit only by the dancing firelight.

But they were not alone here. One of the wounded men groaned, vanquishing the spell.

Rebecca all but jumped back, away from Jacob's embrace. Her eyes, wide with disbelief, reflected flame.

Before she could say a word, Jacob thought it prudent to edge in his defense. "Don't blame me this time. You kissed me."

A burning log shifted in the grate, and a shower of sparks arced onto the mud-stained hearth. The embers' orange glow subsided slowly.

Rebecca lowered her head, but her gaze broadcast a challenge.

"That's a lie. You pulled me to you first, and besides, you didn't seem to mind much." Despite her expression, her husky growl bespoke arousal.

He knew he shouldn't, but still he reached out to touch her cheek. The skin, so smooth and warm, invited him to stroke, caress, to touch all of it . . . of her. With a sigh of frustration, he let his hand drop, knowing that nothing but distance and sharp words could stop this thing that neither of them needed.

"I'm telling you," he said, his voice gruff and impatient. "You start it again, it might get finished."

"You—do you dare to threaten me?" Anger lanced her words, banishing the sound of her desire.

"I'm not threatening, I'm warning. Don't play with fire, Becca. I'm not the hired help. I'm a man, a man who wants you very much."

"It's Rebecca," she corrected. "Or perhaps 'Miss Marston' *would* be better."

With that, she turned to check on her patients.

Behind her, Jacob smiled. He decided that he liked her this way: furious, haughty, and annoying as a thorn lodged in a work boot. She would be far safer, and when all this ended, she'd be far easier to let go.

* * *

Colonel Hall's gaze swept the dark corners of what was once a chicken coop but in recent years had been converted to a ramshackle, filthy stable. He wished they didn't have to stop at the Tate farm, but both he and Simms were chilled to the marrow with the rain and hungry from the long ride. The horses, too, could use a good rest before they resumed their trip tomorrow so he could send the messages. Besides, Nehemiah Tate, though rough in his manner, was as loyal to the cause as any man he knew. Despite the danger of drawing Union retribution, Tate clearly stated that men who slaughtered Yankees would always be welcome guests in his abode.

"I brung ya some hot coffee, colonel." Emmaline Tate's brown eyes were huge and doe-soft, and her words, despite their inelegance, brimmed with nectar.

Lewis Hall knew he'd have to be careful around this one. Young and foolish, she'd made her intentions all too clear the last time he'd stayed at her family's farm.

"Thank you, Emmaline." Eager for the warmth, he reached for the steaming mug. He wasn't quick enough to avoid her touch.

"Got some for you, too," she told Simms. The welcome dropped from both her voice and her expression. In its place, repugnance rose.

Simms, apparently used to that reaction from females, grunted thanks and took the coffee. He raked rain-sodden hair out of his small, dark eyes and slurped.

Emmaline's gaze latched onto Hall's. "Bluejackets been around," she told him.

He grimaced. The last thing he needed was the

delay of dodging a pack of Yankee soldiers. "Looking for anybody in particular?"

Her dark-brown hair swung as Emmaline shook her head. "Don't think so. They told Pa they meant to clean out all these raiders—make it safe for decent folk again. Make it safe for Yankee stealin' is more like it."

"What did your father tell them?"

She grinned, defiance lighting her brown eyes. "He advised that they should go to hell."

"Your father may wish to weigh his words, if only to keep you and your mother safe."

"It's right nice of you to worry on our account, colonel, but us Tates is all of one mind. We'd rather be hung and martyred than bow down to a gov'ment thinks it's got the right to take folks' niggers."

As far as Hall knew, the Tates had never owned slaves, but he did not doubt for a moment that Emmaline spoke for her whole family. He wouldn't have to worry about one of them running to the Yankees while he and Simms were resting.

"The Confederacy commends your loyalty," he told her.

"See you at the house," she said to Hall. Her words dripped with unmistakable intent. She smiled invitingly, then slipped out through the barn door.

Simms pulled the saddle from his mount. "I believe that gal's wetter than this pony. You gonna give her a special private commendation, colonel?"

"She's a child," Hall responded, as if he hadn't noticed the new curves filling the "girl's" bodice. Curves she obviously itched to try out soon.

But he would not oblige her, even for an hour's sport. Lewis Hall had definite ideas about how women should behave, and Emmaline Tate couldn't begin to approach his standards.

As Hall rubbed down his black mare with dry sacking, his thoughts turned to the source of his ideals regarding women. His mother, Lorena Brighton Hall, had been a study in Southern femininity. Raised in a fine New Orleans town house, she had never allowed life on a country plantation to compromise her refined values one iota. Always demure and self-effacing, she'd bent men—including his tough-minded father—to her will with an arsenal of charm and flattery. Lewis smiled, picturing the way she'd so coyly fluttered her ever-present fan, remembering how even on her deathbed she'd managed to elicit promises from her sons to honor the South and all it represented.

If not for that promise, he would not be here today, wondering if what he was doing was honorable at all. And wondering what his mother would think of an impudent hellcat like Rebecca Marston, who inflamed his imagination far more than ill-bred Emmaline could ever hope to do.

Lodged in his imagination, Mother spoke: *Any woman who rushes off to nurse strange men is certainly no lady. Especially not a woman who looks like that.*

He thought of Rebecca's fiery hair cascading past her shoulders, and the way her torn shirtwaist gaped open. No, she didn't look at all the proper lady, but how could he blame her for that? After all, she'd looked respectable enough when she'd been captured.

Just you remember, Mother countered, her refined drawl thick as honey, *blood will always tell.*

And beautiful Rebecca's blood was that of Winfield Marston, a liar and a cheat, a turncoat Yankee who honored his own wealth above all other loyalties. Remembering how deftly Marston had played on Hall's Southern sense of duty two years before, the colonel felt his face heat with shame and rage. The cotton—Lewis Hall and his fellow plantation owners' cotton—which Marston smuggled past the

Yankees' cowardly blockade, had been worth more than twenty thousand dollars.

Dollars that should have brought desperately needed medicines from beyond the blockade. Dollars that could be used to do good now. God had dropped Rebecca Marston into his hands two days before, just as he had dropped the plan into Hall's mind.

Sometimes, Lewis Hall knew, a man had to resort to harsh actions to set things right. Sometimes circumstances forced him to do things others wouldn't understand. Hall only hoped that his old friend, Barlow Pickett, would recognize the perfect irony of setting up the foundation with Marston's ransom money. For Hall's plan to succeed, the Baton Rouge attorney would have to act as go-between and set up an irrevocable trust fund. A fund to benefit Louisianans widowed or orphaned by this war.

Now all he had to do was wait for Pickett to relay Marston's response to his demands. Wait . . . and pray he wouldn't go back to find his men had tired of playing nursemaid and done what they did best to the men and woman in their care.

Chapter Eight

*We stopped at a little tavern where the landlady
was not yet twenty and had a baby fifteen months
old. . . .*

*When we came to pay our bill, the dolt of a husband
took the money and put it in his pocket. He had
not lifted a hand to lighten that woman's burdens,
but had sat and talked with the men in the bar
room, not even caring for the baby, yet the law
gives him the right to every dollar she earns. . . .*

—Susan B. Anthony,
from a letter to
Elizabeth Cady Stanton

A burst of energy kept Rebecca awake and working long after Jacob slept. She was grateful for the silence and for the chance to think without the distraction of his dark gaze settling upon her, disordering her thoughts like a card player shuffling a deck.

But neither the darkness nor the susurration of the deeply breathing men did anything to vanquish her compulsion. Though she'd set herself to the daunting task of cleaning the grimed kitchen, every few minutes she walked through the doorway to check on the three sleepers. She forced herself to examine the others first, to be certain Jonah Pierce was quiet or to replace a blanket that had slipped off Nate Gordon's thin, bare shoulder. But all the while, her heart beat eagerly as she awaited the chance to stare at Jacob Fuller, to wonder what it was about the man that drew her so—and whether that quality could possibly outweigh his vexing words.

A movement on the stairwell made her look up sharply. A red-haired boy stood there, grinning despite his missing teeth. The same boy she had dreamed about upstairs.

The fine hairs on Rebecca's arms rose, and a prickling sensation crawled around her stomach. Did she dream again, or was this a—? She shook her head. He appeared too solid, so solid that she could, with but a few steps, reach out to touch his tousled mop. Real, then?

"Are you—?" she began.

He beckoned with an excited wave, then trotted up the steps. She heard his bare feet thunking against wood. How could a child be here? Whoever would have left him all alone?

"Come back," she called after him. Her heart rose to her throat as she considered following, up into the darkness.

Shaking her head, Rebecca turned and hurried back into the kitchen where earlier she'd found a box of candles, one impaled upon a metal disk with a looped handle. She took it to the fireplace and pulled a twig from the stack of kindling left beside the unburned logs. She lit first twig, then wick before venturing toward the bottom of the stairwell.

Her gaze wandered back to Jacob. Should she wake him? She thought of how he'd laugh if this turned out to be some sort of phantasm brought

on by the late hour and her imagination. With
another toss of her head, she returned her attention to the black maw that gaped above her. Whatever awaited her upstairs, she would go alone.

The rain had long since ended except for the
drips still leaking through the barn's roof. All
around him men snored, but Asa could not sleep.
Not with the want gnawing at him like a starved
rat on an old cob. Not with the thought of some
Big Man's daughter snug and sleeping less than a
hundred yards away.

Licking his lips, Asa rose from his makeshift bed
and brushed some clinging straw from his skin.
He'd get plenty wet crossing the floodwater, but
he'd gotten soaked before for less than this.

He thought about the colonel's threat, a threat
that the other raiders wouldn't risk because they
knew Hall would do exactly as he'd promised. But
the others weren't as smart as Asa, who'd figured
out the way to have the woman and still keep his
balls where they belonged. He grinned at the
thought of it, then scratched at the scar tissue that
covered the space that had once contained his eye.

He'd bring his pistol, but he wouldn't need it
because this time he wouldn't have to overpower
with gun or knife or fist. This time, he'd use the
Marston woman's weapon—words—to force her
surrender. He'd never done it that way, but the
thought left him rock-hard and ready. Unless he
missed his guess, the red-haired bitch would spread
her legs and then tell no one, out of shame. Just
as he'd told no one but his pa when . . .

No. No need to pick at that old scab now. This
time, Asa meant to be the one on top.

Leaving the pup sleeping in its bed of straw,
he removed his shoes. Afterward, he slipped out

quietly, so no one would bear witness to what he meant to do.

How in heaven's name could a small boy navigate such darkness? The candle Rebecca held cast only a tiny circle of dim light, barely enough for her to safely walk, much less search the four rooms. Like the tongue of flame she carried, anxiety flickered inside her. If a child were hiding up here, it stood to reason that he wouldn't be alone. Could his parents be with him, avoiding rebel raiders by secreting themselves inside some hidden panel?

She thought of the young couple from her dream, remembered the echoes of their laughter, and her breaths came easier. Nothing to fear there. She wasn't certain how she knew, but she felt sure of it. As sure as she'd been of anything in all her life.

Nevertheless, when a door creaked behind her, she swung around to face the opening. Inside it lay more darkness and another set of stairs. The attic. Above her, she heard movement.

Taking a deep breath, she muttered, "In for a penny, in for a pound."

She lifted the candle before her and slowly began a new ascent.

Asa held the bundle of his clothes and gun above his head in an attempt to keep them dry. It was a damned good thing the storm had moved through, leaving decent starlight in its wake. A thin sliver of moon hung like a discarded fingernail, giving him barely enough illumination to wade through the dark waters.

Thinking of fingernails, Asa remembered how the first gal scratched him, leaving evidence enough she wasn't near as willing as he'd claimed. Evidence enough to send him to prison for ten years. Would have been more, too, if he hadn't volunteered to join up with the Confederate infantry. But he hadn't taken to the discipline of soldiering, so he'd drifted off to other things . . . and other women, when he got the chance.

Cold mud squeezed through his toes as he emerged dripping near the back door that would take him to the kitchen. Shivering, he hurriedly pulled on his clothing. As he did, he thought about the layout of the house from when he'd searched it, thought about where he might find Rebecca Marston. Downstairs was most likely, sleeping near the men so she could tend them if they woke up in the night. Self-righteous bitch like her would probably do that. But it was possible she thought herself too grand and that she'd chosen to sleep upstairs instead.

Remembering the one remaining bed, he grinned, knowing he'd soon put it to good use. Despite the chilling night breeze against his damp skin, the thought warmed him, and he slipped inside the warmer darkness of the house.

"Hello?"

Rebecca's voice echoed among the attic rafters and returned to her diminished by its journey. Candlelight made dancing shadows from the remnants of the former inhabitants' lives: a rolled rug, frayed along its edges, a mirror with cracks radiating from its center, a few upended boxes, and items too awkward or useless to steal.

But no people at all—not even one small boy.

"Hello?" She spoke louder this time, nearly confident the child had been nothing but the vestige of a dream. In the empty silence that followed, she decided to see if anything here might be worth carrying downstairs.

The first treasure was a spilled box of rags. Grateful to have material for bandages, Rebecca picked up the box to gather them ... and smiled at the discovery of a simple wooden-handled hairbrush.

"Thank the Lord," she said, for her tresses were becoming so tangled, she'd wondered if she'd have to cut them off by the time Father paid her ransom.

After setting down the candle near the mirror, she loosened her hair and started brushing. She hummed a little as she did so, an old melody that obscured the sounds of footsteps mounting the lower set of stairs.

On the stairway, Asa Graves began to shake, the way he always did once he got close. Remembering the smells of sweat and semen, remembering that bad day in the empty stall.

Better to be predator than prey, he knew, *the rapist than the raped.*

Still, those words never kept the images from flashing, lurid as dawn lightning, through his mind. The man said he'd come to look at Pa's stock, though the cows were skinny, scabby, nothing like any self-respecting Montgomery would keep on his fine place. Pa hadn't been around, though, and Asa had felt like a grown man when Hunt, a broad-shouldered fellow with a narrow, close-lipped smile, suggested the two of them "talk business" in the barn.

Afterward, when Pa came in to find his youngest boy crying in the barn, torn and bleeding, his snot diluted by the river of his tears, the older Graves had barely listened. Instead he'd told Asa, "Dry them eyes and don't say nothin'. Nothin' you can do against a Big Man anyway." He'd patted Asa's

shoulder, and then he'd turned away. The last
thing he had said about it was, "Just don't let
nobody think he's made a woman of you, that's
all."

Asa felt his old man's words, sometimes coiled
in his gut, other times writhing like maggots in a
dead bird. Words that had lived with him since a
day imprinted on both mind and body. The day
of his twelfth birthday, a day he'd been trying to
rape his way past ever since.

As he reached the narrow hallway at the top of
the stairs, he wished again for better light than the
candle he'd brought from the kitchen. The idea
of the woman hiding just inside a doorway bothered him. Rebecca Marston seemed just ornery
enough to try to bust him over the skull with anything she got her hands on. Ordinarily, he'd take
care of such a problem with his fists or the pistol
tucked into his waistband, but he couldn't risk
leaving marks that Hall would see—couldn't risk
anything but the words he planned on saying.

Asa was glad he'd left behind his brogans, for
his bare feet made no noise as he walked the dusty
floor. He damn near bit his tongue in two, though,
when he stubbed a toe and tripped on a loose
floorboard. Somehow, he managed to pick himself
up, praying that she hadn't heard him fall. But as
soon as he took another step, he banged his hip
into the corner of a small table he belatedly remembered had been standing in the hallway. Asa swallowed back a string of profanity and moved
forward.

But Rebecca Marston wasn't sleeping in the bed.
All attempts at stealth forgotten, he rushed from
room to room. Panic pounded in his chest. The
bitch had run off on them! He couldn't have been
more shocked. Women didn't do that sort of
thing—not cross snake-ridden floodwaters to slip

away on foot, and certainly not abandon wounded men to do so! Damn it! You ought to be able to count on females to act a certain way—not rabbit off and cause all sorts of trouble.

His mind raced, wondering how long she'd been gone, how to trail her in the dark, and most especially, how to explain her loss to Colonel Lewis Hall. Bastard would likely think they'd had their fun and killed her. The thought of the colonel's fury, of the sort of retribution he'd exact, made Asa want to gather up his things and skedaddle fast.

And then he heard soft footsteps on the stairs above him. Hell! Here he'd been, ready to cut and run, and she'd been in the attic all along! The one place he'd never imagined she would go this time of night.

Yet it suited his purpose, for once he stepped inside the attic door and shut it, her screams wouldn't carry to the first floor far below.

A creak rose up the stairwell, and in the dim candlelight, Rebecca saw a figure moving toward her. Her first thought was that Jacob had come back. Despite her harsh words earlier, a tingling rippled through her body. For if he'd come, he surely meant to kiss her . . . didn't he?

The door clicked shut behind him, but as his face lifted to look at her, her anticipation drained away. Asa's single eye glittered darkly, like a rat's.

Too frightened to shriek, Rebecca clambered backward until she stood on level floor, and turned quickly, desperate to find something, anything, that she might use to defend herself against the man. In her haste, her feet tangled in her petticoat, and both the lit candle and the box of rags tumbled from her hand. Miraculously, instead of catching the loose cloths, the flame vanished instantly. She was plunged into near blackness, with nothing but the hairbrush in her hand.

"Hey there, Miss Rebecca. Didn't mean t'scare ya." His feigned geniality sliced to the core of her, a blade formed of blue ice. His face, floating above the lit candle in his hand, looked more nightmarish than human.

Words knotted in her throat, threatening to choke her. She knew why he had come, at night and alone. Sparks flashed in her vision, as if her eyes were filming with a delicate lacework of hoarfrost.

"Don't you worry, princess. I ain't gonna hurt you none." His monstrous, flame-lit face seemed to float upward and toward her as he advanced. "If you cooperate."

"Oh, dear God . . ." Rebecca managed. Without conscious direction from her mind, her feet shuffled backward, until her heels banged against something—perhaps an empty box.

She managed to untangle a few words from the snarl. "But your colonel said—"

"Colonel ain't got nothin' to do with this, Rebecca. It's just you and me, right here, right now." He moved closer, close enough so he could touch her if he reached forward.

She shook her head and felt the flickering of fury begin to melt her fear. "Go away, you loathsome beast!"

As Asa grinned, his teeth gleamed dully in the candlelight. "I ain't goin' nowhere. Not when I'm this close to where I wanta be."

"Then I hope you're prepared to kill me, because I'm not about to let you—"

She couldn't say it, couldn't even *think* of what he meant to do. She couldn't conceive of anything but getting past this moment. Her heart was pounding violently, and inside her chest she couldn't find room enough to breathe.

"I think you *will* let me," Asa told her.

"Then you're either a madman or a fool," she managed, but her words sounded weak and brittle, even to her ears.

"You want to know how I know that?" Asa set the burning candle atop a wooden box.

Straightening, he reached toward her hair, and Rebecca jumped back, brandishing the brush as if to strike. When Asa hesitated, it occurred to her that he didn't wish to fight her. Remembering the colonel, she began to piece together why. Perhaps the officer had threatened his men with some sort of punishment if she were harmed.

Asa spoke with the voice of Lucifer in the Garden, his words so oily they slithered through her mind. "You'll let me 'cause you want to live once this is over. You want to go back to your fancy mansion and your servants, back to them sort of Nancy boys who'll lift your hand to kiss it instead of your skirts for a quick poke. You'll run back there and lock them gates up so tight, you won't never need to be afraid again. I can see you want it real bad. Bad enough, you'll let me come back every night, so's I can help you out of this mess at the end."

That *was* it, wasn't it? He meant to talk her into some repulsive bargain! She found the very idea infuriating. "I'm not *letting* you do a damned thing."

Despite her assertion, her mouth was dry as chalk, and her heart didn't slow its mad pace one iota. A thought occurred to her with painful clarity. *What if I am wrong?*

Faster than she would have believed possible, Asa closed on her, catching the hand that held the brush in a crushing grip. His other hand skimmed along her ribs and gave her breast a painful squeeze.

With a sharp cry of terror, Rebecca jerked free. She felt the impact as she caught Asa's shoulder with the brush. Yet her blow meant nothing; he only laughed as he stepped back.

"Just a reminder, little princess. We can do this easy, or we can do it hard. Your choice."

Rebecca's stomach contracted, and she knew that at any moment she'd be sick. In her panic, her mind spun uselessly as a gear slipped out of place. She couldn't begin to think of how to stop him from assaulting her.

Unexpectedly, her father's voice came back to her from childhood, from a day she'd come home crying because an older girl had pushed her down.

Never forget that you're a Marston, Rebecca. And the next time you see the little guttersnipe, you damned well show her what that means.

It was the most useful advice her father ever gave her, though her mother complained it was an appalling thing to tell a girl.

Taking a shaky breath, Rebecca straightened her spine and tried hard to pretend Asa was no more than a schoolyard bully. Despite the very real possibility that she might vomit at his feet, she managed to affect Winfield Marston's most condescending tone. "You despicable worm. If you believe for one moment I'll make this easy for you, you're even closer to barnyard filth than your odor implies."

Asa's one eye widened, and she saw his fist draw back. She tried to scramble away, but there was no room.

Then, unexpectedly, he froze, and slowly the fist lowered. Instead of striking her, he gave a bark of laughter, so utterly humorless it made her feel as if she'd swallowed broken glass.

"I got a better idea, princess. Let's see how you

like this one. For every night you don't let me do what I want, I'll make one of them pay. I'll finish every damn one of them Yankee sons of bitches, one by one. Starting with tonight.''

Even in the candlelight, she saw his lip curl in an ugly sneer, and something in his hand gleamed. Could it be a gun? Her bravado shattered, and fear gripped her by the throat.

"I'll be back tomorrow night," he hissed. "And then we'll see who's barnyard filth.''

Asa retrieved the candle. The flame's dance marked his progress down the stairs. A sharp bang echoed in the darkness. Rebecca thought about a soldier she'd once helped nurse, who'd told her that he hadn't felt the bullet strike his body, hadn't known it till he'd felt the wetness on his thigh. Rebecca wondered vaguely if she'd been shot, if blood were pouring from some wound masked by her fright.

She sank to her knees, and for a long time afterward, she knelt there in the inky blackness, too weak with fear to rise again, too terrified to weep.

Asa's mouth twisted in satisfaction as he looked over the sleeping Yankees. Which one of them would die because of her?

Only minutes before, he'd wanted to pound that rich bitch's face to splinters for the way she'd talked to him, but he was glad now, damned glad he'd remembered the colonel's threat in time. Because this, in some strange way, would be even better. What he was about to do would tie Rebecca Marston into such a knot that by tomorrow night she'd be begging him to take her.

Asa ran a tongue over his cracked lips and decided that he liked the idea of her begging.

He looked down at the closest Yank, the curly-headed fella he'd seen outside before. Must be in pretty good shape to be walking on his own. Probably helped out the princess; maybe made her decent company as well.

Asa's lips drew tight against his teeth. She'd likely miss this one most. Besides, he'd kicked off his wool blanket. Asa picked it up and folded it into a square just right for smothering a body.

In the silence of the attic, Rebecca stood slowly, wondering if terror made such a fool of everyone. There'd been no muzzle flash, no bullet. He'd slammed the door below, that's all. Slammed it on his way downstairs.

Downstairs . . . where the men lay sleeping. She whined like a frightened animal as Asa's words burst into memory.

"For every night you don't let me do what I want, I'll make one of them pay. I'll finish every damn one of them Yankee sons of bitches, one by one."

The import of his words detonated in Rebecca's mind. Dear God, she couldn't let him hurt them! She had to hurry, before it was too late!

She missed a step on the dark stairs, fell, and slid down painfully. But that didn't stop her. Instead it was the door, for although the knob turned normally, something blocked it shut.

She pounded hard with both her hands. "Come back! Come back! I need to talk to you. *Please!"*

Another man groaned loudly. As Asa glanced toward him, the other two began to stir.

Shit! That bellyaching would wake the whole lot, and then he'd have to kill them all. That would make short work of his hold on the woman. Besides,

Hall would never believe that all the Yanks died in their sleep the same night.

Quickly, Asa took the blanket and moved from the curly-haired soldier to the man with the singed black beard and angry burns on neck and chest, who was making all the noise. It wouldn't take all that much effort to shut the bastard up for good.

As the Yankee's limbs spasmed violently, Asa heard the other two men's breathing resume an untroubled cadence, in spite of the desperate thumping at the attic door above.

Chapter Nine

*That . . . man . . . says women can't have as much
rights as man, cause Christ wasn't a woman.
Where did your Christ come from? . . . From God
and a woman. Man had nothing to do with him.*
                                    —Sojourner Truth

April 29, 1865

Rebecca threw her shoulder hard against the
attic door; she even clawed at it in an impossible
attempt to escape her dark prison. Why hadn't Asa
come back when she'd called him? Had he left
the house already, or was he downstairs doing the
devil's handiwork right now?

Her body banged painfully against wood, over
and over, until she had to admit she'd never force
the door that way. Terrible images splashed
through her mind, and she found herself praying
frantically, promising anything, *everything,* if only
she could leave here and find all three men alive.

Memory flooded her consciousness—Jacob's
face, his touch, his kisses—and suddenly, the walls
she'd built around her heart collapsed into rubble.

Thick sobs racked her body, and she choked on tears so long absent, she'd forgotten how to breathe amid their onslaught.

At last, after more tears than she'd ever cried before, Rebecca thought to sweep the brush's handle along the narrow crack at the bottom of the door. Immediately, the wood struck another object, and she realized something had been wedged into the gap. She worked for perhaps five minutes before her efforts finally dislodged it, and at last, the attic door swung open. She was free.

But what would she find downstairs in front of the fire?

Faint light leaked in through the second story's bedroom windows. Peering intently toward the nearest, Rebecca realized the sun would soon rise. She moved around the broken chair arm that had been shoved beneath the door at the bottom of the attic stairs, but the edge of a loose floorboard sent her sprawling. Her weight came down on her left knee.

As she lay bruised and panting, she strained her ears for any sounds that might carry from the floor below. For despite her eagerness to rush to her patients' aid when she'd been trapped, she felt tendrils of fear growing like Jack's beanstalk, winding around and choking off her courage. What if she came upon him killing them, and he turned on her instead? Was she truly ready to die for these near-strangers?

Then she wondered, had her brother, Thomas, been ready to die to free black men he'd never known? Had any of the soldiers who'd died these past four years? If they could do their duty, surely she could find the strength to do hers, too.

After whispering a brief prayer, Rebecca picked herself up off the hallway floor. She felt her way to the stairwell, where she could see a square of yellow light. Ignoring the panic that stabbed at her resolve, she forced herself to descend one step at a time.

It was the hardest thing she'd done in all her life.

In Andersonville, Jacob had grown used to shutting out the sounds of weeping in the night. He'd had to, for quiet never cloaked the prison camp. Like hell below, the suffering seemed eternal. Yet if his brother or Seth or Gabe so much as groaned, it woke him, as if his unconscious mind could recognize those closest to his heart.

He heard Rebecca crying hard tears that he knew from the sound alone would leave her eyes as swollen, her face as red and blotched, as Hope's had been in those last days.

"What's wrong?" he asked, pulling himself to a sitting position. At his voice, Nate Gordon woke, too.

"Mister—Mister Pierce has passed away," she answered. The blanket had been pulled high enough to cover his still body, just as Jacob had covered another man the previous morning.

In the firelight, Jacob could see that he'd been right about Rebecca's face. Moisture glistened beneath her puffy eyes. Her professional demeanor had completely failed her, and she continued weeping with the abandon of a child.

"He's at peace now," Jacob offered. He would never forget the way the man had pleaded in the water and after they'd been captured. Surely, death had at least released him from his pain.

"No one could say you didn't do your best, miss," the young private offered. "And if anybody ever does, he'll have to answer to Nate Gordon—maybe even the whole Fourth Kentucky Infantry, if I got anything to say about it.''

"This *is* my fault," Rebecca insisted. "If I'd only—"

Did women think the entire universe—including life and death—revolved around their actions? Jacob couldn't bear to listen to her blame herself again.

"Rebecca—" he began, but Nate interrupted.

"Don't say that," the blond private told her. "Why, lots of folks don't hold with the old ways. You can't think washing off that skunk oil did him in."

Jacob noticed the strain in Nate's voice, as if he were fumbling for anything to say that might appease her. Rebecca stared at him as if he were speaking in a foreign tongue.

"*I'm* feeling better," the private continued, "or leastwise I would be, if you would quit your cryin'. I never could abide a woman's tears."

She took a deep breath and appeared to struggle for composure.

In spite of Nate's attention, Jacob reached out and grasped her hand. She winced, and he looked down.

"What's happened to your fingers?" he asked, for several nails had split and her knuckles were swollen and bleeding.

She jerked free in an instant. "Nothing. I—I scrubbed too hard in the kitchen."

The speed of her denial, the way her gaze slid away, told him she was lying. But why?

"I'm going to reheat what's left of the soup. You two will need to eat," she said.

With the practiced eye of a man who frequently judged the gaits of horses, Jacob noticed she was favoring her left leg as she walked away. What had really happened to Rebecca last night? And why, this morning, was she keeping it from him?

Rebecca's sore fingers quivered as she tried to light the stove with the matches the colonel had left behind. When she'd realized Jonah Pierce was dead, she'd wanted to believe his injuries had killed him. But she could not convince herself, not even with the memory of his request for her to help end his suffering. When he'd spoken of his family, she'd seen a change come over him, a change that said he didn't want to die.

Yet no man survived on wishes, especially with that raider demon about. When Rebecca looked closely at the dead man's face, she'd noticed the blueness of his lips, the trace of wool lint stuck there, the disturbance of the scabbed wounds on his neck—the very wounds she'd bathed so carefully. Not enough evidence for the courtroom, she supposed, but enough for Rebecca to be certain Asa had murdered a helpless man already at the brink of death, probably by smothering him with his own blanket.

And now an Indiana woman named Elizabeth Pierce was a widow, and four young girls were fatherless because Rebecca Marston had refused to surrender honor. The fact of it sank in like a puddle of bile on a costly Oriental rug.

"For every night you don't let me do what I want, I'll make one of them pay." Asa wasn't through with them. Rebecca knew he wouldn't stop till both of the remaining men mysteriously succumbed. She thought of young Nate Gordon, who had promised to defend her honor, and Jacob Fuller, who touched a need inside her that she had never guessed existed. Could she bear to lose them, too, to spend their lives as payment for her chastity?

She thought again of running, trying to escape where he could never find her. But the colonel's threat resurfaced; if she tried to flee, the soldiers would be killed.

Maybe they could *all* escape. Her pulse quickened with excitement at the thought. The weakest of the men had died, and Nate was growing stronger by the hour.

She looked out the cracked and grimy kitchen window. Sunlight filtered through the thin clouds, gleaming across acre after acre of flooded fields. Here and there, the tops of shrubs and trees poked out of the muddy water, but the land's ridges and hollows were well-hidden by the Mississippi's excess.

Movement drew her eye: a man on horseback. The chestnut stopped in water only hock-deep, so Rebecca guessed the rider had chosen a high spot from which to watch. Even from this distance, she could make out the rebel's butternut jacket and the metallic glint of sunlight against his rifle barrel.

They were being watched, of course, from all sides. Escape, too, would mean death.

She couldn't tell which one she'd spotted, but she shivered with the thought it might be Asa. Her stomach rolled violently at the thought of what he would do to her when he returned this evening. Rebecca had a rudimentary knowledge of what passed between a man and wife, but she had never expected to be a participant, much less imagined how it would be to have such acts forced upon her.

Although she realized Asa was a man of average size, he loomed enormous in her memory, his left eye socket clotted with scar tissue, his brown beard as greasy as his hair. She could smell his acrid stench, and she had no idea how she'd bear it near her . . . over her, choking her like a terrible miasma.

Fresh tears rolled down her face, and she wondered if that stench would cling to her forever after Asa had his way. Only then did she fully understand she intended to go through with this devil's bargain. He had broken her.

She whirled toward the approaching footsteps. Had he come for her already? The moment she realized it was Jacob and not Asa in the doorway, her knees weakened with relief.

"You're killing all our matches, Becca." He gestured toward the half-dozen specimens she'd broken from their scant supply. They lay scattered like crushed insects near her feet, and the stove remained unlit.

She let him take the box from her trembling hands. With his first strike, the match flared into life. She thought of thanking him or making some other casual remark, but she could not trust herself to speak.

"You must have seen a lot of men die in your business," Jacob told her. No question, a flat statement.

She nodded carefully, watched him look around until he saw a rag she'd left to dry. Stepping close to her, he used it to blot her tears.

"You couldn't have taken all their deaths so hard," he said.

"But I did," she argued, her voice sounding thick, unnatural, even to her. But at least she'd recovered the use of it for now. "I hid it for a long time, but I took them all to heart. I realized it was killing me, too, a little at a time. I was about to quit, give up, and go home when all this happened."

"I wanted to walk away, too. More times than I could count," Jacob admitted.

"But you didn't. A lot of others did desert," she added, eager for the distraction. If she could only take her mind off what was coming, perhaps she'd somehow survive this day.

He shrugged. "The horses needed me. War's hell on them, even more than men in some ways. Animals don't understand this business, but it still hurts them plenty. Besides, the Army's not much interested in whether or not I approved of their war, and I'd made a promise when I signed on."

"You *volunteered*? Given your opinions, I rather imagined you'd been dragged off screaming."

"It was a good time for me to leave," he said, and darkness moved across his features as if a heavy cloud had slid over the sun. But the cloud passed, and he managed a wry smile. "Somebody had to keep Zeke in line—and safe . . . and I couldn't talk our sister into going. Though God knows, Eliza would've made the better soldier."

Rebecca smiled back, although she still felt as though she might be sick. "I doubt that. I think you were good at what you did. You seem so much more capable than I am, so certain of yourself."

He closed the distance between them until she felt his breath warming her face, helping to dry the still-moist tear trails. "You're more capable than you imagine. These past two days you've held up better than a lot of men I've known."

She stepped back from him and gestured toward her swollen eyes. "Does this look as if I'm holding up? And do two dead men prove I'm succeeding?"

Anger lanced the questions—anger at herself, at circumstance, and at the raider who had pushed her beyond her breaking point.

"You know damned well neither one of them stood much of a chance, Becca."

"Thank you, *Doctor* Fuller." Her voice was icy with sarcasm although she knew he spoke the truth.

Unexpectedly, he advanced on her and captured her left hand. Again, he stared down at the ruined nails and swollen knuckles. "That's twice you've let me call you 'Becca,' and after all that's happened, this is the only time you've cried. Tell me, what really went on here last night?"

Her eyes shot open as he gave her injured fingers a light squeeze. She couldn't answer—*couldn't*—or he'd be sure to interfere. Interfere and get himself—maybe all of them—killed in the process. She didn't doubt it for a moment. And even if some part of her wanted to revert to chivalry, to allow a man to take responsibility for her troubles, the more rational part knew the cost would be too high.

In the back of her mind something whispered that it didn't matter. The lawless raiders would likely murder all their captives, and they would ravish her before she died. But at some point, Rebecca had stopped looking too far ahead. Instead, she concentrated on surviving one crisis at a time. All she had to do right now was ease herself past this one.

"I told you before. I did that to myself by accident." She tried to jerk away from him, but he did not release her.

"You're lying," he accused her. "What I want to know is why."

The room felt suddenly too hot, too close, and she wanted to lash out at Jacob for continuing to press her. Rebecca's impulse to slap him was growing stronger by the second. "You're being foolish. Don't you have enough to worry about without imagining still more?"

"You need lessons. You're the poorest liar I've seen in a long time," he told her.

"Well, you certainly wouldn't be the one to teach me, the way you blurt out every thought that comes to mind."

He smiled. "I keep some to myself. Otherwise,

the hand you're lifting would be across my face right now."

She kicked his shin hard and was gratified to hear him grunt as he released her hand.

"I suppose you saw *that* coming, too," she challenged, "since you're such an authority on what I'm thinking."

To her utter shock, he picked her up and plunked her down so she was seated on the kitchen's worktable. Then, before she could say a word, he pulled up her skirt to expose her legs up to the knee.

"How—how dare you?" she sputtered, and she felt the heat that she knew accompanied her blush.

Jacob stepped out of kicking range to gesture toward her left knee. "Now tell me, did you do *that* cleaning, too?"

Her torn cotton stocking exposed her knee. The colorful bruise blooming there contrasted sharply with the white ruffles that edged her cotton drawers an inch above it.

"I was coming downstairs when I tripped on a loose floorboard," she shot back, pleased that this, at least, was true.

"I don't believe you for a moment," he said, "and let me see that leg."

She reminded herself that he meant only to help her as he ran his hands along the knee joint, then onto her lower thigh, which was protected only by the thinnest cotton layers. But his fingers, as they slid slowly downward, blazed tingling trails, conjuring sensations from when he had kissed her and whispering in her mind that no man had ever touched her there before.

As Jacob carefully flexed her leg at the knee joint, she thought, when Asa came back, she'd have to allow the raider's filthy hands to touch her anywhere he pleased. A cry, more animal than human, escaped her.

"That bad?" Jacob asked.

She nodded and said, "Worse," although she knew that they were speaking of two entirely different things.

Hall saddled his tall black mare, Glory. The horse's head swung around, flashing a narrow white blaze, and she nickered, eager for whatever treat he might have brought her.

"Not this time, girl," he said, patting her neck with real affection. He'd brought Glory all the way from his plantation, and somehow, through all the fighting, both of them remained intact. He meant to get her home as well, to breed fine foals with her long-limbed grace and speed.

He led the mare outside the barn, beneath a sky veiled with a thin layer of silvery clouds. Glancing upward, he was relieved to see they didn't appear to carry rain.

"Ready?" he asked Simms, who was busy with a big bay gelding he called Bushwhack.

"I don't see why we can't just go back to where we sent the telegram from. Jesus, colonel. This Marston bastard's just a Yankee, not some goddamn genius."

Hall hadn't expected Simms to appreciate the nuances of his plan. For one thing, he'd kept most of the details secret.

In his telegram yesterday, Lewis Hall had instructed the Baton Rouge attorney, Barlow Pickett, to reply to South Millsburg, Arkansas, in the name of their favorite schoolmaster, a man now deceased. By moving from town to town, changing names, and using Pickett as a go-between, Hall hoped to confound anyone who might be trying to apprehend him.

"I don't want to end up the guest of honor at a hanging. How about you?" Hall responded.

"I reckon not," Simms answered sourly.

"Then let's get moving. I'm eager to see what Winfield Marston thinks about all this." Hall indulged himself in a fantasy that the old swindler would offer double the asking price, if only he returned his beloved daughter unharmed. Of course, Marston wouldn't do that, but Hall imagined he would nearly break his neck rushing about to pay as fast as possible. The idea cheered the colonel, easing the sting of how he'd been deceived by the old man before. Finally, Marston would have the chance to feel a portion of the impotent rage and humiliation he'd inflicted on so many Southerners.

Nevertheless, two problems remained to trouble Hall. First, he would have to keep moving, far from both his men and the hostages, to retrieve Barlow Pickett's telegrams. The idea troubled Hall, for his threat and the men's greed would only hold them so long, and he had every intention of freeing all of his prisoners once this was over. Which brought him to the second snag. He'd promised his men a cut of a ransom that would never reach his hands. If the raiders found out his true intentions, they'd kill both the Yankees and their own leader.

As he and Simms rode away from the Tate farm, he wondered how he would appease his men. An appeal to their honor on behalf of Confederate widows and orphans would certainly never do. These were hardscrabble irregulars with only the vaguest notions of honorable behavior. Yet he refused to use a dime of Marston's money to buy their cooperation.

Hall patted Glory's black silk neck and thought

of all the dreams he'd had for the foals she would produce on the land his grandfather bought so long ago. But how often were dreams the price of honor?

When they reached South Millsburg, he would look for Marston's answer. Then, once this matter had been settled, he would sell the fine animal he rode so he could give the money to his men.

That amount, along with some other cash he had accumulated, would still fall far short of Marston's ransom. It would, however, be the most hard currency these raiders had ever seen, so Hall dared to hope that it might be enough.

Jacob smiled at the strains of conversation that drifted up the stairwell.

"With all due respect, miss, I've been a grown man from the minute I enlisted. I can make decisions for myself." Nate had yet to give up on the skunk-oil cure.

"This burn is raw and the blisters broken open. I won't have you poisoning yourself with that concoction."

Jacob could hear in Rebecca's voice that she was digging in her heels, preparing to argue until the Second Coming if need be. And just as well. He wanted time upstairs alone, time to look into her story.

What did he hope to find among these abandoned rooms: proof she'd told the truth or proof that she was lying? It would be easier, far easier, simply to take her explanation at face value or to construct some harmless reason she'd kept the real details to herself. Perhaps she'd been especially embarrassed to admit she'd hurt herself through clumsiness, or maybe she was only being stubborn. But he couldn't shake the feeling that the truth was dangerous and ugly—something that would only grow worse if he ignored it.

In the hallway, just as Rebecca had told him, a loose floorboard's edge poked up. Curious, he squatted beside it, then moved it with his fingertips. It lifted easily, and Jacob grinned at the unexpected gift. The former inhabitants must have planned to return. Perhaps they still would once the region was more settled, for they had left behind a row of glass jars secreted beneath the hallway floor. When he lifted more of the boards, Jacob found dried beans and flour, and several jars held real treasures: canned tomatoes, strawberry preserves, even green beans.

"Thank you," he said aloud, thinking of the hours the family must have spent in preparation. He couldn't have been more pleased if he'd discovered sacks stuffed with money. Jacob decided to take only a few of the jars for now, for he had no intention of sharing this bounty with the enemy, and he felt a responsibility to leave some food for the family, who still might come back to reclaim their home.

After removing the items he'd selected, he carefully replaced the floorboards, this time making certain no telltale edge poked upward. But as he stood and turned, the gleam of light against metal caught his attention. He stared in disbelief at the item lying on the floor beneath the hall table, an item he was certain the family hadn't left behind.

It was a revolver—a *revolver!* Quickly, Jacob put down the jars and retrieved it, his heart thudding with elation. This was a lifetime of Christmases and birthdays all wrapped up in one. This, if it were loaded, was their chance!

A bullet filled each chamber of the .44-caliber Army Colt, and it appeared to be in good condition. Yet through his excitement, realization surfaced.

He'd been right about Rebecca. She had lied to him about last night.

His jubilation crashed and splintered at his feet as images flashed through his mind. Rebecca, sleeping in the bedroom. A raider stealing in, using this very gun to . . . But she must have given him a fight. Had she raked those broken nails of hers to gouge his flesh? Had the rebel thrown her down on that sore knee? Somehow in the struggle, he must have lost his gun. But it hadn't mattered, had it? He was bigger, stronger . . . He must have overcome her.

The realization sickened him. She'd been too shamed to tell them she'd been raped.

He wished to God that he was wrong, but nothing else fit. Not her tears, her injuries, her lies. Not the forgotten pistol that lay beneath the table, where it had dropped in darkness.

"The son of a bitch," he swore, tucking the revolver into his trousers, draping his jacket over its butt. Somehow or other, he was going to figure out a way to use this weapon to get all of them to safety. But that wasn't all he meant to do.

He was going to kill the bastard who had hurt Rebecca.

Chapter Ten

We shall some day be heeded, and . . . everybody will think it was always so, just exactly as many young people think that all the privileges, all the freedom, all the enjoyments which women now possess always were hers. They have no idea of how every single inch of ground that she stands upon today has been gained by the hard work of some little handful of women of the past.
— Susan B. Anthony

Despite last night's rain, the island had grown a little wider during the hours of darkness, as if the abandoned farm were slowly reclaiming its remembered borders. The band of water separating the raiders from their prisoners had narrowed by a few feet, lessening the distance Asa would have to wade once night returned.

Staring across the brown ripples, he swore over his missing gun. He must have dropped it in the water last night, while crossing back to rejoin the other raiders. The more he thought on it, the more clearly he could picture the revolver slipping from the bundle of his clothes. He could almost hear its splash, lost among those made by his passing.

He tried all day to convince himself it had happened just that way. He almost managed, too. If not for that voice that had kept his hide intact so many times before, he would have chalked up the loss to hard luck and gone back to using his other weapon—the one he stole off that Union scout they'd ambushed a few months earlier.

But the last time Asa Graves ignored the voice, it had cost him his left eye. He didn't much want to give up another body part to the chance he might have dropped the damned revolver inside.

Asa swore aloud, still watching the house. If their prisoners had the gun, there could be hell to pay— especially if it were discovered that Asa'd been the one to leave the group a weapon.

The pup tucked its tail between its legs and cowered near his feet. It was just smart enough to fear his temper but too stupidly devoted to flee.

"Still frettin' over that red-haired gal?" Macon's voice rumbled, a bear's growl to go with the brown teeth and the ever-present glower. Macon knew of Asa's interest in the ladies. The taller man had joined in with him a time or two, when a woman caught his fancy or he was feeling particularly mean.

"Does seem a hell of a waste, a pretty piece like that, but I like my balls right where they hang," Asa said carefully.

"Me and Carl's gonna cross on over, take them Yanks a bit a cornmeal and one a them squirrels I got this mornin'. Wanta come and take a gander, maybe rile 'em up a bit?"

"Mood I'm in, might be safer for 'em if I stay back. Y'all go on," Asa invited, thinking that this might solve his problem.

In Asa's experience, once folks got an advantage, they could hardly wait for the chance to use it. If one of them Yankee soldiers had the pistol, he'd

likely try to shoot Macon and Carl. If the woman
kept it for herself, she'd wave it around and shriek
till someone killed her. Women were like that when
they got scared, and he guessed he'd scared her
plenty enough so she'd threaten the first raider
she saw.

Another fella might have felt some need to warn
his comrades, but Asa kept his mouth shut. He had
too much to lose by saying something. Besides,
neither Macon nor Carl ever did him any favors.

So as the two rode their horses across the water,
he simply watched and listened for the shots that
meant big trouble. In his mind, he composed a
story in case the worst fell out, an explanation of
how one of the two men had gotten careless with
his weapon.

And then he and Billy and Franklin would have
the excuse they needed to use that woman and kill
the whole bunch the way they should've from the
start.

As much as the idea appealed, Asa was hoping
that instead he'd gotten lucky, and the prisoners
hadn't found the gun. If nothing came of Carl and
Macon's visit to the house, then Asa figured he
could look forward to returning to the princess for
a more private reckoning. One that would take
place in the ink-black hours before sunrise. And
one Rebecca Marston never would forget.

As the dead squirrel dripped bright blood onto
the floor, Jacob glanced up into Rebecca's pallid
face. Across from her, two rebels leered, obviously
enjoying their effect on her. The first, the one with
the brown teeth and heavy brows, held a Navy Colt
at the ready. The second man, tall and auburn-
haired with a graying beard, looked nearly as thin
and lethal as the officer's saber he was brandishing.

From the doorway of the kitchen, Jacob watched them, careful to give no indication of the gun tucked in his waistband or the bloodlust tucked inside his soul. The revolver he'd found gave them a chance, a chance he could ill afford to squander foolishly . . . even if one of these bastards had been the one to creep in here last night—the one to break Rebecca.

No! If he let himself picture their grimy hands on her, let himself imagine her pain and fear and shame, he'd never be able to hold back from killing them. Already his fingers clenched spasmodically, even though he knew both he and Rebecca would likely die in the crossfire. Even if the fellow with the gleaming brown teeth didn't plug them with his pistol and the second man didn't slash them with his sword, the noise would draw the others from across the water.

He had to wait until he had the chance to get her and Nate to safety. No matter how she trembled or how wide her eyes grew.

Don't show them you're afraid, he thought, an echo of his warning as they'd watched the pair approach. He needed her to get up enough steam to scald them, to send them on their way without forcing him to use the gun now.

As if she'd heard and understood, Rebecca drew herself erect and fisted one hand against her hip.

"I just washed that floor, and you're making a mess of it. Now put that squirrel beside the cornmeal and be on your way, if you have nothing more to offer." Her voice was tart as vinegar, but by now Jacob knew her well enough to hear the strain.

The rebel with the saber extended his arm so that the blade's point rested just beneath her chin. "You better hope your daddy hurries up and pays that ransom. My patience ain't too good with sassy females."

The raider with the dark brows and darker grin glanced at Jacob. "Maybe we should have a go at her while her Yankee friend here watches. Might be he could learn a thing or two."

Jacob's jaws clenched, and the muscles of his arms ached with the effort of stillness. He shifted slightly and decided he'd ignore the tall man with the saber to fire on Brown Teeth first. He hoped he was right in thinking he and Rebecca stood a better chance against a blade than a bullet.

But before he drew the revolver, Rebecca stepped back and swatted the sword's tip away as if it were no more than a naughty child's outstretched finger. She then advanced on the man who'd threatened her, head lowered as if she might at any moment paw the earth and charge. Jacob had never seen such fury etched into any woman's features.

"For the past four years, I've heard how the South is fighting to preserve its honor. Tell me, where *is* this so-called Southern honor?" she demanded. "I don't agree with your perverse belief that you have the God-given right to own human beings, but I can at least respect the integrity of leaders like your General Lee, and I certainly understand why anyone might choose to defend his home against invasion. But Mister Lee, sirs, as well as your own mothers, would be appalled— *disgraced*—by your abominable behavior. You two are nothing but lowbred criminals and bullies masquerading as soldiers. You're not fit to breathe the same air as decent people, not worthy to wipe the sweat from the brows of men such as the soldier you have just insulted with your crude suggestion. Leave at once before *I* lose my patience and completely forget my manners."

The two raiders glanced at each other, then quickly looked away. To Jacob's surprise, their feet shuffled and they appeared both sullen and embarrassed, as if a particularly stern schoolmarm had just shamed them before the class.

The tall man, his sword tip drooping, looked up at Jacob with an almost apologetic expression.

"If you boys weren't the enemy, I'd carve out her tongue for y'all."

Jacob shrugged, carefully attempting to hide his pounding heart and the fact that he'd come a hair's breadth from starting a gunfight that would have probably cost them all their lives. "Appreciate the food. One more thing before you leave. Another man died. We'd be obliged if you'd take proper care of him. . . . He was a family man, and I'm sure he would have done the same for you."

"We'll get him out of your way," Brown Teeth offered. Both men looked grateful for the task, an excuse to retreat from Rebecca.

As they gathered the wrapped body and left the house, several things became clear to Jacob. The raiders had only wanted to frighten their captives and indulge themselves in a bit of sport to pass the time. They hadn't come intending to harm anyone—probably because of orders from the officer who'd been here yesterday. But their glances toward Rebecca assured him she had made two bitter enemies, and neither one would hesitate to kill her should the opportunity arise.

Rebecca stood on tiptoe as she peered out the dirt-grimed kitchen window. Her outburst had left a residue of anger, a taste so bitter that she spat her words. "I just know those men are going to toss poor Mister Pierce into the river the moment they think we're not watching. I've half a mind to go out on the porch and insist they bury him where we can see. Once this is over, perhaps I could make arrangements for his body to return home, to give his family a bit of peace.''

Jacob took her upper arm and turned her toward him. ''You're going to have to let this go, Rebecca.''

She stood too close to him, but he left her no room to step back from the warmth of his touch, the concern in his brown eyes. ''But they'll dispose of him as if everything he suffered, everything he was, never mattered.''

''You're right. They'll probably do exactly as you think.''

She liked it that he didn't try to fool her with some falsehood to assuage her feelings. Still, the idea felt like a slap to her sensibilities. ''Don't you think Jonah Pierce deserves a better ending?''

''We all deserve better, but that fact doesn't change one damned thing, does it? It doesn't change his death. And it doesn't change what was done to you last night.''

Her pounding heart sent heat flooding through her veins. What had Jacob guessed?

''I told you before; I hurt myself,'' she protested. But each time she repeated the assertion, the lump in her throat grew more painful and her tears came closer to the surface. All that kept her from dissolving was the stark brutality of Asa's threat.

You can believe this, princess. You don't let me have my way, I'll make you pay. Every damn one of you Yankee sons a bitches, one by one.

As the raider's coarse words rose to the surface, another memory distracted her: her father calling her Princess long ago, when she was small enough to clamber on his back demanding ''horsie rides.'' The image twisted in her stomach. *Father, help me— now!*

''And I told you before,'' Jacob insisted, ''I don't believe you.''

''So once again, this boils down to your assess-

ment of—of what you might presumptuously call
my skills as a liar.''

'' 'My assessment,' as you put it,'' Jacob argued,
''is that you have no skills in that department.''

She threw up her hands, too distraught to continue this pointless debate. ''*What?* Why are you
doing this to me?''

He took her hands in his, careful not to squeeze
her battered fingers. ''Rebecca, I'm not doing anything but trying to help you through this. Tell me
. . . please. No matter what it is, I promise I would
never blame you.''

What was he asking her? She searched his dark
eyes, his handsome features, trying to imagine what
he thought, why he kept dragging her back to the
same relentless questions. She recalled his reaction
to her bruised knee and her torn nails. . . . And
then she realized what he feared.

''Jacob,'' she whispered, overwhelmed by the
depth of his concern for her. Tears, as if eager to
make up for their long absence, once more blurred
her vision. ''I have not been . . . assaulted.''

She held his gaze and watched relief transform
his features. The perfect clarity of his emotion both
touched her and made her uneasily aware of all
she still held back.

''Thank God,'' he breathed, clearly believing her
this time. ''Thank God, Rebecca. I'd hoped it
wasn't true, but—''

''It isn't,'' she repeated. *At least not yet.*

She glanced beyond him, eager for escape. It
would be best to avoid him for the remainder of
the day. He was too close to the truth and too
aware when she was lying. Jacob moved to take out
the food he'd hidden in a cupboard when the two
of them had seen the pair of rebels approach, and
she used the opportunity to slip past him.

''I'm not feeling very well.'' True enough. The

events of this morning had left her temples pounding. "I'd like to lie down for a while."

"Did you eat anything today?"

She shrugged. "I had a little soup earlier. I'm not feeling very hungry."

He nodded. "You go rest, and I'll work on something better for our dinner."

"Thank goodness one of us can cook." Her gaze drifted to the dead squirrel the raider had left atop the table. "Only, if you include that, please don't tell me."

Her culinary tastes didn't run to rodent, but the last two days' fare had left her hungry enough that she knew she wouldn't ask too many questions.

"You have yourself a deal."

She attempted a grateful smile, then turned and left the kitchen. After checking Nate, she started upstairs for the bedroom, her heart heavy with the realization that she'd need all the strength she could marshal to survive the coming night.

Colonel Lewis Hall left Simms outside to watch the horses and hurried toward the doorway of the telegraph office. Just as he reached for the knob, he heard the lock click. Behind the glass, a short, pudgy man twisted the sign in the window to read, "Closed."

But Hall hadn't ridden all day to wait until morning for his answer. He rapped impatiently until the clerk glanced up, his fleshy face crinkling in irritation. With one thick finger he stabbed at the sign and mouthed the words, "Come back tomorrow."

Hall stared at the middle-aged man and moved his right hand to his gun butt. The clerk hesitated, watching the colonel intently, and Hall could almost hear him thinking how the plate glass wouldn't stop a bullet. Within seconds, the man unlocked and opened the door.

"May I help you, sir?"

Hall admired his calm demeanor, the smooth way he pretended that no threat had been implied.

"Is there a telegram for Seabrook Herrod?" he asked, using the false name.

"Oh, yes, Mister Herrod. It arrived less than an hour ago."

Hall tipped the clerk generously before taking his leave. Then, unable to wait for privacy, he opened and read the message.

"Well?" Simms asked. "He sendin' us our money, or we gotta ride all over Arkansas some more?"

Hall's jaw clamped so tight his teeth ached, allowing for no answer, for Marston's response, conferred through the Baton Rouge attorney, was the last thing—the very last thing—he had expected.

FEAR YOU ARE IN COMPANY OF IMPOSTOR. MARSTON ADVISES NO SUCH DAUGHTER EXISTS. NO PAYMENT FORTHCOMING.

An impostor? Hall's mind reeled at the thought. Why in heaven's name would Rebecca have lied about her identity? He thought back to the blond nurse, the one who had blurted, *"She's Rebecca Marston from Philadelphia!"*

Was it possible Rebecca had been posing as an heiress to impress her fellow nurses? The idea appalled him. If it were true, why hadn't this scheming social climber confessed her crime to avoid being held for ransom? Had she feared that no one would believe her? The idea seemed reasonable enough, as did the possibility that Rebecca—if that was indeed her name—might be trying to protect herself from rape. But even so, Hall felt his temper flaming at the thought of Winfield Marston laughing at his error.

"We're going back to get some answers," the colonel said, not caring that he'd explained nothing. Simms's presence barely registered, for Hall's thoughts teemed with the red-haired woman's beautiful face, her elegant figure. Deliberately, he cast aside his attraction with a memory of the sting of her reproachful words. Despite her arrogant lecture regarding his morals, the scheming pretender had played him for a fool. The more he thought about it, the more furious he grew.

Upon his honor, Lewis Hall swore he would make her pay for that mistake.

"We gonna camp tonight outside town?" Simms asked. His gaze kept wandering to the saloon a few doors down.

Hall knew he was hoping for a drink and a hot meal before they stopped to rest. They'd spent a lot of hours in the saddle today, and the thought of food, whiskey, and a good night's sleep tempted him. But the telegram he held pushed him beyond his body's needs.

He didn't have to explain his haste, however, for at that moment, Simms muttered, "Damn."

Hall saw them, too: a trio of men clad in dark-blue uniforms riding in their direction.

"We're starting back right now," the colonel remarked, keeping his voice as casual as possible.

"Sounds sensible enough," Simms said. "But there ain't no more than a couple hours of light left. Can't ride blind in this neck of the woods."

"We'll stop when we can't see. And in the morning, we'll be that much closer."

Closer to some answers, Hall thought. And closer to one more distasteful act of war.

Chapter Eleven

In the beauty of the lilies Christ
was born across the sea,
With a glory in His bosom
that transfigures you and me.
As He died to make men holy,
let us die to make men free.
His truth is marching on.

— Julia Ward Howe

"You was wasted as a farrier," Nate Gordon said brightly as Jacob passed him the bowl he'd just refilled. "Shoulda used you as a cook instead. I know for damn sure I'da fought better if we had decent grub."

"Reckon you'd be more particular if you hadn't spent the last few months living on ground cobs and rancid pork fat." Jacob sat cross-legged a few feet away, then took another bite of the simple stew he'd concocted. He'd been too impatient to cook the beans long enough, so they were still a bit hard, but like Nate, he'd spent too much time in the company of hunger to complain.

Across from him, the blond soldier moved his

spoon from bowl to mouth with hummingbird-quick motions.

"Guess you're feeling better," Jacob commented. "Either that or burns don't much affect your appetite."

The spoon at last slowed its flight and Nate looked up. "Never thought I'd say this, but I'm getting full."

"Three bowls'll do that to a fella."

He looked chagrined, as if he hadn't counted how many times Jacob had carried the bowl into the kitchen to refill it. "Did we—did I leave enough for Miss Marston?"

Jacob nodded. "There'll be plenty left when she wakes up."

A grin slanted across Nate's features. "She's a little bossy sometimes, but I'm sure gonna miss her."

Something in his voice made Jacob look up sharply. "You won't have to miss her. We'll likely be stuck together for a while more."

The private shook his head. "I'm doing a sight better now. Good enough to remember how it felt sitting on that steamboat headed north, headed for home. That's where I'm goin'. I didn't live through a dozen battles, Andersonville, and that *Sultana* blowup to be sent back south to another of them hellholes they call prisons. And I ain't about to wait for one of 'em to decide we'd all be less trouble dead. . . . Just the way they did with that poor fella."

Nate nodded toward the spot where Jonah Pierce had died.

Jacob put down his own food and gave the younger man his full attention. "What are you saying?"

The youth made a show of scooping up another

spoonful and chewing with uncharacteristic thoroughness.

Jacob jerked Nate's bowl out of his hand. "Tell me. Whatever you know—or think you know—you owe it to me and to Miss Marston."

As Nate met Jacob's gaze, his expression grew wary, as if he feared what the larger man might do if he refused. Jacob waited him out in silence, saying nothing to either threaten or absolve, allowing him to work out whatever doubts he had.

At length, Nate sighed. He looked down, unwilling or unable to accept eye contact as he spoke. "I didn't tell you earlier on account . . . well, hell, on account I shoulda done something—at least shouted out—when it was happening. But I just kept my eyes shut most of the way, hoping if I did he wouldn't notice. Hoping he would pass me by."

"Who?"

"I'm not real sure which one it was. I was more'n half-asleep. Thought I heard some footsteps coming downstairs. I figured it was Miss Marston, and I was hoping she'd fetch me that rusty bucket she likes to call the 'chamber pot.' But I'm tellin' you, when I peeked up and saw that reb with the folded blanket, I decided in a hurry that I'd best hold my water. Couldn't see the fella's face, but I saw him leaning over Pierce, saw him holdin' down that blanket. Pierce's arms—his arms and legs—"

Nate's voice broke, and he used his sleeve to swipe at his eyes. He looked up at Jacob then, his features twisting in what looked like shame and anger. With a shake of his blond head, the youth regained control.

Jacob struggled to mask his own reaction, not only to the story of what had been done to Pierce, but to Nate's statement that he thought he'd heard footsteps coming down the stairs. Rebecca's attacker? He recalled her words, her hesitation. *I have not been . . . assaulted.*

He'd believed her then—still wanted to believe her—but the pieces didn't fit. Something had happened last night, something she was hiding.

"His arms and legs was twitching," Nate continued, his eyes shining with moisture, "cause he was bein' killed. Smothered, I guess. And I didn't do a single thing. Didn't even try to shout for help. All I kept thinking on is how bad I wanted to get home."

"How old are you, Nate?"

His voice rode a wave of pain. "What are you sayin', that I'm not man enough to know the right and wrong of what I done? I'm telling you, I am."

Jacob nodded. "Sounds like you've seen enough these last few years to understand life isn't what the preachers say on Sunday. And it isn't what our folks say when they're trying to raise us right. Instead of right and wrong, the way I see it, there's a thousand million shadings in between the two. Some things might be more wrong and some less, but the view keeps changing depending on where you stand."

He picked up the bowl and handed it to Nate again before continuing. "From where I'm standing, you traded a dying man's life for the lives of three people with a chance. One thing I know for sure: that reb didn't come here without a weapon."

The same weapon Jacob now kept hidden. He decided not to mention it to Nate for the time being.

"If you'd done what you think you should have," he continued, "we'd all be dead by now."

Jacob couldn't help wondering if it were true. Did the rebel have another weapon or a compatriot standing watch outside? Or could Nate and Jacob perhaps have overpowered him? He wondered,

too, why he hadn't killed all of them at once. But
there was no way to know the answers and no sense
in distressing the Kentucky private further.

Nate breathed a quiet sigh. "I wouldn't really
run off on you and Miss Marston. I couldn't—only
I was feeling scared, too shamed and scared to
think straight."

Jacob nodded. "Only an insane man wouldn't
be afraid. But you were thinking plenty straight.
Whoever killed Pierce will come back for the rest
of us. And even if he doesn't, the raiders won't
want witnesses to anything as serious as kidnapping.
Not even the victim. We're leaving, all of us, tonight
when it gets dark."

"Do you think ..." Nate hesitated, his nervousness betrayed by the shaking fingers he ran
through his blond hair. "Do you think she'll be
able to keep up?"

He was asking if Rebecca might hold them back,
or if they'd have a better chance without her.

"I'm going to pretend you never said that,"
Jacob told him, struggling to keep his tone neutral.
In truth, Rebecca was in better condition than
either of the former prisoners. But Nate, whose
burns had left him weakest, would never admit any
woman might outdistance him on foot.

Nate nodded his agreement, but he avoided
Jacob's gaze.

Jacob said nothing about the gun he'd found. It
was obvious that fear was sinking its sharp fangs
into the young soldier. He might claim otherwise,
but he was thinking about bolting, running to save
his hide. If Nate learned about the Colt, panic
might even prompt him to try to exchange that
secret for his life. Jacob didn't like to think it, but
in Andersonville he'd seen men's honor fall to
ruin, enough so planned escapes were sometimes

sold out for a shriveled potato or an extra measure of infested cornmeal.

Right now, the only person Jacob trusted was himself, at least until he got some straight answers from Rebecca.

Asa Graves poked idly at a rabbit he was roasting over a weak fire. He watched as the small carcass sweat clear beads of grease, listened as drips popped and sizzled on the reluctant flame. The men had gathered kindling from the barn, but the wood was still damp from the rain the day before. He'd be damned lucky if he could get the meat cooked through.

It barely mattered. In the past few years, he'd eaten so much burned, spoiled, or half-raw food that a decent meal would probably kill him. All he cared about was getting the chore done and passing time until he could finally cross over to take Rebecca Marston.

He reached to scratch the ears of the tan pup that sat beside him, gazing greedily at the roasting meat. What the men had was barely sufficient for their own needs, yet Asa knew he'd slip the animal some of his own portion. Because the hunger that had gnawed at him all day didn't have a thing to do with food. Instead, in the enforced idleness of camp, Asa's thoughts had fixed on what he'd do after midnight.

Always before, his rapes had been crimes of opportunity, brutal and hurried. But later, he'd wonder how much better it would have been if he'd had time to plan; and how much more satisfying if he could spend hour after hour perfecting his acts of humiliation.

As the day wore down, Asa sat cross-legged before the fire, chewing absently at the outer layers of a haunch of the rabbit before tossing its bloody center to the hound. From time to time, he grinned like a fool at his mind's inventiveness, at all the ways he'd thought of to destroy the Big Man's daughter without leaving a mark upon her flesh. And best of all, no matter what he did to her, that bastard Colonel Hall would never know.

This time, when Rebecca followed the red-haired boy upstairs into the attic, he stood waiting at the head of the stairs, his small form silhouetted by the illumination from the window at the room's opposite end. The light filtering through the glass was poor, however, not only because of an accumulation of dirt on the windowpanes, but because dusk was at hand.

Soon night would fall in earnest, and Asa would return. A sick chill rippled through Rebecca's body, but she did not allow herself to take her eyes off the child standing a few steps above her. This time she refused to let him slip away.

He'd scared her half to death only moments before, when she'd felt the peck of his kiss upon her cheek and opened her eyes to see his freckled face above hers. She'd leaped up in a flash to chase the giggling boy into the attic, just as she had last night.

"Where are your parents?" she demanded, breathing hard from the pursuit.

"You're so silly, Mama." A broad grin exposed his missing teeth and lit his brown eyes with mischief.

She felt jolted, as after a dream ending with the sensation of a fall. *Mama?*

"Rebecca?"

The voice was soft but deeply male, just as was the hand upon her upper arm.

She turned to see Jacob standing a step behind her on the staircase.

"Do you see him?" she whispered.

"Who are you talking to?" he asked.

She pointed, and her gaze flicked toward the boy, but just as he had last night, he had vanished once again. Rebecca stood stock-still, her heart pounding.

"I thought . . ." she started to explain before she wondered how she could describe what happened without sounding like a complete fool. She wasn't even certain how to put it into words. Had she been chasing a dream of some sort? Or a ghost? The encounter left her feeling unsettled and disoriented, as if she'd already experienced this moment at some point in the past.

"There's something . . . in this house." She whispered the words, but they bounced against the rafters and returned to her far louder than she had intended. Rebecca felt heat rising to her face. Would he believe her mad?

Jacob glanced beyond her. "You shouldn't find that too surprising. Squirrels and raccoons like to stay out of the rain, too. When people leave a place, they move right in. Where'd you see it?"

She hesitated, uncertain whether she wished to correct him. But pretending she'd seen some sort of animal felt even more ridiculous than trying to explain.

"Not *it*, Jacob, *him*. A little boy." She ignored the strange intensity that sharpened his gaze. *In for a penny, in for a pound.* "I've seen him several times here, but when I try to follow him into the attic, he seems to disappear. At first, I thought it was a dream, but I just spoke to him . . . and he answered."

As Jacob regarded her, the attic temperature seemed to climb. She felt perspiration dampening her hairline. Irritation flashed over nervousness. Was he simply going to stand there, condemning her with silence? She'd prefer even his laughter to this waiting.

"Rebecca," he finally began, "I'm not sure how to ask this, but how long have you been seeing people who aren't there?"

She narrowed her eyes. "You mean, how long have I been suffering delusions? I can assure you, I have never been considered weak-minded, and whatever this is, it's no hallucination based upon hysteria."

Again, there was a maddening pause before he spoke, but his expression held no trace of mockery.

"My grandmother," he continued, "the one who taught me about living off the land, used to say that a house takes on impressions from the folks that lived in it. She grew up in an old place, and she told stories about the smells of baking bread that sometimes rose from a cold hearth, or the strains from an old song that echoed in the chimney. I always thought she was only telling bedtime stories, but maybe they were more than that. She seemed more open than most to other ways of looking at the world."

Jacob smiled, as if his words had triggered some amusing memory. After a moment, he added, "I've felt it myself a time or two—something lingering in old places where people lived and loved and died. Why not here as well?"

Gratitude rushed over her, followed by the quick recognition that if he'd made such an admission, her own reaction would have surely been both immediate and scornful. If his grandmother had been open, did that make her mind closed? Rebecca wondered if she'd been too quick to judge the man before her, too quick to rule him both uncaring and unfit.

Outside of this house, this circumstance, she realized, she never would have come to know the man who stood a few steps below her. She would have seen him only as a man who shod the horses, a man who wore sweat and dirt more in keeping with the beasts he tended than with polite society. She would have dismissed even the possibility of . . . Her mind reached out to him because her hands were too well bred, and she imagined him pulling her against him, enfolding her into his arms, and giving her one more kiss to tuck away. Just one more . . .

Jacob walked up the stairs, bridging the small gap between them, sharing the narrow step. But instead of stopping, he moved past her and into the attic. He had to stoop to keep his head from banging on the rafters. As he peered into the gloom, his gaze lingered on item after item among the remnants scattered there.

She turned, trying to hide her disappointment, but she did not follow.

"What are you looking for?"

He spared her a brief glance. "You ever stop to think why that boy you talked about might be *leading* you up here? Maybe there's something in this attic that's meant for you to find."

"Surely, you don't believe—"

"What? That you're telling me the truth? That you're completely sane?"

She felt a ripple of attraction as he shrugged one broad shoulder. For now, he was all angles, but hard muscles hinted at the powerful man he had once been—and would be again in time.

"You're not lying," he said, "or at least you don't *believe* you are. Not unless you've improved a whole lot on that account since this afternoon."

His words made her recall the reason she had lied to him . . . and the terrible bargain she would make with Asa. She glanced uneasily toward the translucent window and the fading light.

"It's getting too dark up here to see much," she told him, her voice shaky.

"Let's go down and have some dinner," he suggested. "We can bring up candles later and look again."

"All right," she agreed, though neither the food nor the prospect of a search held much interest for her. Though she dreaded the night with all her being, some part of her just wanted to get beyond it, to get on with the business of survival.

Her feet, however, remained immobile, firmly planted on the third step from the top. When Jacob reached her, she couldn't even move aside to let him pass.

"Somebody nail your shoes into that stair?" he asked, cupping her chin with a gentle hand. "You haven't budged since I came up here."

She hesitated, trying to think of how to answer, trying to string words together in some form that might make sense yet tell him nothing.

Before she thought of anything, he spoke to her again. "What is it, Rebecca?"

In the silence that followed, she heard his sigh and felt its warm breath touch her cheek, almost as gently as his fingertips still touched her jaw. He waited for an answer, but she had none. Finally, unable to bear the quiet intensity of his nearness, she whispered, "Please don't do this, Jacob."

"A long time ago, I would have listened to you. But I've been haunted by my own ghost. The last woman I stopped pressing for an answer died."

Old pain edged his voice and deepened into something that brought quick tears to her eyes. She closed them tightly, unable to look into his face.

But Jacob wasn't finished. "She died because she couldn't talk to her own husband."

She heard the raw guilt in his words and wondered how long ago he had been widowed. But she couldn't ask, for opening her mouth meant the risk of blurting out the explanation that he wanted, an explanation that might lead to both their deaths.

Instead, she pulled away and fled downstairs. Their footsteps rapped a clumsy rhythm on the narrow stairs, his bare feet not half a beat behind her own.

As she moved through the open doorway at the bottom of the attic stairs and into the second floor hallway, Jacob caught her arm. Though she tried to pull away, he held her fast.

"Look here," he told her. He jabbed a finger toward the back of the attic door, now open.

Enough light filtered in from the second-story windows to illuminate deep scratch marks on the wooden surface. Scratch marks she had left when she had tried to claw her way free last night.

He spun her toward him, almost roughly. "Are you still going to tell me you hurt your fingers cleaning? Are you going to keep protecting the man who murdered Jonah Pierce? Rebecca, I don't have the patience to keep asking you."

Her breath hissed through her teeth too fast, and her heart leaped like a rabbit in a snare. This morning, she'd concluded that Asa had smothered Jonah Pierce, but hearing it from Jacob made her mind play out the horror of the murder. Asa wadding up the blanket, pressing it hard over the unconscious man's face. Jonah waking to the searing pain of the burns, the horrible pressure, and the panic of suffocation. Fighting, limbs flailing . . . It must have happened that way. Dear Lord, please make it stop-stop-stop.

"*Stop!*" she shrieked, shoving Jacob hard enough to make him take a step back. She glared at him, all her fear transforming into waves of hatred. "Stop making me feel it! Stop asking me, and for heaven's sake, keep your damned hands to yourself!"

Her words echoed in the old house, sounding so angry and desperate that she didn't recognize them as her own. A chill traced the indentation along her spine as she wondered if she would ever piece together the ruined remnants of her shell.

Jacob stood back, his palms uplifted in an unmistakable gesture of peace. As plainly as if he spoke the words aloud, she could hear him wondering if he'd been wrong before, or if a woman capable of such an outburst—a woman who cursed and admitted seeing strange things in this house— could be a woman he might trust.

And though his opinion shouldn't really matter, that unspoken question tore through her like grief. Just as did his slow turn away from her, his steady strides toward the staircase leading to the first floor.

She let him go without her, listened to his feet beat out a downward rhythm on the bare wood of the steps.

A rhythm that was punctured by a cluster of gunshots.

Chapter Twelve

It may seem a strange principle to enunciate as the very first requirement in a Hospital that it should do the sick no harm.
—Florence Nightingale

As the sound of gunfire echoed through the house, Jacob whirled around to look at Rebecca. Already, she was moving toward him down the steps. Her gaze swept over him, and he knew without asking she was reassuring herself that no bullet had struck him.

"Get upstairs right now!" he commanded before he turned and continued his descent, his ears straining for the direction of the fading echoes. They seemed to come from outside, but they were too close to be some of the raiders hunting.

Jacob advanced only a step or two before he noticed the front door standing open—and an unexpected vacancy before the fireplace.

He swore, then shouted, "*Nate!* Damn it, Nate, get back in here!"

The youth's pale face flashed through his memory, and nausea dropped his stomach through its trapdoor. He never should have left the boy downstairs by himself. Fury followed on the heels of fear, both at Nate for running and at himself for ignoring the boy's mounting terror, his clear compulsion to cut and run. If Nate was dead now . . .

But he wasn't. With sickening clarity, the youth's cries split the stillness that had followed the staccato burst of noise.

"Oh, God, help me!" From somewhere outside yet nearby, the words rose in volume, then broke into eerie cries like some sort of wounded animal.

"Nate!" Rebecca called, sweeping past Jacob toward the window.

He tackled her. Too hard, he realized as they crashed short of the window frame. Jacob heard her teeth clack together, her breath rush out with a grunt. His elbow slammed into a floorboard and sent pain flashing up his arm. Rolling off, he rubbed her back until her breathing hitched and started again.

"Sorry, Rebecca, but you can't go charging toward the door or window. They'll be so nervous now, they'll shoot anything that moves." Jacob sat up, but he kept his voice low. For all he knew, the rebels had crossed the water or were crossing it right now. "And I told you to go upstairs."

"I won't leave him out there screaming. I simply *can't*," she insisted. "However did he get out there in the first place?"

Though Jacob couldn't see her face, she was making no effort to disguise her weeping. Outside, Nate was sobbing out a steady stream of prayers.

"That damned fool boy got scared and tried to run," Jacob said, shaking his head in self-disgust. "I should have seen this coming."

Rebecca looked at Jacob and began pushing herself up. "I can't listen to him going on like that. I'm going out to help him. I'm going—"

He pushed her down again. "Like hell you are."

"Let go of me this instant! They know I'm a nurse. Surely, they wouldn't—"

"Being a woman does not make you immune to bullets. *No.* You're staying inside if I have to tie you. Understand that? I'll go get him."

She hesitated. "But you're a soldier. What if they shoot you, too?"

He rubbed his throbbing elbow. "I'll talk to them first, make sure everybody's calmed down. Then I'll carry him in here where we can try to fix him up."

She threw her arms around him and kissed him quickly, unexpectedly, but with an intensity that stunned him. "Don't you *dare* get yourself killed, Jacob Fuller. Don't you dare!"

Her embrace felt warm and welcoming, a moment's respite from the icy bite of fear. The moment ended all too swiftly, and Jacob reached beneath his shirt to pull out the revolver.

Rebecca's eyes grew huge and round as he handed it, butt-first, to her. "Where did you—?"

"Later. Just keep it. Use it if you must, but otherwise, don't let them know you have it. Can you shoot?"

"I—ah—" She shook her head. "I'm not certain how."

He cocked the pistol, pointed to the trigger. "Point it at whichever one you mean to kill and pull this. It's that simple. But don't drop it, or it's likely to go off."

She nodded, her face pale and serious. He half expected her to shrink away from the weapon or decry the thought of shooting someone, but she did neither. Instead, she studied the Colt with intent and sober eyes.

Jacob moved closer to the window and shouted toward the opening. "I'm coming out to get him. Nobody else is trying to leave."

He could feel them watching from somewhere beyond the front porch, could feel their shaking fingers on their triggers, their heartbeats pounding wildly in anticipation. But though he strained his ears, Jacob heard nothing but the sounds of Nate's hoarse sobs.

"Be quiet, Nate!" Jacob called. "If I don't hear their answer, it could get us both killed."

Nate's cries choked back to groans.

"I'm coming out," Jacob repeated. Again, no answer came.

He stood and moved toward the open door.

"Jacob . . ." Rebecca whispered.

Her eyes glowed bright with fear and with something else that gripped his heart. Something he could not afford to think about right now.

"I'll be right back," he said. Raising his hands above his head, Jacob stepped through the doorway and onto the porch. As he walked down the crumbling steps, he wondered if he'd feel the bullet before he heard the sound of its report.

It took only a moment to find Nate lying on his side, his upper body at the muddy edge of the floodwater. His right arm was cradled against his chest, and blood was pumping from his mangled palm, staining his shirt crimson. He ground the reddened fingers of his left hand into his right wrist, pressing hard in what Jacob recognized as an instinctive attempt to block the pain in his right hand.

"Why couldn't you just wait?" Jacob asked as he edged nearer. It was easier to clamp down on his pity and let anger run its course. But he could not forget caution, either. He scanned the area across the water until he saw two men holding rifles. Both barrels pointed toward him.

Neither of the rebels moved a muscle. Instead, they remained as poised as predators, waiting to

Take A Trip Into A Timeless World of Passion and Adventure with Kensington Choice Historical Romances! —*Absolutely FREE!*

Let your spirits fly away and enjoy the passion and adventure of another time. Kensington Choice Historical Romances are the finest novels of their kind, written by today's best selling romance authors. Each Kensington Choice Historical Romance transports you to distant lands in a bygone age. Experience the adventure and share the delight as proud men and spirited women discover the wonder and passion of true love.

4 BOOKS WORTH UP TO $23.96—Absolutely FREE!

Take 4 FREE Books!

We created our convenient Home Subscription Service so you'll be sure to have the hottest new romances delivered each month right to your doorstep — usually before they are available in book stores. Just to show you how convenient Zebra Home Subscription Service is, we would like to send you 4 Kensington Choice Historical Romances as a FREE gift. You receive a gift worth up to $23.96 — absolutely FREE. There's no extra charge for shipping and handling. There's no obligation to buy anything - ever!

Save Up To 30% On Home Delivery!

Accept your FREE gift and each month we'll deliver 4 brand new titles as soon as they are published. They'll be yours to examine FREE for 10 days. Then if you decide to keep the books, you'll pay the preferred subscriber's price. That's all 4 books for a savings of up to 30% off the cover price! Just add the cost of shipping and handling. Remember, you are under no obligation to buy any of these books at any time! If you are not delighted with them, simply return them and owe nothing. But if you enjoy Kensington Choice Historical Romances as much as we think you will, pay the special preferred subscriber rate and save over $7.00 off the bookstore price!

We have 4 FREE BOOKS for you as your introduction to KENSINGTON CHOICE!

To get your FREE BOOKS,
worth up to $23.96, mail the card below
or call TOLL-FREE 1-888-345-BOOK
Visit our website at www.kensingtonbooks.com.

Take 4 Kensington Choice Historical Romances FREE!

YES! Please send me my 4 FREE KENSINGTON CHOICE HISTORICAL ROMANCES (without obligation to purchase other books). Unless you hear from me after I receive my 4 FREE BOOKS, you may send me 4 new novels – as soon as they are published – to preview each month FREE for 10 days. If I am not satisfied, I may return them and owe nothing. Otherwise, I will pay the money-saving preferred subscriber's price plus shipping and handling. That's a savings of over $7.00 each month. I may return any shipment within 10 days and owe nothing, and I may cancel any time I wish. In any case the 4 FREE books will be mine to keep.

KN121A

Name _____

Address _____ Apt No _____

City _____ State _____ Zip _____

Telephone ( ) _____ Signature _____

(If under 18, parent or guardian must sign)

Terms, offer, and prices subject to change. Orders subject to acceptance by Kensington Choice Book Club. Offer valid in the U.S. only.

‖‖‖‖‖‖‖‖‖‖‖‖‖‖‖‖‖‖‖‖‖‖‖‖‖‖‖‖‖‖‖‖‖‖‖‖‖‖

KENSINGTON CHOICE
Zebra Home Subscription Service, Inc.
P.O. Box 5214
Clifton NJ 07015-5214

PLACE
STAMP
HERE

see if Jacob would keep his word. And more than likely hoping that he wouldn't.

"I'm—sorry. I'm—so—sorry. . . ." The words slid disjointed from Nate's mouth, and his blue eyes had lost their clarity. Blood loss and the shock of the injury had plainly left him too weak to move to safety on his own.

Jacob knelt beside him. "I'm going to pick you up. It'll hurt some, but try to keep from screaming. You do, you startle them too badly, and they might shoot us both."

"All right, all right. Just don't leave me out here, please."

"I'm not going to leave you."

Not like you meant to leave Rebecca and me, Jacob added mentally. Later, if both were very lucky, there would be time enough for blame. Besides, he knew that Nate would pay a heavy price for his moment of panic. From the ragged looks of the wound, Jacob guessed it had been a minié ball that struck the boy. In his years as a cavalry farrier, Jacob had seen an obscene number of men and horses hurt in the same manner. As it tore through Nate's hand, the conical bullet would have instantly expanded, destroying bone and tissue enough to kill. It would be a damned miracle if he survived, unless . . .

They could worry about that later. For now, he had to concentrate on getting the wounded man to safety. Nate was heavier than Rebecca, but fear lent Jacob strength to pick him up. He hesitated for several moments, wondering if one of the two raiders would fire now on the chance of hitting two Yanks with one bullet. In the past few years, Jacob had seen sicker acts, most of them committed by the men on his own side.

"Now get your asses on in there!" One rebel's words skated across the water's surface. He punctuated them with a shot that struck near Jacob's feet, spattering his legs with dark brown mud.

From inside the house, Jacob heard Rebecca's shriek of indignation. She shouted a furious reply, but he didn't catch the words. He was far too busy carrying Nate toward the safety of the front door.

As he stepped inside, he asked her, "What the hell are you trying to do, make them even madder?"

But Nate's groans drowned out Jacob's angry words.

"Here," Rebecca said, slapping her hand atop the table. "Let's keep him off the floor and have a look."

As Jacob laid Nate down, he saw the youth's eyes rolling back toward unconsciousness. His face glowed with a spectral pallor, and his flesh felt all too cool.

Rebecca stared at the jagged hole through what remained of Nate's right palm. Shards of bone and cartilage salted white flecks through the gushing redness. She checked him over quickly for more wounds. Finding none, her gaze then sought Jacob's. He knew from her expression that she understood completely that this single injury would prove sufficient to pull a shroud over the boy's face.

"I have some rags in the kitchen." Her words gave away none of the emotions that played across her features. "We'll need to stop the bleeding quickly."

As she turned toward the kitchen, Nate seemed to revive some of his strength. His groans coalesced into something rhythmic, something almost recognizable. Jacob leaned forward, trying to comprehend what he was saying.

"He maketh—maketh me to lie down in green pastures: he leadeth me beside the still waters. . . ."

Nate's words whispered like the hiss of spring rain on pine needles.

"He restoreth my soul," Jacob continued with him as he tore the seam in Nate's sleeve to roll it back. The private's words rose to a cry, but Jacob did not stop. "He leadeth me in the paths of righteousness for his name's sake."

Rebecca returned with a pan of water and an armload of rags. She set them down on a chair, then laid her hand upon Jacob's forearm. Her voice echoed clear and pure inside the mud-stained room. "Yea, though I walk through the valley of the shadow of death . . ."

She turned her attention to Nate's hand and began to wash it. Nate hissed with pain and tried to pull his arm away. Jacob held him still while Rebecca finished, then wound cloth strips tightly around the ruined palm.

As the boy groaned, Jacob knew beyond all doubt the horrible act that it would take to save him. If only he and Rebecca could be strong enough.

Jacob looked into her eyes, but instead of asking her the question in his mind, he quoted, "I will fear no evil, for thou art with me. . . ."

She nodded, answering what he had not asked in words. She smoothed the hair on Nate's pale forehead, and she whispered, "Yes, I am—with you."

"All right then," Jacob told her. "Let's start thinking what we'll need."

Rebecca ground her sore fingertips into her palms. But not even the tiny flares of pain could distract her from the hopelessness of what she and Jacob planned to do. Surely, it could not be successful—not here in these primitive conditions and not by a jaded farrier and a ruined nurse.

When she glanced at Nate, he blinked back, his expression suddenly as alert as if he'd guessed.

"What—what are you doing?" His voice shook, and his gaze shifted lightning-quick to Jacob. "I— I told you, I never really figured on leavin' you behind. It's just that—just that—"

"Shhh." Rebecca stroked his cheek. "That doesn't matter now. I promise, Nate, we're going to do our best to help you."

But she could feel his panic rising like thick smoke through a chimney.

"Lord, it hurts so bad, so bad. Can't you stop it?" Tears leaked from Nate's eyes, then disappeared into his damp hairline.

His fear and pain infected Rebecca like the most virulent of fevers. Her composure dissolved into a gale of trembling, and she wondered how her best could ever be enough.

The first time she'd witnessed the operation, she'd been of absolutely no use, for the sights and smells had sickened her. Afterward, she'd stumbled through one or two of the surgeries, but normally another nurse assisted. Because they all understood she couldn't . . . couldn't possibly . . . Tiny dots swarmed in her vision, their glow pulsing in time to the throbbing at her temples.

Jacob stepped in closer. "She's right, Nate, but you have to know it won't be easy. We'll need to take your hand."

He shook his head. "Like hell! You can't! I won't let you!"

"Tell him, Rebecca. Tell him what will happen if he doesn't listen."

The mention of her name returned Rebecca to herself, returned her to the realization that there was no one else to step in and offer a professional opinion—no one else to help convince Nate that this was the only way. Though her mouth felt packed with cotton, she forced herself to speak.

"You'll die, Nate," she told him. "There'll be fever and pus and a foul odor. And days, perhaps, of pain. But even if you'd been hurt in Memphis and under the care of the finest surgeons, nothing could stop what's been set in motion. Nothing but the—the procedure Mr. Fuller just described."

She saw how quietly he watched her, saw the anguish embedded deep in his expression. She made herself continue, though at that moment she would have signed over her trust fund to anyone who could take this responsibility from her. "If we remove the hand as soon as possible, you'll have a good chance. Amputations below the elbow, especially those performed within a few hours, have a very high success rate. But the longer we wait, the worse the chances."

"No!" Nate cried. "You two don't know what you're saying! You ain't doctors! You ain't God!"

"I swear to you, Mr. Gordon, I have seen more cases like your own than I can count."

But she *could* count them, could count every single one if she but took the time. A parade of ghostly faces flickered through her memory. Many came with voices; many came with names. If she allowed herself, she could recall which limb each man had lost and whether he'd survived it. She remembered letters she had written to their relatives and letters she'd received from some a few months later, after they'd gone home. One, a boy near Nate's age who'd lost his right arm at the elbow, had had his mother transcribe a heartfelt—and heart-breaking—marriage proposal. Another had been so angry he'd sent his surgeon a death threat.

Rebecca swallowed hard and focused on Nate's struggle: terror against reason. She watched fear gain the upper hand.

He shook his head emphatically. "You ain't hacking me apart. I got to find my unit, and I got to get home in one piece! How the hell can I help Pa plow fields with just one hand?"

Jacob inclined his head toward Rebecca. "Give me the pistol, then."

Alarm made her heart leap. "What do you propose to do?"

"You hear him." His voice was flat, betraying no emotion. "Kentucky boy wants to die now that he can't desert us. He wants to take the coward's way. So where is that revolver?"

She had no intention of telling him she'd simply laid it on the floor beside the window when he'd brought in Nate. Not when he was being so utterly ridiculous. "No! We're here to help him, not shoot him, you idiot!"

But her words availed her nothing, for Jacob saw the pistol and strode toward it. Rebecca darted after him, but she wasn't fast enough. Jacob stooped to snatch up the Colt, then stood with its barrel sloping toward the floor. He had only to lift it to be pointing straight at the private—or at her.

"No!" she shrieked. Outrage had her doubling one hand into a fist. Jacob Fuller was no more than a brute, a bully!

"Stop! I promised Pa. I have to get home to help out with the farm. I'm not going to die!" the youth protested.

"Damned right, Nate. Damned right," Jacob told him. "Remember how you promised. Gave your pa your word. But nobody ever said that promises are easy. Are you ready to pay the price for keeping this one?"

In the silence that followed, Rebecca realized Jacob had never meant to kill Nate Gordon, never meant to do anything but bring him to this point. But what did motives matter when his methods were so barbaric? Surely, she could have accomplished the same thing without implying that she'd shoot him. Or could she?

"Yeah . . . *yes.*" Nate's voice gathered strength. "I reckon that I am."

Jacob leveled his hard gaze on her. "And you, Miss Marston? Are you ready to help get this boy home? Are you ready to be strong? Because I've got no use for you if all you'll do is faint or lecture—"

Hating him, she hissed, "I'm a nurse, and I'll do what I must. I have attended before at amputations. Can you say the same?"

He nodded. "I've performed one. It was on a mare. Her lower leg was badly broken, but the owner wanted to keep her for breeding."

"On a horse," Rebecca repeated incredulously.

"A horse that *lived,*" Jacob added.

"Oh, hell," Nate muttered.

Jacob looked at him for a long moment. "Pretty much."

"Yeah, well you were right before on that count," Nate said, his blue eyes closing. "I guess you're even more right now."

Though his words had been directed at Nate Gordon, Jacob's thoughts drifted toward his brother. If Zeke had somehow survived the disaster aboard the *Sultana,* had Seth or Gabe forced him to accept the same choice as Nate? Tucking the revolver back into his pants, Jacob tried not to think of Zeke's weakened condition and his infected ankle—tried not to remember the heat of the flames or the terrible struggle among men all fighting to keep their heads above the river's surface. Yet the awful cries rang in his ears, and the charred memory of smoke threatened to choke him.

He shook his head as if he'd just been doused

with water. He couldn't afford to think about Zeke or his pa, who might well be dead already. He couldn't allow his mind to linger on Seth Harris or wonder what became of Gabe. Like Hope four years before, they were all beyond his power. Instead, he had to keep to a fixed course, to the present, where he might have some impact. And at this moment, his sole concern must be to get Nate, Rebecca, and himself out of here alive.

"Would you come and help me in the kitchen?" Rebecca asked Jacob as she covered Nate with a blanket. Her voice gentled as she spoke to her patient. "Rest now if you can, and try to think of home. Imagine how very glad your family will be to see you."

A few moments before, there'd been blood in her eye, but Jacob could see she'd scraped together some semblance of composure. Still, she worried him. He'd seen one woman pushed beyond the edge, and this one had skated far too close to hers these past few hours.

He followed her into the kitchen.

She turned and faced him, hiding behind the shield of her professional demeanor. "We have no choice but to ask the rebels for the supplies we'll need. First off, a sharp knife—what have you been using to cut the meat you've cooked?"

"Just a shard of broken glass I found on the floor. I've been lucky not to slice myself so far. But it's nothing we can use for this job."

"Very well. We'll also need a needle and some silk thread, though I've heard the Southerners use cotton," Rebecca said, counting off the items on her fingers, "a bone saw, a rope to use for a tourniquet, and a good supply of chloroform—"

"The raiders'll have whiskey. That'll have to do," Jacob pointed out.

"I hope. But what about the bone saw? I can't imagine they'd have anything like that."

"We'll have to ask—and pray they won't laugh in our faces."

"That's a fine idea."

"What?" he asked.

"The part about the prayer." The shield slipped enough so that fear made her words quaver. "Do you realize what it is we mean to do? We're taking off a man's *hand*, Jacob. What if we kill him?"

"If we don't try, we're sentencing him to death anyway. A death by slow degrees."

"Maybe we should use the gun, escape, and go for help."

"You're not talking sense now. If this hadn't happened, I'd thought we all might slip away tonight. But not now, when they're so stirred up. We're too badly outnumbered. Besides, Nate would never make it. Rebecca, we're all the chance he has."

"But I'm just a nurse, and not even a very good one. And you shoe horses for a living! I—I can't do this." Her head shook back and forth, and her words came in a torrent. "*We* can't do this, and don't think you can bully me into thinking any different!"

He captured both her hands in his. "What makes you think I'd do that?"

"You frightened that poor boy half to death with that pistol!"

He nodded grimly. "I won't apologize for that. He's agreed to let us try to save him."

"And you never told me. Wherever did you get that gun?"

"Upstairs hallway on the floor beneath that little table this afternoon. Your visitor must have dropped it last night."

She jerked her hands away. He could sense the

crushing weight of strain, and he knew that if he added just a pebble's worth, she'd shatter. She would tell him everything, but she'd be broken then. Broken so she couldn't help him save Nate's life.

So instead he pulled her into his arms and rocked her like a child against him. Kissing the top of her head, he told her, "It's going to be all right. We'll talk later, Rebecca. Now we have to get Nate through this. We have to work together and be strong."

He felt her nod against his chest. Even so, he continued holding her for several minutes in the near-darkness of the kitchen, feeling as if they'd come into the calm eye of a storm.

"What's he sayin', Billy?" Asa asked the younger raider when he returned from the water's edge. The tall fellow with the curly hair had been shouting something from the house.

"He says they want to parley. Somethin' 'bout that fella tried to run."

Macon hawked up a wad of phlegm and spat. "Shit. Reckon they want us to bury 'em another one? I 'magine that woman thinks we got us a regular Yankee cemetery over here."

"Hell, if that's all, we'll just toss him in the river where we dumped the last one," Asa said. "Won't take but ten minutes."

Billy shook his head. "No, it's more than that. They need somethin' else. He sounded right anxious to talk about it, asked if we'd come over."

Carl idly slashed the leaves off a willow sapling with his saber. "You can count me out. Damned if I'm goin' to get all soaked and then get chawed on by that bitch."

Asa grinned at him. "She scare you? Hell, she

gives me any back sass, I might just borrow that
sword off a you and whale her ass with the flat of
the blade. She won't be able to sit down for a
week!''

The others laughed, clearly delighted with the
image.

''Tell you what,'' Asa said to Billy. ''You tell him
I'll parley—but with *her*. He wants somethin' offa
us, he can send her over here . . . alone.''

''Absolutely not,'' Jacob told her. ''There's no
way in hell I'll let you go into their camp.''

Rebecca drew in a deep breath. The thought of
crossing the water alone and on foot to meet the
raiders was the stuff of nightmares, and she was
paralyzed by the idea of going to Asa, by the possibility he might demand she satisfy his vile urges
there and then.

Yet wouldn't he come for her anyway in a few
hours? And if she did not do this, Nate would surely
die. She swallowed hard, though her throat felt as
if a peach pit had lodged in it. It was time now to
have courage, time now for brave words.

She couldn't say them. Instead, she closed her
eyes and hated the coward she'd become. What
had happened to the girl who had so passionately
argued with her father—even when he'd threatened to throw her to the wolves—to pay the women
in his textile mills a living wage? What had happened to the woman who had fled a safe existence
to act on her convictions and help aid the war
effort? Her failure as a nurse was hard enough.
Would she be able to survive the death of her true
character as well?

Taking a deep breath, she straightened her spine
and reached for the door handle.

''Who are you, Mr. Fuller, to *let* me do anything?''

she asked. "I make my own choices, and in this case, I choose to go."

Though they'd lit candles, the light was still dim. Nonetheless, she'd have to be blind to miss the disbelief in his expression.

"You are the most stubborn, exasperating female I have ever known! You're right. I shouldn't give a hard-times token what becomes of you." His bewilderment gave way to a glare. "But I do, Rebecca. I do."

Nate called from across the room. "He's right. You can't go over. It wouldn't be safe. Them boys ain't civilized; they're rebels. They'll likely abuse you the minute you get over there alone. I'm not proud I tried to run, but it was *my* mistake, not yours. My mama didn't raise me to allow a lady to risk herself for me."

"You shouldn't have to die for a moment of panic," Rebecca told him. "And you certainly shouldn't have to die on behalf of some antiquated notion of a woman's honor."

Jacob put his hand on the door to keep it from opening. "A lot of men have died for less these past four years."

"Those men died for principles!" she shot back. "And I'll not have you demeaning their memories by saying otherwise. Now remove your hand. I'm going while Mr. Gordon still has a chance. I assure you, their colonel will allow no harm to come to me. He may be on the wrong side, but he *is* a gentleman."

Jacob stared at her, and dropped his arm. "Was *he* your visitor last night, Rebecca?"

"Certainly not! Do you—do you actually believe I am *entertaining* callers? What sort of woman do you take me for?" She pulled open the door and then stepped through it. Across the span of water, a campfire beckoned. She wondered if she'd make it to the other side.

"Right now, I'm not so sure I could answer that in language you'd approve of," Jacob told her.

"Then don't bother answering at all," she said.

"All right, Miss Marston. You go. But know this. If they hurt you . . ." There was a long pause, as if he weren't certain himself what he would say. Finally, he finished. "If they so much as *touch* you, I'm going over there to kill them. No matter what the cost."

She turned her head to look back at him, and she found that she believed him utterly. But she couldn't answer, not then, or her courage would completely fail her. So instead, she simply nodded and started walking toward a campfire that flickered like the fires of her personal hell.

"She's comin', sarge! She's comin'!" Billy let loose with a rousing rebel yell.

The hound pup howled in chorus, and Asa laughed, amused.

"She ain't the Queen of England," he reminded Billy.

The boy shrugged. "Close as I'm ever like to come. Rich lady with all them big words and fancy manners."

Asa suppressed a grin, thinking how he'd make her regret all her advantages, make her feel like filth.

"Y'all run back to the barn and let me talk with her. Whole bunch of you together are enough to scare a decent woman half to death."

Macon leered. "Yeah, and I reckon she'll feel real comf'table with you, Sergeant Graves."

"I ain't gonna hurt her. You heard what I told Hall."

Macon turned to the others. "I'm layin' odds old Asa will be ball-less 'fore the week's out."

They were still discussing their bets as they headed toward the barn, laughing as they schemed ways to watch the action yet stay out of the way.

But Asa would have the last laugh long after all of them were snoring. Not here, where it would cost him, but inside the house, where none of them would hear a goddamned thing.

Her bare feet slipped on the muddy bottom, so that before she knew what was happened, Rebecca was spitting river water, her sodden hair dripping in her eyes. She shoved it out of her face as best she could and used the firelight to reorient herself. By concentrating on Nate's need, she made steady progress. Or perhaps her speed was the result of her memory of the snake.

Either way, she arrived on the opposite shore soaked and filthy, but otherwise no worse for wear. She peered at the figure seated beyond the fire, but she couldn't yet make out the face. Even so, she knew it wasn't Colonel Hall. This man lacked his dignified posture, and with his manners, he would have stood at her approach.

All too soon she discerned the ruined eye, and she knew she faced the one person she least wished to see. If he expected her to cower, he'd be disappointed, she decided. She had a job to do, and she meant to do it well.

"We'll need some supplies to save the boy one of your men shot. Or did you do the deed yourself?" she asked, her voice an accusation.

Asa didn't rise from his seat by the fire. Instead, he shrugged. "Didn't shoot him, but I sure as hell woulda. We warned all of you not to try and run."

"He's little more than a child."

The same shoulder rose, then dropped. "Ground's full of even younger fellas. Can't stop to ask 'em all if they been weaned."

The leggy hound pup plopped down in front of her and whined, its tail fanning the damp sand. When she ignored it, it returned to Asa's side and licked his hand. Asa idly rubbed the hound's ear.

"We need to amputate the boy's hand, but we'll require your cooperation," Rebecca said.

"Amputate? You mean you're gonna cut it off here? *You*?"

"With God's help and Mr. Fuller's. Otherwise, he will certainly die."

Her words brought Asa to his feet. As he stepped nearer, it was all that she could do not to retreat.

"Well, now." His one eye glittered in the firelight, and he came so close that he might touch her if he reached out his hand. "Seems like you need more than God and this Fuller's help, or you wouldn't o' come here. You want cooperation? So do I."

Rebecca's muscles quivered with the overpowering desire to turn and run—or at least to strike him. She did neither. Instead, she answered, "You made your point this morning. You made it very well."

"Do I got to repeat myself, maybe with your Mr. Fuller?"

As she shook her head, her world careened. *Not Jacob.* Rebecca fought past her horror. Taking a deep breath, she said, "Get me what we'll need to save that boy, and then I'll . . ."

She closed her eyes, unable to speak the words that signaled her capitulation. But he must have understood them anyway. His fingertips grazed her cheek, and she heard the sharp, desirous intake of his breath. She could not help flinching, as if she'd been struck by burning embers.

"You will, won't you?" he hissed. With one finger, he traced a pathway from her chin to her torn neckline. "Tonight, then, you'll wait for me in the attic."

Unable to bear his touch, she stepped back out of reach. "Tonight I'll have to stay beside the boy, if he's to live."

His head shook. "Tonight you'll get so tired, you'll hafta go upstairs a coupla hours before sunup. Hear?"

"What—what happened to . . ." she began. "Might I speak to your colonel?"

Asa's grin was pure malice. "He left me in charge for a spell. Now we got ourselves a deal, princess?"

"You, sir, are the most despicable human being I have ever had the misfortune of knowing. The very thought of you—" The words—and more than that, the images—caught in her throat.

He laughed. "You wait and see. The thought of me won't come near to doin' justice. Now tell me what you need 'fore I decide I can't wait."

It took her several moments to recover sufficiently to speak. "We—ah—we'll need whiskey, first of all, a good, sharp knife, a needle and some thread, and something we can use to saw through bone."

"Hell, woman. You want us to give you our whiskey? I'd sooner get the boys to pass over their guns." He stared hard at her, appraising.

Remembering the pistol Jacob had found, she was careful to make no mention of firearms. Instead, she said, "I thought we had a deal. Besides, didn't your colonel charge you with keeping us alive?"

"*You're* the hostage. What makes you think he gives a damn about a bunch of Yankee riffraff?"

"I believe he does care, and I'm a decent judge

of character. For instance, I found yours apparent from the start.''

Asa grinned. "You're a hell of a woman, princess. Soon as I get to thinkin' I got you beat down, you're off and running that trap of yours again. We'll get you your whiskey and the needle and some thread. I don't much like the idea, though, of givin' the enemy a knife.''

"What do you suggest? That we chew off the wounded hand?''

"With your mouth, I wouldn't imagine that would be too hard. How 'bout this? I'll send over a man to keep watch. He'll take care of the knife until you need it. Then, soon as you're done, he'll bring it back.''

She nodded agreement. "What about the saw?''

He shook his head. "We ain't been doin' too much carpentry of late. Can't think of anything that—wait. How 'bout an axe. Macon found an axe back of the barn.''

She shuddered at the thought. "Dear Lord, we're going to kill him. . . .''

Asa shrugged. "If you want, I'll do the honors now so he won't suffer.''

She shook her head. "No. I'll take the axe. But God help us, and God bless that poor boy.''

"She comin' back yet?'' Nate asked.

Jacob stood in the doorway, peering into the darkness. "I've told you ten times already, I can't see well enough to know. If you'd be quiet, maybe we'll be able to hear splashing as she walks.''

"I told her not to go. You heard me, Fuller. I told her—''

"Quiet! I have to listen for her!'' Jacob fought to rein in his temper, fought not to take out his fear and frustration on Nate. But his mind was filled with images, each one more vile than the last, of Rebecca and those . . .

No. He wasn't going to think it, and he'd be damned if he would sit here and blame himself for allowing her to go. Yet he did, and he could not help wondering if they were trading away her life for the chance Nate might survive. So he strained his ears for the sounds that marked her passage, even though he understood—and dreaded—that he might hear her screams instead.

Nate groaned, though Jacob could tell he was trying to keep silent. If Rebecca's absence had accomplished nothing else, it had distracted the private's attention from his ruined hand. But the pain of such an injury could only be kept at bay for so long. Whether or not Rebecca managed to gather what they needed, Nate's suffering would stretch this night out into a nearly endless hell.

As he returned to watch for Rebecca from the porch, Jacob felt his anger at Nate begin to ebb. Not only because of the boy's pain, but because his concern for Rebecca seemed so genuine. Nate had truly meant it when he'd told her not to go, and the note of fear in his voice each time he asked about her rang true.

As well it might be, for without her they would both be dead. Nate, of his mangled hand, and Jacob, of a bullet, for he'd meant exactly what he'd told her in those moments just before she'd left.

His brooding was interrupted by the muted sounds of conversation. Quiet as it was, he shouldn't have heard it at all, but the night and the water had a way of buffeting sound in all directions, something he remembered from his hours floating on the river, clutching a plank of wood to save his life.

"Be careful not to slip and drop those." Rebecca's voice held neither hostility nor fear, just her normal note of bossiness.

Jacob felt a jab at the thought that she must be speaking to the colonel. Remembering the way the man had looked at her, he tried to convince himself that Rebecca would see him only as her abductor, nothing else. Yet her earlier words came back to haunt him.

"I assure you, their colonel will allow no harm to come to me. He may be on the wrong side, but he is a gentleman."

A gentleman, and not someone beneath her . . . as *he* was. Cursing himself, Jacob realized he was thinking like a jealous beau, as if he had—or even wanted—some claim on Rebecca Marston.

No. He might as well be honest with himself, at least. It might not make a lick of sense, but he did want her—and badly. The taste of her lingered in his mouth, and the memory of her body in his arms inflamed him. He wanted to sink down into her, to . . .

Jacob took a deep breath. If he didn't stop this line of thought, he was going to have to dive into that mudhole to douse his overheated body.

"Here, over this way," she told the person with her.

The light from a thin sliver of the moon stitched its way through tree branches to dapple the dark water. Two shapes moved closer through that dim light, then emerged onto the island.

But the person beside Rebecca was definitely no gentleman. He swore fierce complaints against the idea of getting soaked on account of "some goddamn Yankee and a woman what don't have no idea of her place." Jacob recognized him as Brown Teeth, who'd come over earlier in the day. In one hand, the rebel held the same Navy Colt he'd carried that afternoon. The other gripped an axe.

"We'd best not let Nate see that," Jacob suggested, keeping his voice low so it wouldn't carry through the open doorway.

As if he'd heard his name spoken nonetheless, Nate called, "Is Miss Marston back yet?"

"I'm here, Mr. Gordon!" Rebecca answered. "I'm here, and I'm all right."

She inclined her head toward the raider and explained to Jacob. "They've sent him here to keep watch over the weapons. For some foolish reason, they suspect we might have the time or inclination to misuse them."

Sounded like a reasonable precaution to Jacob, though he hadn't yet forgotten the man's crude threat to Rebecca earlier. Despite the calmness of her words, he could tell from her expression that she had not forgotten either.

"How about that whiskey?" Jacob asked. "Seems like we ought to start out Nate with a few drinks."

Rebecca nodded and passed him the flask she'd carried over, along with the hunting knife.

"Hey, don't point it at me," Jacob told her.

She turned it around to offer him the handle. As he took it, their hands touched, and even that brief contact sent a wave of longing coursing through his veins.

Brown Teeth slung the axe over his shoulder and stepped up onto the porch. Swaggering through the doorway, he glanced toward Nate, who stared at him from atop the table, then leered back at both Jacob and Rebecca.

"This could be worth a soakin' and a night's sleep after all. Don't imagine I'll ever get to see another Yank chopped into kindling." With that, the raider swung the axe, which split a wooden floor plank with a resounding crack.

"You ignorant bastard!" Jacob advanced on him so quickly, he might have struck the man before he had the chance to fire. But Rebecca grabbed Jacob's arm in an effort to restrain him.

"No!" she cried. "No more shooting, and no fighting in this house."

She turned a furious glare upon the rebel, who by now had his gun pointed in their direction. Ignoring the weapon, she marched over and jerked the axe out of the floor with a strength that took Jacob by surprise.

"You, sir, will say nothing. Nothing whatsoever, or you may find yourself short an appendage of your own."

"Rebecca ..." Jacob warned. Though only moments before his temper might have cost him his life, he was appalled that she would risk herself so foolishly. He could still hear the axe blade striking the floor, the echo lingering in the room like a haze of gunsmoke. It was a sound bright with promised violence, like the rumble of artillery or the command to charge.

The raider's heavy brows drew dangerously close. "You'd best watch who you're threatening, missy."

"I could tell you the same thing. Now sit down in that chair." She used the axe to gesture toward one. "And enjoy this little show to your heart's content, but say nothing more until it's over. *Nothing.* Do you understand me?"

Instead of answering, Brown Teeth moved toward her deliberately, slowly, and then pulled back the hammer of his Colt. Jacob's hand reached back toward his own hidden revolver, and he wondered if there was any chance he might be fast enough.

She felt the cold gun barrel against her breast. The raider watched her intently, doubtless hoping she would entertain him with a display of terror and regret. But Rebecca was still wildly furious about the man's casual cruelty to her patient. Or perhaps that accounted only in part for her recklessness. Perhaps her promise to meet Asa had made her careless with her life.

A glimpse of Jacob, whose hand was edging in an ominous direction, and the memory of Nate's pale face, reminded her that she gambled with more lives than just her own.

"Perhaps I expressed myself a bit directly," she told him, although every word tasted bitter as bile. "What I meant to say is, won't you please take a seat? If you're hungry, I believe we still have stew left from this afternoon."

"And they say Yankee women ain't hospitable." His leer was dark and menacing, but the raider backed off, slowly lowering the gun. He dragged the chair closer to the fireplace, then stooped to toss on an extra log. After turning around the chair, he straddled it to sit. "Think I'll pass on that meal and just sit back and see if this fella takes it like a man."

Jacob had to give Nate credit. The wounded soldier looked once at the raider and told him, "You just watch me, reb."

Maybe it was only youthful bravado, but having the enemy right there might give Nate the strength he needed to maintain his composure. Jacob found himself praying silently that though the boy might lose his hand, he might keep his dignity. Jacob tried to picture a day when, after a safe span of years, Nate Gordon would mesmerize his children with the tale of how he'd bravely faced this awful moment, of how he'd looked the enemy in the eye and scored an unlikely victory.

Then, as if to remind them of his youth, Nate

asked Rebecca if she thought his Baptist parents would forgive him for indulging in the sin of alcohol.

"It's purely medicinal in this case," she said without a trace of hesitation. "Your own minister would say the same thing. Now please drink."

Jacob was relieved to see Nate had to choke back the first few sips. Inexperienced as he appeared to be with drinking, he wouldn't have to take in much to feel its effects. Still, there would be a period of waiting while the whiskey dimmed his senses, an awful period while he, Nate, and Rebecca would have time to anticipate how irrevocable their decisions were—and how very, very hard.

Already, Jacob could see Rebecca's pallor, the way it made the scattering of freckles across her face appear that much darker. Her dress left a wet trail along the floor, and he could see her shivering.

"Let Nate rest here for a while," he told her, "and come out to the kitchen. You need to get dried off and have something warm to eat before you drop."

They needed to talk, too, to plan exactly how they would remove Nate's hand. Jacob had the basic idea, but he needed to hear Rebecca's description of how surgeons went about this business. At the thought, fear slashed through his midsection, so razor-sharp that he half expected his entrails to slide out onto the floor. Sucking in a deep breath, he reminded himself that he, too, must stay strong.

"Knife stays here," the raider warned. Despite his own wet clothes, he looked comfortable in his seat near the fire. His jacket was steaming slightly, making him look as if he'd just crawled up from hell. "So does the axe."

He made no move to follow.

Rebecca glanced from the rebel to Nate. "You call if you need us."

Nate nodded and drank deeply from the flask. He coughed and made a face at the taste, then nodded toward Brown Teeth and said, "Don't worry. I won't give him too hard of a time."

His laughter was part alcohol, part desperation.

The rebel, for his part, shook his head and smiled. "You know, I got a boy 'round your age and just as cocky. You favor him a mite."

Rebecca brought some rags with her into the kitchen and tried uselessly to blot her sodden dress.

"Here. Let me help," Jacob offered. When she did not refuse, he attempted to find some safe place to pat her down with a torn scrap of flannel. But every inch of damp cloth reminded him of what lay hidden, and he was embarrassed to find himself tracing the curve that ran beneath her arm down to the flare of her hip. He hadn't felt so awkward since that first time with Hope, when he'd still been too young to guess that it was already too late to save her.

His fingertips accidentally touched the pale flesh near her collarbone, exposed by the torn neckline. "You're so cold, Rebecca. Why don't you eat?"

"Maybe in a few minutes. But what I'd give right now for a change of clothing." She looked directly into his eyes, and her unwavering gaze ignited a fire beneath the surface of his skin.

Foolish, to feel this sudden lust while so much hung in the balance. He couldn't remember feeling this terrible urgency when first he'd met the widow who became his wife, couldn't remember ever feeling anything like this in all his twenty-eight years.

Yet he did, and its intensity could not be denied. "I want you, Rebecca," he blurted out, before he even guessed what he was saying.

Her skin flushed pink and she stared toward the floor. How odd to see this fiery, outspoken woman suddenly turn shy. But if attraction made ill-considered statements burst from his mouth, perhaps it wasn't so strange that it had the opposite effect on her.

"I'm sorry for being so direct," he told her, feeling more foolish by the second, "but I'm an honest man. There's something happening between us. I tried to pretend it wasn't; tried to think of all the reasons why it couldn't work. Only right now, I can't think of anything but holding you against me. I can't think of anything but making love to you."

She recovered enough to raise her gaze to meet his. "When men are frightened, they propose, although I must say, most of them are more—ah, more conventional in their wording."

"You think I'm just scared?" he asked. He was, but he took such care to keep that part of him hidden, he hated like hell that she could see it.

She nodded. "Of course. Only a fool wouldn't be frightened. The two of us are about to hold a boy's life in our hands. I'm afraid that I might swoon."

Jacob grimaced. He'd always had to be strong: strong for Hope, then for his brother, strong for both their friends. But inside, doubt always flickered, no matter how he tried to smother it with common sense. Funny how before her, no one else had guessed. "I was thinking I might get sick all over the proceedings."

"It worries me to death to think that I might cry . . . and in front of that horrible man," she admitted.

Heedless of her wet clothing, he reached out and took her in his arms, pressing her so close the dampness bled right through his uniform. "Nate's just a kid, and he says he's going to show that rebel. Hurting like he is, he means to be brave. I don't see how we can do any less, Rebecca."

"But how?" she whispered, her breath soft and warm upon his neck. "How?"

"Maybe now's the time for praying. I sure wouldn't turn my nose up at any help that we could get."

It was not the kind of prayer they taught in churches, as the two of them stood locked together, holding one another tight. But Jacob felt it far more sacred than any prayer he'd uttered in his life. Perhaps it was only his imagination or the living, breathing spirit in his arms, but when it was finally over, he felt as if the two of them might just stand a chance.

Chapter Thirteen

*Disease is an experience of the so-called mortal
mind. It is fear made manifest on the body.*
                                    —Mary Baker Eddy

By the time Rebecca and Jacob came out of the
kitchen, Nate Gordon slept upon the table, a whole
boy waiting to be maimed. Thunder murmured
like Rebecca's doubts, and a wave of dizziness swept
over her. Even if he survived, she realized, he would
forever carry with him the consequences of what
they did.

Back at the hospital, someone else had made
the terrible decisions. Someone who knew better,
someone who'd been trained. Or so she'd always
liked to think, though Drew had told her how
uncertain he had felt—until the sheer volume of
experience began to numb his rawness.

Alcohol, too, had been a part of the hardening
process, as had laughter in the form of the macabre
jokes he'd liked to play. But despite it all, he'd
confided how the images rushed back at him on
those nights when his exhaustion went too deep
for sleep. And on those nights when he awoke from
dreams too frightening to recount.

Rebecca had listened to him often, but she hadn't truly understood. She supposed that despite all her bold statements to the contrary, she imagined a man more qualified to make the grave decisions and lead the bloody charges. Remembering Drew's admissions and Jacob's abrupt declaration in the kitchen, she realized now she had been wrong. Men weren't immune to doubts; they only felt a responsibility to hide them.

Glancing at the rebel, who watched in edgy silence, she vowed not to admit hers either. Not only for Nate, who dozed, still clutching the flask, but to avoid giving the raider any opportunity to mock her weakness.

Even so, she felt like a young sapling, bent double until she must either snap or spring free of her bonds. Yet somehow, she did neither as she and Jacob began their work.

Jacob looked up at the raider. "We could use your help to hold him down. Just in case he starts to flail."

"Why the hell'd I want to do that?" The voice was gruff, but his dark eyes flicked toward the private's face. After a shrug, the raider rose and tried on his fiercest scowl. "Might just as well, I suppose. Got nothin' better to do to pass the time."

Positioning himself near Nate's feet, the rebel grasped his ankles and muttered, "You don't gotta die on my account, boy. It's enough you won't be runnin' for a spell."

Nate only groaned softly, though mercifully, he never fully roused during the ordeal that followed: the tying of the rope tourniquet, the delicate cutting of the knife through muscle and blood vessels. Only Jacob's terrible swing of the axe, which Rebecca had to turn her face from, brought a half-conscious shout of protest, which quickly subsided into moaning.

For all her blinking, for all her admonitions about the judgment in the raider's gaze, the crack that followed the blade's fall still loosed Rebecca's tears. But she need not have worried—at least about the Rebel—for before the echo died, he slipped with a quiet thud onto the floor.

Jacob's gaze met hers, his brows raised in grim amusement. As she sutured the first of several major blood vessels, he covered the lost hand and then took it through the front door. When he returned, he retrieved the unconscious raider's gun and removed its bullets.

"Where's the rest of that rope?" Jacob asked her.

"You're going to tie him? We can't possibly attempt an escape now. Not with Nate in this condition."

"I know you're right, but you heard this bas— this . . ." He seemed to struggle for a word he might use to describe the man and not offend her. Giving up, he sighed. "You've heard him talk. Hurts my feelings not to serve him up a fraction of the grief he's caused."

Rebecca spared the raider the most fleeting of glances. Despite his horrible threat this afternoon, despite the callousness with which he'd treated Nate, she felt herself emptied of emotion, a broken vessel with its contents splashed across the floor.

Her fingers, seemingly as detached as the private's right hand, worked deftly, independently, freed of the shaking that had plagued them. She thought, *Thank God. Thank God I cannot feel it anymore.*

Perhaps this was the numbness of which Drew had spoken, the detachment that allowed others to carry on so well. Or perhaps her pain had only been deferred to a time when she might feel it without costing a man's life.

"Leave him be. You can live with your hurt feelings," she told Jacob. "Heaven knows, we're all living with worse."

The two of them worked in silence for a long time. When her fingers cramped, he took over, using careful stitches to complete their work.

After checking their handiwork, Jacob said, "There's going to be so much pain. I know you don't think much of it, but the willow bark tea could ease it some."

She nodded. After they'd improvised an entire amputation, this seemed a small concession, unworthy of the strength to argue.

From the floor, the raider groaned.

Jacob nudged him—none too gently—with a toe. "We thought while we were chopping, we might as well take your leg, too."

"What the hell?" the man roared, sitting up abruptly. He blinked at both his feet in disbelief, then swore at Jacob.

Jacob shrugged. "You got off easy, and you know it."

The raider reached for his revolver.

"Looking for this?" Jacob held out the weapon, then strode to the front door. "Go find it."

He hurled it off the porch. Rebecca thought she heard a splash.

"You curly-headed bastard!" Awkwardly, the Rebel stood, then staggered.

"Be careful," Rebecca warned him. "It seems that you're still dizzy."

He glared at her. Then, as if he'd just remembered, he glanced back toward the private.

"He make it through? Not that I got any use for Yankees, but—well, hell, he *is* a kid."

"He's lost a good deal of blood," Rebecca explained, gesturing toward a pile of sodden rags.

"But his breathing is steady. If there'd be any way to get him morphine . . ."

"I—uh—I'd best get back to camp," the raider said, turning his gaze quickly from the blood-soaked cloth.

Cautiously, Jacob handed him the axe and knife.

The raider moved toward the doorway. "I'd be obliged if you didn't make no mention of my—uh—my legs goin' out from under me. And I'll see what I can do about some morphine for—what was it you called him?"

"Nate," Rebecca answered. "His name *is* Nate Gordon, and he's going to make it home to help his father with their farm."

Jacob and Rebecca carefully moved Nate to the floor, where they elevated what was left of his right arm and did all they could, over the next few hours, to make him comfortable. As they worked, Jacob wondered if to an outsider the two of them would look like a pair of worn-down plow horses, struggling to make it to the end of each row while steadfastly ignoring the totality of the field. Rebecca's eyes in particular looked empty as she replaced Nate's bandage—bereft as she stooped to feed another split log to the fire.

"I can't think of anything but holding you against me," he remembered telling her. *"I can't think of anything but making love to you."*

He wondered if the tide of blood had washed his words away as if he'd never said them. Just as well, he thought, since she'd dismissed them as another desperate man's proposal, nothing but the voice of fear. If she'd known him better, she would understand he was not the sort of man to make such a statement lightly, not the sort of man to change his mind.

He'd have to teach her that about him, but not now, while she looked so hollowed out by emotion and fatigue.

"You should go to bed now," he told her. "Go away from this and sleep for a few hours. It would do you good to let those damp clothes dry, too."

She didn't look at him or answer. Instead, her gaze traveled up the stairwell, into the utter darkness. She didn't move a muscle to follow it upstairs.

Outside, thunder curled around the house, a sinuous sound that made him glad to be indoors.

"I'll get you a candle so you won't stumble in the dark," Jacob offered. But as he did so it occurred to him that her hesitation and her silence could not be cured by candlelight.

"Are you afraid of something up there?" he asked, his voice only slightly louder than the murmur of the rain. He wondered if at last she'd tell him what had happened.

She shook her head, too quickly. "I'm more concerned about leaving Mr. Gordon."

"He's sleeping soundly. You said yourself his color's looking better. But if you'd like to sleep down here . . ."

"Oh, no. I couldn't do that. Not if I'm to dry this dress."

"You think you couldn't trust me if you stripped down to your—"

"Please, Mr. Fuller—Jacob. Have you already forgotten what you told me earlier?"

"Not for an instant, Rebecca, but just because I want you doesn't mean I'd get it in my head to . . ." He paused, overwhelmed by the thought that someone else had been upstairs last night . . . with her. And not only that, though that was plenty, but she'd claimed that she'd seen something. A boy, she'd told him in the attic. Of course, she was afraid.

"Let me come up with you," he offered. "Just to check on things. Then I'll come straight downstairs afterward; I promise."

Her unwavering stare reminded him of the first night they had met, when he'd been so very cold and she had looked so desperate. Desperate, but already mesmerized by some force that neither of them understood.

"What if . . . what if that's not what I want?"

He swallowed painfully, too surprised to answer. Outside, the rain redoubled its assault on the old house. From somewhere he heard water dripping, but it barely registered.

He went to the kitchen for a candle while she checked on Nate again. After pausing by the fire to light the wick, he took her hand.

She lifted her eyes to look at him, but this time her gaze went deeper, longer. This time, she whispered, "Yes."

Rebecca's legs quivered so violently, they could barely carry her upstairs. The enormity of what she had just offered struck her, and her knees loosened suddenly.

Jacob caught her arm and steadied her. "Don't worry, Rebecca. You'll be safe with me."

She wondered what he meant. Was he vowing to be gentle or promising to ignore her shameless overture? As he helped her up the stairs, she thought again about the impulse that had prompted her to speak so boldly. About the aching need that had opened like a chasm, demanding to be assuaged before her ruin.

For surely Asa would destroy her. And just as Nate must have, she felt fear eating away at her core. As he had run away, she must run to Jacob, the only place in all of this she felt secure.

Once they reached the upstairs hallway, Jacob walked ahead of her, the candle raised before him. Both its warm light and the cooler brilliance of lightning flashes illuminated his passage through the upstairs rooms. He returned to her and gently took her hand.

"Come into the bedroom, and I'll help you out of those damp clothes."

A bolt of fear forked through her. Had she made the wrong decision? Despite her misgivings, she followed him, no more able to govern her emotions than to catch a shaft of lightning.

Jacob placed the flickering candle on top of the scarred dresser, where the cracked mirror reflected its yellow light. Rebecca caught a glimpse of her own form, stiff with indecision, and of his, so tall and muscular.

Jacob turned to her, distracting her from their reflection. He stepped close to her, so close that her first instinct warned her to move back. But a second impulse, even stronger, urged her to venture forward, to claim this man, if only for the hours she had left. Yet she stood rooted to the spot, listening to the sounds of the heavy rain upon the window, the rhythmic scraping of her breath.

Jacob's hand moved to the remaining buttons of her shirtwaist. Remembering Asa tearing at them, she could not help flinching.

He drew back his hand, then reached out to run his fingertips along her jawline. "Rebecca ... I would never hurt you, and I'd kill anyone who did."

Sensation rippled through her with his touch in dizzying waves of longing that made her ache for more. Yet she remained powerless to move, save for a tear that trickled a hot pathway from the corner of her eye.

One by one, Jacob unfastened each button. Then

he carefully slipped the dark sleeves free of her arms and helped her step out of her wool skirt. As his dark eyes appraised her, she shivered in the chill room, conscious that for the first time, she stood before a man wearing only her chemise and corset. She wondered dimly if he found her lacking, a pathetic, dried-up spinster. She grasped at the desperate thought that she might be sufficiently repulsive to dissuade the raider, too.

"My God," Jacob breathed, "but you're so lovely."

He reached toward her, then stopped abruptly. Changing his mind, he used his outstretched hand to rake his curls.

"I can't do this," he told her. "I have to go downstairs. God help me. I want you more than I've ever wanted anything in my life, but this is wrong. There's nothing I can offer a woman like you. Nothing but regret."

As frightened as she'd been, the thought that he would leave her sent a jolt of terror through her heart. That he would leave her and that Asa would be the next man through this door.

"You can offer me this night," she whispered, tears stinging her eyes and tightening her throat. "You can take me through this hour. . . ."

As if her words had burst the dam of his restraint, he pulled her to him almost roughly and claimed her with a kiss that shook her to her core. There was nothing tentative or questing in it—nothing but a blazing hunger that made the ache inside her deepen into agony, a fire that could only be quenched by his lips, his hands, the contact of their bodies.

She was wrong, she realized. The closer they pressed, the hotter the flames that leapt inside her, igniting all misgivings and reducing them to ash.

He framed her rib cage with his large hands, then allowed them to drop dangerously toward her hips.

Rebecca was shocked to find her own hands just as busy, stroking the hard muscles of his upper arms and later pushing against his back as if she were trying to pull herself inside the shelter of his body. She had never felt so desperate, so burdened by the imperative to hurry toward her fate. Jacob might as well be a precipice, and she'd just made a leap.

God help her when she struck bottom, but for the moment, Rebecca felt nothing but the exhilaration of her flight.

She heard her chemise tear, and she shrugged out of it, impatient with its restrictiveness. Her underthings went just as quickly, until she stood wrapped in nothing but Jacob's firm embrace.

His hungry mouth traveled to her neck, and she moaned, losing herself in this storm of new sensation, allowing it to obliterate all thought. Even as he kissed her, his hands traveled to the tightness of her breasts, and she felt the shock of his thumbs against the hardened tips.

"Please, Jacob," she breathed, asking for she knew not what. And then a quick intake of breath rasped beyond all other conscious thought.

He scooped her up and took her to the bed. After laying her down gently, he joined her within moments, as naked as she was.

At the sight of his aroused male form, her mouth went dry, and a thrill of apprehension raised gooseflesh.

"Oh, dear." As the rain murmured against the house, thoughts flooded her brain, most of them terrified. She became acutely, embarrassingly aware of her nudity and her location—in bed with a man.

A flash of lightning revealed his smile. Despite

the briefness of the illumination, she sensed as much as saw the sadness in it.

"It's not too late to change your mind, Rebecca," he whispered. He lay on his side before her. His hand cupped her breast, and he began to kiss her neck once more. As his mouth moved ever lower, he added as a warning, "But it's about to be."

She meant to tell him she'd made a terrible mistake, to ask him to go away. But at that moment, his lips found her nipple, and he began to suckle, sending unimagined pleasure coursing through her body. Again, anxiety deserted her, along with reason. She was his, only his, with nothing to fear so long as he continued.

"I want it to be too late," she whispered. "I want you to show me . . . teach me . . . everything."

When his fingers found and stroked the hot center of her, she gasped anew. She moved against him without shame, instinct carrying her further and further from her mind and into a new realm, one that only her body understood. But that ancient knowledge served her well, so that when he moved above her, she felt such a sense of expectation that she wanted to cry out her desire.

He kissed her tenderly, then gazed into her eyes, though she understood from his quivering that he was eager.

"I've dreamed of you like this, beneath me," he whispered. "I've dreamed of rocking deep inside you until we both . . ."

He grew silent as another flash lit up the room, as Rebecca pulled him toward her. And when he entered her, there was a tearing pain, but it was borne away by wave after wave of pleasure. Pleasure so intense, it washed her off of her foundations and carried her to sea.

* * *

Asa grasped the barn door to keep the wind from tearing it away. But the gust signaled the storm's last gasps, and the distant flashes were receding in the distance. The rain had softened, and above his head he saw a few clear patches with starlight winking through them.

He'd been sitting with only the pup for company, apart from the others in the darkness of the barn. He'd listened to their snoring and the storm sounds, all the while thinking of the Big Man's daughter in that old house, reckoning how much time would have to pass before he could hie himself over there.

He grinned, wondering if she thought the spring squall would keep her safe all through the night. Wondering if she'd given in to sleep, or if she lay trembling now beneath her blanket, awaiting his return. Both thoughts had their appeal, but no matter what the case, Rebecca Marston's time was up.

He meant to cross the water. And to cross the colonel, too.

April 30, 1865

Jacob's eyes flew open at the soft slap of footsteps on the wood floor and the echo of old laughter. Shadows shifted, chased by the candle's unsteady light. But whatever he had heard must have been no more than sleep trying to steal over him. He and Rebecca lay curled together, utterly alone.

Jacob moved closer to her back and kissed her temple, then smiled at her sweetly female sigh. Didn't sound much like a harpy out of hell now— just a woman wrapped in the warm cocoon of her contentment. And not just any woman, either, but his Rebecca, who armored a tender heart with sharpness, who had trusted him enough to let him past her barricades.

It was a good place, he decided, a place he never wished to leave. Emotion welled up in him, pushing past his scars. He felt overwhelmed by a fierce need to protect the woman in his arms, by the desire to make love to her again.

Rebecca had been sleeping for some time now while he'd lain awake beside her, grinning like a fool at the thought that he'd been the one to bring her pleasure, that he had moved her beyond the dark place where she'd been hiding and into dazzling light. Just as she had moved beneath him, so alive she vanquished every fear, every memory of death, so wonderfully exuberant and warm he had exploded with the joy of it, unable to hold back. At the thought, he wanted her again, wanted to consecrate survival, to sanctify what they had found.

Yea, though I walk through the valley of the shadow of death . . .

He could hear each nuance, every inflection of her voice as if she'd just repeated the biblical words, reminding him the two of them had emerged together from that valley through an act of love. He was surprised to realize it was love for him, a great glowing sphere that lit the path ahead. A path beyond their differences, into a shared future.

He gently kissed her neck, hoping she would awaken, praying she would feel the same.

"I love you, Rebecca," he whispered, not caring if she heard him, for he meant to repeat it till she did. To hell with the fear pounding in his heart, the pulsing beat that warned he spoke too soon. Before, he'd kept his feelings to himself until it was too late—too late for Hope; too late, perhaps, for Zeke and their best friends. He might declare

himself too early, but never again was he waiting
until no chance remained.

"Mmm . . ."

She wriggled against him, so catlike in repose
that it made him smile anew. Then, as if someone
held a lit match to her sole, she jerked and gasped,
sitting up abruptly.

"What's wrong?" he asked. "Did you have a nightmare?"

She didn't answer, but he could feel the tension
in her muscles, could feel the way she strained
against his embrace. And in that moment, Hope
resurfaced, her shadows overwhelming even the
possibility of light.

"You have to go downstairs now," she told him,
in Miss Marston's voice and not Rebecca's.

His heart froze. She was *dismissing* him, as if he
were a servant, as if what they had done meant
nothing at all to her. As if she hadn't felt even a
fragment of what he felt for her.

"Please . . ." she urged him. But this time, he
caught the note of fear. "I never should have
slept."

Remembering her reaction to the death of the
first prisoner, he asked her, "Are you worried about
Nate? I just went and checked him a few minutes
ago. He's sound asleep, and there's no fever. See,
I brought up a new candle." *So I could watch you
in your sleep.*

"You have to go," she repeated.

"What's wrong, Rebecca? Did I hurt you somehow? Did I—?"

"It's nothing, nothing to do with you." She
climbed out of bed and slipped on her chemise,
then hurried toward the window, gazing out
through the filmy curtains. In the candlelight, he
could see her shivering.

And all the pieces spun together: the claw marks

on the attic door, the gun he'd found lying in the hall, her clear terror earlier, and most disturbingly, the way she'd flung away her virginity, wasting it on a man so far beneath her.

He'd been an idiot to imagine she might love him. She'd only thrown herself into his arms to escape her terror.

"Who's coming?" he demanded. "Who's coming here tonight?"

She spun toward him, her expression frigid. "He'll kill you if he finds you here. Leave, Jacob. Please go now, before it's too late."

"It's the colonel, isn't it? I'll kill that pompous bastard!"

She shook her head. "It's not him. It's . . . another of the raiders. That horrible man with the ruined eye, the one I heard called Asa. Please understand, Jacob. He would have killed you. He would have murdered both you and Nate, one for each night I refused. Just as he killed Mr. Pierce when I would not give in last night. And then when I went to gather what we needed for the surgery—"

"You'd already made a deal with him," Jacob interrupted, each word deepening the pain, "when you let me—"

"Yes." Her voice was tight, controlled, as if her feelings were glazed over with a sheet of ice. "I— I thought somehow it might be easier if you were first. . . . I'm sorry if I hurt you. It was never my intent."

As Jacob dressed, anger boiled up in him. "Why in God's name didn't you tell me this before? I asked. I did everything but beg you."

Leaving his shirt unbuttoned, he reached for the pistol he'd left on the floor beneath the bed. He checked the chambers to reassure himself that it was loaded. When he glanced at Rebecca, she was staring at him.

She shook her head. "My mistake wasn't in keeping silent before. It was in telling you just now. Put away the gun, Jacob. Put it away now."

"If you think I'm going to go downstairs and pretend to sleep while some rebel forces you . . ." He shook his head violently, as if to dislodge the images his words had conjured. "If you believe that, you really don't know me at all."

"I do know who you are, Jacob. I know. But you can't do this. I may have made a devil's bargain, but it's the only way."

"Like hell it is!"

"Don't you swear at me."

He glowered at her. "I'll damned well swear all I like. When you came to me, I thought . . ."

He turned away from her, disgusted that he'd ever imagined there could be anything of value, anything permanent between them. She'd only turned to him when she was in need of comfort, when she had nothing left to lose.

He heard her soft steps on the floorboards just before she laid one cold hand on his shoulder. "You've shown me time after time that you're a decent man, a man of honor. You don't have to throw away your life to prove it."

"I'm not letting him touch you. Do you understand that?"

"Understand this, you stubborn fool. If you shoot him, the others will come running. And they'll kill all three of us." Her voice rose on a gush of anger. "I choose to do what I must so I can live through this. So that all three of us can live. And you have no right to take that choice from me."

He wheeled toward her, his temper running fast and hot. "You gave me that right when you allowed me in your bed."

He never saw it coming, but he heard the sharp clap of her palm at the same moment pain flared in his cheek.

Lowering her hand, she hissed. "Aunt Millicent was right. When a man sleeps with a woman, he believes he owns her. Understand this, Jacob Fuller. You're very much confused if you believe that I belong to you—or any man. And rest assured, I'll never repeat the mistake of making love with you again."

She watched, her heart pounding in her chest, as Jacob stalked from the room and slammed the door behind him. She still had no idea of what he meant to do: whether he would lie in wait or feign sleep while Asa climbed the steps.

The only thing that she was sure of was that she'd made a terrible mistake. If she hadn't been so overwhelmed by loneliness and fear, she never would have fallen willingly into his arms.

Liar! That was only an excuse, only a small part of all she felt for Jacob Fuller. He *was* a decent man and a man of honor, as she'd said, but he'd grown to be so much more than that to her. From the first moment she had seen him, she'd felt an attraction so sharp-edged it made her bleed inside. Their conversations and their kisses sliced into her more deeply, and surely their lovemaking had slashed an artery.

Perhaps that was why she felt all the emotion bleeding out of her—why she felt so empty, so bereft. For now, in the darkest hours before dawn, she had pushed away a lover to trade him for a rapist. And in doing so, she knew she'd broken Jacob's heart.

Chapter Fourteen

Cautious, careful people, always casting about to preserve their reputation and social standing, never can bring about a reform. Those who are really in earnest must be willing to be anything or nothing in the world's estimation.
—Susan B. Anthony

Asa's head jerked and his heart sank the moment that he heard the whistle. Colonel's whistle, he realized—the signal meant to sound like some sort of a bird so no one would shoot the members of the group as they approached.

Goddamn it, not now! Not when he'd already pulled off his jacket and set one foot in the water.

Whistle didn't sound like any goddamned bird he'd ever heard, he thought irritably. But it could be that the trilling notes were soured by the realization Hall was back. That would make Asa's plans for Rebecca Marston far riskier—maybe even impossible tonight.

He swore, somewhat too loudly.

"That glad to see us, sergeant?" Hall asked.

Hall led his horse nearer as Asa hurried to slip into his shirt.

"Got anything to eat, Asa?" Simms's voice sounded road-grimed and fatigued. He explained, "Colonel here wasn't of a mind to stop."

Maybe they'd be snoring heavy in ten minutes, Asa thought. Maybe they would leave him time enough.

"Lost a bet to Cole," Asa lied. Almost immediately, he remembered that the greyhound-thin raider had left with Billy earlier, supposedly to scout for food. He shrugged off the fact as unimportant. "I figured you'd be back tomorrow around noon. Did the Big Man ransom her already? We all rich men yet?"

The idea occurred that maybe they'd get to split Cole's and Billy's share. Maybe there would be enough to buy himself a new start somewhere west.

"It's late," Hall said, "and we rode hard to get here. I'll need a meal and a good rest before we talk about that."

Asa would swear he heard frustration in the colonel's voice. He wondered what the hell went wrong. But one thing was for damned sure: Hall wouldn't tell the likes of Asa until he was good and ready.

"Where are the other men?" the colonel asked.

Simms took both horses and grumbled an offer to get them fed and bedded down. Hall grunted his agreement—a sure sign of his exhaustion, since normally he would tend his mare himself.

"Most of the boys are in the barn now." Then Asa gave a brief report on the Yankee's attempted escape and Billy's lucky shot. "Macon was over with 'em earlier. They took the fella's hand off, and I sent him to keep an eye out on the knife and axe we let 'em use."

Asa didn't mention the revolver that they might have. No way in hell was he admitting that.

"Do you mean that *nurse* performed an amputation on her own?" Hall asked.

Asa chuckled and wagged his head in disbelief.
"Seems like nobody ever told that gal she's just a
woman. She said something about havin' that other
Yankee help her. There's only the two of them
river rats left. Other one died off this morning."

Asa felt great satisfaction in his own part in the
man's demise. He half expected the colonel to say
he was going to check on his precious lady hostage,
but Hall only stared in the direction of the dark
house, saying nothing. Behind the structure, the
sky had lightened to an iron gray, the first harbinger of morning.

Asa cursed his luck, but at the same time he
realized that something big had changed. Maybe
it was no more than wishful thinking, but he had
half a notion that Miss Rebecca Marston wasn't
under Hall's protection anymore.

The two of them stood together, both gazing
across the span of water. From the branches of a
nearby tree, a morning bird cried as if to teach
them its authentic song.

Jacob lay beneath his blanket, the revolver
gripped so tightly that his fingers ached. He
thought of how he'd warned himself against Rebecca, thought of how he'd recognized her fundamental weakness—one that would inevitably break,
leaving her as shattered as the woman he had wed.

He'd never been so wrong in all his life, he realized. Just as Rebecca's red hair had first fooled
him, so had the pain that glimmered in her eyes.
She might damned well be hurting, but her fragility
was all illusion, a mirage atop the bedrock of her
strength. But if stone was strong, it was equally
unyielding, and equally unthinking, as in Rebecca's
case.

Jacob had seen men follow orders, had seen them

lead the charge into artillery fire that would rip limbs from their bodies and tear their flesh to shreds. A shudder swept through him as he recalled their unfocused eyes, the ice that hardened their words before they rode into the fray.

They knew they wouldn't come back, and yet they still went, convinced the officers had had no better choice. Convinced that their deaths would mean something.

Yet they never did. For however many died, more men came to fill their ranks. However many horses had to be destroyed, more were confiscated from the locals, then sacrificed to the unending butchery.

Jacob swore aloud at the stupidity of it all, and at whatever misplaced sense of duty drove wave after wave of men to self-sacrifice. Just as Rebecca Marston meant to sacrifice herself.

Jacob had made a decent enough soldier, doing the best he could for the horses amid long stretches of boredom and shorter bouts of fierce insanity. But after Andersonville, after the *Sultana,* he found something in him changed, and he could no longer stand by idly and allow such madness to continue. Particularly not when it involved Rebecca Marston.

"I'm taking myself back," she'd told him, as if her heart were some bauble too hastily given. As if she could undo what they had shared. She might well never again yield her body to him; she might even hate him for all time for his presumption, but she could not keep him from protecting her as best he could. It was clear enough they would never share a future, but he would damned well do his best to see her safely home.

Through a filmy window, he could see the sun was rising. Something had to have gone wrong with Asa's plan. Jacob sighed, relieved he wouldn't have to kill the bastard yet, but knowing that whatever had delayed the man would not long prevent him from coming back to claim his prize.

Tucking the gun back into his waistband, Jacob went to check on Nate.

"Get better fast," Jacob told the sleeping youth, for despite the makeshift amputation, they would have to leave here. All of them, tonight, before it was too late.

Rebecca had washed and dressed, yet she stood shivering in her still-damp clothing, watching through the window as the light increased. She'd stared for hours, she supposed, watching as the eastern sky silvered and then reddened into a deep blush. And now that the edge of the sun's disk had made its appearance over the flooded field behind the house, there could be no denying the long night had finally ended.

Dawn meant morning, didn't it? Dawn meant that Asa wouldn't come. Surely, with his emphasis on her cooperation, he would not dare make his appearance during daylight.

Rebecca closed her eyes, exhausted at the thought of more hours spent in dread, awaiting his arrival. Hours she would have to pass with Jacob, who must surely hate her by this time.

She thought of going to him, of trying once again to make him understand. The hand that had slapped him tingled, and she thought of what she'd said and done to push him away.

Leave it be, she told herself. She'd been weak enough in her loneliness without returning to him now.

She closed her eyes tightly, yet images assailed her, each one more sensual than the last. She thought of all they'd shared, and it was as if it was all happening again: his hands upon her body, his kisses falling on her neck, his body moving over her, moving her toward . . .

Dear God, she'd been a fool to think not knowing might be unendurable. Far worse was the pain of realizing she would never again lie with him, never hold him to her breast. For after Asa used her, she knew she would be ruined for Jacob, just as she'd be ruined for any other man.

Was that the life she meant to buy with her submission? A life spent cowering inside her father's mansion, listening to him berate her about the price of her disobedience? She thought about his anger before she'd run away, of his intolerable threats if she would not bow before his will. No doubt he'd remind her daily of the ransom, and if he ever learned she'd been despoiled . . .

And what if she conceived? Could she bear her family's shame and her inevitable banishment from home? Even worse, how could she begin to guess if such a child were Jacob's or that monster's?

Picking up the hairbrush from the dresser, Rebecca hurled it into the cracked mirror. Then she watched with satisfaction as a large shard fell out and shattered on the floor.

"I *won't*," she told her fragmented images within the web of cracks.

Within moments, she heard the thud of footsteps and the bedroom door flew open. Jacob stood before her, his pistol drawn and at the ready. His face was flushed, and he was breathing hard.

"I won't do it," she repeated. "This arrangement is entirely unacceptable. I can't bear the waiting, and I will not bear the consequences."

Jacob lowered the revolver. "It's about time you came to your senses."

"Please put that thing away." She gestured toward the gun. "I can barely think with you waving it about."

"What do you expect, making all that racket? I thought one of the raiders must be crawling in your window." His gaze lingered on the mirror and the hairbrush that now lay among bright shards of glass. "I hadn't reckoned you might be up here throwing a tantrum."

She glowered at him.

"Come on downstairs, Becca, and let's try to have a civilized breakfast. We're going to need to talk about what we'll have to do to get ready for tonight."

"Tonight? Surely, you don't believe I intend to bed you again—"

He shook his head. "You've already made that clear as rainwater, Rebecca. Way I figure it, we've been stuck together these last few days, and the circumstances would push a saint to—never mind that. It was a mistake. We can barely speak without arguing. There's not much future in the whole idea."

Rebecca tried to control her expression, tried not to let him see how his words stung. Certainly, Jacob was making sense, she told herself—only saying what she'd told herself. Still, his words echoed again and again: *"It was a mistake."* So much so, she didn't hear the first part of what he said next.

". . . we can't afford to wait any longer," Jacob told her. "If the three of us are going to survive this, we'll have to take our chances on escape."

Rebecca shoved aside his rejection to concentrate on the idea of fleeing this place. But her mind brimmed with bloody images of what had happened yesterday when Nate had tried to run. She thought, too, of Nate's weakened condition and of the raiders with their ready guns, of the unfamiliar, swampy territory. Not to mention the snakes swimming in the water, slithering on the land. She shuddered, but she said nothing because she knew Jacob was right.

No matter how long the odds against their flight, at least they'd have some chance. A chance they'd be denied if they stayed here.

As the morning wore on, Jacob wished more than once for hot black coffee to help lift the fog of his fatigue. He'd barely missed the brew during his months of privation in Andersonville, but for the past few days, he'd longed for a steaming mug. Today especially he'd wished for it, for after leaving Rebecca's room, he'd sat, revolver poised, at the bottom of the stairs. There he'd strained his ears for any sound that might mean Asa had come to collect on his unholy bargain.

Jacob noticed Rebecca stifling yawns as they discussed their plans, and he imagined that, like him, she had been too tense to sleep. Apart from their fatigue, however, both took a businesslike approach to conversation, carefully avoiding any reference to what had passed between them. Though their words were brittle as thin ice, at least they remained civil. And if Jacob missed the sparks that flew from Rebecca's tongue, he told himself he was a fool.

The two of them stayed busy making preparations, along with keeping Nate as comfortable as possible. While Jacob packed provisions in the kitchen, Rebecca went to feed Nate, who had just awakened. The swinging door remained ajar, so Jacob could hear their conversation.

"If you aren't feeling up to eating, you could simply say so." Irritation lanced Rebecca's words. "This skirt is filthy enough without you flinging stew onto it."

Nate shouted something unintelligible in re-

sponse, and Jacob resisted the urge to intervene.
Rebecca wouldn't want his help, just as she had
made it clear she wanted nothing further from
him.

"This time, take the spoon, Nate." Her voice
gentled once again, into what Jacob recognized as
her nursing demeanor. "You're going to have to
learn to use your left hand, so let me help you,
please."

"The right hand still hurts somethin' fierce, even
though it's gone." This time Nate's words were
clearer, though his voice was so strained, he barely
sounded like himself. "I thought at least—I
thought at least I'd be shut of the pain."

"There'll be pain at the wrist from the surgery
for some time," Rebecca told him. "But even after
that heals, you may feel what seems to be sensation
in the missing hand. Sometimes it will be discomfort, sometimes an itch or tickle. I'm afraid there's
nothing to be done about that part."

Next, Jacob heard Nate grumble, "You may as
well just shoot me now."

"I am very sorry that you lost your hand, but
certainly that's no reason to give up—"

"I heard you two talkin'. You and him are gonna
leave me here, ain't you? You're gonna leave me
to get killed. Ain't hardly worth the effort to try
an' save a fellow with one hand."

Jacob poured more beans into a cloth sack and
wondered if the jar of flour would survive their
journey. Or if they would live long enough to need
it.

Rebecca told Nate, "If you're going to eavesdrop,
you ought to do a better job of it. We have absolutely no intention of going without you."

To her credit, she did not bother reminding the
boy that he'd been the one to try that yesterday,

nor did she need to. There was little chance that Nate, with his oozing stump, had forgotten.

"You ain't leavin'—" he began.

"Shush!" Rebecca hissed. "There's someone coming."

Steps clumped onto the porch, and Jacob scrambled to put away the food he'd taken from the cache upstairs. If the raiders saw the food he'd found, they'd steal it. If they realized he was preparing for escape, they might shoot him on the spot.

"Jacob!" Rebecca warned.

The front door flew open, banging the wall with a loud crack. Jacob finished hiding the provisions and carefully approached the kitchen door, his hand on the butt of the revolver. Peering through the narrow opening, he watched and waited to see what would happen. Once again he reminded himself their best chance was in escape and not gun battle. Even so, he'd be damned if he'd let Asa . . .

Rebecca backed away from the man coming through the door. Jacob was surprised to see, instead of Asa or either of the men who'd come yesterday, the black-haired, bearded officer striding toward her, bearing down on her like an oncoming train.

What could possibly have happened to dislodge the bastard's smooth civility? Rebecca tried to dart away, clearly frightened by whatever she saw in his expression, but he moved damned fast for a man with such a heavy limp. He grabbed her arm so tightly she cried out.

"Take your hands off her, you stinkin' grayback!" Nate struggled to rise, though his face paled with the effort.

Hall drew a revolver with his free hand. "Sit down, boy, unless you want to lose the other one as well."

Nate froze, making no move to obey.

Sit down, Jacob ordered mentally. The pup seemed bound and determined to get himself killed. Better for all of them to wait and see what the officer wanted, even though Jacob itched to do the raider some serious damage for handling Rebecca so roughly.

"Do as he says," Rebecca told Nate, her words strained but struggling toward control. She was trying, Jacob realized, to calm Nate.

When the boy complied, she turned an icy gaze on the colonel. "I'd imagined you fancied yourself a gentleman, a cut or two above those criminals you lead."

The colonel shoved her hard enough that she fell. Rebecca landed on her bottom, but she made only a muffled grunt.

"I'm gentleman enough when I am dealing with a lady."

"What . . . ?" Her question trailed off in confusion as she stared up at the bearded officer. "Hasn't—hasn't my father paid you? Surely, you didn't expect he could get the money here immediately. I'm certain such a thing would take—"

"Quiet!" the colonel exploded. "This charade has gone on long enough. I will *not* be taken for a fool, Miss Marston, or whatever it is you're calling yourself today."

What the hell was going on? Jacob couldn't comprehend what the Southern officer was saying, but it was clear that something had gone badly wrong. Had they waited too long to attempt freedom?

"How dare you, sir!" Rebecca said rising to her feet. "Have you taken a fever? Because you certainly have returned a different man. Tell me, what is it you're babbling over?"

"Who *are* you?" he demanded.

"Why, I believe you truly are delirious." Her

tone grew guarded, almost wary. "You know exactly who I am, or none of us would remain in this uncomfortable situation."

"I know who you *claim* to be, madam. Now what I wish to know is why."

"First of all," she explained, "it was my friend who told you my identity, but only after she was frightened half out of her wits by that—"

"She told us your name, and you never denied it. Did you think to buy your friends' lives with your lie? Or were you caught up in some earlier mischief where you'd passed yourself off as a person of quality?"

She was *not* Rebecca Marston? Confusion swirled in Jacob's mind.

Rebecca gave a sharp bark of laughter. "You don't believe I'm *me*? This is ludicrous!"

The colonel pulled a paper from his pocket and thrust it in front of her. "Winfield Marston claims no such daughter. I have it here, in writing. He will not pay for your return."

She peered down at the paper, then shook her head emphatically. "No. He wouldn't say that. There must be . . . there must be some mistake."

No trace of humor lingered in her voice. Once again she stepped back, as if she thought she might be struck.

Jacob wanted to believe her, but the facts did not add up. What sort of a father would deny his flesh and blood, would leave her to the mercies of an outlaw band of rebels?

The colonel advanced on her, threatening as a cougar just before the pounce. "So I ask you once again, madam. Who are you, and why have you perpetrated this deception?"

"My name . . . is Rebecca Wells Marston, and I *am* the daughter of Winfield Marston. How ridiculous to think I lied. I can't begin to imagine why

anyone would do such an outrageous thing." She
shook her head, and even from this distance, Jacob
saw tears shining on her face. "I don't understand
this. My father . . ."

Again the officer grasped her arm, and this time
Jacob had had enough. He didn't care who the
hell she was, he wasn't about to stand here and let
a man abuse her while he hid in the kitchen. Hoping he could resolve the matter without resorting
to the gun, he replaced it beneath his shirt and
strode into the parlor.

"Let go of her right now," he ordered.

The raider glowered at him. "This is none of
your concern."

"Like hell it isn't."

Beside the fire, Nate said, "We ain't gonna stand
for you manhandling Miss Marston."

Ignoring the wounded private, the colonel
turned his weapon toward Jacob, making him feel
a fool for keeping his gun where it would do none
of them any good.

"Sit down," the raider commanded. His gaze
flicked to Nate. "Both of you stay out of this
matter."

Jacob ignored the order. "I may not be a gentleman, but I'll be damned if I sit here while you hurt
her."

The click of the gun's hammer sounded unnatu-
rally loud inside the room. Jacob realized he was
behaving much as Nate had. Still, he couldn't make
himself obey the rebel officer.

The revolver's barrel swung from Jacob to Nate,
then back. "Which one shall I shoot first, *Miss
Marston?*"

"You may as well shoot me," Rebecca snapped,
"because my story *isn't* changing. I refuse to invent
some lie to appease you. Whoever sent that tele-

gram has made a terrible mistake—or is lying to you for some reason."

The colonel lowered the gun's muzzle and regarded her coolly. "There's another possibility that we have not considered."

"What could that be?" she asked.

"Is there some reason your father might not want you returned?"

Rebecca paced the confines of the sparsely furnished bedroom, too overwrought to rest—or even sit.

Of course she had denied the possibility. The very idea that Father might have abandoned her to rough criminals was far too painful to consider.

Yet the idea wouldn't leave her mind after the colonel departed, promising to return once he'd decided what to do with them. Could it be her family didn't want her back?

Not her entire family, no. Her mother was undoubtedly still hatching schemes to pawn her off on some unsuspecting bridegroom. And Aunt Millicent had written often, keeping Rebecca abreast of the latest squabbles among the leaders of the women's suffrage and abolition movements. She was eager for her niece to return and take up dress reform, her latest cause. Her brother's annoyingly perfect widow, Prudence, had her hands full with the twins, and she would welcome Rebecca's help at home even as she preached the gospel of proper female subservience.

But Father was another matter. She thought back to their last conversation, and several snatches kept repeating. *"I forbid it, absolutely. . . . If you persist, I wash my hands of you."*

She remembered, too, an earlier discussion, when she'd tried to persuade him not to fire some

women who had organized to demand better wages
at one of the mills.

"*Of course I must go through with it,*" he'd insisted,
"*no matter how painful. I warned them what would
happen, and I stand by my word. It's essential in business
and in life, Rebecca, for a man to say only what he
means and to mean exactly what he says. Anything less
is unpardonable weakness.*"

He had fired those women, though their requests
had been both reasonable and easily within his
power. Rebecca had accused him of being heartless, but she'd never guessed the extent of her
father's callousness. Surely, he must guess she
would be brutalized or murdered. Just as surely,
he must have made his decision and kept it from
the women of the family.

The patriarchal tyrant! Rebecca wept bitter tears
into her hands and finally sank down upon the
bed. She was never going back there, never. Not
while Winfield Marston reigned like Satan over
hell!

But what would happen to her now? Surely, at
the very least, the colonel would withdraw his protection, making her easy prey for those among the
raiders such as Asa. Even worse, she could not
dismiss the possibility he would murder all of them
outright to keep them from bearing witness against
her kidnappers.

She prayed some measure of civility remained
to the Southern officer. After all, he'd been the
one to order the steamboat survivors pulled out of
the river, regardless of the complications that act
entailed. Despite his anger today, she sensed, near
the end of their discussion, a softening of his attitude as he began to suspect her father might be
the one who lied.

Perhaps he would delay his decision, giving her,
Jacob, and Nate a chance to flee this house. With

no ransom forthcoming, it was possible the raiders wouldn't bother giving chase.

Wasn't it? She hoped she was doing more than lying to herself.

Wiping away her tears, she felt exhaustion overtaking her. Before she'd quite decided whether to return downstairs, Rebecca dropped into the dark arms of heavy sleep.

As he brushed dried muck from his black mare, Colonel Lewis Hall cursed himself for a fool. A wiser man, one less attached to pride and honor, would have taken the debacle with Winfield Marston as a warning to steer clear of the scoundrel for all time.

Instead, Hall had leapt at the chance to avenge himself with all the enthusiasm of a child impulsively grasping a serpent by its tail. Now that the snake had turned and bitten, he had learned how sharp the fangs, but it remained to see how potent the venom.

Between his effort and his worry, Hall was growing warm, so he paused a moment in his brushing to remove his jacket, which he draped over a split rail just outside the barn. Turning back to his labors, he once again called to mind Winfield Marston, with his receding silver hair, his muttonchop whiskers, and a paunch that bespoke an overaffection for fine foods. Marston had beguiled Southern planters with his talk of sympathy for those affected by the Union blockade, but in hindsight Hall remembered how cold and flat the Yankee's voice, how utterly gray and emotionless his demeanor.

In stark contrast, Hall pictured the woman he had come to think of as Rebecca Marston and the bright swathes she brought to mind: the rich red of her hair, the clear blue of her eyes, and the ivory of her face sprinkled with freckles like a dusting of cinnamon. Though he could not claim to truly know her, he felt certain her vibrant coloring was a match to her intensity of spirit—an intensity altogether missing in the man she claimed as her father.

Yet if she was not a Marston, who else could she be? In spite of her unladylike frankness and profession, she was obviously well educated and familiar with propriety. Just as clearly, she was bright enough—and willful enough—to carry off this subterfuge. But why?

Hall swore under his breath, frustrated that he could see only one practical solution to this problem. He knew the noose of the Union drew tighter every day, and he understood his part in this conflict was nearly at its end. The question of victory, he admitted to himself, had already been settled. What remained was the matter of how he would live with what he'd done these past four years. If he ended the war a murderer of a woman and wounded, unarmed soldiers, could he claim to be a better man than the Yankees he despised?

He needed time to unravel the knot of this abduction and to decide how he might defuse the rage his men would feel when they learned that there would be no ransom for the "lady" they had guarded in her moat-ringed castle. But for a long while his mind lingered on that other, more perplexing puzzle.

If Rebecca was Winfield Marston's daughter, how could he possibly abandon such a jewel?

Chapter Fifteen

The Queen is most anxious to enlist every one who can speak or write to join in checking this mad, wicked folly of "Women's Rights," with all its attendant horrors, on which her poor feeble sex is bent, forgetting every sense of womanly feeling and propriety.

—Queen Victoria
From a letter to Sir Thomas Martin

Rebecca's dreams were lenses, magnifying doubts. Her mind revisited the difficult days after Thomas had been killed and the trying months after his widow and the twins had come to live in the grand rooms of the Marston mansion. She remembered how well, how seamlessly Prudence and her mother helped each other recover from their grief by gossiping about social inanities, shopping for new frippery, and planning luncheons. Rebecca had been grateful that the two had found each other, at least until she'd overheard her mother telling Prudence, "I feel as if you're the true daughter of my heart."

Prudence, whose mother had died only a year before, had basked in the warm glow of Harriet Wells Marston's affection. Indeed, she grew steadily

greedier for more, even coming to treat Rebecca
as an unwelcome rival.

For all her grasping shallowness, Prudence possessed a singular talent for cruelty. Leveling Rebecca with her narrow, cat-eyed gaze, she would
make seemingly casual comments, such as, "I'm
so delighted I could be the one to give your father
heirs and your mother grandchildren to spoil,
since they'll clearly get them from no other
quarter."

In the interest of family harmony, Rebecca made
a halfhearted attempt to reform the young widow,
though she would have much preferred to drown
Prudence in the nearest water closet. But Rebecca's
first—and final—effort to educate her sister-in-law
on social inequities and the latest on the abolition
front was met with a dismissive wave of her hand
and a sharp click of her tongue.

"Really," Prudence would say, "I'm continually
amused by these spinsterish diversions of yours."

Not long afterward, Rebecca had left to take up
nursing and Aunt Millicent had decided to move
into the family's New York town house to be closer
to her friends. Was it possible that not just her
father, but her mother, had decided the family was
better off without them both? Had Prudence, too,
participated in the decision to proclaim Rebecca
an impostor?

Tears soaked into the folded blanket she was
using for a pillow. One warm rivulet tickled along
the channel formed beside her nose.

Gradually, Rebecca became aware of the gentle
stirring of the air in the bedchamber. Next, she
heard leaves whispering together, perhaps moved
by the same breeze.

As if the bedroom window had been left open.

Her heart froze in mid-thump at the thought,
then lurched into a drumbeat. She came awake

completely, and her gaze shot to the window. But instead of Asa climbing through, she saw only the worn white curtains blowing, rippling lazily.

Yet she could see the grimed glass of the window still. Clearly, it remained closed. So what had stirred the air?

"Mister Fuller?" she called softly, hopefully. Though she disliked the idea of the man traipsing through the bedroom, spying on her as she slept, the alternative—one of the raiders—was too frightening to imagine.

But instead of Jacob, the head that poked around the doorframe was a child's. The red-haired boy looked at her through eyes gleaming with tears.

"I want Papa," he whispered.

As Rebecca climbed out of the bed, she stretched her hand out toward him, silently begging him to stay. "Please—let me help you find him."

He stared at her intently, sending a feverish chill chasing up her spine. But at least for now he did not flee.

Despite her excitement, Rebecca tried to keep her voice slow and gentle. "First, please tell me, who *are* you?"

He sighed, a strangely adult sound coming from a gap-toothed child. "Andrew, of course. Can't you remember anything?" The boy's head shook in obvious frustration. "I want my papa."

"Tell me more, and I'll do my best to help."

He turned away from her, then shot a frown over his shoulder. "Seems to me like *you're* the trouble."

"The trouble? What on earth . . . Stop, Andrew! You wait right there—"

But her words echoed in the near-emptiness of the bedroom, for the child had turned and run away. She could hear his footsteps receding down the hallway, and she knew even before she caught

sight of the closing door that he was once more
leading her into the house's attic.

This time, however, she was on the rascal's heels.
She could imagine no reason she could not catch
the boy. After all, her legs were longer, and she
could move quickly enough when she set her mind
to it. And right now, her attention was completely
focused on getting to the bottom of this mystery.

Flinging open the attic door, she raced up the
flight of stairs, her eyes straining to catch a glimpse
of the fleeing child. As she reached the top step,
light shining through the dirty window silhouetted
his wiry form. The boy appeared to be frantically
attempting to shove his way between a pair of
wooden boxes. One toppled over, filling the air
with dust and the floor with yellowed papers.

"Stay right there," she pleaded.

His head moved, turning toward her. Like the
rest of him, it was a dark shape without detail, a
shape against the light. And as she stood transfixed,
the figure broke into tiny motes and settled with
the dust.

A keening howl arose, a drawn-out cry of protest,
and it took Rebecca several moments to realize
she was its source. She clamped down on the cry,
hoping that Jacob would not come running to her
aid. For if he did appear, surely he would demand
an explanation.

And then whatever would she say?

Her knees rebelled against the effort of supporting her, so she sank down to sit on the top step
and stared at the place where the boy had been.

Had been. That explained it, didn't it? The child
was someone who had been here, probably with
the parents she had dreamed. Perhaps they had
all died within these walls. . . .

"You're so silly, Mama," the child had accused her,

and the memory made the fine hairs rise upon Rebecca's neck.

He mistook her for his mother for some reason. Why was that? She recalled his tousled red hair, so similar in color to her own. Maybe that was it. Perhaps his mother had had red hair, too.

She realized she was considering the possibility that she had seen a ghost. Not simply an impression of a former inhabitant, as Jacob had supposed, but an actual departed spirit. She'd always thought herself a rational creature, immune to flights of fancy. But what logic, what science, could possibly explain what had happened here? The boy had disappeared before her eyes!

Rebecca shook her head, unable or unwilling to believe the child was dead. She remembered the surgeons she had worked with, men of science every one. How would they explain this?

Unfortunately, she knew beyond a doubt. She could almost hear her cousin's voice, sounding amused and condescending in her head.

"Just a touch of the hysteria, Rebecca. Frequently, a woman's more delicate nervous system is beset by these disturbances of the imagination and emotion. Fresh air, good food, and a bit of rest will set you right, and of course, not too much excitement."

Rebecca snorted rudely, unable to accept that explanation either. She might be suffering from more excitement than any sensible human being would like, but she had not imagined what she saw.

Think logically, she told herself. If she discounted the possibility that the child was a ghost or that her mind had conjured his appearance, that left only some other, unknown explanation.

Something she had not yet imagined was at work inside this house.

* * *

Jacob's muscles strained with effort as he hauled the rope. The wooden bucket attached to the pulley leaked, but it was still the most efficient way they had to draw water from the cistern.

Though he was thirsty, instead of drinking from the vessel, Jacob hauled his dripping burden to the kitchen, where he could more easily scoop out a cup. But as he carried the bucket, he heard a tapping, and he wondered if he'd hauled up some stones with the water.

Peering inside the bucket, he was surprised to see a glint of yellow. He took a moment to push back his sleeve before reaching in to scoop out the two hard bumps his fingers touched. He set aside the first, a small, tan pebble, to stare in admiration at the other.

He was no expert on jewelry, but he saw at once it was a woman's ring. The nicked rose-gold band had been engraved with a delicate pattern, much of which had been rubbed to no more than a suggestion of its former floral detail. A wedding band, he realized, one that had been worn for many years. Had its owner been the same woman who had so carefully hidden the food he'd found upstairs? He wondered, too, if she had lost this ring some time ago or if she had hurriedly tossed it in the cistern.

Disjointed images assaulted his senses, each a fragment of a new whole taking shape, surrounding him, and becoming his reality. Somehow, inexplicably, he was watching from outside himself, watching as he stood upon the front porch of this house. Only the beams supporting the porch roof stood straight, and white paint coated the walls behind him. And the man who stood there, the man he understood to be himself, had hair streaked with silver, and solemn blue-gray eyes. The years had lined the man's face, and worry creased it further. Beside him stood a woman, tall and thin, stooped slightly with age. Her white hair, nearly dry and smelling sweet with recent washing, undulated in the warm breeze and made him think of the silky milkweed down floating across meadows.

The scene shifted, and Jacob's perspective careened into the man's, so that he could feel the old woman's hand clasping his, then squeezing, so he could see the swift approach of a dozen or more riders. Their horses trampled wilted cornstalks, tearing down the drying feed crop, and the breeze carried the metallic taste of blowing dust. The woman's hand squeezed harder just before she spoke.

"They might take all else, but they aren't getting this," she vowed. She released him to twist at the gold ring, but her knuckles had knotted in the familiar way of farm wives. Undeterred, she shook her head. "I'm going in to get some lard. They *won't* have it, I tell you. No one will have it until I'm good and ready."

The husband who was both Jacob and not Jacob looked after her, then returned his gaze to the approaching riders, who wore a ragged mix of homespun shirts and uniforms, some of which were blue. Union deserters, he decided. Thieves who would steal to prove their honest nature. Cowards who would kill to affirm their courage and their loyalty.

He raised a rifle and sighted one of the riders down his barrel.

Jacob stumbled with a wave of dizziness. Shaking his head, he wondered what the hell was wrong with him. Even as a child, he'd never before experienced such a . . . Could one rightly call the thing a dream? It seemed too real for that, and when he looked down at the ring again, he felt a ripple of unease.

He tried to convince himself the ague had caught up with him after his long months in the prison pen and his dousing in the river. He thought about the chills and fever that had weakened Zeke even before his brother hurt his ankle. The idea made a simple flight of fancy seem all the more appealing.

Remembering his grandmother's theories, Jacob supposed there was another possibility, that those who had once lived in this house had left an imprint so strong that both he and Rebecca somehow felt its echoes. He wondered if it might be possible that the people he had seen were as real as the ring he now held in his palm. With it came a woman's voice, the same voice that had spoken to the old man on this very porch.

"I'm good and ready now. You take it, but remember, it won't mean a thing until you pass it on."

The hair rose on his arms, his neck. Pass it on to whom?

But the old woman's voice fell silent, and Jacob would almost swear he felt the house let out a long breath and settle, down into the dreamless slumber of decay.

After several minutes, sitting on the top step in the attic became uncomfortable. After several more, Rebecca's discomfort grew, and her mind filled with frightening images from the night that Asa made his horrible proposition and then locked her in the attic. Her fingertips were still sore and scabbed from her frantic efforts to escape while he'd gone downstairs to murder Jonah Pierce.

With a shudder, she rose to her feet and dusted off her skirt. She'd been deeply shocked by the child's disappearance, but in comparison to Asa, the boy's presence seemed benign—perhaps even pleasant.

She conjured the grin he'd bestowed on her earlier and smiled to herself, warmed by the memory. She'd always been fond of children, especially her brother's precious four-year-olds, Tom and Win. After her brother's death, when they had come to live in the Marston mansion, their laughter and mischief so delighted Rebecca that it nearly made up for their mother's tiresome presence.

Aunt Millicent had observed Rebecca's affection and warned her against becoming overly attached. *"Nephews and nieces are all well and good—assuming you keep them at a reasonable distance—but children of your own will tie you down like anchors. You'll never be anything but a nursemaid and a slave if you live your life for a husband and a family. We have work to do, Rebecca, work that will make all the difference in this country."*

Rebecca did not mention that Aunt Millicent had never kept *her* at arm's length. Instead, she'd been swept away by the woman's passion and by the certain rightness of so many of her beliefs. But somehow, something had shifted for Rebecca, beginning with the knowledge that either an escape attempt or Colonel Hall's actions might end her life this very day. The thought of her own death both frightened her and filled her with regret, but not for the reasons she once would have imagined. Much to her surprise, she found she didn't care so much about the social reforms she had not yet accomplished. Instead, her heart ached for those people she might never see again: her aunt, her mother, her two nephews (though Prudence could go rot, taking her petty cruelties with her), and her friends. And tears welled in her eyes at the realization that she would never again hold a man close to her heart, would feel neither his desire nor his love. She would never again see Jacob Fuller. Not that she would see him even if they suc-

ceeded in their plan to escape. She had no plans
to bother with a man who would call their relationship a mistake, even if she *had* provoked that
response with her own words.

Without conscious decision, Rebecca walked to
the box of papers the boy had overturned. Though
she knew it was unlikely, she wondered if the spot
where he had vanished would yield further clues.
Also, she could not help wondering if anything in
the box, now on its side, might possibly prove useful. Perhaps, at least, she'd carry down a handful
of old papers to help with kindling a fire.

A glance toward the window told her the day was
waning, and here inside the attic, the light was
barely adequate for reading. Even so, she realized
immediately that she could not think of burning
any of these papers. The embellished script on
several marked them as important documents.
Though they appeared in poor condition, she felt
certain they must be important to the family that
once lived inside this farmhouse.

As she picked up those few closest at hand, they
began to flake, creating a small blizzard of musty-
smelling yellow fragments. The topmost sheet read
"Certificate of Marriage." She peered more
closely, curious to see the date.

"May 4," she read, though the year had flaked
away. Her gaze swept across the ornately printed
names of husband and wife, and her heart thun-
dered with the shock of recognition.

"Jacob Fuller" was the groom's name, and his
bride's, "Rebecca Marston."

She gasped as the letters swam inside her vision.
No, of course those names weren't right. Why, right
now she could see the husband was Jacob *Marlow*,
not Fuller, and the wife . . . She blinked back the
moisture in her eyes, only to see the entire sheaf
of papers collapse and flutter toward her feet.

"No!" she cried, trying too late to hold the aged document together.

The red-haired boy's frown sprang to her mind. *"Seems to me like you're the trouble."*

What on earth had he meant? And why did she now feel so certain that this certificate was what the child meant for her to see?

Asa wasted no time in lifting Hall's jacket when he spotted it hanging unguarded just outside the barn. It was easy to see the deal was going rotten. The sour expression on Hall's face as he'd gone into the outbuilding was proof enough of that. But the bastard, as always, was stingy with the details. The colonel never told the men a damned thing they didn't have to know.

Several of the men had spread out to keep watch on the house, and Asa recognized the murmur of voices inside the barn as Hall's and Simms's. That ought to give him a few minutes to find out what was what.

Asa's fingers riffled through a wad of Yankee currency. He longed to stick the money into his own pocket, but Hall would string him up faster than he could whistle "Dixie." Instead, he kept searching until he found what he had hoped for: a single telegram.

Maybe this would shed some light, thought Asa. He stuffed it into his own jacket, then walked behind the barn, where he'd be out of sight. Colonel'd have his hide if he caught him looking at it, and if any of the others saw him, they'd likely raise some sort of fuss, too.

Even so, as Asa unfolded the paper, he wished he'd rounded up Carl or maybe Macon. Both read better than Asa, and some of the words on the telegram were damned tricky.

Fear you are in company of . . . What the hell was that word, *i-m-p-o-s-t-o-r?* Asa didn't have a clue, so he read on. *Marston advises no such daughter . . .* Asa skipped the next hard word before struggling to decipher more. *No payment . . .* There was one more word he couldn't make out, but it didn't matter. He knew enough to understand that Winfield Marston of Philadelphia didn't mean to pony up the cash.

"Goddamn it!" he swore.

"Sergeant, what the hell are you doing with my private message?" Colonel Hall's voice boomed behind him, and he snatched back the paper Asa had been holding.

The pup tucked its tail between its legs and darted away at Hall's tone. Just as startled, Asa nearly jumped a foot, but anger flashed over the brief stab of fear.

"I was findin' out what you been keepin' from us," he told Hall. "We got a right to know we been wastin' our time playin' wet nurse to a nest of Yankees and a woman who ain't worth a cent."

Hall sighed. "True enough. Asa, we've been together for some time. Believe me when I say I had no intention of hiding this from you. I simply needed time to decide how this situation should be handled."

"How 'bout we take care of it the way we always do? You turn your back and let what happens happen, in the name of the Confederacy and ol' Jeff Davis."

"It's not that simple. This war is . . ." Hall shook his head. "Since Lee's surrender, it's only a matter of weeks before the remnants of our army are swept aside. What purpose could it serve to butcher a woman and a couple of soldiers who have clearly suffered?"

Asa glared a challenge. "Revenge, for starters.

Look what those Yankee bastards done to us. To
all of us. We've seen the burning. We've heard
the widows cry. Them bluejackets come through
stealin' everything that ain't nailed down and—"

"I begin to wonder if our methods have been
so very different. I begin to ask myself what kind
of men this war has made of all of us."

"Easy for you to fall back on playin' the gentleman," Asa accused. "You got somewhere to go
back to and a pocket full of greenbacks to help to
smooth the way. What do we got, colonel?"

Hall looked serious and thoughtful, a different
man from the one who had so often used his knife
or gun to sort out trouble. He asked, "Will you
have more if you kill those three people?"

"I'll have one thing more," Asa told him, turning
away from him to walk around the barn and toward
the water. "I'll have my turn at that gal before she
dies."

He had nearly reached the water when Hall
grasped his arm as if to turn him.

Asa was having none of it. He had the colonel
figured. Hall wanted to play the hero, then woo
the woman like the princess she thought herself
to be. He'd forbidden them to touch her while he
charmed his way between Rebecca's legs. Or maybe
it was more than that. Could be he and Simms had
worked out some sort of scheme to cut the rest of
them out of their share. Both ideas flashed through
Asa's mind as he spun around with his fists flying.

His first blow caught the colonel hard in the
left temple and sent him staggering. Christ, Asa
thought. He'd just done a damned-fool thing. Hall
had only meant to stop him, but now the colonel
would for sure go for either gun or knife.

Before Hall could recover, Asa jumped him, and
both fell and rolled into the scummy water. Asa

heard Macon's shout, followed by those of at least one other man.

The colonel's fist sank into Asa's belly, setting off what felt like an explosion in his gut. Hall's leg swung over and flipped him, and Asa's face was shoved into the mud. He felt its grit grinding into his skin, and he realized the bastard meant to drown him in three inches of water. But the depth would hardly matter if Asa sucked in the sandy muck.

Jacob was drawing another bucket from the cistern when he heard the shouts across the water. Rushing to the doorway, he called quietly, "Rebecca!"

She wiped her hands on a rag as she came from the kitchen. "What is it?"

"Come out here and take a look."

Though the light was failing, Jacob made out the signs of struggle along the opposite shore. Raised voices, though unintelligible, added to the appearance of some sort of fight.

"They're not worrying about guarding us right now. This is our chance," Jacob told her.

"I'm worried about Nate. He's still in so much pain."

Nodding, Jacob said, "We'll have to help him the best we can. Listen, Rebecca. There won't be a better time."

She nodded, her gaze intent and solemn. "I know that. And I'd rather go now—even if we're shot—than suffer through another night of waiting."

He could almost hear her thinking, *waiting to be raped, waiting to be murdered.*

She was right.

The two of them swiftly worked to gather the few

items they'd prepared. Then Jacob hoisted Nate
to his feet.

"I'm not sure I . . ." he began. Fear and pain
clouded his blue eyes.

"You were ready enough to get back to your unit
the other day. Let's see what you Kentucky boys
are really made of."

Nate nodded. "I'll do it."

Rebecca joined them. "We all will, together."

The three of them slipped out through the back
door, and Jacob prayed to God that no rebel had
them in his sights.

Chapter Sixteen

I never hear the word "escape"
Without a quicker blood,
A sudden expectation,
A flying attitude.
        —Emily Dickinson

As he struggled to free himself from Hall's grasp, Asa sucked in a mouthful of muddy water. Immediately, he started choking, gagging, as his lungs spasmodically reacted to the intrusion.

In the blackness behind his eyes, bloody motes blossomed into gold-edged explosions, and even worse, a flash of memory erupted. A memory of being held down by a larger man, of having his legs forced apart, and . . .

No! Asa twisted and bucked, his strength infused by a scalding gush of terror. He was a man himself now; he'd proven it a score of times at least. He'd be damned if he would *ever* be the one held down again. No Big Man made a woman out of him!

He threw off his attacker and stood, seeing not Hall this time, but Montgomery. Seeing Montgomery and being back there, torn and bleeding, sniveling like a girl. Hearing Rebecca Marston liken him to barnyard filth just as if she *knew* all about it, as if they *all* did.

With a scream of rage, Asa flew at the Big Man who'd held him down. Out of the corner of his eye, he saw others running, their mouths open, though the roaring in his ears prevented him from hearing what they said. And he knew in one horrifying moment that this time Montgomery had brought his friends to watch his humiliation. This time, he'd brought others to take turns.

Still, despite Asa's rage and horror, the Big Man again overpowered him and knocked him off his feet. And Asa was almost glad when his face was shoved under the water. Almost glad, because that meant the bastards couldn't see his tears.

Rebecca glanced anxiously at Nate, who waded just behind her, the water lapping brown up to his waist. His face was tight and set in the expression of a boy determined not to cry.

"Keep the elbow bent and your—" She'd been about to say *"hand,"* but she caught herself in time. "And your wrist elevated to reduce the seepage."

She'd tied his sling so tightly that he could hardly do otherwise, she realized. Her biggest worry was that he would stumble, soaking the stump in muddy water.

Nate nodded, slowing his pace a fraction. Jacob, who was ahead of them, probing with a stick to check for drop-offs, looked over his shoulder.

"We need to put as much distance as possible between ourselves and the house before we lose the light," he said.

"I know," Nate agreed. "Just let me catch my breath a minute."

Rebecca said nothing, though like Jacob, she felt

impatient to move on. The water seemed to stretch forever in this direction. They had chosen this route to throw off pursuit, but it also made their escape less comfortable.

She stubbed her toe on a stump or stone and wished again for the protection of her shoes, which she'd tied together and hung around her neck. At least she could put them back on when they climbed out of the water. Both Jacob and Nate were barefoot, as they'd been when they were pulled out of the river.

Despite the exertion, Rebecca felt chilled and burdened with wet clothing. Her arms ached from holding up her blanket-wrapped bundle in an attempt to keep it dry. She was especially careful because she was the one who held the precious matches—their only hope of warmth.

"Near as I can figure, we're headed north and veering toward the main river."

"Do you see any sign of solid ground?" Rebecca asked. She saw trees jutting from the water along with the tops of shrubs in spots, but without some dry place, how would they rest or warm themselves?

Jacob pointed. "The ground's sloping upward this way. Maybe we'll find a ridge before long."

"Or there'll be soldiers looking for us," she suggested hopefully.

"Maybe." Jacob nodded, but he didn't sound too optimistic.

Nate continued wading forward, but he soon lagged behind. Rebecca glanced westward frequently, as if her concern could slow the sun's descent.

But each time she looked to her left, the bruised sky darkened slightly, and above their heads, she could discern the first bright stars.

* * *

Panting with exertion, the colonel held down Asa's head until the man stopped struggling. Hall winced as the hound stopped its furious barking to sink sharp teeth into his leg. He moved to swat it away, only to have strong arms haul him to his feet. His stomach tightened at the sight of Carl and Franklin. God above, were his men all turning against him? But as soon as he was standing, they released him and he saw that they wore identical expressions, stony masks of indecision.

With unhurried movements, Macon dragged Asa from the water and rolled him onto his side. He didn't appear to pay attention to whether the man breathed. Instead, he and Simms watched Hall, clearly waiting for some sort of explanation. Pain throbbed at Hall's temple, and each breath sent agony flaring through his chest. He suspected a cracked rib or maybe worse.

But still, he needed to produce some answer, some explanation for drowning a comrade most of the men had known far longer than they'd followed Hall. They needed a reason not to turn on him for killing one of their own, and they needed it this minute.

The flare of Simms's small eyes warned him that someone stood behind him. Glancing back, Hall saw Asa gagging, retching, and struggling to rise.

"There's not going to be a ransom," Hall said quickly, before his sergeant could do the honors. "Marston is refusing."

The colonel didn't add the man's reason, which seemed more unlikely each time he thought about it.

Macon glared a challenge. "How do we know you didn't already get the money?"

"I was with him," Simms said. "Only thing he got was some telegram."

"Could be in some bank somewhere, in his name," Macon countered.

"Are you accusing me?" Hall asked. His hand floated just above his gun. Even that small motion sent a shaft of pain arcing along his battered ribs, and he knew he was a dead man if it came down to a gunfight. Oh, he'd kill Macon, all right, but his authority, which had held these renegades together for five months, had broken. And nothing in this world would mend the damage.

Macon's lip drew back in an ugly sneer, exposing his dark teeth. He stared at Hall for several long beats. Macon might have been considering what he knew of Hall's character, or he might have been considering the fact that Hall could kill him before dying.

Hall softened his focus, allowed it to take in the others' hands. But there was no way he could tell who else might try to beat him to a draw.

Billy and Cole rode up, and even though neither of them knew what had just happened, Hall felt the odds against him lengthen.

Macon broke the silence. "Saddle your horse and git on down the road, colonel. Take that as your due. But show your face again and you're a dead man. And that you can believe."

Asa's eye stung so he could barely get it open. He remained on all fours, rocking and concentrating hard on keeping down the contents of his stomach. The stupid dog was licking desperately at his face until he roughly shoved it away from him.

"Jesus, Asa," Simms hissed. "What the hell went on?"

Knees threatening to give out, Asa sat heavily in

the mud. The world spun, and a buzzing clogged his ears.

"Graves?" another man asked, loud enough to cut through the wasps' nest worth of noise.

Someone roughly shook his shoulder. Asa flopped onto his side and drew his knees up toward his chest. His arms rose to protect his aching head.

"Shit," said one of the others. "Hall's drownt whatever sense he ever had."

For several moments, they left him alone. Asa struggled to think on when and where he was and tried to separate twin nightmares. Then, unexpectedly, a torrent of water struck his head. Gasping and sputtering, he sat up to keep from drowning.

Macon held an empty pan, still dripping. "I ain't askin' you again. What the hell went on?"

Asa shook his head to clear his face and eye of water. He noticed Cole had come back; several yards behind him Billy held their horses.

The other raiders stood around, looking expectant.

"Ain't gonna be no ransom," Asa told the others. "He knew it, and I found out he's been keepin' it from us."

Carl grimaced. "Hall just told us. And if that sharp-tongued bitch was my daughter, I wouldn't pay the ransom neither."

"Cheap Yankee bastard," Simms complained. "She's still his kin. A woman's papa oughta pay to get her back."

"Ain't you heard?" asked Billy. "Them Yankees eat their young."

Several of the men laughed, but not Asa. Instead, he told the others, "Since Old Man Marston ain't sendin' us the money, I still figure we oughta get somethin' for our trouble. How 'bout you?"

As a group, the raiders gazed across the water to the house.

"Reckon we ought to at that," Simms said.

Billy piped in, "Tell 'em what we saw, Cole."

The boy's uncle scratched an auburn beard shot through with silver. "There's Union cavalry headed this way, a whole damned mess of 'em. They ain't near far enough for comfort, either. We need to move on out."

"Got a good stout tree here, big enough to hang them ones inside before we go," Carl suggested.

"Yank bastards don't deserve to die right off," Asa told the others. "First I wanta make 'em watch us teach a certain princess why she oughta show respect for Southern men."

Macon shook his head. His bushy eyebrows were drawn lower than ever, and his feet shuffled as he spoke. "Don't hardly seem worth the trouble. Colonel said the Yanks was gettin' close. I say we skedaddle, leave those up in the house right where they sit. We get caught killin' them three, especially that woman, and we're dead for sure."

Carl laughed. "Ain't like you to cut Federals so much slack. You fall in love or somethin', last night at that house?"

"Hell, no," Macon snapped, but Asa could see there was more to it than the man was saying. He'd kept unusually quiet about the details of last night's amputation.

Simms spat in the mud. "If y'all don't have the balls to take care of them Yankees, I'll be glad to do the honors. Three bullets won't take no time, and then we can move out."

Jacob hadn't bothered much with praying since the night that he lost Hope. He'd figured that if God hadn't listened to all his weeks of pleas and promises, he was dead, stone deaf, or utterly indifferent. And if God didn't care about the suffering of a sad, sweet woman like Hope, chances were he wouldn't give a damn about the fool who'd left a gun within her reach.

But just because Jacob was too mule-headed to ask for help during the long months of his imprisonment didn't mean he couldn't change his mind. So he muttered a silent prayer as he turned and waited for Nate and Rebecca to catch up to him. Nate waded in near-silence, his expression grim as that of a corpse. Both his face and Rebecca's glowed moon-pale in the near darkness, but it was hers that caught Jacob's eye and held it. Exhaustion was as evident in her features as her gait. Every time he looked at her, he could see more of her strength had ebbed away in the cold water.

"We need to get you out of that skirt and petticoat," he told her. "They're catching the current like an underwater sail."

He expected her to blast him for making such a discourteous suggestion. Instead, she nodded her agreement, testimony to either her fatigue or a growing practicality.

"Perhaps you could assist me." Her voice was barely loud enough for him to hear.

When Jacob reached Rebecca, she sagged into his arms. He felt her shivering against him.

"I thought we were finished." He spoke quietly against her ear. "And here you are, asking me to take your clothes off for you."

His spirits sank when she didn't answer. It was a sad day when he couldn't pick enough of a fight to bring the temperamental redhead to a boil. Right now, he'd settle for a lukewarm fit of pique.

Just when he'd given up on the idea, Rebecca murmured, "Swine."

It wasn't much, but Jacob felt encouraged. His spirits soared still higher when Nate emerged from his stupor to say, "That's land over there. Do you see it? Dry land!"

Jacob swung his gaze to follow Nate's outstretched pointer finger. He squinted, but the poor light made it impossible to tell.

"I don't see it," Jacob said. "Are you sure you're not—"

"Yes!" Rebecca cried. She was pointing in the same direction. "It's there! It's real! We can build a nice, warm fire—"

"And then sleep," Nate interrupted.

Jacob nodded, still uncertain, but unwilling to argue with what could be an answer to his prayers. Despite his hopes, however, he wondered if Nate might have been mistaken and if Rebecca had confirmed the error out of desperation. Jacob had seen soldiers do the same thing, swearing to the veracity of whatever rumor held the promise of an end to war, of going home.

"We'll walk in that direction for a while, but let's not stray too far off northward. I don't want to waste too much time if it's not—"

"Mister Fuller can't see it," Rebecca told Nate, "so he thinks we've gone soft in the head."

"Must be he's longer in the tooth than he looks if he's too blind to see that ridge." Nate quirked a lopsided grin at Rebecca, the first glint of humor in his pain-filled day.

"I thought I saw a little gray in those curls," Rebecca answered.

"Long in the tooth, my eye," Jacob muttered, squinting harder. "I can see it now." *Almost.*

They made slow progress in the direction Nate had indicated. With every step, stars brightened in the sky above and the features of the pair beside him dimmed. Jacob's senses, too, abandoned him, so he could no longer be certain whether they had walked five minutes or five miles from the spot where Nate first spoke.

God help them all if the private had been wrong. Jacob imagined wading hour after hour through the darkness until, weakened by exhaustion, they succumbed to sudden, unseen ditches or unexpected currents as they reached the main channel of the river.

For the second time that day, he whispered a prayer.

Once the animals and men were ready, the raiders started toward the farmhouse. Asa noticed that Macon lagged behind along the water's edge.

"I still think we ought to move on before them soldiers get here," Macon said, showing his mud-colored teeth.

The others ignored him, crossing the band of floodwater, which had narrowed in spite of last night's rain. Macon mounted his gelding and trotted in the opposite direction, leading both of the stolen army horses.

Like hunting wolves, the others split up to cut off their prey's escape. Simms, Carl, and Franklin took the back door while Asa, Cole, and Billy burst in through the front. It took them less than a minute to realize that their prisoners had escaped, and five minutes longer to confirm it by searching every room, including the dark attic.

"They couldn't have been gone too long. Fires are still burning," Carl pointed out, gesturing toward the kitchen stove and fireplace. "Musta just slipped out."

The group moved outside and spread out, but in the poor light, they saw no sign of their missing prisoners.

"We'll go after 'em, then," Asa insisted.

Panic knifed through him at the thought that Rebecca Marston might win. He couldn't let her get away from him. Couldn't let her make it back inside locked gates, where she could laugh over his threats or maybe even pay someone to hunt him down.

No, it couldn't happen because he would be damned if he gave up.

Cole shook his head. "Macon was right. We ain't got time. I'm tellin' you, we better get out of here before them Yanks catch up."

"But we know they're comin'," Asa insisted. Frustration was eating away at the remnants of his control. "We'll ambush the bastards, and then we'll go after the prisoners—"

"Not this time," Cole said. "There's too many."

The others were edging toward the door, talking about joining up with Macon.

"But I ain't through with her!" Asa shouted.

When no one met his eye, Asa could see that this was it—the end of their loose confederation. He wasn't too surprised; until Hall's arrival, members had come and gone as it suited them. Without the colonel to plan strategic raids and give them orders, nothing remained to bind them to each other.

The others returned to their own mounts and rode off, leaving Asa's horse behind. Didn't bother him a bit. With the others gone, he'd be able to find Miss High-and-mighty and pay her out right proper.

Before this night was over, he would damned well be the one on top.

The ground began to rise. Jacob staggered as his drenched body, no longer buoyed by the water, began to emerge upon a muddy ridge. All at once, he felt as if his limbs had turned to lead. Desire overwhelmed him, an undeniable need to lie down upon the land and close his eyes until . . .

"Jacob—Mister Fuller."

Rebecca's voice was sharp, demanding. Jacob wished that she would go away and annoy somebody else.

She shook his shoulder hard. "I need you to help me start a fire."

He couldn't remember ever meeting such a woman for giving a man orders. He rolled onto his side, away from her.

"We're all tired, cold. We have to build a fire," she repeated. "It's dangerous for you to go to sleep now."

Dangerous? How could a little sleep be—

Something hard prodded his ribs. Rebecca was kicking him, he realized, and from the feel of it, she'd put her shoes back on.

"Damn it, Becca," he complained as he sat up. If there was anything dangerous around here, she was it.

"That's *Miss Marston*, Mister Fuller." Her voice lanced through the darkness. "Now come and help me, please. My fingers are too cold to use these matches properly. Besides, I'll need help feeding the kindling we brought into the flame. The sticks I've found are so damp, we may have difficulty."

He sighed and raked his fingers through his hair. "Where's Nate?"

"Just over there," Rebecca said. "He's sound asleep, poor thing."

"You save any of that sympathy for me?"

"Why? Did someone lop off *your* hand with an axe, too? Now please hurry, Mister Fuller. I'm chilled to the bone."

She took his hand and led him higher, to a drier strip of bare land. The thin moon and stars com-

bined their strength to silhouette a thick tangle of
branches to their right. As he fumbled with the
matches, she prepared the frayed cloth scraps she'd
brought.

"It bothers you when I call you Becca," Jacob
told her.

"Yes, I'm sure I've said that several times."

A match flared to life, but as Rebecca attempted
to feed it, the flame died.

"Well, I'll tell you what bothers me," Jacob told
her. "You calling me *Mister Fuller* like I'm no more
than some acquaintance—even after everything we
shared."

"You're only irritated that I woke you. Let me
remind you, *you're* the one who said what happened
was nothing more than a mistake."

"But it *still* happened, and pretending I'm the
hired help won't undo a single kiss. At least . . . at
least you need to call me Jacob." Yellow light rose
up between them, and each of them reached forward.

This time, the flame caught, and Rebecca placed
it on the bed she had prepared. The two of them
sat in silence, feeding the fire carefully, nurturing
its growing golden glow.

Jacob admitted to himself that Rebecca had been
right about their need for warmth. But as the damp
wood sent pale puffs of gray smoke skyward, he
hoped like hell the raiders weren't out hunting
them by starlight.

Because if they were, the fire would surely point
them in the right direction.

Rebecca could see Jacob more clearly now, could
see the amber flickering in his eyes as he watched
her. As the raider's had the night before, his jacket
and trousers steamed with his nearness to the fire.

"You should take those off to let them dry," she told him.

Beyond the ring of firelight, frogs peeped and insects sang their age-old rhythms. Something stirred faintly in the bushes, perhaps only a light breeze.

"We all should take our clothes off," Jacob countered. "You especially."

She folded her arms across her chest. "I've never seen you as the help . . . Jacob. But if I did, I'd dismiss you for that impertinent remark."

"If I ever doubted for a minute that you're Rebecca Marston, that comment seals it for me. I only meant you have more layers than Nate and I put together, not that there's anything under them I'm anxious to see again."

She bit back a smile. Though she was certain she'd never in all her life looked so bedraggled, she recognized the hunger in his voice.

"I'm gratified to hear that you're no better a liar than I am," she told Jacob. "Now, shall we undress Mr. Gordon first?"

Soon, they had their assorted garments spread before the fire. For modesty's sake, Rebecca retained a layer of her underclothing, but both men relied on only blankets.

Yet even wrapped inside a worn quilt, Rebecca still shivered, though she had moved nearer to the fire.

Jacob scooted closer, just behind her, and wrapped his strong arms around her shoulders. "No sense wasting body heat."

"No." She shook her head, and she meant to shake him off as well. This was foolish, reckless . . . and yet he felt so good, so solid holding her. Within moments, his warmth began to permeate her chill.

She sighed. "I don't suppose there's any harm

in being practical, as long as we remember that we're only keeping warm."

Yet in his embrace, her body began tingling in anticipation, traitorously hoping he'd ignore what she'd just said. All traces of fatigue vanished, replaced by a frisson of excitement. She had to force herself to keep still when what she really wanted was to turn her head and feel his lips on hers.

Don't complicate things, she warned herself. Not now, when they had built a fragile peace, as well as an understanding that what they had filled was only a temporary need.

Yet as fatigue quieted her urges, disjointed images fluttered through her mind: their two names written on a certificate of marriage; the paper as it crumbled into dust; the red-haired boy's frustration as he told her, *"I want my papa."*

Rebecca shivered, despite the warmth of Jacob's embrace. He pulled her even closer, sending dangerous impulses thrumming through her veins.

Her neck arched toward him, degree by slow degree. *Foolish, to risk so much. . . .* She searched instead for something she might do to stop this before it was too late.

"You mentioned before that you'd been married." Instantly, she regretted asking, for his body tensed against hers.

"I'm sorry, Jacob," she added quickly. "I shouldn't have presumed—"

"It's all right. Could be it's something you should know now."

He left the rest unspoken, but she knew what he meant: *before we make the same mistake again.* She kept still and silent, waiting for him to decide what he would tell.

"I was nineteen when I met her," Jacob began, his words soft and warm against Rebecca's neck.

"I was tending the horses in her barnyard, but they were restless on account of the activity. Folks were crawling over that farm like ants, previewing farm equipment and the property before the auction.

"I heard her weeping inside the barn, and I knew that she had every right to. Both her husband and her little son had taken sick with influenza and died the month before. She had no other family, and the bank called in the loan since there was no man to work the fields. So Hope had no choice but to watch the vultures pick her clean."

"That poor woman ..." Rebecca whispered, imagining how it would feel to lose everyone—and everything—she loved. A stab of memory reminded her that her own father's betrayal might have placed her in a similar position.

"As soon as I could, I went to her," Jacob continued. "She was older, nearly thirty, and it made me feel like such a man when she threw herself into my arms and cried."

Rebecca felt his head shake in denial.

"All I wanted to do was make things right for her. I didn't understand that it was already too late," Jacob said. "She moved into town after the auction, set herself up in a little house, and took in sewing. I kept stopping by to see her, to check on how she was doing."

He stopped speaking, until Rebecca guessed he'd changed his mind about sharing the story. In the fire, a chunk of wood collapsed upon itself, chasing a swarm of embers skyward with the smoke.

Jacob cleared his throat. "I thought—I thought when Hope invited me into her bed, it meant she loved me, even though she never said it. When she agreed to marry me, I figured that was her way of telling everyone, including me, the way she felt.

"My family said she was too much older and still too sad about her loss. I wouldn't listen to them, though, because I had the fool idea that I could make her happy, that I could undo all the pain inside of her.''

Rebecca's vision swam with unshed tears, and she thought of what a fine man he was, despite their many contrasts. Even as a boy little older than Nate Gordon, his impulses had been kind and decent. She wanted to tell him that, or better yet to kiss him gently, again and again, to make him see that the future could be different.

But she'd already hurt him once, just as she had been hurt. Better to let their wounds heal than to reach out and risk new suffering. Heaven knew, he'd already suffered pain enough.

"After we were married, Hope grew even quieter," Jacob continued. "I didn't understand though—or maybe I simply didn't want to see. I figured that if I was happy, she was, and I made all sorts of excuses for the way she shut herself apart from folks. Even from me. Until one day, I went to the forge to help Sven with some shoeing. When I came home, I found my wife had shot herself to death."

Rebecca's tears spilled as she felt his grief and horror. "Oh, Jacob. I'm so sorry. But surely, you can't blame yourself."

His voice hardened. "I can and I do. She used my pistol, a pistol I had bought in case I ever needed to put down a badly injured horse. But I didn't carry it with me. The house was close enough to the forge that I could run and get it if it was needful. So Hope took my pistol, and she used it to end her suffering . . . because she knew I'd never be enough."

She turned her face toward his. And the words that came surprised her, for they flowed as quick as thought and true as anything she'd said in all her life. "Jacob . . . I believe you *are* enough—and more."

And with that, at long last, she kissed him with all the sweetness welling in her heart.

Sorry bastards would have to come up missing just as it was getting dark. Asa thought about his options as he climbed to the attic to get a better look.

He could barely see through the lone window, so he overturned a wooden box and smashed out the filthy panes. After clearing away the shards of glass, he hung out the opening.

The thin crescent moon and sparse stars barely lit the sprawling darkness, but still Asa remained in the awkward position, in the hope that his single eye would adjust to make do with the poor illumination. The idea occurred to him that he'd been making do as long as he remembered, in ways the Marstons and their kind had never dreamed of.

He was done with that now. Done with the whole idea of giving in to accommodate his betters. Asa thought again of how he'd taught Colonel Hall that lesson, and he thought again of all the ways he'd school the rich bitch on that very point.

But first he had to find Rebecca Marston.

Jacob felt Rebecca's warmth surge through his body, sparking not only a flood of sensation, but one of memory. Perhaps his words had resurrected Hope's ghost, for he recalled in sharp detail how easily comforting her had given way to making love, an act he realized now had been meant to thank him. Or perhaps Hope had been reaching out through her pain, reaching out with her body if not with words or trust.

He thought, too, about Rebecca and how she'd first allowed him in her bed. Once again, the wrongness of her reasons spiked through all else—the idea that she'd come to him out of fear or desperation . . . just as Hope once had. Now that he had told his story, did Rebecca kiss him out of sympathy? Would he once again accept whatever crumbs a woman offered?

He pulled away from her, though every fiber in his body howled with frustrated desire. He looked into her face, cast golden by the firelight, and he used his thumb to wipe a smudge of dirt off her cheek.

"I don't need your pity," he said, more sharply than he'd meant to.

"Maybe I need *you*," she whispered, not sounding for a moment like a spoiled socialite.

"Like you needed me before?" he asked. "To get you through the night?"

He read the hurt in her expression so clearly, it might have been a headline. But Jacob resisted the impulse to kiss away her tears, to serve a woman only as temporary comfort. From now on, he would insist on more than that. He had to, to maintain his sanity.

Rebecca stood, her red hair surging loose about her shoulders. "You're not only cruel, Mister Fuller; I think you're a damnable coward, too."

He could have argued with her, could have reminded her of how he'd survived the war, imprisonment, and a steamboat explosion. But he knew on a different level, she was right. He was afraid of the feelings she'd stirred in him. Afraid to risk the hell of grief he'd plunged into in the wake of Hope.

She stalked away from him and sat at the fire's opposite side, where the flames' light played upon the old quilt wrapped around her body. Something in her posture—or perhaps it was only guilt—put him in mind of an abandoned child.

He realized abruptly that since he believed her to be Rebecca Marston, that was very much the case. Jacob cursed himself for dwelling on his past pain and forgetting hers was in the present.

He stood and walked to the place where she was sitting, staring into the fire. She didn't bother to look up. He would swear he felt waves of fury rolling off her, breaking against him.

He squatted down beside her so she would have to turn her head to avoid his gaze. "I'm sorry. Sorry for a lot of things."

Instead of looking away, as he'd supposed, she glared at him, lowering her chin the way she did when she was angry. "Sorry you can't comfort me again, or sorry that you did it in the first place?"

The acid in her words stung, but he supposed that he deserved it.

"I'm sorry that I took advantage of your innocence . . . and your fear."

"Don't be ridiculous. I'm not some dewy-eyed schoolgirl that you preyed upon. I'm perfectly willing to take responsibility for my own decisions." Her voice softened, and she reached out to take his hand. "And I *did* decide."

He allowed her to draw him down beside her. She looked into his face with an intensity he'd never before seen, not in his mother or Eliza, and surely not in Hope.

"Yes, I was afraid," Rebecca admitted. "I didn't know—I still don't know—if any of us will survive this. But there was more to it than that. Over these past days, I've seen something in you . . . something so very rare. Make no mistake, Jacob. I wanted you then, and I still need you now."

He wanted to believe her, wanted to believe the

past and the present could be enough for him. But he knew it wouldn't. He had to have a future, too.

"We're from different worlds," he said, then shrugged in defeat. "Maybe I *am* a coward, afraid of how I'll feel once this is over and you're gone."

"Where would I go, Jacob?" she asked. "To my father, who very clearly meant what he said about disowning me if I left to be a nurse? Or back to the hospitals, so every death can tear another chunk out of my heart?"

She tossed another stick into the fire, then turned to look at him so hard it made him itch. "I may have lost a great deal, but I still have some pride. I won't beg you, Jacob. . . . I won't even ask again."

His heart pounded as he fought the impulse to enfold her in his arms. She believed what she had told him; he could hear it in her voice and see it etched in her expression. But she believed because she needed to, not because her feelings were real or permanent.

Giving in to her would not be kindness. Sooner or later, she would mend fences with her family and return to the privileged life she'd known before the war. A life with no place for a farm-raised farrier from Indiana. And he'd be left with nothing but another set of scars.

So instead of holding her, he steeled himself and said, "If you're looking for a last resort, I won't be that for you. It didn't work before, and I don't see it working this time."

With that, he stood and moved to the fire's opposite side, where he lay down. But despite the leaden weight of his fatigue, several empty hours passed before he fell asleep.

Chapter Seventeen

The best protection any woman can have . . . is courage.

—Elizabeth Cady Stanton

May 1, 1865

Rebecca wrinkled her nose at the cold dampness of her skirt and shirtwaist, which she'd donned again in consideration of the lightening predawn sky. Silently, she counted to ten, her eyes squinched shut with revulsion at the musty smell and gritty, soiled fabric against her skin. Once they found help, she swore to herself that the first thing she would do was insist the filthy clothing be incinerated in the nearest ash can.

The second thing would be to put as much distance as possible between her and Jacob Fuller, so she could forget she'd ever dared to dream that they might have a future. She prayed they would soon reach safety, not only to free her from the fear the raiders would recapture them, but so she could put everything about these past few nightmare days behind her.

Her gaze drifted to Jacob, sprawled haphazardly in sleep. Abruptly, she shifted her attention toward the glowing coals and used the last stick to poke the dying fire. Tossing in the branch, she sighed with the realization that her life would never be the same. She had changed with this experience, discovered things about herself she never had imagined. Never again could she pretend that causes and not people mattered or that she would be content within the bloodless realm of intellectual debate. She had watched a cousin die; she had helped perform an amputation. She had even, God forgive her, moved beneath a man and welcomed passion.

Yet she had suffered losses, too. Just as surely as Nate had lost his right hand, she had lost her heart, a part of it to Jacob Fuller, another to her father's cruel betrayal. She thought about the colonel's telegram and his angry question: *"Who are you?"* No longer was she certain of the answer. She didn't feel much like Rebecca Marston anymore.

Whoever she was, however, enough of the nurse remained for her to check her patient. As soon as her hand touched Nate Gordon's forehead, she groaned with disappointment. Sweat dampened his hair, and his flesh burned with fever. There would be no moving him this morning.

After cooling him with damp cloths, she decided she might as well pick up more firewood. Whatever the day brought, they would likely need to keep the fire from burning out completely.

Rebecca stood slowly, stiff from a night spent sleeping on damp earth. She remembered that Nate and Jacob, who had both spent time in Southern prisons, had survived not days but months in far worse conditions. She smiled to herself as she imagined both of them returning home to soft,

clean beds, good food, and loved ones. Surely, both
had earned it after so much suffering.

She looked up sharply at a noise coming from
the nearby underbrush. Her heart thumped at the
crisp sounds of disturbed leaves and twigs. Edging
closer to the spot where Jacob slept, she meant to
wake him and warn him to take out the revolver.

But the next sound she heard, an angry *chi-r-r-r*,
changed her mind. She recognized the sound from
family outings of her childhood, when she and her
brother had slept outdoors near their estate along
the Delaware River.

Stepping carefully to avoid giving away her presence, Rebecca moved closer to the noises until she
spied two ghostly figures squabbling beneath the
thick branches of a bush. At the sight of the ringed
tails and the masks, she laughed—until she realized that the two raccoons were fighting over the
strewn contents of a pack of food Jacob had carried.
With their clever paws, the creatures had somehow
removed the lid from the jar of flour, which
explained the snowy dusting on their fur.

"Get away from here!" she scolded.

The two stared up at her, their black eyes glittering with greed. One licked its chops and chirred
at her before both turned and disappeared into
the dark mass of the bushes.

"Wretched little thieves!" she called after them.

She bent to search among the scattered items.
Back at her family's estate along the river, she and
Thomas would have found the raccoon raid amusing. But then, she and Thomas would have trooped
inside for one of the cook's delicious breakfasts.
She sighed, thinking wistfully of the delicious tastes
of poached eggs, buttered toast, and tea, not to
mention the luxury of having a full stomach.

Stubbornly, Rebecca pushed aside the thoughts

of a good breakfast. There was no point in dwelling on what she could not have. . . .

Like Jacob. Somehow, she would have to put him from her mind.

With a light shudder, she straightened, only to come face to face with the mist-shrouded figure of a man. Her heart leaped with the thought that he had changed his mind.

"Jacob?" she called softly. She warned herself not to rush into another humiliating declaration. For all she knew, he'd come only to investigate the noise.

He moved with shocking speed, and in the instant before he lunged toward her, Rebecca realized the figure was not tall enough for Jacob, but exactly the right size to be the rebel she feared most.

Jacob woke to the angry hissing of some sort of creatures speeding through the camp. By the time his eyes caught up with the sound, the bushes were waving in the wake of the animals' departure.

"Wretched little thieves!" he heard Rebecca say, from somewhere nearby yet out of sight.

Jacob glanced around to where he'd left the pack of food, and groaned. He'd been so damned tired last night, he hadn't thought about marauding animals. Hurriedly, he pulled on his clothing, intent on helping Rebecca salvage whatever the beasts had left. A glance reassured him that Nate still slept.

Reaching for the revolver, he realized it was missing. Could Rebecca have taken it with her on her way out of the clearing? The idea surprised him, for she'd appeared uncomfortable when handling the weapon earlier. He warned himself to be careful not to startle her and get himself shot.

"Rebecca?" he called, walking in the direction he'd last heard her voice. "Rebecca, it's just me."

But though he quickly came upon the scattered remnants of the food pack, he could not find Rebecca anywhere.

Too shocked to scream, Rebecca turned and bolted. As she ran, she realized that Asa had been holding a gun, pointing it directly at her chest. Perhaps if she had not been so startled, she would have tried some other tactic, but her every instinct shouted the imperative for flight.

She prayed that she might lose herself in the morning mist. She imagined hiding like a rabbit in a thicket, waiting in mute terror while the raiders combed these woods. But first, she needed distance to put space between herself and the awful bargain now come due.

Something crashed through the brush at her right, and she thought her heart would explode through her chest wall. Turning her gaze toward the sound, she glimpsed the white tail of the deer an instant before it bounded out of sight. With a shaky sigh, she continued, praying the startled animal might confuse her pursuer.

Brambles snagged her skirt and branches caught her shirtwaist, yet she did not slow her pace. Ignoring the stinging scratches, she chose a path that led her deeper into the overgrown woodland, away from the floodwaters and away from both Jacob and Nate. If she could lead her pursuers astray, perhaps they would not find her two companions. After all, from the very start she'd been their intended hostage.

But that had been when they believed she had value. Now, with her father's refusal to acknowledge her existence, she knew they only had one use for her.

Rebecca strained her ears, listening for the sounds of cursing or tramping in the brush behind her, but all she heard was her own labored breathing. Pain forked along her rib cage with each gasp, and her limbs trembled like the last dry leaves clinging to an October oak. She realized she could not run much farther, so she began to look for somewhere she might hide.

Jacob tried to convince himself that Rebecca had run after another furry bandit, or maybe she'd slipped away from camp for perfectly natural reasons. He grimaced, imagining her fury if he charged through a clump bushes and disturbed her privacy.

That's not it at all. The same sense that had warned him Rebecca was keeping a dangerous secret earlier now whispered that something was dead wrong. He followed a narrow trail leading through branches that swayed as if they had been recently disturbed. A few steps farther in, he found a trio of long, red hairs hooked on a broken twig. Soon after, he came across several dark threads dangling from a thorn. Rebecca had come through here, and she'd done it in a hurry.

Had the raiders caught up with them? A group of half a dozen or more men would surely be making enough noise for him to hear, and besides, at least a few of them would have gone after him and Nate. Jacob wondered if, instead, one or two of them had come with the specific intent of recapturing Rebecca. But why? The colonel claimed her father had refused to pay, so who . . . ?

Rebecca's words echoed the answer: *"It's not him. It's . . . another of the raiders. That horrible man with the ruined eye, the one I heard called Asa."*

Certain he was right, Jacob closed his eyes and groaned. Asa's desire for Rebecca had nothing at all to do with ransom.

As he raced along the winding pathway, Jacob thought again about the missing pistol. Would Rebecca remember enough to use it, and more important, could she possibly shoot down an armed, experienced man?

Swallowing hard, Jacob vowed to find her. He only prayed that she had not been swiftly captured and taken away on horseback, where she would be beyond his help.

At least the hound pup wasn't altogether worthless. The animal crouched before a thicket, wagging tail high, front paws low. Several joyful barks proclaimed that the young hunter had found its quarry.

Asa felt his mouth twist into a smile as he crouched down and peered into the tangled mass of briars. Near its base, a shallow opening formed a passageway toward the center. He caught sight of a woman's foot and the delicate outline of her ankle, but vines concealed the rest of her.

She'd picked a decent hiding place. If not for the pup, he could have searched for weeks and never found her. But despite the wicked thorns, her refuge wouldn't stop a bullet.

"I know you're in there. Time to come out now," he said.

Not surprisingly, she didn't answer, as if she believed that silence made her invisible.

"We had a deal, princess," he told her. "It's time for you to pay the price."

The pup yapped again, until Asa shushed it with a harsh rebuke. Before he'd surprised Rebecca, he'd seen the surviving Yankee soldiers sleeping

near a fire's dying coals. He'd retrieved his lost
revolver, which he found beside the curly-headed
one, but he'd decided to delay the pleasure of
executing both men. He'd wanted to surprise the
woman while she was alone, and he could always
pick off the others later. He didn't want them hearing him, however, and interrupting the proceedings with the princess.

"An agreement executed under duress is certainly not binding," she called in a voice that put
him to mind of sour milk. "I refuse to move from
this spot."

Asa wondered what the hell she was talking
about. Didn't she realize big words and fancy ideas
couldn't help her here? Yet he hadn't expected
her to meekly crawl out of the thicket and willingly
spread herself before him. In his experience, some
women went limp and quiet, others wept, and still
others fought like hellcats. Rebecca Marston would
definitely fit into the last group, only she'd try hard
to talk him into a coma if she could.

Asa pointed one of his two guns in her direction.
"You're gonna come out now, or I'm gonna have
to shoot you."

"Go ahead," she countered. "As I'm certain you
intend to murder me anyway, I'd prefer not to
suffer your disgusting attentions first."

Goddamn woman could argue the bark off a
tree. He wished now that he'd killed the soldiers
earlier, so he wouldn't have to worry about noise.
He'd fire into the bramble, maybe wing her, and
she'd scramble out fast enough.

"If you come out, I promise I won't shoot you,"
he told her, thinking that he might like strangling
even more. Impatience boiled to the surface. She
would damned well pay for all her stalling.

Her laughter was mocking, like all the Big Men

and their kind. "Why on earth would I believe that? Do you take me for a fool?"

That was *it*. Fury pounding at his temples, Asa dropped to elbows and knees and began to crawl in after her. She drew back her legs, but apparently, she could move no farther.

Thorns tore at Asa's hair, his hands, his jacket. Ignoring the pain, he pushed forward until he got a firm grip around her ankle. She shrieked and tried to jerk away, but he held fast and began to drag her toward him.

Rebecca fought to free herself from Asa, but for all the good it did, his hand might have been bolted to her leg. Panic ripped through her as she began to slide in his direction. She screamed until her throat felt shredded, and she grabbed a handful of vines and tried to use them to pull herself away from her attacker.

The thorns bit deeply into palms and fingers, but she held on tight. Still, inexorably, she lost ground. Her ankle throbbed, and she feared that at any moment, bones would snap inside it. Clearly, this thicket wasn't going to save her.

Tears stung her eyes as she released the vines and twisted her body. Desperately, she drew back her free right leg, and as Asa dragged her toward him, she kicked him fully in the face.

Terror must have made a gift of strength, for Asa released her suddenly, his hands flying to cover his nose, which spouted scarlet.

"You *bitch!*" he bellowed, his last shreds of control swept away by the torrent of his blood. "You goddamned bitch, I'll kill you!"

With that he reached behind himself, and Rebecca knew he meant to grab his gun and fire. As the dog barked beyond the thicket, Rebecca realized she would be dead in seconds.

Her mind flooded with a desperate hunger to see Jacob one last time. That desire flared to fury, stripping away every civilized impulse. She leaped at Asa, her intent so murderous she didn't pause to consider either his weapons or his greater size and strength. Instinct prompted her to rake at his face with her nails.

Asa howled in pain and rage as she tore at the sensitive flesh beneath his right eye. Dropping the weapons, he balled a fist to punch her left shoulder, then the right side of her face.

Her head snapped, and she rolled onto her back. Vision swimming, she felt dazed and numb with pain. She tried to rise, but her body was limp and unresponsive, drained of energy. She choked back a sob at the sound of Asa's laughter and—far worse—the sensation of his hand sliding up her skirt to stroke her inner thigh.

"Now this is more like it," the rebel whispered. "You keep real still and quiet, and mayhap I won't head-shoot you when I get done. Don't worry. I won't be long. Two, three hours at the most. Just long enough so I'll always remember what it's like to have at a princess. Just long enough so you'll get a proper taste of hell."

His hand crawled higher. Rebecca couldn't move, but still, hot tears rolled along her temples, salty rivulets of her defeat. Her mind struggled to piece together a prayer, but the fragments wouldn't hold together.

Asa laughed. "We'll see who's barnyard filth when I get finished. Open your eyes, gal. I want you to know exactly what you got comin'—and exactly who's on top."

Rebecca shook her head and screwed her eyelids

even tighter. She didn't want to see or feel or think. She didn't want to live through—

"Get off of her, you bastard!"

Rebecca's eyes flared wide at Jacob's voice. She wanted to warn him about Asa, tell him about the guns. But her voice refused to heed her, and she felt as if both mind and muscles had been dipped in paraffin. The entire world, it seemed, had slowed down, so that when Asa reached for one of the revolvers and began to spin around, his movement seemed artfully composed, a travesty of dignity and grace.

With Rebecca's name blazing through him on a lightning shaft of terror, Jacob tackled the raider. As the two men rolled away from her, Jacob struggled to pin the outlaw's arm and gain control of the weapon. The raider managed to flip over, spilling both of them to the ground. Asa's speed and strength stunned Jacob. Until that moment he hadn't understood how badly his months in Andersonville had weakened him. He fought to hold down the rebel's left wrist, to keep him from raising the revolver, from pointing it at him.

"Jacob!" A blur of red hair distracted him, along with Rebecca's shouted warning. "Look out!"

Jacob saw it then. Asa held a second pistol in his right hand, but his grip was awkward. The raider swung it, club-like, toward the side of Jacob's head.

Releasing his grip on Asa's arm, Jacob swung his fist with all his might.

Pain cracked sharp against the side of his skull, and another exploded across the knuckles of his left hand as they slammed into Asa's face. Jacob struggled to control his arms, his fists, yet a black wave swept up and over him, carrying consciousness away.

* * *

As Jacob slumped to the ground, Rebecca dove, reaching for the second revolver, which had fallen to the ground. His face a bloody mask, Asa raised the muzzle of his revolver toward her, his movement slow and clumsy, as if he were badly hurt.

She froze, her fingertips still inches from the gun, to watch in horror as his aim swung past her and then wavered back and forth like the needle of a broken compass.

"Goddamn it, woman!" he screamed, his voice crackling with panic. "Where the hell are you?"

Rebecca saw then that his single eye was shut, apparently as a result of either her nails or Jacob's blow. She realized then he couldn't see her, that he was waiting instead to hear her voice so he could aim and fire.

She stared at the revolver, so close to her grasp. Revulsion filled her at the thought of touching it, of using it to shoot a man.

Jacob groaned, and at the sound Asa whirled in his direction.

When a gun spoke, long seconds seemed to pass before Asa swayed and flopped backward, a crimson river flowing from his neck. Rebecca heard his gurgling struggle, heard the phlegmy rattle of his final breath, but the sounds spun out like the strands of spiders' silk that sometimes fluttered in the wind.

Only then did she realize that she had been the one who held the weapon; she had been the one to fire. To save Jacob's life, she realized. To save both of them.

Alive, alive, her mind sang. . . . But what of Jacob? The question stabbed through her, along with a jolt of the purest terror she had ever felt. She didn't want to look at him, didn't want to touch him for fear that the impact of the gun against his skull had left him dead.

She hesitated for a score of seconds, until apprehension overwhelmed the paralysis of terror. Finally, too weak to rise, she dropped the gun, then crawled until she knelt beside him.

Seeing him so still made Rebecca want to shout his name and shake him. Instead, she forced herself to take a few moments to assess his condition. A thin trickle of blood had run along his temple, then meandered in front of his ear and along the square jawline. Not a lot of blood for a head wound, and when she checked she found the scalp cut to be small. She could easily see the rise and fall of his chest, and noted with relief that the breaths appeared deep and regular.

Yet it was impossible to know what, if any, damage had been done beneath the surface. She tried to focus on the fact that she'd seen unconscious men wake with no more than a headache and a bit of lingering confusion. Still, she could not help recalling other men who'd lain silent for days or even weeks before they died.

"Jacob?" she said softly, close beside his ear. "Jacob, please try to wake up."

When he did not respond, she took his hand in hers.

"Jacob, squeeze if you can hear me," she said, repeating his name in an effort to gain his attention. She pinched the top of his hand in another attempt to rouse him.

Her attention fixed on Jacob, she barely registered the approaching footsteps. By the time she turned to look, the colonel was kneeling down beside her, so close that she could hear the crackling in his knee.

"The sergeant's dead," he told her, but there was no accusation in his words.

Rebecca stared at him. Had they come so far, suffered so much, only to be taken prisoner again? No, she told herself. As her father might have put it, they *damned well* hadn't.

"We aren't returning to that house." Resisting the temptation to touch her throbbing cheekbone, Rebecca straightened her spine and looked straight into the officer's gray eyes. "This man is hurt, and I have another injured man back beyond the bushes. I refuse to allow either to be taken back."

The Southerner ignored her. Instead, he shook Jacob's shoulder roughly. "Quit malingering, soldier. Time to move out now."

The unconscious man did not so much as twitch.

Rebecca glared into the officer's well-formed face, now smudged with the outgrowth of whiskers and lined with fatigue.

"I assume you have a horse nearby," Rebecca said. "We'll use it to move this man close to the other. I'll need your help with the lifting."

The colonel sighed. "You missed your calling, Miss Marston. You were born to command legions. In this case, I defer to your authority."

"So you're back to believing I am Rebecca Marston?"

"Let's say I've decided to trust your honesty more than your father's. I've already been deceived by him before. Nevertheless, I had difficulty believing that even a swindler could sacrifice his own flesh and blood."

Rebecca's natural inclination—and her habit, among strangers—was to defend her father's honor, but the words stuck in her throat. He had abandoned her, so why should she care what this man called him? Instead, she explained, "I infuriated him by going to work for wages and nursing soldiers."

The colonel nodded. "I'm not surprised. The whole idea of a lady lowering herself to such a task is appalling. It's a sign of the degeneracy of the Northern culture that women have been a part of the Yankee war effort."

Rebecca felt her hackles rising. "I don't recall asking what you think of my behavior, nor am I likely to, since my opinion of your own conduct is so low."

The man gestured toward Asa's body. "Tell me, did the soldier kill him, or did you?"

"I stopped him from shooting Mr. Fuller and myself. He'd already struck me—and tried to do far worse."

"Then you had sufficient cause."

"I won't say I'm sorry that he's dead." She refused to lie about that, though she'd noticed that the colonel had retrieved both of Asa's guns.

"Nor am I. But you must understand . . . Rebecca. I, too, have had reasons for the things I've done. I only regret that you were hurt." As he reached for her, his hand curved to caress her cheek.

She grasped his wrist and roughly pushed his hand away, unable to bear the thought of being touched without her leave.

"There's a difference between reasons and excuses. You and your men were not defending life and limb when you abducted me, terrorized my fellow nurses, and murdered my poor cousin. Do you expect me to forget that and fall fawning at your feet because you're experiencing a bit of human feeling?"

He arched an eyebrow. "I'm never certain what I expect—or want—from you."

When she looked into his face, she saw no cruelty, only wistfulness. In spite of this, his comment chilled her. His actions and attitudes had been so

erratic that she could not help but wonder if he
might use the weapons to try to force his wishes
on her.

Eager to change the subject, she reminded him,
"We'll need to move Mr. Fuller to the camp with
Mr. Gordon now. There's water nearby and the
coals from last night's fire. I'll help you lift Jacob."

"That won't be necessary," the colonel told her.
"You're obviously hurt, too. Can you even see out
of that eye?"

Her vision *was* dimming as the area beneath her
right eye swelled. She gave in to the temptation to
probe the area carefully with her fingertips, but
even that gentle touch made nausea yawn before
her like a chasm.

As the pain faded, anger rose. She felt like walking over and kicking Asa's corpse. Glancing in the
direction of his body, she saw the hound pup close
beside him, whining and licking his face as if it
believed its action would rouse its motionless master. With a shudder of revulsion, Rebecca turned
away.

"I'll be fine," she told the colonel. And she
would, she swore, for she had to be certain that
both Nate and Jacob were attended. Though both
men worried her, she welcomed the distraction.
Anything to keep from thinking of Asa's hands on
her, of what he'd meant to do.

The colonel retrieved his horse, which had been
tied nearby. With some difficulty, he slung Jacob
over the mare's back and proceeded in the direction Rebecca led him. Once Jacob had been
returned to a place near the fire's coals, the colonel
explained that he was going to find Asa's horse
and bring it back.

As the officer vanished into the brush, Rebecca
wondered what had happened to the other raiders.
Maybe they had given up after hearing there would

be no money. She sincerely hoped that was the case, for despite his unpredictable behavior, the colonel appeared to be abiding by some code of honor. She only hoped he wouldn't suddenly find "sufficient cause" to turn on his three Union captives, then excuse their murders as another of his "regrettable events."

She turned her attention to Nate and found him sleeping peacefully. His head, though still warm, felt a bit cooler than it had earlier. It was still too early to be certain, but it appeared the fever was easing its grip.

After leaving him, she dampened a rag and settled beside Jacob. Carefully she washed away the drying rivulet of blood. As she did, she kept seeing Asa's gun barrel slamming against his skull, kept hearing the awful clunk of metal against bone.

Dear God. Tears burned in her eyes, despite the knowledge that she could ill afford to lose control.

She thought back to their conversation late last night, of her prideful promise: *"I won't beg you, Jacob. . . . I won't even ask again."*

She understood now that she had lied, that she would ask again and then again. Because she loved who this man was, loved him beyond all pride or reason. She wanted to be with him, to wend together through the pathways of ten thousand conversations, to love together through the darkness of ten thousand nights. It didn't matter that she'd known him only a scant handful of days, because she truly *knew* him, recognized in him some crucial element she couldn't do without.

Her mind swirled, confused by the suddenness of change. Whoever would have thought, when she had first defied Winfield Marston, that she would discover that a common-sense farrier like Jacob Fuller had more nobility than all the hypocrites in Philadelphia? Whoever would have dreamed that she would learn her own father was less honorable than a Southern officer who abducted her at gunpoint, then went on to save a group of dying Union soldiers? She felt as if her world's skin had been peeled and then reversed, depriving her of so many comfortable assumptions.

The shift was so overwhelming, so frightening, and so sudden that for a moment she wished she could return to an earlier, easier time—a time when she could claim a place, even a spinster's awkward perch, within the realm where she'd been raised. Certainly, it would be easier than finding herself stranded in this new land, cut off from the delusion that her father was a good, well-meaning man—one she could change through the application of reason and example.

Yet if she had been marooned on the island formed of the abandoned house, she had not been left alone. There had been Jacob, always Jacob, and there had been the boy.

Their boy. The possibility trickled along the indentation of her spine, branching out and flowing along the myriad channels of her body, until the rightness of the idea saturated every cell.

She took the newfound knowledge and held it up against Jacob's earlier suggestion that a house took on impressions of those who had come before. Was it just as possible, she wondered, that the reverse could be as true? Had what she seen been a shadow, not of the past but of the future, of some potential set in motion within the past few days?

"I want my papa." The boy's voice returned to her again, hurt and wistful and not a little angry as he let her know that he blamed her for the lack. As if she'd driven off his father. . . . Rebecca glanced at Jacob and shivered. Or as if she'd let him die . . .

A few yards away, a bird sang a score of notes,

then paused until an answering call came from the distance. A whir of wings marked the first bird's exit as he sought out either a rival or a mate.

Bending forward, she kissed Jacob's temple and felt the pulse of life beat warm against her lips. She meant it as a promise. She would do all she could to be certain he survived this, and beyond that, she would try to find the words to convince him that unlike his wife, she didn't want him because she wished to escape a painful past.

She wanted him for the future the two of them would forge together.

Jacob woke to a pair of sensations at odds with one another: the first a relentless ache, the second warm and welcome. Rebecca was kissing him, he realized, though he could not say how he knew, for the pain in his head prevented him from opening his eyes. He tried to will her not to break the contact of soft lips pressed to his temple, of gentle fingers wrapped around his wrist.

"Tell me, do you share such intimacies with every patient?"

The familiar male voice startled Jacob, and he felt Rebecca pull away. Who was speaking to her? Certainly not Nate or Asa. Another of the raiders? Yes, he was certain it had been their officer, the colonel. Had he come and put an end to Asa's attack? If so, were the others here as well?

Despite the knowledge that the officer's presence had probably saved their lives, the man's question galled Jacob. Yesterday the rebel leader had been furious with Rebecca, convinced she had been lying. But today his words were both mocking and flirtatious, reminding Jacob of the fleeting hunger he'd seen in the man's eyes when he'd looked at Rebecca after she had fainted.

"The lips are very sensitive to temperature," Rebecca answered hastily, as if she'd been embarrassed to be caught kissing a soldier. "I—I thought it best to see if there is any sign of fever."

"Now I understand the popularity of female nurses," the colonel stated. "Why, Miss Marston, how lovely you look blushing!"

The colonel was calling her Miss Marston again, Jacob realized. Apparently, he'd believed her explanation yesterday. Worse yet, the interest in his voice was unmistakable. Jacob wanted to knock the rebel upside down, but he could not imagine how he'd stand without assistance. Cracking open his eyes required a Herculean effort.

"Could it be—?" the officer continued.

Rebecca cut him off. "*Enough.* If you've nothing better to do than mock me, perhaps your energies would be better spent resurrecting the fire. There's a chill this morning, and we'll need to strain some drinking water."

Jacob wanted to cheer. *He* might enjoy Rebecca's bossy nature, but he was almost certain that the Southern officer, with his grand manners, would take offense.

"Do you never tire of issuing men orders? Have you never heard of 'please' or 'thank you'?"

"Why waste time when there's work to be done?" Rebecca snapped. "Besides, aren't you the same man who excused every atrocity you and your men committed in the holy name of war? If you can use this war to explain my cousin's murder, surely I can use it to dispense with a few tea time niceties."

"I feel certain you were better brought up than this and that you'd be quite charming under better circumstances."

"How nice of you to give me the benefit of the doubt." Despite Rebecca's words, her voice remained as flat and cool as a mirror's surface. "Now are you going to tend that fire or not?"

"I'm always glad to help a lady," the colonel answered.

He must be here alone, or surely he would have ordered another of the raiders to assist. Yet despite the irritation in the officer's tone, Jacob thought he detected a certain measure of admiration, too.

God help him, was it more than admiration? Had this rebel driven off his own men for the chance to court the woman whom he'd taken hostage? The idea seemed ridiculous, until Jacob recalled something else the man had told him.

"Make no mistake. Winfield Marston is the enemy and not his daughter. But we'll do what we must to be repaid . . . .

Might the colonel's idea of revenge include seducing the man's daughter? The more Jacob thought about it, the more certain he became that he should tell Rebecca about the man's intentions.

The throbbing in Jacob's head stepped up its pace, and swirls of nausea filled his stomach. Concentration soon fragmented, the shards spinning into darkness.

His last coherent thought was that he must tell Rebecca for her own good . . . and not because he meant to keep her for himself.

Chapter Eighteen

Whilst you are proclaiming peace and good will to men, emancipating all nations, you insist upon retaining an absolute power over wives. But you must remember that arbitrary power is like most other things which are very hard, very liable to be broken—and notwithstanding all your wise laws and maxims we have it in our power not only to free ourselves but to subdue our masters, and without violence throw both your natural and legal authority at our feet.

—Abigail Adams
From a letter to John Adams, May 7, 1776

"It won't help to keep checking them. Please sit down, Miss Marston. Rest."

The colonel's voice was smooth and warm, reminding Rebecca somehow of the deep amber of old whiskey or the flames of the campfire. Benevolent, but commanding all the same, in that confident manner that brooked no disobedience. She imagined he spoke the same way to his dogs, his horses, and female family members.

She understood the type well. By virtue of his race, his gender, and his social standing, he would

consider authority his birthright. And though he
would wield it with more finesse than her father,
the thought still filled her with the same sense of
injustice, the same need to rebel.

She shook her head and returned to check on
Jacob, who slept deeply, as he had throughout the
past two hours since Asa had struck him. Both his
pulse and respiration maintained strong, healthy
rhythms, so she continued to hope—to pray—that
he would soon awaken.

As she rose to walk to Nate, a wave of dizziness
engulfed her, and she staggered. The colonel
caught her by the arm and led her to the log he'd
dragged beside the fire.

"I'm not letting you get up until you rest," he
told her, settling beside her on the log. "There's
no reason to bustle about until you collapse as
well."

He sat far too close for comfort, his long leg
against hers. She wanted desperately to scoot away,
but her mind kept returning to his weapons, so
Rebecca tried instead to distance him with words.

"I have not been 'bustling about.' I've been
attending to these men."

"So who's attending *your* wounds?"

Once again, he reached up to touch her face
where she'd been struck, but Rebecca jerked her
head back.

"No!" She could feel herself shaking like a spar-
row in a gale. Yet not even fear could still her angry
tongue. "I will not be pawed again, sir, not by you
or any of your men."

Regret shadowed his features. "I meant to keep
you safe."

"You meant to get my father's money."

"True," he admitted.

"Why? I mean, why his in particular? Am I right
in thinking this was something personal?"

"Oh, yes. Winfield Marston arranged a trade. Cotton for his mills in exchange for medicine for the South. He had the means to run the blockade, but it turned out he had only the will to run it one way."

She closed her eyes against his words.

"What's wrong?" the officer asked her. "Is it too hard to imagine?"

"It's not so difficult at all, I'm afraid. I only wish it were. Perhaps if I were the 'ideal daughter,' I could delude myself enough to argue." Tears welled in her eyes, forming a shimmering haze around the fire. "Once upon a time, I would have, in spite of whatever information came my way.

"Sometimes I even tried to play the part of conscience, but he said he didn't need one in his business." When she laughed, the sound rang brittle, humorless. "What a fool I was. My father must have been relieved for the chance to be rid of his spinster daughter with all her uncomfortable ideas. No wonder he refused to acknowledge my existence."

The colonel took her hand in his, gently so as not to crush her fingers. "Your father is a great fool not to realize what he tossed away . . . Rebecca."

She looked at him as if for the first time. How was it this near-stranger could see what she had so long missed herself?

"I am no longer your abductor," he said quietly. "I swear it. I want you to think of me as Lewis Hall."

A lump in her throat prevented her from arguing or answering. She sensed that by trusting her with his name, he was handing her his life to do with as she wished.

She struggled to remind herself that his orders had led to her ordeal, had led to Drew Wells's death. The puddle of her cousin's blood expanded, hot and sticky . . . yet it could not entirely engulf her growing sympathy.

Looking down, she realized she had not released Hall's hand.

Their words flowed like leaves atop a clear stream, leaves spinning in the same pleasant current that carried him along. Jacob floated on the sounds of voices, floated until he was able to pick meaning out of movement, and his pleasant mood dissolved.

"Your father is a great fool not to realize what he tossed away . . . Rebecca."

Jacob waited for her to respond with some caustic remark, or at least to tell him that she understood his game. But she did neither, and at length, the Southern officer continued.

"I am no longer your abductor. I swear it. I want you to think of me as Lewis Hall."

Jacob committed the name to memory. Headache or not, he had no intention of forgetting the man who'd held them captive, even if that man had also saved his life.

Experimentally, Jacob moved his head, then braced himself as pain slammed through his skull and tried to drag him under. Fighting the rising tide of blackness, he gritted his teeth and opened his eyes a fraction.

The sight that greeted him took his mind off his physical discomfort. The rebel sat close beside Rebecca near the fire, and he'd enfolded her hand in his own.

Jacob's full attention riveted to their joined hands, he began to shiver as if he'd been plunged into ice water.

Let go! Jacob heard his younger self shout, though no sound rose to his ears. As if from a great distance, he watched himself attempting to pry Hope's fingers from the gun. She was holding the revolver at an awkward angle, backwards, with her thumb hooked around the trigger. Apparently, that position made it easier to shoot herself. . . .

Through the heart. That was where the pain shot as his vision cleared enough to watch Rebecca allowing their enemy to hold her soft, pale hand. A hand that Jacob, too, had held. A hand that once caressed him.

"Let go," he said aloud.

"What?" Rebecca asked him.

She moved to kneel beside him. To his surprise and great relief, she took his hand.

He squeezed hers in return, not wanting her to break the contact. Not wanting her to go back to touching the Southerner. Colonel Hall, Jacob remembered. He'd given her his name.

"How are you feeling?" Rebecca asked him.

Her voice soothed Jacob like one of his grandmother's old songs, but Rebecca's face—her beautiful face—had changed. A livid bruise had spread across the cheekbone, which had swollen to the point that he could barely see the slit of her right eye.

She was hurt because he'd been unable to protect her. She lived—they both lived—because of the colonel's intervention, the same man who now dared to woo her within Jacob's hearing.

And why not? The gentleman warrior and the Eastern heiress had a great deal in common. Colonel Lewis Hall might be a Southerner, but Jacob would wager his little house in Indiana that the man, with all his fancy talk, had come from money. Like Rebecca. Undoubtedly, this war had offered Hall his first tastes of dirt and sweat and blood. Like Rebecca once again.

"Jacob, are you all right?" Rebecca asked,

reminding him that he hadn't answered her before.

"No," he told her honestly. He wasn't. Because although his head would heal, his heart had sunk down deep, down into a bottom blackened with decay.

May 2, 1865

Despite Nate's and Jacob's injuries, both insisted—along with Colonel Hall—that Rebecca ride the ugly roan horse that Asa had left tied. Rebecca had sensibly suggested that the three of them take turns astride the animal, but she soon saw that both Jacob and Nate would rather drop in their tracks than displace her.

Foolish, stubborn men, she thought, but oddly enough, the idea was infused with real affection. They might be wrong to believe a swollen eye and a few bruises made her an invalid, but she knew beyond a doubt that they cared about her welfare.

Unlike her own father . . . She sighed deeply and noticed Nate's gaze flick toward her. A moment later, he began to sing:

> *Ring the good ol' bugle, boys, we'll sing another*
> *   song,*
> *Sing it with the spirit that will start the world*
> *   along,*
> *Sing it as we used to sing it fifty thousand strong,*
> *While we were marching through Georgia.*

Nate sang of Sherman's invasion in a voice of impossible bravado—as much, she suspected, to goad the colonel as to cheer her.

Colonel Hall scowled and urged his mount to trot ahead of them. His chivalry slipped a fraction as he cursed under his breath.

"You have a fine voice," Rebecca told Nate honestly. "But no more war songs, please. I'm weary of them, aren't you? And perhaps I'm tired, too, of thinking that the right or wrong of it was all reserved for one side."

Purposely she glanced at Jacob, for her own words brought to mind his earlier insistence that she keep in mind the war's costs before glorifying its ideals. She still believed in those ideals, still wanted to believe that those who died or suffered had done so in the name of freedom and unity. But in the past few days, she'd been confronted with too many reasons for doubting that any geographic region of the country could lay claim to all its virtue.

If Jacob could read her mind, however, he gave no indication. Instead, he looked every bit as irritated as the colonel.

"So you're taking up for Johnny Reb now?" Jacob asked, swinging a thumb in Hall's direction.

The tan hound pup trailed him like a shadow. Though Jacob had feigned indifference to the "rebel cur," Rebecca had seen him scratch its long ears at least twice this morning. Since he'd been darting black looks in her direction all morning, she was almost surprised he hadn't kicked the animal instead.

"I'm taking up for no one," Rebecca said, annoyed at his assumption. "I'm simply speaking my own mind."

"I wonder."

"You wonder *what*, Mister Fuller? Whatever it is, simply say it and be done with it."

Her tone must have been a bit sharper than she'd intended. She saw Nate wince in an exaggerated matter in Jacob's direction—one of those annoying confidences between men.

"I know some other songs, Miss Marston," Nate

said, evidently intent on defusing the tension. "How about 'Camptown Races' or 'Hard Times, Come Again No More'? Or maybe somethin' to set you grinnin'. You like 'My Wife Is a Most Knowing Woman'?"

Without waiting for an answer, he launched into the first verse.

"Mister Gordon," Rebecca interrupted. Glaring with one eye swollen nearly closed was difficult but not impossible.

Nate glanced at her and snapped shut his mouth abruptly.

"You're looking very pale," she continued. "I *insist* that you take the horse and ride ahead a while."

"But you—" Nate began.

"I'm feeling nearly jostled to death by this animal, and I would welcome a chance to stretch my legs," Rebecca explained, and it was true. Attempting to sit a man's saddle in a ladylike fashion was uncomfortable for both her and—she assumed from its fidgeting—the horse.

Nate nodded, and she saw that he truly did look tired. "All right. I won't turn down the chance, then."

Miracle of miracles, Rebecca thought. But she slid down from the roan's back with a sigh of gratitude and was half-surprised to find Jacob helping her to keep her balance. The welcome sensation of his large hands on her waist sent regret pulsing through her, along with a wave of shame at the memory of how he had rejected her two nights before. Tears stung her eyes—tears that she prayed he would not see.

Jacob turned her toward him and reached up toward her cheek. He did not touch it, but he said, "Every time I look at that, I wish that rebel was alive so I could kill him all over."

"You'd have to fight me for the honor, black-smith," Nate boasted.

Rebecca smiled at the youth, once again impressed by his resilience. Already, the promise of returning home was easing the terrible loss of his right hand.

Jacob turned to help the private into the roan's saddle. As he did so, Rebecca glanced at Nate's bandages and was gratified to see that they had not bled through.

Nate made a clucking sound and urged the horse to trot ahead a respectful distance. In a few moments, she heard him whistling "Marching through Georgia."

Jacob glanced after him. "I guess Nate aims to test the limits of the colonel's so-called affection for you."

"Affection? Is that what you imagine this is all about?" It dawned on her that he was jealous, that he had the unmitigated gall to worry about Hall's motives after he had rejected her himself.

Jacob shrugged, and the two of them began to walk side by side. "It's hard to say what Hall's about for certain. There has to be some reason he shot down his own man and offered to escort us all to safety."

"Jacob, Colonel Hall wasn't the one who killed that man."

"Then who did?" Comprehension swept his features. *"You?"*

"I barely knew what I was doing," she admitted quietly. "All I remember is his gun swinging toward you. Then, somehow he was falling, and the other gun was in my hand."

"I'm sorry that you had to do it." When she said nothing in response, he added, "But I still think the colonel's sweet on you."

"Perhaps he's simply the honorable man he

claims to be. He genuinely regrets some of the things he's done in the name of his homeland, and he's trying to put some of them to right."

Jacob shook his head and grunted a denial.

"Why is it so hard for you to imagine a man acting upon principle?" she asked him. "You've obviously done so on more than one occasion I can think of."

"This isn't about me. It's about Hall, a man who hates your father enough to risk everything on the chance of revenge. What makes you think he hasn't decided that seducing you would work as well as ransom?"

Embarrassment at his suggestion boiled into anger that quickly erupted into words. "*You* might not want me, Jacob Fuller, but is it so inconceivable that any man could have feelings for a pathetic, shrewish spinster?"

He looked at her as if he had been slapped, and suddenly, in his dark brown eyes she saw everything: the uncertainty, the fear, and . . . yes, even the love that he was feeling. He'd bricked all of it behind a wall of jealousy, but her words, her need, were battering that defense, weakening the bulwark that was keeping him from her.

When he didn't answer, she glanced down, unsure of how—or whether—to move forward. She watched, as if from a great distance, as their bare and muddy feet tramped through a layer of last year's leaves. For several moments she let the cool dampness and the rhythmic slapping sounds carry her along, let the odors of decay mingle with the sweeter scents of new spring growth.

But at length, she found the courage to lift her gaze to meet Jacob's, only to find him steadily watching her. He took her by the hand and stopped her.

"How could you . . ." he began, seeming to struggle for each word. "How could you ever think I would believe no man desired you? How could I, when every time I look at you, every time I hear your voice, I want you more? The other night, when I was hurt, I saw the way he looked at you; I heard the way he spoke your name. And when I opened my eyes a little wider, when I saw your hands . . . together . . . I wanted to crawl over there and thrash the man to pieces."

Jacob ran his free hand through his hair, disordering the ringlets. "Then I got to wondering if he might really love you and if maybe you would be better off marrying a man who could take care of you the way you deserve—"

"I am not a pet, Jacob. I don't want to be 'taken care of.' I don't want someone who feels an obligation because my father has behaved so—so appallingly toward me. And I certainly don't want to be shackled to a man who believes that decent women have no right to express opinions or do any sort of useful work."

The world seemed to shrink in scope, drawing so tight that it contained only the two of them and this moment in time.

"So what *do* you want, Rebecca? Tell me, and I swear to you that I'll do all I can to . . ."

The illusion of aloneness shattered at the sound of a gunshot from up ahead, where both Nate and Colonel Hall were riding.

Rebecca looked that way, then glanced back at Jacob.

"Wait here," he told her just before he hurried in the direction of the shot.

She hesitated for only a few moments before running after him.

* * *

Moving cautiously behind a screen of brush, Jacob altered his course to move forward from an unexpected angle. It was possible that Hall had fired on Nate or perhaps just fired past him to silence his rude song. Whatever the case, Jacob didn't want to get shot by charging into the situation without first assessing it.

Peering between two slender pine trees, he saw a scene as astonishing as it was welcome. In a narrow clearing lit by green-tinted shafts of sunlight, Colonel Lewis Hall stood several paces from his horse. The rebel's elbows were pointed skyward, and his fingers were meshed behind his head in an unmistakable attitude of surrender. Not far from him, a pair of mounted Union soldiers held their weapons pointed at Hall's chest.

It was over, Jacob realized. They were safe now, and Hall would no longer be free to pursue Rebecca.

"You heard me," said one of the soldiers, a beefy, ruddy-faced man, who sat glaring at the colonel. "I said throw down your weapons, or the next bullet's going through you."

Perched astride the roan horse, Nate blinked in confusion at the two soldiers, as if he could not believe that his ordeal had finally ended.

"You also told me if I move, you'll shoot me," Hall said to the soldier. "So which is it to be?"

Jacob cleared his throat, not wishing to startle the armed men. Making sure his hands were visible, he stepped into view.

Hall's gaze shifted to take him in. Jacob thought about the man who had saved his life by ordering his men to pull him from the river, the man who had helped Rebecca tend him after Asa knocked him senseless.

Would he have done the same for helpless enemies? Jacob thought of how his months in prison had left him steeped in bitterness, and to his shame, he was not certain of the answer.

"Maybe I can help out," Jacob volunteered. "I'll take his guns for you."

He did so and then brought the revolvers to the red-faced man whose jacket marked him as a sergeant.

"What's your story, soldiers?" he asked both Nate and Jacob.

Jacob gestured with a thumb toward Nate. "He and I were aboard the *Sultana* when she burned—"

"The *Sultana!*" exclaimed the younger soldier, a tall and gangly fellow not much older than Nate. "We about gave up on findin' any more of you boys livin'."

Jacob swallowed past a knot inside his throat at this reminder that his brother and his friends might be among the dead. He forced himself not to bombard the men with questions. First, he had a debt he must discharge.

He nodded toward Hall. "This fellow was kind enough to stop on his way home from the war and pull us from the river. We were mighty sick, but he stayed with us, and—Johnny Reb or not—the man kept us alive."

Nate turned toward Jacob, and their gazes locked for several seconds. The younger man opened his mouth as if to add something, but Jacob gave his head an almost imperceptible shake.

The mounted soldiers didn't notice. Instead, the younger man gestured to a point behind Jacob's right shoulder. He heard the slight rustle of movement from the same direction.

"So where does *she* fit in?" he asked.

Jacob glanced behind him to see that—as he might have expected—Rebecca had ignored his order to stay put.

"Wait. Are you Rebecca Marston?" the sergeant

blurted out, his attention suddenly riveted on her. "There's fifty men out combing the area for any trace of you! Two nurses reported you'd been taken prisoner."

"I was," she explained. A long pause followed before she pointed toward the colonel. "But not by this man. He—he found me after I'd escaped the others. I was lost out here."

Hall closed his eyes, no doubt to say a prayer of gratitude. As well he might, since Jacob and Rebecca had just conspired to save his life.

"So you're sayin' this reb's some kind of hero?" the sergeant asked them.

"I wouldn't go that far," Hall interjected. "I did only what I believed I had to do."

"You can go ahead and put your hands down now," the sergeant told him. "Sorry we can't give you back your weapons."

The colonel looked from Jacob to Rebecca and then back toward the sergeant. "That's all right. The war is over. I hope I need never hold a gun again. All I want is to go back home to raise my crops and horses."

"We'll need to take you with us," the sergeant told him, "so we can get your story down on the report."

"Please," Rebecca interjected, "don't delay him any longer. I ask you . . . let him go."

The sergeant hesitated, then glanced in the direction of the private riding with him. "I suppose it would cut through some red tape to say we found the other three alone."

The younger man shrugged. "Fine by me. I don't cotton to tramping through these marshy woods any longer than I have to. Sooner I get back to the barracks, the happier I'll be."

The sergeant gave a nod toward Hall, who returned it before gracefully remounting his black mare. Ignoring all the others, he looked straight at Rebecca.

"Miss Marston, I shall not forget you."

Jacob wished at that moment that he'd allowed the officer's arrest.

Rebecca answered, "Colonel, rest assured I also won't forget *everything* that you have done."

Whether it was her emphasis or the expression on her face, something made Hall shift his gaze, and for the first time Jacob had observed, the Confederate officer truly looked defeated.

With a barely perceptible nod, Hall turned his horse southward and disappeared between the trees. The hound pup started after him, then looked back, whined once, and bounded back to Jacob's side to lick his hand.

"Well, girl," Jacob told it. "I suppose if you're going to stay, you'll need a name. Think I'll call you Turncoat."

But it could be, he reflected, the half-grown dog wasn't such a traitor after all. Perhaps, just as with humans, questions of loyalty were not so clear as they appeared upon first glance.

Chapter Nineteen

The old idea that man was made for himself and woman for him, that he is the oak, she the vine, he the head, she the heart, he the great conservator of wisdom . . . she of love,—will be reverently laid aside with the other long since exploded philosophies of the ignorant past.

—Susan B. Anthony

May 3, 1865

It all looked the same as the very day she'd left, Rebecca realized, from the blue of the spring sky to the army wagon to the brown of the two horses pulling it. She could almost hear the broad tones of the ward matron's voice and the rippling notes of Sarah's laughter. She could almost see her cousin's smile, and the way the sunlight warmed his brown hair with auburn tones.

But Drew was dead now, killed in accordance with the orders of the same man she'd helped set free just yesterday. She wished she could explain to Drew how things were so much more complicated than they seemed upon first glance—that in a few short days, circumstances had forced her to look longer, deeper, beyond the glittering surface to places where the currents flowed among cool shadows.

The wagon clattered along the road into Riverport, Arkansas, where she'd once lived and worked. In the distance, between the righteous white-walled church and its humbler neighbor, Buck's Feed & Hardware, Rebecca glimpsed a mud brown stretch of the Mississippi River flowing past. She glanced at Jacob, who sat beside her, and she realized he and the others must have floated past this very spot after their steamboat met its end upstream.

Thank God Jacob had come to her, she thought, and she gave his hand a squeeze. He returned it and gave her a smile that faded quickly, replaced by a strained look. He was thinking of his brother and his friends, she guessed, and worrying about what he might learn of their fates.

As the horses' hooves clopped closer to the grim face of the hospital where Rebecca had once worked, Rebecca remembered that it had been a grand old home before it had been seized from a secessionist and used to shelter sick and wounded men. Someday soon, God willing, it would be a home again, with all its floors scrubbed free of bloodstains, with all its windows thrown wide to release the echoes of old screams. . . .

And the ghosts of so many lost soldiers, like those that haunted her.

Staring at the two-story brick building, Rebecca whispered, "Time to go home now. . . ."

"Rebecca?" Jacob asked her.

She was surprised to realize the wagon had stopped and he was standing beside it, reaching to help her step down onto the walk. Accepting his offer, she waited, her gaze upon the hospital so intent that she barely heard Nate complain, "I ain't helpless. You don't have to hand me down like some lady."

"I'll take your little mongrel with me to the stable around back and shut her in a stall for the time being," the driver told Jacob. After accepting the animal's rope leash, the soldier said, "Go ahead inside. We sent ahead a messenger, and you're expected."

Before the group could reach the entrance, the door was flung open and Eleanor's broad form filled the opening. The ward matron's face glistened with tears. Rebecca squinted, sure that some trick of the light had fooled her, for until Drew's death she had never seen Eleanor weep, in spite of the ebb and flow of lives around her.

"Rebecca Marston! Why, in all my born days, I . . . I never—! Oh, dear child!"

Eleanor's short legs drove her forward like a steam engine, but it was Rebecca's longer strides that closed the gap between them. The two women embraced, and Rebecca realized Eleanor was weeping for the miracle of her return—and for the terror in the clearing that they had somehow both survived.

"Are you—are you—well?" Eleanor ventured, her voice fading to a whisper on that last word. She patted Rebecca's bruised cheekbone. "Did— did they . . . ?"

Understanding the woman's concern that she'd been violated, Rebecca shook her head. "I was struck once, but otherwise I'm unharmed."

But not unchanged, she thought. She would never be the same.

Through a haze of her own tears, she glimpsed a blond head in the open doorway.

"Sarah!" Rebecca cried.

Sarah stepped backward, into shadow, the shaking of her head barely visible. "I—I never meant . . ."

Rebecca disentangled herself from Eleanor and hurried toward her friend, all the while remembering the many times Sarah had walked her out of the wards to take some air or distracted her with laughter. Remembering how she and Drew had looked at each other on that final afternoon . . .

"Sarah, please come here," Rebecca said.

"I—I'm so sorry," Sarah stammered. "I never meant to tell them who you were. I was so very frightened. For the past week, I've been so—"

Rebecca crossed the threshold, and Sarah cringed as if she expected to be struck. Instead, Rebecca wrapped her arms around her and kissed her on the cheek.

"It's all right, Sarah. Everything's all right now."

"Yes, that appears to be the case." The deep voice echoed cold against the marble of the entryway. "Your mother and your aunt will be relieved."

It was a voice that Rebecca would know anywhere, a voice sharp-edged as splintered ice. Her father's voice.

Forgetting everyone around her, she whirled toward him. Unlike her friends, he made no move to embrace her and gave neither word nor gesture to indicate his feelings regarding her reappearance. Instead, he stood like a man striking a pose for a heroic statue: head high and expression stern.

Rebecca glared at him, remembering the terrible words printed on his telegram: *Fear you are in company of impostor. Marston advises no such daughter exists. No payment forthcoming.*

She felt her face flaming with anger and humiliation.

"Come to collect my body, have you?" she demanded. "Were you thinking I'd behave much more acceptably once I was planted in the family plot?"

"Don't be ridiculous, Rebecca. I came as quickly

as possible to direct the rescue efforts. But seeing as how that will no longer be necessary, I shall take you to Memphis and then home ... once you've had the opportunity to clean up and change those rags you're wearing."

Rebecca dug her nails into her palms. She thought back to her mother's insistence that no lady—even if she were being stabbed to death with knitting needles—ought to create a public scene. But those admonitions burned off in the white heat of Rebecca's rage.

"I am *not* ridiculous. I am *not* a dabbler. And I am *not* going anywhere with you," she insisted.

"I am prepared, Rebecca, to give you another chance. I imagine that your ... ordeal ... has taught you the lunacy of this idea of yours of running off to war to work for wages like a common— well, not at all as any decent woman should."

"You insult my friends," Rebecca told him, gesturing toward Sarah, who looked embarrassed, and Eleanor, who had one hand fisted on her hip and an angry gleam in her eye. She noticed, too, that Jacob had come in and was watching her intently.

Winfield Marston ignored her complaint and continued. "Young lady, as a gentleman and as your father, I swear an oath that this offer will never be repeated. If you will but apologize, everything— *everything*—will be restored."

That second "everything" would be her inheritance, she supposed, the carrot her father dangled as a substitute for love. Would he never understand how little money mattered to her?

"You swear this as my father," Rebecca said. "Let me tell you about that man. I knew he wasn't perfect, but I believed him to be good and honorable: a man who could be moved by an impassioned argument; a man who felt a pride he couldn't show for his daughter's determination. A man who truly

loved his family, for all he didn't say it. I believed
so many things . . . with so very little cause.''

Her father stood before her, his jaw working, his
graying muttonchop whiskers quivering as if he
wanted to say something. Rebecca hesitated, waiting, yearning for him to say something, anything,
to bridge the gap.

Instead, he straightened his spine and told her,
''I will not be spoken to in such a manner. I am
your *father!*''

''You have a hell of a way of showin' it, mister!''
Nate cut in.

A sense of utter calm dropped over Rebecca like
a shroud. ''Perhaps you'll find my sentiments
clearer if I express them in the same terms as your
message to my abductors: I fear that I am in the
company of an impostor. No such father exists. No
apology forthcoming.''

He reached for her at last, the blue eyes behind
his spectacles thrown into stark relief against his
pallid face, his mouth gaping like a fresh-caught
fish. But for Rebecca, the gesture came too late.
She turned away and fled down the hallway toward
the safety of the sunroom, which was nearly always
crammed with boxes of supplies.

Perhaps there she could find bandages enough
to blot her streaming tears.

''My—my *message?*'' Marston stammered.

''Yes, yours, you heartless son of a bitch.'' Jacob's
gaze drifted to the two women, both of whom
appeared stunned by the exchange they'd witnessed.

''I'm sorry for my language, ladies,'' he hastily
apologized, though his temples throbbed with his
desire to pound Rebecca's father into paste.

The elder of the two steered the blonde away.

"Don't you have duties to attend, Sarah?" she asked gently. "Perhaps you could take this young man to one of the wards and have Doctor Wyatt check that bandage."

"I wouldn't say no to some decent grub," Nate conceded.

After the two left, the ward matron said, "If you'll excuse me, gentlemen, I'll go see to Rebecca."

Winfield Marston grumbled, "I'll take care of her myself," and turned to follow.

Jacob gripped his arm and held him like a vise. Clearly, he wasn't about to listen to his daughter, but he'd damned well understand the hell that his hasty words had unleashed. "You sent the rebel raiders a telegram denying that you knew her. It's a wonder they didn't slit her throat on the spot. As it was, you saw her bruises. What you did was a damned disgrace."

Though Marston was several inches shorter than Jacob, he was perhaps forty pounds heavier and looked to be in robust condition. Jacob half expected the man to take a swing at him; he almost hoped that Marston would.

Instead, the older man jerked away his arm. His pallor faded to chalk white, and his fingers trembled even as they absently stroked the fullness of his silvery sideburns.

"Dear God . . ." Marston groaned. His blue eyes looked distinctly watery. "Such a foolish, grasping woman. What the devil has she done?"

A foolish, grasping woman? Obviously, this bastard didn't know his own flesh. "Rebecca? She's done nothing except try to survive this all as best she could. And while doing that, attempt to save the lives of wounded men. I've seen your daughter work beyond exhaustion and refuse food when there were men in need. I've seen her hold a dying soldier's hand and help perform an amputation. I've seen her restore hope."

Marston shook his head, but Jacob ignored him, plowing forward with the same tenacity he'd once used to plow his father's fields.

"I've been honored to know Rebecca Marston. She's a woman who deserves the best life has to offer, and that sure as hell does not include an arrogant swindler who won't even acknowledge her to save her life."

Marston straightened his spine. After removing his spectacles, he stared into Jacob's eyes for several beats.

"You—you love her, don't you?" Beyond the incredulity came the demand. "*Don't* you?"

"Don't *you?*" Jacob asked in turn.

To his surprise, Marston nodded stiffly. "I do, and I don't give half a damn if you believe it. But I believe I asked the question first."

Never in his life had Jacob been so aware of his appearance. Though he, Nate, and Rebecca had all done their best under camp conditions last night, all three wore mud-stained clothing frayed at seams and hem. Their persons looked nearly as bedraggled as their clothing, with dirt beneath their nails and hair that hung in limp disorder. Under the best of circumstances, Jacob suspected Marston would be horrified to know a common Union soldier loved his daughter. In his present condition—and especially after he had spoken so bluntly to the older man—Jacob would be lucky if Marston didn't pay someone to have him shot.

Even so, he answered honestly, unwilling to deny a truth that shook him to his soul. "I'm in love with her."

"And she has given you some indication that she feels the same?"

Jacob simply nodded, as if the gesture could

begin to express the complexities of his relationship with Rebecca.

His face grim, Marston looked Jacob up and
down. Shaking his head, the older man grumbled,
"For ten years now, her mother has been attempting to . . . with all the very best that society
has to offer. Well, never mind that now. It seems,
sir, that I have a favor to ask of you."

Sir? Jacob couldn't wait to hear what "favor"
the man wanted.

"If you truly love her, you must convince her
she should see me. She doesn't understand at all.
Neither of you does. I'd like the chance to explain
to her what's happened. Bullheaded as she is, she
won't listen to a word if I simply force myself into
her presence. That's why I need your assistance."

Jacob stared at the sincerity blazing in the man's
blue eyes. The same man who had hurt Rebecca.
Could he possibly be telling the truth now?

And if he could produce some explanation, some
excuse Rebecca would accept, would she forgive
her father and return to Philadelphia?

Jacob hesitated. Would Rebecca leave, forgetting
all they'd shared these past few days?

Marston spoke again. "I'll pay you well, if that's
what it will take."

"Like hell you will," said Jacob. "Whatever I decide to do, I'll do for Rebecca. But not for money.
Not ever."

"Then help me for her sake."

Turning his back on Marston, Jacob said over
his shoulder, "I'll think about it."

But first, he meant to find a bath and a hot meal.

Bathing and a single dress should not make so
much difference. Yet in the soft lamplight of early
evening, both changed everything.

Jacob had always found her beautiful, no matter how disheveled or exhausted, no matter if mud grimed every inch of her. But now, hours after their arrival, she struck him speechless when she answered the door of the room that her friend Sarah told him had been provided for her use.

Rebecca wore a full-skirted azure dress made of some expensive fabric Jacob didn't recognize, trimmed in delicate lace that no doubt cost more than he earned in a fortnight's work. Though her feet remained shoeless and her unbound hair was still damp with its fresh washing, she might have been a star, she looked so far above his reach. And now he knew that it was up to him to set her back in the heavens, back where she belonged.

He only wished it wouldn't hurt so, especially when she cast a surprising coquette's smile in his direction. She ducked her head and gazed at him through long chestnut-colored lashes, a glance that bespoke drawing-room flirtations and polite society, not the fiery whirlpool of emotions that had pulled both of them inside.

If only he had seen her in her fine things first. Then he would have understood how truly unattainable she was. He would have heeded the warnings of his memories of Hope.

"Quick," Rebecca said, "come in before someone sees you. They wouldn't think me decent."

To demonstrate, she poked out her stockinged toes and wriggled them.

He stepped inside and closed the door. She stared at him as if she were looking at a stranger. Was that how she saw him now, in her fine things?

She leaned close enough to rub her hand along his freshly shaved cheek. Her touch sent heat sparking through him and tested his resolve to keep his hands to himself.

"I was right," she told him, showing a flash of

straight, white teeth. "I always thought you'd clean up nicely. It's too bad, though, they put you in a uniform. I'd like to see you in civilian clothes."

Jacob shrugged. "I'll muster out soon enough, and this uniform is some kind of improvement. You—uh—you cleaned up nice, too. More than that, I mean. You're beautiful, Rebecca."

She waved off the compliment. "Sarah dragged this over from my chest in the dormitory, and Eleanor insisted on ironing it herself. I'm afraid it's ages out of style, but I've been wearing a sort of uniform myself for quite some time now. I'm finished with that now."

"So you aren't going back to nursing?"

She straightened her spine in a manner that reminded her of her father. "I don't intend on going *back* to anything. I mean to move forward, Jacob. Have you . . . ?"

"Have I what?"

"Have you found out anything about your friends?"

He shook his head. "Not until tomorrow when I go to Memphis."

She reached out and took his hand, then squeezed it. "You mean when *we* go."

His heart, too, felt that squeeze. "Your father wants to see you. He has some things to say to you."

The mention of her father dimmed the spark in her blue eyes. She shook her head emphatically. "I'm certain that whatever it might be, I don't wish to hear it. He washed his hands of me once; I have the perfect right to do the same."

"You can always hear him out and then leave if he insults you. But somehow I don't think he will this time."

She fetched a buttonhook from a valise and sat in a straight-backed chair between two of the room's half-dozen beds. Apparently, this bedroom had once served sick and wounded soldiers. Its emptiness was yet another sign that the war had wound down to a conclusion.

Rebecca slipped on her shoes and began fastening the buttons. "Why should this conversation be any different from the last?" she asked.

"Maybe this time you'll give him the chance to say his piece."

She looked up at Jacob, one eyebrow raised. "You think that he deserves that chance?"

Jacob sighed. "I can't tell you that. All I know is that *my* pa might be dead by now, and there are things I never told him. Things I never heard him say."

Thinking of those things, he prayed he would have that opportunity. After a brief pause, he continued. "Don't throw away the chance—even a slim chance—that your father might give you something that you need to hear."

After finishing with her shoes, she nodded. "All right, then. I'll see him. But it won't change a thing."

Some part of Jacob hoped it wouldn't. For if things changed, he knew he'd never hold Rebecca in his arms again.

It was only fitting that Rebecca and her father met in Drew Wells's office, for in a way her cousin had been the catalyst that prompted the explosion between the two of them. By helping her to come west—mostly to annoy Rebecca's mother—Drew had prompted her father's ultimatum.

But stubbornness, both hers and her father's, had surely lit the fuse.

Rebecca could barely look at the battered army desk without seeing Drew leaning against it, his feet crossed in a manner that reminded her so much of the devilish child of years past. She felt him watching, smirking at them, as she and her father sat stiffly in two threadbare parlor chairs. Between father and daughter sat a small table with two cups of tea and an untouched basket of oatmeal cookies. Remembering Rebecca's fondness for them, Eleanor and Sarah had quickly baked a batch. Yet this evening, the scent turned Rebecca's stomach.

What appeared to be Drew nibbled on a cookie, his appetite undiminished by death. *"Can't wait to see how this plays out."* Inside her mind, his voice sounded cheerful, as if this family crisis had been staged for his amusement.

She narrowly avoided the impulse to order him away. But when she next glanced in the desk's direction, he had vanished anyway. Of course.

She would have to do something about these flights of fancy, lest she lose her mind. Or was her agreement to see Father proof that she already had?

As if on cue, the man reached for his cup of tea, then spoke.

"I believe I understand what happened," her father began, "and for my part in it I sincerely apologize to you."

Rebecca searched her memory for another occasion when he had apologized to her or anyone; she could not remember a single episode. But the uniqueness of the event did not lend it value. How could mere words begin to excuse such a betrayal?

But instead of telling him that, she dropped a lump of sugar in her tea and stirred it, recalling her resolution not to shout or accuse. Listening was all she'd promised, and at this moment, it was all she had to give.

"The news of your abduction came as a terrible

shock," her father continued. "Your mother took
to her bed weeping as if her heart would break. I
wished I could do the same. One child is more
than enough to lose to any war. . . ."

Her mother, weeping for her? Rebecca had
almost imagined she would be relieved. Now she
could give all of her attention to Perfect Prudence,
the daughter of her heart.

But even to Rebecca, the thought sounded cruel
and childish. Harriet Wells Marston might never
understand her daughter, but she loved her. Otherwise, she would have given up years ago on the
hopeless task of finding Rebecca a suitable husband—something she believed a necessity for her
child's happiness.

Pricked by guilt, Rebecca asked, "Did you send
a wire to Mother to let her know I'm safe?"

Her father nodded. "I had a man ride with the
message to the telegraph right after our—ah—
conversation in the entry hall. I had him wire your
aunt Millicent in New York as well."

Her silence broken, Rebecca could not contain
the question foremost in her mind. "Tell me,
Father, about that other telegram. . . ."

No need to say which one. They both knew. The
cold words of his message to Hall hung between
them, a fanglike row of icicles.

"I never sent that message."

She stood, sloshing hot tea from her cup in her
haste. First a weak apology and now an outright
lie!

"Wait—please, Rebecca." Her father rose to his
feet, too. "You must believe me. As soon as possible,
I began the journey, first to Memphis and then
here. I never received any message from your captors. Indeed, I had no idea where to reach
them. . . . But if I had, I swear to you, I would have

paid—and dearly. I would have given all I had for your safe return."

"But you said if I persisted, you would wash your hands of me. You swore it. I remember, as I always will."

He sighed, but his gaze never left her. "You have no idea how it is to spend so many hours deafened by the ringing of one's own foolish words. I only said them in the first place because—because I was afraid for you. Afraid you would be harmed."

He reached out and touched her bruised cheek delicately, as if it were the wing of the rarest butterfly. "As you were . . ."

She jerked her head away, still not quite believing.

"If you didn't send the telegram, who did? Who in heaven's name could have—" Abruptly she broke off, because she realized exactly who it was who didn't want her back in Philadelphia, where she might regain the affection of her parents, the warm embraces of her twin nephews, and her portion of an inheritance imagined lost.

"I'm so delighted I could be the one to give your father heirs and your mother grandchildren to spoil, since they'll clearly get them from no other quarter."

"Dear God . . ." Rebecca whispered. The venomous little witch wanted *all* of it: all of Father's fortune for her children, all of Mother's attention for herself!

"It had to have been Prudence," her father said, confirming her realization. "Your mother seemed so distraught, so fragile, that I asked my attorney to put everything past Prudence. I knew that Prudence disliked you. Frankly, I always thought her jealous of your intelligence. But I never thought, never imagined such a terrible betrayal. Forgive me, Rebecca. Please forgive me for trusting her."

"What will you do to her?" Rebecca whispered, thinking immediately of Tom and Win.

A movement to her right drew her gaze. As if the thought of Thomas's children had conjured him, the red-haired boy called Andrew sat there, his feet crossed atop the desk. He smiled at her, a cookie clutched in his right hand, and the sight of his missing front teeth made her stomach drop.

She thought she'd left him behind in the old house. A sense of unreality threaded through her mind, intense as the deep throbbing of a wound. It was unthinkable, that ghostly child and her flesh-and-blood father in the same room.

Despite the buzzing in her brain, Rebecca made out Winfield Marston's voice. "You must come home with me and face her. I've a mind to have the schemer thrown into a female penitentiary."

Rebecca shook her head. "As vain and grasping as Prudence might be, she's a good mother to her sons. I won't be the one to take her from them."

Her father stared at her in disbelief. "Such a vile deception cannot go unpunished."

"That's what the man who ordered me abducted said," she told him bluntly. "Only he was referring to *your* deception. Something about cotton . . . and medicines you never did deliver."

He waved it off as if it didn't matter. "Oh, yes, the cotton for the mills. I won't trouble you about the details, but suffice to say that the blockade runner I sent ran into . . . unexpected difficulties."

"So you didn't uphold your end of the bargain."

He scowled at her. "I attempted to do so on more than one occasion. I have mills to keep supplied, and even though I found dealing with our enemies distasteful, it's hardly good business to acquire a reputation for breaking one's word. But I don't see your point, Rebecca. What does this have to do with Prudence?"

"I want you to work this out with her, for the children's sake. Her husband and her parents are all dead, and I believe that you and Mother have come to mean everything to her. So much that she wanted you both all to herself."

He snorted. "You've always been an idealist. It was the money all along, I tell you. But I suppose something can be arranged. I don't want to lose Thomas's boys, and I certainly don't wish to harm them."

"Promise me, Father, that you won't have her arrested the moment that my back is turned."

He shook his head. "If I live to be a hundred, I will never comprehend the way your mind works. But you needn't worry about me doing anything behind your back. You're coming home with me."

Chapter Twenty

Truth is the only safe ground to stand on.
—Elizabeth Cady Stanton

May 4, 1865

"I appreciate you riding with me instead of in that fancy rig your father's hired. I don't mind telling you, I'm plenty scared," Jacob admitted as the army wagon entered the outskirts of Memphis, Tennessee.

Somehow, though, *scared* seemed too tame a word to describe what he was feeling, but he was too impatient to search his swirling brain for the right one.

Rebecca laid her hand on Jacob's arm. Apparently, she was undisturbed that the buckboard was open to the view of passersby. Perhaps the thought of going home emboldened her. She hadn't said much about the outcome of her talk with her father, but Jacob had seen them this morning having breakfast. He had seen Rebecca take his hand in both of hers and bless him with that beautiful smile that could only mean forgiveness and home-coming.

Homecoming. He thought of facing his without her . . . and maybe without his brother and his friends as well. Very soon, he would find out. Turn-coat licked his hand, but Jacob was too nervous even to scratch the hound pup's ears.

"I've been praying for them," Rebecca told him, as though she'd read his mind. "I've been praying you'll find all of them alive."

Jacob nodded. He wanted to tell her he'd been doing the same thing, but he felt an irrational fear that, if he tried to speak of his desires, they would elude him in the same manner beads of quicksilver from a dropped thermometer darted away from closing fingers.

He wished Nate had not remained at the hospital in Riverport. Right now he could use some of the young man's chatter, or maybe even one of his camp songs. Anything to take his mind off the possibility that he would arrive in Memphis to find Zeke, Gabe Davis, and Seth Harris all dead—or, even worse, missing without a trace. Anything to distract him from the fact that Rebecca soon would be as lost to him as if she, too, had died.

The soldier driving their rig drew the horses to a halt. "Would you like me to take you to the depot, miss?"

Rebecca shook her head, but she did not remove her hand from Jacob's arm. "No, thank you. The train won't arrive for hours, even if it's running on time. I'd like to accompany Mister Fuller to the soldiers' home."

"Thank you," Jacob managed. It would be diffi-cult enough to check the lists of survivors from the loss of the *Sultana* without having to do it by him-self. Besides, every moment Rebecca delayed leaving would be one more that he could savor in his memory.

The soldier nodded and turned to cluck to the horses and flick the driving lines to get them moving.

"Jacob, I've been wondering," Rebecca began.

Her voice sounded tentative, almost naked without its routine bossy tone. *Naked.* The word burned in Jacob's consciousness as he remembered Rebecca's creamy flesh beneath him.

Lord . . .

"Just before we were found, you were asking me a question," Rebecca continued, "a question about what it is I want. We were interrupted, but still . . . Don't you want to know my answer?"

Panic sliced through the thick layers of his terror. She was telling him, right now, that she would leave. As if he hadn't guessed already.

He shook his head, and that quickly, whatever barrier had dammed his words collapsed. "Please, Rebecca, not here, not now. Don't say it right this minute. Give me . . . just a little more time, just a little—"

"I want *you,*" she interrupted. "There. You've made a liar of me. I said I wouldn't ask again. But it comes down to this. I love you far more than Philadelphia, far more than my old life. It would be a sin to keep that from you, don't you think?"

Jostled by the bumps and ruts rolling beneath the wagon's wheels, Jacob stared at her in disbelief. Was it possible he'd heard her wrong?

But the dryness in his mouth, the pounding in his chest suggested that her words and their meaning were as real as anything he'd ever known.

"I'm not certain what went on between you and my father," she continued. "But he likes you, Jacob."

"He said that?"

She shrugged and did a surprisingly good imitation of the old man. " 'I'll say this for the insolent bastard. Whatever he sees in you, it's not your trust fund.' " Her voice rose to its normal tone. "With Father, that qualifies as high praise. Even more important, he didn't argue when I told him I was staying. At least not for very long."

So she was willing to walk away from everything she'd known, everything she had. The realization turned Jacob's mouth to dust.

"Rebecca . . ." he began, and he wondered how to tell her that he had nothing for her—*nothing*—not even a penny in his pocket. Not even a . . .

Words rose out of memory, an old woman's words, floating to the surface, sweet as cream: *"I'm good and ready now. You take it, but remember: it won't mean a thing until you pass it on."*

He swallowed hard, and then he reached into his pocket and drew out the band. A simple golden circle, with no beginning and no end.

"I found this at the old house," he explained to her. "It would seem it's meant for you, for *us*, seeing as how much I love you, how much I want you, too."

Rebecca cried out so sharply people walking along the sidewalk paused to look. Heedless of their scrutiny, she threw herself into his arms. He could not resist the urge to kiss her, to kiss away the years of pain and loneliness that both had known.

When he felt the hot dampness of her tears against his skin, he pulled away, praying he had not somehow been mistaken. But Rebecca was smiling through her tears, her fist clenched tightly around the golden ring.

Jacob noticed people were still watching, but that fact barely registered. "Will you come with me to a little town in Indiana? Will you be my wife? My wife and, God willing, a mother to our children?"

"Just what *is* it you'll do there?" Rebecca asked, her voice suddenly serious.

"You—you know that," Jacob stammered. "I've told you I shoe and doctor horses."

Rebecca's smile widened. "I know a little about doctors. Perhaps I can be your nurse—*and* your wife, of course. We can take care of that last part after I see my father off this afternoon. Or perhaps we can convince him to delay his trip until just after the wedding. We may have to tie his mouth closed during the objection portion of the ceremony, but it would be nice to have at least one family member present."

She kissed Jacob a second time, and from somewhere on the street, he heard a whistle and hands clapping. The wagon lurched slightly and then stopped.

"We're here," announced the soldier. "Uh, Miss Marston? Mister Fuller?"

Sheepishly, they thanked the grinning young man and accepted his best wishes. Moments later, Jacob helped Rebecca from the wagon and picked up the small valise of clothing she had taken from her room in Riverport before their boat trip to Memphis.

Hand in hand, the two of them walked toward the main entrance to the soldiers' home, and Jacob braced himself to face whatever he would find.

Rebecca could feel the tension radiating from Jacob, would have felt it even had he not stopped stone-still before the door. She took the time to tie the dog to a small tree, then returned to find Jacob standing in the same spot. Instead of urging him forward, she touched his elbow.

"Whenever you're ready," she told him patiently.

If he heard, he gave no sign.

Behind them, a pudgy, clean-shaven man in Union blue said, "Excuse me," in a highly annoyed tone.

Jacob hesitated for several moments. Then, just as Rebecca was about to ask him to move to one side, she heard him sigh, setting free a long-held breath.

He stepped through the door. Rebecca followed, ignoring the impatient grumbling of the man who'd been delayed. Repeatedly, he rustled his thick sheaf of papers.

The lieutenant—Rebecca saw it from his uniform insignia—edged around them in an attempt to hurry past, and nearly bowled over a rather handsome younger private with short blond hair and eyes of sparkling blue.

"Step lively, soldier," the junior officer said in lieu of an apology.

The private looked inclined to argue, whatever the man's rank. But as he opened his mouth, his gaze snapped suddenly to Jacob, the blue eyes widened, and his jaw dropped even farther.

"Gabe—my God! Gabe Davis!" Jacob rushed forward, and the two men embraced like brothers.

Tears welled in Rebecca's eyes as Jacob's laughter filled her ears.

"Still picking fights with officers, I see!" Jacob said, pulling away to give Gabe's shoulder an amiable thump.

Fortunately, the officer in question had already hurried past.

A petite black-haired young woman stood nearby, smiling radiantly at both men. Her arm rested in a sling, and Rebecca noticed bruising around the high neckline of her dress. She wondered if the young woman had been injured in the explosion of the steamboat.

"I—I thought you were dead!" Gabe exclaimed, still staring at Jacob in what appeared to be an attempt to memorize his features. "For days and days, I've been searching, looking for your body. My Lord, Jacob, it's so damned good to see you standing on your own two feet."

Heedless of his bandaged hand, Gabe took Jacob's and pumped it enthusiastically.

"Oh, yes," the blond man straightened, and his gaze sought out the woman's. He smiled at her— a smile warmed by joy. "Jacob Fuller, I'd like to introduce my wife, Yvette Augeron—or I should say, Yvette Davis. My wife."

He repeated the words "my wife" as if these were the finest the English language had to offer.

Jacob looked at Yvette and gave a whistle of surprise. "Well, I'll be. You're the—you're the young lady from the *Sultana,* aren't you?"

"Oui, Mister Fuller, and I am very happy we have found you well." Both the South and the French language accented her rich voice. But there was, too, a note of caution, as though she wasn't certain Jacob would be pleased to see her here.

Jacob offered her his hand. "I'm glad to meet you, Mrs. Davis. I couldn't be happier for you both."

Gesturing toward Rebecca, he added, "And I'd like you both to meet Rebecca Marston, my fiancée."

With a shrug in Gabe's direction, he added, "I don't work *quite* so fast as you."

In short order, introductions and congratulations were exchanged, and Jacob briefly explained that he'd been delayed after floating far downstream. But like a clock, their talk wound down to the hardest questions, those yet to be asked.

Silence stretched between the two men until

Jacob finally broke it. "What about my brother, Gabe? And what of Captain Seth?"

Gabe looked down at the hem of his wife's skirt.

Yvette suggested, "Perhaps we all should take a walk outside. To someplace where the two of you might speak in private."

Jacob shook his head. "No—please. Please just answer me, Gabe. I—I don't know how I can ever ask again."

Gabe looked up and into his friend's face. "Seth's gone. Two days ago they pulled him from the river. We're taking him home, so he can at least make it back to Indiana."

"After everything that ... *hell*. Seth." Jacob closed his eyes, and the color fled his face. Rebecca stepped forward to grasp his arm, to try to brace him for the rest.

"I know, Jacob," Gabe agreed, his young face lined with strain. "I know."

He took a deep breath, perhaps to bolster his strength to say the rest. "Your brother, Zeke— Zeke's the same as you were. Missing, but it's been so long. Too long, I'm afraid, and he was pretty weak. I'm sorry, Jacob. Sorry that I couldn't find him for you."

Jacob nodded. At length, he whispered, "It's all right, Gabe. I know you did your best. I'll find Zeke myself. I'm going to bring him home."

"I've been in contact with your sister," Gabe added. "She wanted to come, but she's busy helping with your father's convalescence."

"Pa's still alive?"

Gabe nodded. "Maybe learning you survived this will be the medicine he needs."

"I suppose," Jacob allowed with a shrug, but he sounded unconvinced.

Rebecca's heart ached at his grief. He'd joined the army to keep Zeke safe, and she sensed that forever after, he would regret that failure as bitterly as he regretted his wife's death. Doubt coursed through her. Could she somehow serve as consolation after such great loss?

The lieutenant who'd earlier bumped Gabe bustled back into the entry. He told them, "I have transfers to supervise *if* you people will move out of the way. Now step aside."

Gabe glared in his direction. "I thought they schooled you officers in manners. I guess you never got to *please* and *madam.*"

Jacob added nothing, but his mouth was set in a grim line.

Instead of arguing with Gabe, the lieutenant glanced at the two women present. His brown eyes blinked. "You're correct, private. I'm terribly sorry, ladies. I was so caught up in updating the survivors' list that I'm afraid I wasn't paying much attention."

"Survivors?" Yvette asked quickly. "There are others?"

The man nodded. "From the *Sultana.* A few more came across the river from Mound City, Arkansas, today. Two were quite badly injured, so no one knew their names before."

Jacob grabbed his arm. "Please, tell us. Tell us who they are."

The lieutenant began riffling through his sheaf of papers before Gabe snatched them from his hands.

"What—what are you doing?" he demanded.

"Yes—yes, there it is!" Jacob shouted, peering over Gabe's shoulder at the list. "Fuller, Ezekiel—survived! *Survived!*"

"But what—?" the lieutenant repeated.

"My *brother,*" Jacob told him. "My brother is alive!"

The lieutenant smiled at him, at all of them, infected by their joy.

"Oh, *that* one," he said with a nod. "The one who's eating everything in sight. Says he's trying to 'outgrow his big brother' before the two of them meet up in Memphis."

"Can you tell me," Jacob asked him, "how *is* Zeke?"

The lieutenant's smile stretched into a broad grin. "I think I can do better. I'll take you to him now."

Jacob shocked Rebecca by lifting her in his arms and spinning her around. Her hair slid free of her chignon and fanned out all around her shoulders.

And Rebecca felt, at long, long last, her love spill free, too, through the shattered remnants of the stone wall she had once built around her heart.

ABOUT THE AUTHOR

Gwyneth Atlee lives in The Woodlands, Texas, with her husband, son, and a retired racing greyhound. Gwyneth is the author of *Touched by Fire, Night Winds,* and *Canyon Song,* and *Against the Odds,* the story of Jacob Fuller's friend, Gabe Davis. She loves hearing from readers at P.O. Box 131342, The Woodlands, Texas 77393-1342 or via E-mail at *gwynethatlee@usa.net.* Learn more about her upcoming releases and sample excerpts at *www.gwynethatlee.com* on the Web.